HOPE
AND
GLORY

KATHERINE SUTCLIFFE

JOVE BOOKS, NEW YORK

HOPE AND GLORY

A Jove Book / published by arrangement with
the author

PRINTING HISTORY
Jove edition / February 1999

The Penguin Putnam Inc. World Wide Web site address is
http://www.penguinputnam.com

ISBN: 0-515-12476-1

A JOVE BOOK®
Jove Books are published by The Berkley Publishing Group,
a member of Penguin Putnam Inc.,
375 Hudson Street, New York, New York 10014.
JOVE and the "J" design
are trademarks belonging to Jove Publications, Inc.

PRINTED IN THE UNITED STATES OF AMERICA

10 9 8 7 6 5 4 3 2 1

Seated at night in my secret study,
Alone, reposing over the brass tripod,
A slender flame leaps out of the solitude,
Making me pronounce that which is not in vain.

With divining rod in hand, I wet the limb and foot,
Set in the middle of the branches.
Fearsome awe trembles my hand,
I await,
Heavenly Splendor!
The Divine Genius sitteth by.

He who is called prophet now, once was called seer.

—MICHEL DE NOSTRADAMUS

HOPE
AND
GLORY

PROLOGUE

England, 1164

The old castle had never been more animated nor more lively than on that evening, when Godfrey de Gallienne waited in Wytham's great hall for word that his son had been born. The idea that the child might possibly be a daughter had never occurred to him. A daughter indeed! What use did he have for a daughter? The seed of his loins would beget no other than a fine young warrior who would, like himself, learn to hunt the wild boar, to go hawking, to hold a fief, to defend his king, and if necessary, to lay down his life before the Holy Sepulcher and redeem his father's soul before the furnaces of Hell, as surely he would be forced to do. For while Godfrey de Gallienne was vassal to God and his king on the battlefield, he had as certainly turned his black, burning eyes toward the Devil on occasion if it meant victory in the face of defeat.

He ceased his frantic pacing as his wife's screams echoed about the keep's walls. "For the love of Mary," he whispered aloud, then throwing back his dark head, he clenched his fists and roared, "Priest! Bring me the goddamn priest!"

The steward hurried forward, and bending to one knee, said urgently, "My lord, the priest is out of chapel, attending to other business."

The earl laughed, sounding slightly mad to his own ears, surely mad enough to make the frail steward quail slightly as he found himself glared upon by his sire. "What do you mean my priest is about *other* business? What other business could be more important than his lady?"

"Sire, your blacksmith's wife is also birthing at this very moment. She, too, finds the babe difficult to deliver. They called the priest some hours ago in hopes his prayers would ease the woman's torment."

Godfrey de Gallienne moved away from the steward and walked to the window overlooking the grounds. Bonfires and torchlight turned the night to day. The screams and laughter from the revelers rose up in a shrill cacophony that made his aching head pound all the more. Already the people were beginning to amass their collection of gifts at his threshold. Meager though they were, they were proof of his vassals' tremendous loyalty and support. Proof, too, that they held his wife, the beautiful and demure Alais, in highest esteem.

Thinking of his fair young wife, the earl swallowed back his emotion, and said gruffly to his attendant, "Bring me the hag, man, and be quick about it." There came a silence in response. Without turning to the steward, he repeated more forcefully. "The hag. Bring her to me."

"Perhaps I should fetch the priest instead, sire."

"I would not take him from my blacksmith's wife. You know me better than that."

"As you wish, my lord."

When he was certain the servant had departed, de Gallienne turned away from the window and allowed his dark eyes to sweep the hall. The babe's cradle, graceful in form, had been prepared already and was placed near his chamber's entrance. A fire had been lit on the open hearth, and the water in which the child would be bathed as soon as he was born was warming. It appeared that all had been readied for the blessed event: the best coverlets prepared, fresh rushes strewn over the floor. Their finest possessions had been exhibited, for the son of the great lord and fierce warrior de Gallienne would know all that would some day be his upon his father's death. There were gold and silver cups, enamelware, ivory, and richly bound books displayed upon the cupboards. All safeguards had been taken to assure an uncomplicated birth, yet complicated it was. For the last twelve hours the midwife had remained at Alais's bed, rubbing the laboring lady's belly with ointments to ease her travail, encouraging her with comforting words.

But the difficulty had not released its foul, pale grip on his lady. Word had soon spread throughout his serfs that the child was being stubborn, and many had come to his door and, on bended knee provided what humble assistance they could impart. One had suggested that all doors, drawers, and cupboards in the keep be opened, and all knots untied. Another gifted him with a gemstone of jasper which was said to hold great childbirth-assisting powers. Even the dried blood of a crane, along with its right foot, had been delivered to safely speed the process of birth.

Nothing had worked so far. *Nothing!*

Again, his wife cried out in pain.

For the love of Almighty God, he had slain a thousand men on the battlefield, would have spit in Satan's eye without fear of retribution; yet the sounds of his frail lady's anguish rent him like the blade of his own mighty sword. The moment he had laid eyes on the lovely little woman-child, daughter of his peer, Raoul de Cambrai, he had been smitten by love. He had worried that Alais, only fourteen at the time, might be repulsed by a man of his years, that being eight and thirty, but she had smiled shyly from atop her prancing palfrey, and, maiden that she was, had blushed so prettily in encouragement that he had wasted little time in offering for her hand in marriage. The union between the two mighty lords had done much to settle discord within the region. Young King Henry had been thrilled with the alliance of his most trusted and respected landlords. Their combined vassals would surely become the very backbone of his dwindling armies.

But power and greed had nothing to do with the devotion—yea, love—Godfrey de Gallienne had felt for his wife these last twelve months. She was all that was good and kind and dear in his life, which had been embroiled in war and bloodletting for as long as he could remember. He would gladly give up all that he had once held as important, land and power and riches, to spare her one more moment of pain. He would sacrifice his own life, if he could, to spare hers.

For now, one year exactly after their wedding day, she lay in her birthing bed, pinned to the mattress in pain, and near death, and all she could think of was whether or not she would give him a son.

A roar of the crowd outside the castle brought his mind back to the present, and at once he realized he was no longer alone. He half-turned to see the woman, stooped at the shoulders, shuffling from foot to foot in the shadows. Her filthy hair hung in long black strands around her face, and her gnarled hands grasped her pouch to her breasts as she gazed at de Gallienne and bared her nubby teeth in a smile.

"Sire . . ." She wheezed and the fire on the hearth danced in sparks that scattered over the rush-strewn floor and smoldered. "You wished to see me, my lord?"

He moved to the trestle table and dropped to the bench, indicating a place opposite him, waiting impatiently as the old woman waddled her way to the seat and sat upon it. Without looking at him again, she spilled the contents of her leather bag onto the table, studying the placement of the leaves and polished, colored stones and bits of bone. As de Gallienne regarded her with open malice, she cocked her head at him and raised her eyebrows. "It seems I was right, does it not? Did I not foresee that the lady Alais would bear you a child on the exact night that marked your marriage of one year? What is it you want of me now, my good lord?"

"Will she live?"

The question hung suspended along the rafters of the high-ceilinged room.

"Well?" he bellowed. "Tell me, hag, before I cut out your tongue. Will my lady die this night?"

"I fear you will cut out my tongue if I tell you what you don't wish to hear."

"You have my word of honor, bitch. Now out with it. Does my Alais live or die this night?"

Bowing her scraggly head, the hag studied the articles strewn over the tabletop. Her mouth was firmly set as she looked at him again. "There is trouble ahead for you, sire. Great trouble. I see the noble house of de Gallienne falling before a powerful king."

Leaning near her, his handsome mouth pulled back in a sneer, he said, "Blast your soul to Hell. Godfrey of Gallienne falls before no king. Henry is king, and Henry is my friend. Now tell me what I want to hear before I do as I have so threatened."

"But hear me out," she rasped in an urgent, grating voice, "and heed me well, my sire. Did I not predict that you would find success on the battlefields of Chaumont? Did I not predict that you would find your life's love on the very eve of your greatest conquest? Alas, did I not foretell that your son would be born on this very night?"

Cursing through his teeth, de Gallienne shoved away from the table, and as his wife's scream ripped through the hall, he plunged his hands through his thick, black hair and squeezed his eyes closed. "Witch, tell me what I want to hear before I have you burned at the stake!"

"Aye!" the old woman cried angrily. "Yer lady love will live, for now, but at the cost of all that you hold holy and dear."

"Cease speaking in riddles and say what you mean."

"Your son will destroy her."

His eyes slightly wild, he looked at her directly and said through his teeth, "But you just said she would live through the birth—"

"Aye, and she will. But the warrior she bears you will bring your destruction, and hers. He will ravage the land and your wife, and people will be left bloodied behind him like lambs of slaughter. He will raze the great line of Gallienne and bring about the fall of all England with his treasons!"

The earl drew back his hand and slapped the hag hard, sending her to the stone floor where she cowered, her bony arm upraised to protect her face from further abuse. She glared up at him with glittering, yellow-brown eyes as blood oozed from a cut on her lip. "You asked for the truth, my lord, and I have given it as I see it."

"You are a liar!"

"Nay! The son of your loins will be born a heretic and he will die a heretic!"

With a roar he drew his sword and prepared to strike her with it. Cowering, trembling, she threw herself at his feet and wept. "Have pity, my lord Gallienne. You did but demand me to look to your future as I have faithfully done many times before. I have but told you the truth as I see it. Killing me will not change your destiny. The stars have decided your fate."

"To Hell's fire with your stars!"

As he raised his sword, intent on felling the woman who would so disparage his son, Alais's cry of intense pain stilled him. Heart hammering, he stared toward the chamber opening, his blood freezing in his veins at the horrible sound. Then . . .

The child's husky cry resounded through the hall, and forgetting the hag for the moment, he hurried to the threshold and there looked frantically upon his wife—his lovely wife, white of face, the bed soaked in blood.

"Godfrey," she called weakly. "My dearest lord and husband . . ."

He threw down the sword and the reverberation echoed against the walls. He hurried to his wife's bedside and, going to one knee, took up her fragile hand in his.

"The child," she pleaded. "Tell me, my lord, have I given you your heir?"

He looked briefly toward the midwife who, having tied and cut the umbilical cord, raised the screaming babe for his inspection. The midwife's face beamed with pride, yet in his own heart his joy lay as cold and dead as the future that stared back at him in the form of a red, wailing infant—the infant that had almost cost his dearest Alais her life, that in truth may yet rise up to destroy her—destroy them all, if he was to believe the wretched soothsayer.

Closing his eyes, he turned back to his wife and, lifting her delicate white hand, pressed it to his lips. "Aye, my lady. You have given me a son."

As tears leaked from her eyes, she smiled in relief, but her brow was yet troubled. "Make haste to bathe him," she struggled to say. "Clothe him in his robes and rush him to chapel. He must be baptized before this night is over."

"There's time," he hurried to assure her.

"Nay, there's not, my lord. I fear this fitful birth an omen of doom. Cleanse his soul before it's too late. Mayhap God will smile more kindly on our son and his birth if he be baptized as quickly as feasible. Quick—quick to the font and cleanse away whatever demon has beset him!"

"But, wife, preparations have yet to be made—"

"Then make them, my lord husband, for I shall not look upon our son's face until his soul is saved in the name of God and Heaven!" She turned her sweat-moistened head from him then, and as the midwife hurried from the chamber, he kissed Alais's hand then followed, slowing as he caught up to the midwife; then he watched the harried, buxom woman bathe the babe with the warm water, place the squalling child upon the trestle table and begin to gently rub him all over with salt, then tenderly to cleanse his palate and gums with honey.

Looking to the shadows, he found a servant hovering at the door. De Gallienne beckoned him nearer and said quietly, "Have you word yet on the blacksmith's wife?"

"Aye, my lord. The smithy has a son."

"Is the child and his mother faring well?"

"The child is weak, my lord. It seems the cord was wrapped about his neck. The priest fears he will not live beyond the hour."

Closing his eyes, de Gallienne said wearily, " 'Tis a fateful night that brings lord and serf, bound by such a common thread as birth, to their knees." Shifting his gaze to the crying babe, he ordered, "Have the priest hasten to the chapel and prepare for baptism." As the servant turned to leave, he caught the young man by his arm. "Tell him I will bring my son alone to the font, and will name the godparents later at the official rite on the morn."

"I will tell him, sire."

As the servant hurried from the hall, he turned back to his son, who by now had been dried with a *bouquerant* and wrapped in swaddling bands. As the midwife carefully placed the babe in his powerful arms, he looked upon the moon-shaped face and head full of curling black hair, and felt his heart break. "See to my wife," he hoarsely ordered the servant.

She curtsied and complied, leaving Godfrey de Gallienne

alone in the immense hall to contemplate his son, and the future the hag had so bleakly foretold moments before. Tipping his face to the shadowed rafters overhead, he closed his eyes and swallowed back the grief that made him tremble as weakly as the child who stared up at him through the slits of its swollen eyelids. Then, as tenderly as possible, he raised the baby to his lips, pressed a kiss upon its brow, and vowed, "In the name of our merciful God, our king, and my wife . . . I defy you, stars!"

Word spread quickly among the revelers that a child had been born to their overlord, yet be it male or female they did not know. The merriment ebbed to a waitful silence as all watched the closed doors of the great hall in anticipation for some word from Godfrey de Gallienne, for until he made the actual announcement of the birth the event would not be acknowledged. Serf and knight and sergeant-at-arms stood shoulder-to-shoulder, their keen eyes watchful for some sign of their lord. Minutes passed until an hour had come and gone, and whispers were beginning to circulate that all was not well in the house. Rumors were rife of the soothsayer's predictions. Several curious villagers broke free of the spellbound audience and scurried to the hag's hut on the verge of town to hear for themselves what she foretold of their overlord's future. Finding the hut deserted, they set it afire and hurried back to the great hall where the others yet waited.

Then word reached them that the blacksmith's son had died barely an hour after he was born. Their own beloved lord was seen hurrying to his hut to offer his condolences to his highly esteemed vassal, for in truth, the two had been as thick as thieves as they were growing up. It was only one of the many reasons they so highly respected and revered their overlord. He was as kind and generous as he was fierce and mighty.

Two hours passed before the massive double doors of the great hall were thrown open. Soldier and serf alike stood at attention, their faces lit by the scattering of torches through-out the crowd. A child cried and its mother hushed it. The yapping of dogs in the distance was muffled by its owner's harsh command. No soul dared move or speak until Godfrey de Gallienne stepped through the shadowed interior of the hall to stand before them, tall and broad of shoulder, the highly polished mail across his chest reflecting the torchlight like soft candleglow. He looked every bit the warlord, fa-mous for his conquests on the battlefield.

Yet, there *was* a difference, and not one man who had fought valiantly at his side throughout the years failed to see it, that glint of madness that turned his hawkish gray eyes the color of cold, dead ash. It was enough to make the blood course like ice water in their veins.

Girard de Roussillon, his second-in-command, hastened to step forward, pausing as Godfrey drew his sword, and raising it high, pointed to Heaven and declared, "It is a son!"

As a great cry of happiness rose up from the mass, Girard placed his hand over his heart, and staring into his lord's strangely emotionless face, called out, "God save you, sir, in the name of your son who was born this night, and is so little. Tell us what name we shall bestow on him."

"He will be called Roland . . . Roland de Gallienne! Be glad and rejoice, for he is born, the liege lord of the lands you hold. He is born who will give you the richest furs, the vair and the gray, splendid armor, and priceless horses." Staring straight ahead, he added, "In fifteen years my son will be a knight!"

A great halleluia arose then, and with it much rejoicing. Few noticed as their lord slowly descended the steps, his movements wooden, his dark eyes glazed. Taking the hilt of his sword in his hands, he then drove the weapon deep, deep into the ground.

Turning his tear-filled eyes to the black sky, he whispered, "It is done. Merciful God in Heaven, have pity on our souls."

ONE

France, 1189

Despair! Despair! Despair!

Blood and woe.

Murder and melee.

Qui en Dieu a fiance il ne doit estre mas. He who puts his trust in God has no need for anything more.

So mocked the engraving on Roland de Gallienne's finely honed and blood-caked sword.

They would fight no more, Roland had decided, until their wounds and grievances and pride had been healed in a place of sanctuary, free from the threat of death. For that reason he had turned his men away from the campaign in Poitiers, and directed them toward the Abbey of the Miracles.

The town of Déols lay still and silent beneath the blanket of fog that had settled so heavily along the earth just after nightfall. Somewhere above the cloak of gray mist spread out over the stars, an eerie moon shimmered through the clouds, casting dim light and heavy shadow over the craggy, broken ground around them. For well over an hour the beleaguered army had cautiously meandered its way up the twisting, curving slope toward the infamous Déols. King Henry's battalion would not be welcome there, at the abbey. Two years before, prior to Richard Coeur de Lion's having sided with Philip Augustus in this tedious war, Richard had headquartered his army at Déols while he occupied Châteauroux. His mercenaries had pillaged the town, and once ready to move on, Richard had ordered his men to burn the town and the abbey, lest they should be used as a base for an attack on Châteauroux. The sacrilege had been prevented, however, by a strange incident that night.

A group of frightened townsfolk had gathered to pray before the statue of the Virgin outside the abbey's south door, when mercenaries sacking the town before it was burned came and jeered at them in their habitual godless fashion; for all who fought for pay were under formal sentence of excommunication. One of them threw a stone at the statue, breaking the arm of the infant Jesus, which, to the terror of the onlookers, began to flow with blood, while the impious soldier was struck dead. Once news of this miracle reached Châteauroux, Richard's men became terrified. The prince countermanded his orders for the burning of the town and abbey, and the next evening, the statue was seen to move and tear its veil. Richard himself had ridden to Déols to inspect the happening, and had returned to his camp white-faced and humbled, and willing to testify upon the Holy Sacrament that the miracle was truth.

In view of this miracle of God, the kings, Henry and Philip, had been convinced by two cardinals to make a truce for two years. The truce had yet to be acknowledged, however, before Lusignan rebels in France, reputed to be subsidized by Philip Augustus, were again causing riot across Henry's lands. Unrest had risen to new levels when word reached Henry in England that two of his English knights were seized as they returned from a pilgrimage in Compostela. This had been in response to Richard's taking of Count Raymond's minister, Peter Seilun, who had advised the count to murder and castrate some Poitevin merchants. Finally, in July of 1188, Henry, King of England, had been forced to set out for France once again.

So, the war had escalated, and whatever friendship and trust that once lay between the two powerful leaders was now history, and both sides had felt the blow of defeat time and again.

But the end was near. Roland knew this. With any luck his friend Henry would at last sit face-to-face with the arrogant Philip Augustus and agree on a treaty that would, hopefully, leave England and France at peace. Such a contract would not come too soon to suit him, for knight he may be, but he was mighty weary of fighting—be it for God, or king, or all the fair virgins in Christendom. After three long years away from England and his home in the midlands, he was ready to return, despite the equally annoying and bitterly galling obligation awaiting him there—that of marrying the homely and wasp-tempered Hildegard, daughter of his father's most powerful, and troublesome, baron, Arnold of Cheswyck.

God's teeth, had his soul not found an everlasting penitence in the fiery furnaces of Hell he might have stood intentionally before Philip's army and invited them all to take their best shot with their straightest lances, for he would rather look into the wan face of cold death than gaze upon his betrothed's countenance for a single night. Saints, but she was ugly.

As if sensing his crippled mood, the great black destrier he rode tossed its noble head and snorted, prancing sideward along the ancient path, coming much too close to the precipice, which, when looked upon in the dark and dreary fog, seemed to plunge to the very depths of perdition. Sitting straighter, Roland glanced over his shoulder at the long line of soldiers trailing behind him, their heads fallen forward in fatigue, the groans of the wounded and dying drifting over the landscape like the moans of ghosts. A knight could find no more loyal or valiant vassals than those who had attended him the last many months, for each man was under no obligation to fight for longer than forty days a year, which is why Henry had so often been forced to buy the services of mercenaries. Yet because Roland had chosen to remain so faithfully at Henry's call, so had his men. They all deserved sainthood, as far as he was concerned. Once he returned to Wytham he would make certain that each knight and his vassals were substantially rewarded.

At last Roland saw the town and the abbey, which appeared to grow up from the rock foundation on which it had been constructed, its massive walls reaching high toward the heavens and built of stone the same hue as the earth. From each of its tiny windows a speck of yellow light could be seen, shining forth like beacons of God through the bleak condensation. The huts of the village were shrouded in darkness, however, attesting to the lateness of the hour. No doubt their arrival in Déols would cause much in the way of distress among the townsfolk. The army would all be wise to look to their backs during their stay.

By the time they arrived at the abbey's gate, the weather had gone from bad to worse. A cold wind had risen and the fog had grown denser. Though the army yet wore the mail and helmets of combat, the frigid air bit into their flesh and their wounds with enough ferocity that each man was hard pressed to will back his impatience as they gazed up at the cold gray walls and awaited Roland's next move. He was not altogether certain that most of his men would approve of his intruding on the abbey at such an hour, though he knew there were many who were eager to confess, and many others who were mortally wounded and close to death, deserving their last rites. Still, they were all aware of the sup-

posed miracles that had taken place here before. They also
remembered the quick death that had come to the foolish
soldier who had thought to desecrate the holy ground. Pilgrims from as far away as Spain and Italy were arriving at
Déols every day in hopes of witnessing for themselves the
weeping shrine. And there had been other rumors as well:
rumors of a living saint sheltered within the abbey walls, a
saint who was said to hold the power of healing, and who,
if he was to believe the hearsay, possessed the ability to
foretell the future with a clear and startling accuracy. Mayhap
his coming here had more to do with curiosity and some
secret desire to renew his belief in such heavenly blessings
than a need to rest and lick his wounds before meeting Henry
at Le Mans, Roland thought. He was well aware of his own
waning faith, as were his men. And there was his refusal to
confess before going into battle. After all, confession was
demanded from knights before performing any solemn act of
their lives, and most particularly before going to battle. Some
had even attested that such a denial, nay, insult, in the face
of God was no doubt the reason for their recent failures on
the battlefield.

Mayhap that was true. But to go to his knee and confess
before a God he had come to question seemed a sacrilege in
itself. How could he pretend otherwise when he had witnessed so many stalwart and God-fearing comrades die horribly beneath the sword, his own young squire included not
two days past. The fine lad's blood still stained the tunic he
wore beneath his mail. He had refused to wash it, but wore
it like a hair-shirt to remind him that in war there is but death
and destruction that is mindless of age and beauty and good.
Beneath the bloodied sword, *all* were punished.

He was about to order Roger de Ferres to dismount and
see to the awakening of the abbey, when several of his
horsemen approached him through the dark.

"Sir," came a young man's voice. "Why came we here

to this place? 'Tis known we will not be welcome.''

"Agreed," said another. "In truth, 'tis a disturbing place."

"Why so?" he asked briefly.

"The air is frigid, yet the summer is nigh upon us. Mayhap God will frown on our invasion upon His holiest ground."

Roland wearily removed his helmet and shoved his gloved hand through his unruly black hair. "Yea," he responded softly. "Still and all, we come not to invade, but to rest and heal our injuries. Surely God would not frown on that."

"But, sir . . ." The young man shifted nervously in his saddle. "I've heard stories . . ."

"Stories . . . ?"

"Of an angel. The pilgrims on the road mentioned she is harbored within these walls, protected by the abbot himself."

Roland flashed the vassal a kind and understanding smile, the same smile that had won him many friends—both English and French—on the long and often bloody roads of England and France; a smile that had caught the eye of many a comely wench as well.

"You are free to remain outside the abbey if you so wish, Albert. Myself, I would rather face the Pope's anger than trust my fate to a lot of furious peasants with pitchforks."

Albert Gozbert looked uneasily at his companions, who regarded him in return with an impatient eagerness to get on with their quest. Resignedly, he slid from his mount and moved through the fog to the abbey gate. There he hesitated only briefly before pounding on the wooden structure so hard that the sound echoed through the fog. Again and again he struck, until at last an irritated voice called out, "Who dares to disturb this abbey at such an hour?"

Roland moved his destrier closer and replied in a raised voice. "It is Roland de Gallienne, and in the name of our king, we request sanctuary inside this abbey."

"What?! Did I hear you correctly? Do you mean our King Philip?"

Roland's mouth curled in a smile. "Nay, I do not."

A long moment of silence ensued. Then, "Request denied. Go away and leave us in peace."

"Unless you wish me to set my men free to find respite in this village, you will allow us inside."

Another silence. "This should be discussed with the abbot, of course."

"Of course."

They waited for some time before the barricade was drawn back and the gate opened. A misty shape moved toward them, swirling the fog, causing the usually dauntless stallions they rode to toss their heads and prance nervously, to whinny and paw the hard earth while their riders struggled to control their unusual behavior. When the figure at last stood motionless before them, he waited until the men had gained control of the uneasy beasts before speaking.

"Sir Roland, what brings you to Déols?"

"Are you the abbot?" Roland inquired.

"No. The abbot wishes me into inquire over your reasons for this invasion."

"You may tell His Magnificence that Roland has no wish to invade the abbey, or this village. We wish only to rest amid this place of God. Our wounds are many, and our spirits are weary. Many of my men are dying and call out for the confession."

"But we have heard, Roland de Gallienne, that you and your men are heretics and are to be damned by excommunication from the church."

Roger de Ferres dug his spurs into his mount so the animal lunged toward the robed official, yet the cowled figure stood unmoved by the knight's outburst of anger.

" 'Tis a lie!" Roger cried. "Who has spread such slander

about Roland de Gallienne? I will face him myself and cut out his tongue!''

Roland, having never taken his eyes from the dim figure, responded with less vehemence, but with enough authority so he was certain the official would not mistake his irritation for less than it was. "Roger is correct. 'Tis a lie, and were I to face my accuser he would sorely regret spreading the false tale.''

"If the tale prove to be false, then I beg your pardon. However, before the abbot invites you inside he must be given your solemn vow that, once entering our most sacred grounds, you and your men will agree to adopt the holy strictures of the abbey as long as you remain here.''

"You have my oath.''

"And what sort of reward do you intend to offer our meager sanctuary in return for its generosity to your weary men, Sir Roland?''

Smiling unemotionally, Roland replied, "Our penitent souls, of course. What greater reward could God ask from a lot of possible heretics?''

There was silence from the cloaked figure, then it turned and disappeared through the thickening fog. The thump of the slamming abbey gates sounded in the darkness.

"Seems even the good abbot is not beyond an attempt to enrich their paltry existences,'' Roland said dryly.

"So it would seem,'' Roger replied.

The gates were thrown open in that moment, and a voice called out, "You may enter.''

Because of the late hour, they were not greeted, as was the norm, by the usual monks who lined up in ranks to welcome their more aristocratic guests. Nor were they met by the abbot. Instead, the hosteler, a stout, white-haired man who moved quickly despite his rotund size, led them all to the line of dormitories where they were shown some forty straw mattresses, each with its individual latrine. Roland was then shown to a tiny stone cell, set apart from the dormitory, where he found a bed that was little more than a long, wide niche in the wall that had been covered with a thick mat of sweet-smelling straw. He was given a candle and abruptly informed by the intense and highly aggravated hosteler that Mass would be at daybreak; then he was left alone to contemplate the state of his circumstances.

As bone-weary as he felt, he could find no respite in the dreary cell. Instead, he paced the cramped, suffocating room, his mind tumbling with his troubled thoughts.

Three years. Three long years since he had last seen his beloved England, his home, and his father. Word had reached him only a fortnight ago that his father's health had deteriorated to a greater extent than it had been when they had last met face-to-face. If he lived to be one hundred, Roland thought he would never forget the look of madness that had shone so frighteningly clear in Godfrey's eyes. In truth, it was as if his father were staring into the face of the Devil, so terrified did he become when looking upon his own flesh and blood.

Yet, even then, on that fateful night, Roland had not been a stranger to his father's odd behavior. As a young boy, before his father had sent him off to squire with King Henry in London, he had witnessed a kind of suspicion and fear, and occasionally anger, when in his father's company. All his life he had stood by and watched confusedly as Godfrey poured all his interest and devotion on Harold, the younger of his two sons, while the ill-tempered, surly, and irreverent Harold had treated everyone, from his father to the lowliest serf, as if they were little better than horse dung. Even Henry, who had truly loved few people in his life—Godfrey being among the very few to whom he would have entrusted his life—was hard pressed to understand Godfrey's reasons for disliking and distrusting his elder son to the point of refusing to acknowledge him at all on occasion.

Once, as Roland and Henry relaxed after a particularly gruesome battle, Roland had reflected on his relationship with his father, and cautiously tried to feel the king out about his ideas on Godfrey's behavior. Henry had shrugged and looked at Roland sympathetically.

" 'Tis hard to know a man's mind when the man is incapable of knowing it himself. I am a sad evidence that a bond between a man and his sons does not always hold true when it comes to loyalty, my young and trusted friend. Remember well that you are the greater, and stronger, of his sons, and continue to stand by your father no matter what. Patience is an admired virtue and one for which you will be amply rewarded in Heaven."

Frowning, Roland glanced wearily about the cell, and thinking of Heaven, thought, too, about his mother. He didn't remember her well. He'd been only six when she died giving birth to Harold. She had been warned against having a second child because the birth of her firstborn had nearly killed her. She had never fully recovered from Roland's birth; therefore, when complications set in with Harold, all of Wytham had prepared for the worst.

Mayhap there was the cause for Godfrey's turmoil. Roland's godmother, Mary Goodman, wife of the blacksmith, Royce, who was his godfather, had quietly mentioned once that the earl's behavior might possibly stem from guilt over agreeing to Alais's tremendous desire to give him a son toward whom he might feel more inclined to hold affection.

Once, when he'd imbibed too much wine, Roland had stumbled his way to Matilda the hag's hut and paid her a tidy sum to look into her crystals and tell him why his father so despised him, and, more important, why his father appeared to fear him so greatly. She had snatched up his coins with her clawed hands and informed him that Godfrey blamed him for weakening his beloved Alais so irrevocably that she never recovered.

Finally, it had all come to a head the night his drunken father had succumbed to Harold's insatiable lust for battle and had allowed his younger son to persuade him into waging a number of unsuccessful attempts on neighboring estates, with whose earls Godfrey had continued to maintain friendly relations . . . until then. When ordered to take up arms and join them in their melees, Roland had refused, and had been foolish enough to stand in his father's way.

No one stood in Godfrey de Gallienne's way aside from Henry Plantagenet.

Father and son had come to blows. Or rather, father had inflicted the blows, grabbing up a club from the wall and sending it crashing against the side of Roland's head so hard that he had been knocked unconscious, waking up moments later to the pain of a throbbing temple and the sharp point of his father's sword pressing into his jugular. Towering above him, his eyes wild with that frightening madness that had lately given him the nickname of "the Lunatic," Godfrey had looked on the verge of murder. Had the calm voice of his godfather not intruded, Roland suspected his father might surely have killed him, encouraged as he was by Harold, who was laughing hysterically somewhere in the distance.

Afterward, the lines had been drawn. Godfrey's vassals had been ordered to choose the man to whom they would continue to hold liege. Many of the younger and more inexperienced had sided with Roland. Most of the older knights and vassals had remained with Godfrey, due mostly to loyalty, not because they thought his outrageous behavior befitting his station, or because they approved of or even understood the immense dislike he had always shown toward his elder son. As several had quietly mentioned to Roland later, they had fought at his father's side for scores of years, had watched the mighty warrior when he was as powerful as King Henry, and Henry's greatest asset. Now, due more to pity and some spark of diminished respect, they chose to remain at his side as long as he needed them.

Wearily, Roland ceased his pacing, removed the sword from his hip, then struggled with the heavy hauberk until he had pulled it off over his head. He crossed the cell to blow out the candle, then dismissed the idea. Habit, no doubt. He was too accustomed to sleeping near the open fires of his camping army during their long campaigns. Even if he happened to take to his tent on occasion, there was some sort of light provided in case he was forced to grab up arms before dawn.

Finally, he lay on the bed, staring at the ceiling. The soft chanting of praying monks came to him as he closed his eyes and attempted to drift off to sleep. Little by little he felt his body relax. Sweet Virgin, how long had it been since he had last slept without fear of assault? For that reason he had driven his wounded and weary men hard the last days to reach the abbey. Here, they could rest body and soul while they awaited Henry's next directive.

A noise . . .

He rolled his head slightly, but the heavy hand of sleep pulled him deeper into his dreams . . . Deeper . . . Until the doors of his subconscious were thrown open, allowing the tumbling sleaves of misty memory to intrude, brushing his face with cool, ephemeral strands that brought shivers to his slightly sweating flesh. Beyond the gray curtain of his dreams there was movement. He could just make it out as the figure crept along like a shadow against the gray stone wall, a vague, shapeless form with no face and some bright and glittering object in its white, long-fingered hand. It seemed to hesitate at the edge of his dream, drifting in and out of his vision like smoke in the grip of a wind; then, very slowly, it appeared to float toward him until he was almost certain he could see two blazing orbs that were eyes, burning down into his with such ferocity he could almost feel the heat and the hate, emanating from within the smooth white skull of certain death.

Yet, if this be death, why then did the faint scent of sweet flowers tease his nostrils? Where was the stench of worm-eaten flesh and rot that had so often pervaded his senses of late? Why did he sense that this harbinger of untimely woe was as gentle and kind as she was beautiful? Yet ... yet ...

He drifted through the dream, and around him the fires of penitence danced upon his men's grim and ravaged faces as they, in their bloodied mail, knelt before their improvised altar, and in silence, offered their souls to Him who had died on the Cross. He continued to stand aside from the faithful, distanced, his eyes drawn to the withered form of the hag who cowered at his feet, lifting her crystal in the palm of her hand.

"Look and beware," came her craggy voice. "Look and beware, Sir Roland. There. There!" She pointed her gnarled finger at the brilliant, blazing stone that grew brighter and hotter and more beautiful than anything he had ever witnessed, so startlingly beautiful he could but gaze at it briefly before throwing up his hand to shield his eyes.

"Look and beware," she cried. "Beware the unearthly light, for in it you will find naught but despair. Despair and woe and death, my young sire. Despair and woe and death!" She threw back her dark head and cackled in laughter while the light in her palm grew brighter, and brighter still until he was stumbling backward through the mists, and the faces of his army had turned to glare at him with condemning eyes, their mouths chanting, "Heretic. Heretic. Heretic. From the Devil you came, to the Devil you will return ..."

"Murderer."

The soft sound brushed his temple like a breath, and as the fog closed in around him again he saw the hooded, formless creature and smelled her tempting fragrance as she rose high in the air above him, and beyond her shoulder the star pulsed like a living ember, orange and yellow and red, rising like the sun, streaking the dim light with fire.

Beware the unholy light, for it will bring you despair and woe and death. Beware . . . beware . . .

"Murderer. Heathen. Son of Satan."

Heart thundering in his chest, he opened his eyes.

"Murderer!" the faceless, hooded creature above him screamed, then the bright light moved like a streak of lightning, and before he could attempt to escape, the dagger sluiced down, burying into the flesh of his shoulder.

With a howl of pain he grabbed for the avenging figure before it could strike him again. His hands grasped only air, and had the agony of his fierce wound not felt so horribly real he might have been tempted to believe the attack a part of his odd and frightening dream. Yet, the dagger protruding from his body, the mind-searing anguish of the injury, could not be mistaken for anything but what it was.

Gritting his teeth, he wrapped his blood-slick hand about the jewel-encrusted hilt of the weapon and jerked it out of his shoulder, swallowing back the pain that would have caused a lesser man to cry out. Rolling from the bed, he fell to one knee before stumbling to his feet and to the doorway, plunging into the dark, damp night just in time to see the figure of his would-be assassin fleeing through the scant light of nearby lanterns, dissolving into the shadows.

His attempt to call out fell silent as hurt tore through him, robbing him of breath and strength. Denying the agony, he shoved himself away from the cell and into the night, forcing himself to run, to follow the cloaked figure the best he could over the tree-lined courtyard, beyond the vegetable gardens, through the botanical gardens, and around the buildings of the balneary, and infirmary. If he could believe his eyes, the cloaked figure was making haste up a long, narrow curvature of steps leading to the high tower and adjoining walls. Though the fire in his chest was great, and the loss of blood immense, he struggled on, driving himself up the steep stair-case, pulling himself up by his bloody hands, one yet grip-ping the dagger, until he reached the summit of the perilous edge and sank against the tower wall, which seemed to plunge toward a fathomless black abyss. Here the wind screamed in his ears and dashed his breath away, tore at his tunic and teared his eyes. The very clouds brushed his burn-ing cheeks and sank their wet, cold fingers into his flesh, making him shiver all over.

The blackness was as suffocating as the pain, pressing down on his shoulders so that his legs trembled and his mind blurred. The idea of lying down upon the cold stone floor and dying seemed appealing in that moment, but the thought of succumbing to the eternal night without first confessing his sins to a priest was abhorrent, which made him laugh at the hypocrisy of his traitorous soul. Nay, he would not die yet. Not until he found the unholy murderer who so cowardly masqueraded in monk's rags and attempted to slaughter men in the name of God.

The shriek rose up from behind him so suddenly that he had little time to react with more than a swift turn to meet his adversary face-to-face. He stumbled backward from the impact, managing only to grab hold of a thin, pale wrist as the phantom attempted to snatch the dagger from his hand.

They tumbled together to the stone floor, Roland landing hard on his wounded shoulder, causing him to cry out and twist away, gripping the bloody tunic in his fingers while doing his best to free his mind of its pain and confusion. There was a scrambling behind him, and too late he realized that he had dropped the dagger when hitting the floor. In-stinctively, he rolled just as the blade was driven hard onto the stone where his chest had been.

He rolled again and felt the tip of the knife penetrate the flesh of his cheek, drawing a thin burning trail of blood down his face.

Again he rolled as the *whoosh* of the blade sounded near his ear.

Again and again the knife cast sparks into the dark as it connected with stone. And now the howl of anger and frustration rose up from the cowled featureless figure as it slashed and slashed its way nearer to him as he retreated, slipping in his own blood, to the brink of the waist-high wall.

There was no escape but down into that cleft of black uncertainty below. Through the fog he could just make out the spectral shape looming nearer, the stained dagger winking with some reflected light he was desperate to discover.

"Who are you?" he shouted, breathless with an uncommon fear that was greater even than the ache of his injuries. "For the love of Almighty God, I have a right to know who would butcher me in this sacred house!" Then the dagger was rising again and he was leaning back and back until there was nothing but air to hold him . . . then he was reaching out in a last desperate attempt to stop his fall, and for a moment, a split instant, his fingertips grabbed at the cowl, dragging it back, unveiling . . .

He tumbled backward, over the wall, did his best to claw for a handhold, fingertips digging into the slippery stone ledge as his feet scrambled for a toehold in the rampart. No use. His own weight pulled him down, and as his fingers lost their grip on the stone he closed his eyes and slid down the uneven face of the abbey, vaguely aware of the sharp surface of the stones peeling away his tunic and flesh, the roar of the wind like the roll of a distant marching army in his burning ears.

Falling.

Falling.

There came the splintering of wood and the piercing of something sharp into his body, the rustle of leaves—dear God, a tree had broken his fall—down—down, the sharp crack of breaking limbs shattering the quiet, spilling him like a bouncing walnut toward the ground, the flash of the abbey wall rising in and out of his vision—he grabbed for it—anything to stop the descent—his hands clutched and held something smooth, so smooth.

At last he was able to curl his arms around it, whatever it was, to press his sweating face into the icy, flawless plane while his knees rested upon some sort of ledge that, although knobby, was equally comforting.

Closing his eyes, Roland tried to steady his breathing while, little by little, he felt his strength begin to wane, and as unconsciousness closed in upon him his grip slowly relaxed. He was going to fall again, and he didn't care. Not now. He was too tired. He hurt too badly.

Yet he did not fall, but settled into a bed that felt cold and comforting against his back.

Darkness threatened his bleary mind, yet he forced it back one last time and opened his eyes.

Dawn tinged the bleak sky with fingers of yellow and purple and vermilion, casting a nimbus of gold over the towering abbey walls high above him. At last, he turned his eyes to the shimmering white form where he lay.

The blood-streaked face of the Virgin Mary gazed down at him, her marble features gentle and soft with compassion. He lay in her lap, against the baby Jesus with the broken arm.

Two

The refectory was generously illuminated by many torches placed in sconces on the walls. Rows of empty tables were lined up across the room and dominated by the abbot's table, which was set perpendicularly to the monks' on a broad dais. On the opposite side was a pulpit that would be occupied by a monk who would read aloud the *Edent pauperes* before starting their meal. He was just taking his place as the abbot, following the ancient counsels of Saint Pachomius, wrapped his white cloth around Roland's wet hands, which had been washed in the lavabo in order to dry them.

"Murder?" The abbot scoffed. "Surely you jest, good knight. Murder in this abbey? Preposterous. We are men of God here." The abbot, tall and thin, his height surpassing that of most normal men—aside from Roland de Gallienne, who stood perhaps a hand taller than he—gazed pensively at his guests as they watched the entrance of the many monks into the refectory. His eyes regarded the knights in a sharp and penetrating way, obviously disapproving of their presence at his abbey. His nose was long and slightly hooked, his cheeks hollow, giving his countenance the appearance of sneering when he spoke in a subdued manner, as he was at that very moment.

In as quiet a voice, Roger de Ferres said, "The figure swept upon Roland like a demon, slashing with the murderous dagger into his shoulder. See for yourself, if you like. The wounds are there as evidence. Had I not been awakened by my own odd dreams I no doubt would have missed my lord's cry for help. As it was, I only found him after an extensive search. By that time the crime had been perpetrated, the damage was done."

The abbot's head turned; his dark eyes regarded Roland fixedly. "You look well enough."

Roland did not respond, but kept his attentions on each of the monks as they filed into the room and took their assigned places along the linen-covered tables. Standing behind their chairs, they remained motionless, their cowls lowered over their brows, revealing little of their faces, their hands tucked under their scapulars as they waited silently for the abbot to pronounce the Benedicite.

The abbot continued. "Would you recognize this alleged murderer if you saw him again?"

Roland shook his head. "I doubt it. They are all dressed similarly, in robe with cowl." He motioned toward the robed monks. "The hood, of course, was drawn up over his head, obscuring his face."

"But he must have been very tall and powerful. See you any man among these who resembles him?"

"In truth, abbot, he was neither tall nor overly powerful."

"But to overcome you as you say he did—"

"He came at me in my sleep. A very drugged sleep at that, I might add. Now that I have had time to consider it all, I would swear that I had somehow been under the power of some substance capable of producing visions, or I might have awakened before the attack."

"Exactly my thoughts," Roger added. "I spoke not long ago with the hag—"

"The hag?" the abbot inquired.

"The crone. The seeress. Our reader of the stars. She knows much in the way of herbs and their effects on our minds. I spoke to her of my dreams—"

"Which were?" The abbot's thin mouth curved in a smile.

"I and my men all had the head of a dog." He raised his eyebrows as Roland frowned. "She told me that mayhap the wicks of our candles had been greased with wax from a dog's ear. By breathing the smoke of those wicks we perceived ourselves as the beasts."

"Roger de Ferres," the abbot replied in an even tone, "You make us sound as if we are a coven of witches instead of Christian men. Spell casters and murderers? Nay, I think not."

A burst of laughter erupted from the long table where numerous soldiers sat apart from the silent monks, who partially turned and regarded them in dismay over their un-Christian outburst. "Need I remind you of your oath, Sir Roland?" the abbot said.

"Oath?" Roland repeated absently. His gaze was locked on the small figure of the hooded and concealed monk who had just entered the refectory through the kitchen door, head bowed and frail hands gripped together at his waist.

"Since matins your men have played havoc within the abbey. Their noise and behavior is more befitting a lot of jongleurs than repentant soldiers."

"Theirs has been a long and wearisome battle." Roland's cold, penetrating stare bore into the abbot. "Mayhap they find this reprieve from the constant threat of death a holiday. But . . ." His gaze swung back to the monk who remained near the door. "I'll remind them of my oath. I'll inform them, too, that they may well be safer in the village come nightfall."

"It is well known that at eventide the time of danger commences, for the Devil is abroad in the night."

Roland thought of telling the stern abbot that the Devil was abroad night *and* day, as was his experience these last years of fighting, but he didn't. He was too interested in the timid monk who, after several minutes, had still to take his place at the table. In truth, the small figure had yet to turn his way, but continued to show Roland his back each time he found himself under Roland's perusal. Bending closer to Roger, he said, "I'll have a word with that one."

Without responding, Roger moved before the door, his stance wide and prepared in case the monk decided to flee his way.

Despite his soreness, Roland moved gracefully toward the cowled shape, the clink of his sword upon his belt the only sound in the suddenly silent refectory; armed soldier and robed monk watched his procession with both concern and curiosity, their gaze shifting often from one to the other in anticipation.

When no more than several lance lengths separated them, the figure suddenly spun and dashed out through the kitchen door.

"Hold!" Roland commanded.

In two long strides he reached the door and rushed into the kitchen, which turned out to be a vast smoke-filled hall crowded with servants—peasants of the village who worked in the abbey for a wage. They stopped their preparation of foods to gape at him as if he were some fang-toothed dragon dropped without warning into their midst. Many fell to their knee in obeisance. Others sneered, and from nowhere a handful of radishes went sailing by his head.

A movement at the far end of the room caught his eye. The monk, having hidden behind a stone and mortar column, dashed again, knocking over a great table loaded with greens, barley, turnips, and carrots. Roland vaulted it easily and

made for the distant doorway through which the figure had
absconded, throwing back the hastily closed barricade so
forcefully that the walls shook from the impact. In this chamber the walls were lined with enormous ovens and fireplaces,
each belching reddish flames. Huge black pots were boiling
their contents into the hissing coals, and spits of beef and
swine carcasses were spewing grease over the walls and
floor. In truth, he wondered if he had somehow fallen
through a door into Hell, so hot was the infernal room. The
heat rose up in roiling clouds to drive him back as he
shielded his face in the crook of his upraised elbow to better
see his surroundings. It simply wasn't possible that the monk
could vanish before his very eyes, yet—

The scream came from behind him, and before he could
spin he was hit hard and driven toward the open fire where
a side of cow was charring over the licking flames. His hands
caught the arch of the heated stone facing of the fireplace,
and though the force in his spine pressed him nearer the
flames, it was the searing of his hands that caused him to
throw back his dark head and roar with pain. With all his
strength he threw his weight backward, swung his elbow
hard as he could toward his attacker—connecting fiercely
against bone just as his feet slid on the grease-covered floor
and he fell hard, jarring his wound so severely that he was
momentarily paralyzed by blinding hurt.

"Roland!" cried Roger's voice.

Groaning, Roland rolled away from the blasting heat, at
last feeling the effect of the fire as it virtually singed his flesh
and tunic from his body. He grabbed Roger's hand as his
friend helped him to his feet. They stumbled toward the open
door where the abbot watched impassively, surrounded by a
band of agitated, wide-eyed monks.

Face sweating, shoulder and hands throbbing with pain,
Roland met the dour-faced abbot with his fists clenched and
his dark features enraged. "Deny now that there is a mur-

derer amongst you, abbot! You have seen with your own eyes—''

''I saw nothing, Roland de Gallienne. Only a heretic pursuing his own demons, perhaps.''

Roger took a maddened step forward, his fingers gripping the hilt of his sword. Roland stayed him with a lift of his hand. Quietly, he said, ''Do you tell me 'twas my conscience that drove the dagger into my shoulder, caused me to tumble over the high wall of this abbey this morn, then attempted moments ago to roast me like that damned spitted swine yonder?''

''You must draw your own conclusions, Sir Knight. Look about. Do you find this cowled, murderous monk anywhere about you? I and your friend can vouch that this supposed perpetrator of unmentionable sin did not retreat through this door, or we and the peasants beyond would have seen him. To where, then, did he escape?'' He motioned toward a closed door on the far end of the room, near the bread ovens. Roger hurried to it, and though he shoved hard on it, it wouldn't budge. The abbot reached into the folds of his robe and extracted a ring of keys. ''That door remains locked during the preparations of the bread and meats so that the godless infidels about our village may not somehow sneak into the kitchens and pilfer that which will feed the mouths of our holy brethren. As you may well see, Sir Knight, the other walls are lined with fire. But for the opening there—'' He pointed one thin finger directly up, to the narrow portal high over head. ''—there is no other way out. Do you imagine that this murderer winged his escape through there?''

Roland studied the high aperture and the dark smoke rising in clouds through the outlet. Finally, he lowered his eyes, like cold steel, back to the abbot. He smiled, just a slow, emotionless, curling up of his lips. ''You're right, of course. Your pardon, good abbot. From here on out I'll do my best

to contain my aggravated and grieving conscience until I'm
again on the battlefield.''

The abbot regarded him a long while without moving or
blinking, his mouth pressed in a firm line and his hands
gripped tightly together. Finally, he spun, causing his flowing
robe to swirl about his slippered feet, and headed back to the
refectory. In a moment his voice sounded out the Benedicite.

"Benedicte, omnia opera Domini."

O, all ye works of the Lord.

Roland kept to his cell most of the day, too weary and sore
to join his men as they took leave of the abbey in order to
visit the village. Many soon returned, grumbling and in black
moods, for Roland had not been wrong in his assessment of
the peasants' anger over their presence at Déols. Aside from
a few lusty wenches who cared more for a coin than the
opinion of their peers, the peasants had spat at their feet and
refused to hawk their meager wares to the knights. Some had
called them murderers, infidels, defilers of the righteous.

At last Roland was forced to walk into the village in order
to keep a watchful eye on his men, as their tempers were
chafed and smoldering, their patience tried to their endurance
by the lot of jeers and jibes the villagers heaped upon them
as they strolled in search of a diversion to help pass the long
and uneventful hours of the over-warm day. His own for-
bearance was tried again and again by the filthy slurs they
hooted as he passed, and when one of his soldiers grew tired
of the ridicule and kicked over a water barrel, then flung a
scrawny lad face down into the mud, Roland only laughed
and turned away, as if he had not witnessed his man's transgression.

There were a great many visitors in the village, pilgrims
who had traveled far to stare for hours up at the statue of
Mary in hopes of witnessing for themselves some small miracle. Roland himself walked by and stood at a distance, his

arms crossed over his chest as he regarded the bloodstained features of the serene Virgin who had caught him in her arms hours before. He noted soon enough that the good abbot had not yet ordered his monks to remove Roland's blood from the statue. He thought of informing the pious worshipers that the blood they looked upon as miraculous and holy belonged only to that of a knifed vassal of King Henry, the despised sire who would overthrow their beloved Philip Augustus if he could.

By the time he walked back to the village, the shadows had grown long and preparations were being made to shutter the ale houses. Roland noted that the abbey's almoner was hurrying toward the monastery with his tumbrel of foodstuffs and clothing he had been dispensing to the town's indigent. It was then that he noticed the crowd that had converged around a square, which was clustered by small huts and a stone wall that stood as high as his head.

A line of people—men, women, and children—stretched down the road leading into the town of Déols. His long stride slowed when, as he neared them, his eyes registered their sorry, impoverished state. Many were old and obviously ill. They all gripped what appeared to be offerings or gifts in their arms; their countenances, though greatly fatigued—for no doubt they had trekked great distances—were anxious, yet resolute.

Addressing an old woman, he asked, "Why are you standing here?"

"The saint," she replied in a breathless, pain-laced voice.

He recalled the rumors he and his men had heard on their journey to Déols. As the line of people shuffled forward, he bent to retrieve the woman's crate of goods and dragged them up behind her. "What have you in this box?" he inquired.

She turned her faded eyes up to his and regarded him with an interested lift of her thin eyebrows. Her pleased smile registered her appreciation over his assistance, and his appearance. "Cloth," she replied. "Woolens and linen and the finest silk to be found in my village, good sir."

Noting her twisted hands, their painfully knotted joints showing signs of severe inflammation, he frowned. "Do you spin it yourself?"

She nodded, and tucking her hands into the thin and tattered folds of her skirt, as if to hide their grotesqueness, she replied, "I do. Or did until this cursed ailment crippled my fingers so I can no longer weave."

"And that's why you've traveled all this way? In hopes this supposed saint will relieve this affliction?"

"I have great faith that it will be done," the woman said. "I've brought my very best cloths, as you can see, all fine enough to dress our Heavenly Mary Herself. Mayhap He will see these gifts precious enough to grant me the cure I seek."

"I pray He does," he responded softly. Bowing slightly, he then took his leave, moving at will down the long line, his sharp perusal noting each treasure placed near the pilgrims' feet as they awaited their turn before this implied miracle worker. When he reached the wall, he measured it well with his eyes before slipping into the shadows and sidling along the stone barricade that shielded the goings-on within from the eager witnesses. When he was certain of his privacy, he gripped the wall ledge with his blistered hands and heaved himself upon it, landing lithely on the balls of his feet. Shielded within a lair of tree limbs and wildly twisting vines, Roland focused on the activity below.

Cursed luck that he should find his view frustrated by the high backing of the splendid chair in which the figure sat. Crouching, he moved slowly along the wall, his leather shoes gripping the stones well as he did his best to remain hidden within the leaves. At last he was forced to stop, or risk disclosure.

He noted first that the abbey's chamberlain stood just in-

side the gate, admitting only one pilgrim at a time. Beside
him was a cart where each gift was placed. The cart was
pulled by an ox, which was driven to the monastery when
the tumbrel became full, which it appeared to be, for just
then a novice hurried forward with a birch switch and, catching the dumb animal by its ear, led it out of the square and
up the bumpy road toward the abbey. Slowly, very slowly,
Roland's eyes shifted back to the chair.

He could see little, for the hood of the robe had been
uplifted to hide the brow, indeed, most of the face of the
mysterious (spiritual?) figure. White, delicate hands were
placed upon the shoulders of a bent, stooped man whose
upturned face, regarding this ephemeral creature in open awe,
was sublime in its wonder and amazement. A boy no more
than half a score and three years sat cross-legged on the
ground, dipping a quill time and again in an inkwell as he
scribbled in a large bound journal with gilded pages. His
blond hair kept spilling over his brow as he wrote, but never
did he stop in his task, just tossed the flowing thick curls
back with a fling of his head and continued jotting whatever
it was the soft voice of the saint was saying, be it to the
scribe or the old man kneeling before the throne, Roland
could not guess from his distance.

At last, the enfeebled man moved stiffly to his feet and
turned toward the chamberlain, who showed him the way
out. The cloaked figure, in apparent fatigue, drooped back in
the chair and remained motionless for a time, until the boy
had completed his writing and closed the book. The lad
spoke briefly to the chamberlain, who then walked to the
people still awaiting their turn to see the saint and informed
them that they would have to wait until the morrow for their
audience. Roland watched this all very carefully before looking once again toward the throne, and the mysterious figure
draped in the brown robe. Though the boy remained, the
purported saint was gone.

• • •

He did not sleep, but lay in the dark on his stone bed in the sweet-scented rushes and listened to the sounds in the night. There was the chorus of chanting prayers that eventually trailed into a yawning silence. Occasionally there came the distant laughter of his men enjoying their games of dice, which the abbot had forbidden them to play during the daylight hours. Try as he might, Roland could not force himself to think of the future, when he would again raise up his sword and shield in defense of Henry. Nor did he wish to dwell on the fact that someone within this abbey had attempted to murder him, although this night he rested with his weapon in easy reach. After all, he and death had become constant companions these last many months. He looked not at mortality as an end to any pleasurable experiences, or even a fare-thee-well to loved ones—alas, there had been few of those in his five-and-twenty years on this earth. Rather, he saw it as a peaceful end to a life of dark turmoil, an existence that robbed the youth of his innocence and planted, instead, the seed of greed and mistrust in his heart. Nay, he would not think of dying this night. Instead, he forced himself to recall the wretchedly ill and impoverished people he had seen in the village that afternoon, their anguished faces alight with a faith he had lost long ago. What irony that he, who had secretly wished for the life of the cloister as he was squiring in King Henry's court, had become one of the mightiest and most dangerous knights to ever charge the king's foe upon a destrier . . . and who had broken the first and greatest commandment of chivalry: *Thou shalt believe all that the Church teaches, and shalt observe all its directions.*

He left his bed and stood in the dark cell, shrugging against the chill, wincing at the deep ache he could feel in his shoulder where the dagger had thrust. Thrice the phantom had attempted to kill him, yet each time the attacker had vanished like mist. The hag had warned him days before to

guard his back, for there were those among his men who
would look upon his failing faith as a portent of doom for
them all. Try as he might, he could not imagine any of his
men committing such treason. And the slender figure garbed
in monk's robes who had attempted to roast him that morning had belonged to no fierce knight in his army. In truth,
the slim creature could have been no larger than . . .

The howl of a wolf brought his mind back to the present,
and he walked to the doorway, slightly ducking to avoid
hitting his head against the low overhang. Dressed in only
his tunic and chausses he stepped into the night.

Odd weather. All day it had been overly hot, almost stifling, yet the cold had moved in again with the moon, and
with it the wind, swirling through the trees like a covert sea
tide, pulling the leaves and limbs back and forward as if they
were no more than tender seaweed in a fierce current. The
meticulously planted hedges along the cloister rattled, and
the flowers that had bloomed bright red in the sunlight but
glowed pale and colorless in the dark were now whipped
round and round, scattering snowy petals over the ground at
Roland's feet. Then the wind died, and what few clouds had
covered the moon suddenly vanished, pouring white light
over all.

What a strange silence did grip the dense air in that moment. Not a breath remained to stir the tiniest leaf on the
tall, thin beeches that crowded the path to the main church.
The crickets, bedded within their lair of lush grasses, had not
yet quickened to their nightly serenade. Standing within the
deep shadow of the pilgrims' hospice, Roland looked hard
over the abbey's grounds . . . for what? Gripped in this odd
anticipation, as if he were waiting on the battlefield for his
foe's imminent attack, he felt his keen perceptions throbbing
with expectation. A chill crept up his spine, and recalling
vividly the sense of premonition that had gripped him the
night before, he stepped swiftly into his cell and retrieved

his sword, the steel singing sweetly as he drew it from its sheath.

Again, he left the small cold cell and stepped into that bleak eventide, prepared to meet whatever foe stalked these sacred grounds in the form of frail murderous monks. He did not hesitate in the shadows, but moved into the moonlight whereby he could be seen from any rampart, and slowly, so slowly, raised his sword high in challenge.

He sensed, rather than saw the presence of an entity he could not name, though his eyes searched hard through the midnight darkness for some form or movement. Then he heard it: the song. Lyrical and hauntingly beautiful, the Latin phrases drifted through the air like an angels' choir, yet the resonant quality belonged only to a single voice, a woman's, enchanting and luring, fading then rising as if on the wind.

Impossible, of course. No women resided in this monk's haven.

Ave Maria.

He turned toward the church. The great façade and the arched ceiling rose up in a dark mass, the rare, colored glass in the window a shimmering thing reflecting the moon's glow from above. The door was unlocked, an oddity, for the sacristan would have bolted it long before now. It moved easily at his touch. He slipped inside, hesitating as he noted the altar looming out of the darkness at the far end of the nave. A single candle burned there, casting soft, flickering light into the shadowy foyer where he stood. For a moment, just a moment, he thought he saw a figure there, knelt before the tabernacle, but it faded as he neared it, little by little swallowed by the moonlight pouring into the room through the window.

Then the song again, soft and unearthly, a resonance of piety that filled up the gloom and dankness and vibrated along the nerve endings of his impious soul.

Ave Maria.

He focused hard on the dim, shimmering visage before the altar, the cowled head bowed and the hands, like alabaster, gripped in desperation—or reverence; he could not tell which. And though compelled to move forward, he could not. He stood frozen as an unaccustomed fear trailed up his back with wintry touches, making the finely honed tip of his sword tremor lightly upon the stone floor where it rested near his foot. Then, in what seemed like an illusion, as this must have been, an illusion brought about by some magnification of his profane guilt, the robed head slowly turned; the cowl slid back.

His breathing stopped.

It was a woman, or rather a girl, whose face was as incomparable in beauty as it was disturbingly tragic. And the eyes, oh, the eyes, like bright fires weeping crystal tears.

Little by little the image disappeared, and with it the song, leaving his ear pounding with the discordant silence that filled up the nave. The burning candle flickered and went out, leaving him to stare, unblinking, into the complete darkness, the smell of the spent taper heavy in the motionless air.

He turned and left the church, only vaguely aware that he could not lift his sword tip from the ground. It made a harsh, grating noise as he dragged it upon the stone steps and path.

Finally, he stood in the hush of the courtyard, and somewhere beyond the high walls of the monastery, a lone wolf howled, a haunting wail in the silver night.

THREE

The boy sat with his legs crossed, balancing the tablet on his lap as he waited to scribe every word whispered to him by his sister. His joints ached with cold, for although the wattle on which he perched was thick with sticks and weeds, it did little to alleviate the chill seeping up from the floor. Having grown weary of the wait, he sighed and rubbed the back of his neck. "There is a problem?" he asked.

Silence.

Frowning, he looked up and regarded the girl, who gazed blindly into a candle flame, her chin propped upon her hand. "Hope?"

"Hush. I'm thinking."

"Dreaming is more like it. I fear my sister's thoughts have drifted beyond yon monastic walls."

"I'm weary, Daniel. Nothing more."

"And troubled. You're unhappy over the English intrusion."

"They have no business being here."

"*We* have no business here, yet here we are."

"*They're* a lot of infidels, Daniel. Their very presence defiles these sacred grounds."

"There is more defiling these grounds than King Henry's armies and we both know it. I've long since lost the ability to discern between good and evil the last years." He tossed down the tablet, causing a puff of dust to scatter around his knees. "We've been led to believe these last years that the English are the Devil incarnate, that they're butchers and evildoers, just as we once believed that the abbot was the incarnate of God."

"One mustn't condemn the entire tree if one apple from it be bad."

"Would that not hold true of armies as well? And kings?"

Lifting one brow, Hope turned her gaze on her younger brother. "Are you defending the curs, Daniel? Need I remind you that they murdered our mother, burned Déols to the ground, and would have killed us as well had we not found our way to Châteauroux."

"Châteauroux." He spat on the floor, then leapt to his feet, dragging the reams of paper with him. "I hardly call the dungeon in which we've been imprisoned a glorious Zion. We live like worms, Hope. *Maggots.* Yet you excuse the abbot's brutality because he *says* he represents God. Well I, for one, don't believe God condones daily thrashings and the starving of his servants. My back yet throbs from his lashes. And you—" He placed one hand on her shoulder, and she flinched. "God help me, Hope, but I would kill him with my bare hands were I given the opportunity. How the fiend can so unconsciously lay strap to your fair flesh is beyond my ability to comprehend."

" 'The deliquent will be brought to terms by harsh beatings, so they may be cured of the sloth of disobedience.' "

"So says the abbot."

" 'Tis the rule, Daniel."

Daniel wedged aside a slab of rock, carefully placed the tablet into the secret niche, then slid the stone back into place, perfectly hiding the papers. Again he looked at his sister, who regarded him with luminous blue eyes. "I fear you forgive too easily, sister, at least where the abbot is concerned."

"My lot has been determined. This burden I bear must be used to help, and not destroy."

"No burden, Hope. A gift. Not from Satan. From God. Would Satan allow you to heal a child? Would he give you the power to lift the shield of blindness from an old woman who needs her eyes to sew for her livelihood? The abbot would have you believe that you're evil in order to benefit himself and Châteauroux's coffers. Thanks to you this monastery has become the wealthiest in Philip's domain. The last thing the abbot desires is for his 'saint' to suddenly up and disappear. Where would his treasuries be then? I doubt he would relish the idea of again feeling the pinch of poverty, no matter how meager an existence is expected of a monk."

"You prattle too much, Daniel. No wonder the abbot flogs you. Remember: 'In speaking there is no escape from sin.' "

"Deny I'm right and I'll be silent . . . I thought not." He dropped onto the wattle and stretched out his long legs. "You hate him as much as I."

"Daniel!"

"Sorry. I occasionally forget you aren't capable of hate."

Hope focused again on the candle flame, watching the dark thread of smoke stream into the overhead darkness; then she shivered. "I *am* capable, Daniel. To believe otherwise is foolish."

"Ah, yes. Which brings us back to the English."

"Curs. All of them. They reek of malice. The very sight of them fills me with revulsion."

"That's my girl. Purge thyself of anger and I vow you'll sleep better tonight."

"I'll not sleep as long as they occupy this place."

"They seem docile enough. Even friendly."

"Stay away from them, Daniel."

Propped on one elbow, Daniel chewed on a weed and regarded Hope closely. "Have you had a vision? If so, tell me. I'll write it in the book—"

"This is not a vision for the book. It has nothing to do with the future . . . at least, not in *that* way."

Daniel slowly sat up. "Why didn't you tell me?"

"I prayed I was wrong."

"When have you ever been wrong?" Daniel moved to a stool across from Hope and sat down. He stared at her through the flame, then reached for her hand. "Was there much pain?"

She nodded.

"When did this occur?"

"Five eventides ago."

"What happened? What did you see?"

Shaking her head, Hope took an unsteady breath. " 'Tis forbidden to discuss it until the moment has come and gone, else the pain will return more severe than before."

"Has it something to do with the English?"

She nodded and entwined her fingers with his, gripping fiercely. His brow creasing, Daniel whispered, "Did you foresee their coming to Châteauroux?"

"Yes."

He studied her closely, then said, "They've come. Would you not be free to discuss it now?"

She thought for a moment, her eyes closed as she awaited the first hint of pain in her head. Nothing. Her shoulders relaxing, she opened her eyes and stared hard into her brother's young face. "I was preparing the tripod, and when I lit the candle wick, the flame . . ." Her voice faded and her eyes grew frightened. "Brother, the flame sprang forth as black as perdition. And that's not all. As I touched it in fear and awe, it shattered like glass onto the table. As I watched, the fragments melted like ice into crystal pools. Within the pools I saw reflected images of soldiers carrying King Henry's banner."

"Did they war?"

"No."

"Did they rape?"

"No."

"Pillage?"

She shook her head.

Daniel sat back in the chair and released his breath. He shrugged and grinned. "Then I see nothing to warrant this apparent emotional flux you're experiencing."

"But what could it mean?"

"I'll tell you exactly what it means. Yon army is led by a knight known as the Black Flame."

"The Heretic!" she spat.

"So some whisper. But I question the rumor."

Leaving her chair, Hope paced the cell. "Hated infidels. Their cruelty is dwarfed only by their arrogance."

"I've witnessed little arrogance in these men. In truth, they appear weary and bloodied. Why else would they ask for respite in one of Philip's monasteries?"

"You defend them like they're idols, Daniel." She looked at her brother, and noted the distant look in his eyes. Her anger softened as she lightly touched his fair hair and smiled. "Yon soldiers fill your head with dreams of chivalry, I think."

"Were I free I would be fighting for Philip by now."

"And taking up shield and sword against the much-maligned English?"

"Is it not a man's destiny to fight for his true beliefs? Honor, truth, liberty? They fight for their beliefs just as we do."

"You're too young to dream of fighting."

"Younger men than I have died on the battlefield!" He jumped from the chair, grabbed the ink-moist quill from the table, and raised it high in the air, spattering ink across Hope's chin and forehead. "*Mademoiselle!* Sir Daniel of Déols has traveled far to liberate you from this drab dungeon of dispair. *En garde,* loathsome enemy, and beware. Send me your fiercest armies: I will defeat them. Release your most dangerous dragons: I will slay them."

He punctured the air with his mock sword, then danced backward just as the door of the chamber opened. The abbot stepped in, a thin leather strap in one hand. Daniel hurried to Hope's side, placing his body slightly before hers.

The abbot regarded them without smiling. "It seems you have a penchant for disobedience, Daniel. Did I not state that you were to remain away from your sister unless granted my approval?"

"And I told you that I would see and speak to my sister if I desired to do so."

"Daniel," Hope whispered. "Silence. You'll only make matters worse."

"Indeed," the abbot said. "I wonder when young Daniel will learn to respect our degrees of humility—one of the most important demanding that we restrain our tongue and keep silent."

"Never," Daniel replied. "I'm no monk and therefore I don't ascribe to your rules. Neither will I keep my head bowed and my eyes toward the ground. I serve only one Lord, and that is God."

His eyes narrowing, the abbot said, "Self-will has its punishment, my son. Perhaps a month spent in the oubliette contemplating your disobedience would benefit us all."

Hope stepped between her brother and the abbot. "Daniel means no disrespect. The ignorance of his youth occasionally spurs him to speak when silence would benefit him better. He thinks only of my welfare, which is commendable in itself, is it not? To put the well-being of another before his own?"

The abbot lifted one eyebrow and regarded her sharply. "The boy is old enough to take responsibility for his actions, not to mention his sins."

"Daniel has committed no sin that I am aware of."

"No?"

Hope took a step back as the abbot moved closer. Still, she remained a shelter between him and Daniel, her shoulders back and her chin lifted obstinately.

"Is it not unlawful to have anything which I have not given or allowed?" the abbot asked.

"Are you claiming that he's guilty of such a disobedience?"

"Is it not a sin of this Rule to take that which is not freely offered by me?"

"If he's done so, then tell me."

"Tablets have been pilfered from the stores. As well as quill and ink."

"What would Daniel do with tablets and quills and ink, other than to perform that which the abbot so requires of him: writing down each and every donation gifted to Châteauroux by its pilgrims."

"What indeed?" The abbot cocked his head, and his mouth turned under. "Perhaps I was wrong to think of him as the culprit. Perhaps I'm looking at the guilty one this very moment." Extending his arm, he touched Hope's brow with one thin, crooked finger, then held it up toward the light, studying the dark smudge on his skin. Daniel gasped quietly. Hope lifted her chin a little more and met the abbot's burning eyes directly—her look one of challenge.

"It seems the demon of deception has roused in your heart, my dear Hope, not to mention the wicked vice of thievery."

"No!" Daniel attempted to shove Hope aside. "It was I. I took the tablets and quill—"

"He did not!" Hope cried and struggled to keep her place

between Daniel and the abbot. "I took the tablets, Father. And the quill and ink as well. I desired to scribe my thoughts and feelings on my life at Châteauroux—"

"Silence!" Placing his hand on Hope's shoulder, he pushed her aside roughly so that she fell to the floor, then grabbed Daniel around the throat and squeezed so fiercely that Daniel's face flushed purple and red. He gasped for air, and, getting little, clawed at the abbot's hand, fighting for release as the abbot's composure became a mask of contempt.

"Thou shalt keep your tongue from evil and your lips from speaking guile. Let no one in this monastery follow his own heart's fancy, and let no one presume to contend with me in an insolent way. But if anyone presume to do so, let him undergo the discipline of the Rule. He shall not steal, nor shall he entertain deceit in his heart, or he shall feel the punishment of my rod."

The abbot moved toward the door, Daniel's feet floundering across the stone floor as he attempted to gain a foothold, his head fast becoming dizzy from lack of air. The abbot threw open the door, then flung Daniel as if he were a rag doll against the wall across the narrow hallway. Stunned, Daniel slid to the floor as the abbot slammed the door and turned back to Hope.

She slowly stood, willing strength into her legs as her gaze fell to the leather strap he still gripped in one hand. "You must know by now that your beatings no longer intimidate me, Father. Nor will they win a respect for you that I don't feel."

"Speak up, demon. Thy voice is timid."

"There is no demon here . . . Father, other than he who masquerades himself as abbot."

He slapped her across the face with the strap. Her hand flew to her cheek, but she refused to whimper or cry. "Careful, Father. How will you explain to yon pilgrims that your saint and miracle worker deserved such a lashing? Were they to learn that she is less than worthy of sainthood, would they not be reluctant to lavish this abbey with their riches? I fathom you wouldn't care to be too closely scrutinized by Philip and the Pope. They might learn that their abbot is pilfering as much for himself as he is for his monastery."

His jaw worked and his fingers clamped around the strap harder. "Granted. However, few would question my whipping of a boy."

"I told you: Daniel is innocent—"

He drove his fist into her belly. Hope bent double and fell to her knees, clutching her midriff as vomit rose in her throat.

The abbot twisted his fingers into her hair and yanked her head back, grinning down into her eyes. "Bruises are well hid beneath the cowl and robe, as are lashes. The strap would cut your soft skin cruelly, would it not?" With that, he grabbed the shoulders of her woolen robe and dragged it over her head.

Naked, Hope scrambled across the tiny chamber and huddled into a shadowed corner, her knees drawn up and her arms locked across her breasts. Her hair spilled down her body and gathered around her buttocks like a reflective pool.

The abbot moved toward her, his breathing audible in the sudden thick silence. Hope glanced from the strap in his hand to the robe that had become tented by his arousal.

"Do you think I care that your ignorant brother took from my stores without permission?" he asked, dragging the robe up his legs. "My anger lies not in his unlawful manner, but in your wickedness which brings the wrath of the Heretic and his army upon this sanctuary."

Shaking her head, Hope cringed further into the corner, unable to escape the image of the abbot with his robe hiked, his swollen organ rising from between his thin, hairless legs. "I—I don't know what you mean, Father. I've brought nothing—"

"Do you deny it was you who skulked in darkness to Roland's chamber and drove a dagger into his shoulder?" He snatched a handful of her hair and dragged her to her knees. "Do you deny you swept upon him atop the tower and attempted to murder him a second time? Because if you do then I must assume it was your brother, and therefore pay a similar visit to him . . ."

Roland inspected the wound on his shoulder, wincing as Roger painted the ragged, healing flesh with a thick, foul-smelling concoction the consistency of ox dung. "No doubt the injury will fester, Roger. The hag would like nothing more than to murder me, I think."

"I would rather the hag be doing this instead of me, Roland. This is far too much to ask of a soldier, much less a friend. God's teeth, but I'll stink for a fortnight."

Gently rotating his shoulder, Roland flashed his second-in-command a telling look. "At least you can bathe. Try wearing the mess under your nose for a fortnight."

Roger laughed and wrapped the shoulder with bandage cloth. "I wager you'll not be wandering amid the village ladies during our stay. That should keep you out of trouble."

"My interest doesn't lie in what trouble awaits beyond the abbey walls, but what awaits within. The abbot is lying to us, Roger. He's hiding a fiend amid these monks."

"What the abbot does here is no business of ours, Roland. We'd be wise to concentrate more on our objective and less on saints and ghostly murderers."

"Easy for you to say. You aren't standing there with a hole in your shoulder and half your life's blood staining yon tower walls."

"You've suffered worse, friend. Need I remind you?"

Roland stiffly stood and moved to the door. The night was heavy with impending rain. His plans to leave Châteauroux at sunup would be delayed if the roads became impassable.

Sighing, he leaned against the door frame and crossed his arms over his chest. "Am I insane, Roger? Did I imagine that the frail monk attempted to roast me like a boar today? Could the entity who drove a dagger into my shoulder have been one of my own men? Do you know of any who would care to murder me in my sleep? Have I become so loathed by my own army during these battles that they would turn against me and Henry?"

"They grow wearied, yes. But no more than you or I."

"They blame our recent bad fortune on the rumors of my losing faith in God." Roland looked back at his friend. "Mayhap they're right."

"You've not lost faith, Roland. You've simply lost hope and the belief in the fight. As have many of us. After all, it's been too many seasons since we were last in England. I have a wife and children whom I haven't seen in three years."

"You're under no obligation to stay. Nor are the others."

"You know our first loyalty is to king and country . . . and to you. Our wives will be there when we return."

Roland grinned. "And hopefully with no children younger than three years."

"I have nothing to fear there, my skeptical friend. My dearest Gwyneth would dry like dust before she took another into her bed. She adores me. I'm quite certain Hildegard will feel the same about you . . . eventually."

Roland flinched as Roger laughed. "What's wrong, Sir Knight? Hasn't the prospect of marriage to Hildegard yet become palatable?"

"Roger, occasionally your friendship bites like an asp."

"And with that, I'll take my leave." Roger stepped around him just as a cry of alarm sounded from the dormitory.

"Thief! Stop! Someone sound the alarm. A fiend has just made off with my dagger!"

Just then a figure darted through the dark. Albert trailed at a distance, doing his best to drag his chausses on as he stumbled over stone and hedges. Dressed only in his own chausses, Roland struck off over the grounds, Roger close behind as they followed the culprit through the shadows and into the black, meandering ambulatory surrounding the apse. The fiend ducked through a portal that led down a curving stairwell barely wide enough for Roland and Roger, as they were forced to slow or further risk injuring Roland's shoulder. At last, they came to the bottom of the stairs, pausing in the pitch darkness that felt both hot and cold, the air so suffocatingly thin that they gasped for a solitary breath.

His voice a whisper, Roger said, "I fear the only soul to reside this deep in the earth is either a worm or a cadaver. I venture to guess a worm could hardly manage to outrun us. May I suggest we return to the surface? I like it much better when I can *see* my foe rather than simply feeling him . . . No? I was afraid of that. You were never nervous of the dark, while I—"

"Quiet."

A sound. A foot treading lightly on dry straw somewhere in the distance.

Arms outstretched, his hands flattened against the damp walls, Roland felt his way along the passage, doing his best to shut out the sound of his and Roger's breathing least he come face-to-face with the fugitive.

At last there came a thread of illumination, just enough for Roland to focus on the distant threshold: a door ajar, allowing the light to creep across the entry to some chamber from which the sound of weeping escaped.

Cautiously, Roland and Roger approached it, stepping into the dim light that felt like an assault on their eyes after the intense darkness. A figure huddled in the distant corner, its features concealed by the monk's cowl drawn low over its brow. Then the face slowly rose and the familiar eyes locked with his.

"Murdering jackal," Roland growled, just as a howl of rage erupted and a body flew at him from the shadows, a dagger slashing near his face. Roger let out a yell of surprise as Roland caught the attacker's wrist and flung him against the wall, pinning the writhing body against the stone, only then capable of discerning that the culprit be a boy.

"Filthy, butchering English," the boy sneered. "I'll kill you. Then I'll kill the abbot for what he's done to us. Depraved pig, I'll see his soul roast in Hell before this night is finished."

Roland wrenched the knife from the boy's fist and flung it to the floor. Then he swung the thin body toward Roger and shoved. The boy sprawled into Roger's arms with a squawk of outrage and immediately began thrashing, jabbing with his elbows and kicking with his bare feet.

"I'm not certain I've ever encountered such ferocity in such a wisp of a child," Roger laughed.

"I'm not a child," the boy cried. "I'll face you man to man and we'll see who's more ferocious."

"Ho, ho, Roland. We've got quite the little dragon on our hands."

Roland focused his gaze on the cowled figure crouched against the distant wall. "Dragon he may be, but *there* is the culprit who tried thrice to murder me." He moved toward the figure, whose face was once again hidden within the cowl. "I would know those eyes amid a score of others, for even though I've looked into the face of hatred a thousand times I've never encountered such evil in the purest sense."

" 'Tis the saint of Châteauroux!" the boy yelled. "God will strike you dead if you harm her. And if He doesn't, then I will."

"Saint?" Roland threw back his head in laughter. "Since when do saints let blood?" Roland twisted his hands into the robe and lifted the body from the floor.

The cowl slid back, revealing the spray of pale hair framing frail and fair features . . . and eyes brilliant and crystalline as gems. They flashed, not in fear, but in challenge as she hissed, "Infidel!" then spat in his face.

FOUR

The abbot set aside his cup of wine and regarded Roland fixedly. "You come into my abbey and demand respite. Your men terrorize and bully the God-fearing peasants of the village. You make wild accusations concerning my monks, and now you claim that I have imprisoned a child and perpetrated some cyclopean ruse on King Philip and the people of this country by passing off the girl as a saint." His mouth thinning, the abbot added, "Such accusations demand that I consider anathema for you and your army, Sir Roland. I wonder what those men would do when suddenly discovering themselves publicly condemned as heretics with complete exclusion from Christian socicty."

"Your threats of excommunication and anathema don't frighten me. I've looked the Devil in the eye too many times to fear the verbal lash of a mere mortal—blessed though he may be or may not be, by God."

"I refuse to allow you to remove the girl from this abbey. Should you attempt to do so, the people of this village—indeed, this entire country—would see you crucified and burned on a stake. Philip himself would see you hanged from a gibbet."

"I wonder what the people of this village, not to mention your beloved king, would think of their abbot abusing their saint?"

The abbot raised one eyebrow. "I don't know what you're talking about."

"Her face is slashed and bruised. The boy Daniel declares that you beat her . . . and worse."

"It's my right and obligation to punish those who disobey the rules of this abbey." The abbot gestured with his hands toward the dagger on the table, its blade yet stained with blood. "She attempted to slay you. I would be remiss to do less, would I not?" He left his chair and moved away, his body casting a narrow shadow across an ambry. His back to Roland, he said, "Would it not also be remiss of me to use her certain . . . powers for the good of God and mankind?"

"I see no powers other than her ability to spit and claw like a cat. I suspect any powers she may harbor are simply products of your own imagination and greed. It's well known that this monastery has become exceedingly rich since your saint took up residence here. No doubt Châteauroux's wealth exceeds Philip's own. To remove her would bring an end to your favor with Philip, not to mention the Pope."

"To allow her the freedom to unleash her abilities on mankind is to bring about the destruction of the people. As abbot of Châteauroux, it's my responsibility to thwart evil, not cast it upon the wind to scatter like pollen to every corner of the land." The abbot turned. "To take her from my control would bring the ruination of life as we know it. Satan will reign. Surely, even a heretic such as yourself would be reluctant to unleash such evil power on the world."

"Wouldn't a heretic such as myself welcome the opportunity to harness such power, if such a power existed?"

The abbot narrowed his eyes.

Roland moved to the door and stopped, looking back. "My men will be taking their leave of Châteauroux at first light. At that time I intend to grant the girl and her brother their freedom. My thanks for your gracious hospitality. Mayhap our paths will cross again.''

''The only path you'll traverse, Roland de Gallienne, is straight to Hell—especially when King Philip learns of your transgression.''

Roland raised one eyebrow and slightly bowed. ''As I said, Abbot . . . mayhap our paths will cross again. *Adieu.*''

Roland stepped from the abbot's chamber and released his breath, little realizing until that moment how close he had come to losing his patience, not to mention his temper. Thrashing the abbot would hardly grant him favor with either king, not to mention the Pope, if he could believe the abbot. Henry was Roland's friend, but he would not look favorably on such a transgression if it meant an escalation of war between England and France. Rumor had recently reached Roland's army that Henry, along with growing more feeble and ill by the day, was losing heart and patience with the war. Even as close as Roland and Henry had been through the years, his old friend would not be pleased by the possibility, indeed, the probability that he might suddenly find himself in boiling water with the Pope.

Roger approached, his face concerned. ''A word, Roland.''

Shoulder-to-shoulder, they moved along the ambulatory, their faces lit briefly as they passed through the dim yellow light of flickering sconces on the walls.

''I take it your visit with the abbot didn't go well,'' Roger commented.

''Unless you consider excommunication for myself and all my men polite conversation between two gentlemen. How are the girl and her brother faring?''

Roger's step slowed. ''While I question the truth of her ability to perform miracles, I confess that I'm confounded by certain aspects of her behavior, not to mention the odd objects Albert collected from her cell.''

"Have you learned their names?''

"The boy is called Daniel. The girl is Hope.''

The girl, lost amid the folds of the gray woolen monk's robe, sat on her mat on the floor, regarding Roland's men with blatant loathing. At Roland's entrance, she scrambled back into a corner and made a sound like a cat.

His voice low, Roger said, "I'd wager my chausses that she's a lunatic. Her brother seems only slightly more sane.''

Albert entered the cell, his arms full of oddities, which he placed at Roland's feet. "She said she refuses to leave Châteauroux without these, Sir Roland. What do you make of them?''

Roland stooped and regarded the tripod, the collection of odd-scented candles, and numerous bags of strongly scented herbs—familiar odors he had come to recognize as medicinals used by the hag Matilda. There was whortleberry, borage, black mustard, and corn cockle, among others.

Roger pointed to the tablets stacked near Roland's knee. "We discovered these in the boy's possession. He was attempting to hide them amid robes and blankets.''

Roland squinted to better see the scrawled messages on the tablet.

"It says,'' Roger whispered, "that in the fifteenth century an explorer of Italian descent will prove to all mankind that the world is *not* flat, but spherical as an egg.''

Roland frowned. "Then she *is* a lunatic.''

"And that's not all, Roland. There is page after page predicting plagues, fires, earthly upheavals, and catastrophic wars, all in different centuries.''

"Hopelessly mad,'' Roland whispered back, his attention drawn again to the girl staring at him from the corner of the cell, most of her face hidden within the cowl. The image of the apparition he had witnessed earlier in the chapel—its voice a hauntingly beautiful soliloquy that had made his blood run cold—roused before his mind's eye with a clarity that made him shiver.

"What do you make of it, Roland?" Roger asked.

Roland stood and moved slowly toward the girl, his gaze locked with hers, which seemed to cut into him like the dagger she had plunged into his shoulder the night before. Cautious, he bent to one knee before her.

"We won't harm you," he said in a gentle voice.

She neither moved nor blinked, just continued to grip the cowl closed over the lower part of her face.

Roland touched the rough robe with his fingertips, the ridiculous notion occurring to him that if she truly was a saint she deserved to wear something far less abrasive to her fair flesh. "A saint deserves to be dressed in flowing robes of gold and silver thread," he whispered. "To be adorned with fine gems that might reflect the fascinating color of her eyes."

Her eyes widened momentarily, then narrowed. She slapped his face so hard he rocked back on his heels.

Grabbing her wrist and twisting so that she cried aloud and fell at his feet, Roland said through his teeth, "On the other hand, shrews and devils deserve nothing more than horsehair shirts and thistle girdles. I have a quantity of both that would fit you perfectly, I think."

"Stay away from her!" Daniel shouted, struggling mightily to escape from a pair of Roland's soldiers, who laughed at his tenacity, further agitating the boy's anger as he was dragged into Hope's tiny cell.

"It seems our little dragon yet breathes smoke, Roland," Roger said. "Perhaps a plunge in a cesspit would dampen his temper."

"Release him," Roland ordered.

"What?"

"I'm perfectly capable of defending myself from a child."

"I am not a child!" Daniel sneered, stumbling as the soldiers suddenly released him. He fell hard against the wall, hitting his head and bringing blood upon his brow. The soldiers guffawed and slapped their knees until Roland silenced them with a look.

"Since when have my men laughed over the injury of a child?" he admonished, bringing both men upright and silent. To Roger he said, "Give the word that we take leave of Châteauroux at daybreak. If you can rouse her from her drunken stupor, have the hag concoct one of her foul ointments for the boy's head. I fear the cut is deep."

The men departed, leaving Roland to regard the cloaked, silent girl who continued to watch him with open malice. The boy, obviously addled by the blow to his head, sat with his back to the wall, head cradled in his hands and blood trickling between his fingers.

"I mean neither of you harm," Roland said. "You needn't fear me or my men unless you continue with your obsession to do away with me. The abbot appears to be the foe here, not I. Now tell me: why have you thrice attempted to murder me? I have a right to know."

"You have no rights," the girl replied, the anger of her words muffled by the cowl over her mouth. Yet her eyes continued to blaze with a sort of unnatural light that made them translucent as artesian water. "You're filthy English dogs and were I able I would cut you from ear to ear and watch you bleed to death in the dirt. Then I would spit on your corpse and leave it to feed the crows."

"Hardly words I would expect to hear spewing from a saint's lips. I suspect that if you're blessed as the abbot claims you to be, you would be forgiving me my sins instead of condemning me for them."

"Your condemnation will come, Sir Roland de Gallienne— friend of Henry, son of the lunatic Godfrey. Surely as your mother died giving birth to a cur, your destruction will come like a bolt from the turbulent sky as you sleep unprepared for your fiery—''

She grabbed her head suddenly, her fingers twisting into the cowl, causing it to spill to her shoulders, releasing a fall of blond hair that draped down her back to the floor. Roland caught his breath, as much struck by her incredible beauty as he was over her unsettling behavior. Even as he watched, her small body appeared to contort in excruciating pain and her brow began to sweat.

"Away!" Daniel cried, shoving Roland aside as Daniel flung himself onto the floor by his sister and wrapped his arms around her. Turning his blood-streaked face to Roland's, he beseeched in a calm but surprisingly authoritative voice, "I care not what you subject me to. I ask only that you grant my sister a moment of privacy."

"For the love of God, what has come over her?"

"It will pass soon. But not without quiet." Pressing Hope's head against his shoulder and stroking her hair, Daniel met Roland's eyes directly and added softly, "Please."

Reluctant, Roland stood and backed toward the door, unable to take his eyes from the girl, who continued to groan and hold her head as if it might shatter. How small she seemed at that moment, how vulnerable and childlike. Hardly the image of a murderess. Or a saint.

Just what the blazes was she?

Who was she?

What emotion had he seen in her eyes that would rouse this disturbing desire to rescue her from something she obviously had no desire to be rescued from? At last, he stepped into the passageway and into the shadows, his back pressed against the wall as he listened to Daniel try desperately to soothe his sister.

"Relax. The pain will pass if you clear your thoughts. Think of Mama. Of our house in Déols. Of the freedom we're soon to enjoy again once we leave here. Imagine, Hope, that soon we'll return home and look upon the faces of our friends again. There, there. Is it better yet?''

"Yes,'' came the weak response.

Roland listened harder.

"Your head, Daniel. What have they done to you?''

"I have my own temper to blame.''

"There's so much blood. Let me help—''

"No! You mustn't, Hope. You know what it could mean—''

"I won't see you suffer, Daniel.''

"But—''

"Quiet. Be still and close your eyes.''

How long Roland stood there, braced against the wall, his senses tuned to every sound from the cell, he could not fathom. An odd lethargy gripped him, dragging him into a place much darker and colder than the damp passageway in which he loitered, spying on the little dragon and his unsettling but beautiful and troubled sister.

"Roland? Roland, are you sleeping?''

His limbs heavy as lead, Roland turned his head toward Roger, who regarded him with concern.

"God's teeth, man, you look like one in a trance. Are you ill? Why are you propped like scaffolding against this wall?''

Roland glanced around. "I'm . . . not certain, Roger. One moment I was listening to yon conversation between the girl and her brother, and the next . . . I must have slept . . .''

"The men are mounted and prepared to depart.''

"Already?''

Roger smiled. "The dawn has broken, dreary as it is. If we hurry we may make the next village before the rains come.''

Roland roused, wincing at the stiffness that had settled in his shoulder.

Closer to Roland's ear, Roger said, "The men grow nervous. I fear they've listened too long and intently to the village gossip, not to mention the dozen or so pilgrims waiting beyond yonder monastic walls to see her. Whatever you may or may not believe, there is little denying that yon village believes she's saintly, and is prepared to stone us if we remove the girl from this abbey. Rumor is word has already gone out to Philip of our intentions, and you know what that means. If you harbored any hopes of spending the next days or weeks avoiding confrontation with Philip's armies, specifically Lacurne, you may be regretably mistaken. In short, my friend, you'd better have a bloody good reason for removing her from Châteauroux—at least in the minds of your army."

"The girl and her brother are obviously being abused. Is that not a sufficient enough reason?"

"Sufficient enough to invite the condemnation of the Pope? Listen to me, Roland. For some time the men have suspected that you were one step away from hellfire and damnation because of your refusal to confess before battle. They believe that our recent defeats were God's way of punishing you for your lack of faith. To so blatantly thumb your nose at the Church would be the ultimate insult." Putting his hand on Roland's shoulder, Roger said, "Will you consider what I've told you, Roland? If you think of her as nothing more than a comely little baggage of problems who attempted thrice to murder you, you'll have no problem leaving her and her hotheaded brother to their fate here at the abbey. From what I've seen of her behavior, she and the abbot deserve one another."

Roland raised one eyebrow and his mouth thinned in a sarcastic curl. "Is she comely, Roger? I hadn't noticed."

"I saw your expression when the cowl slid from her head. Had she looked like a buzzard you would have cuffed her when she slapped you."

"Need I remind you that we took an oath upon our knighthood, Roger, to respect all weaknesses, and constitute ourselves the defender of them. The girl and her brother are being kept here against their will.''

Roger stared at Roland without speaking, then stepped aside, allowing Roland to move to the door of Hope's cell. The sconce on the wall was little more than an ash, casting an amber glow over the floor where the girl and her brother huddled on a thin mat, sleeping. Roland moved silently to where Hope, her back propped against the wall and her hair framing her face like a silver cloud, slept without any apparent discomfort. Daniel, stretched out on the floor, rested his head in Hope's lap.

Roger moved up behind Roland and caught his breath.

Roland raised his hand to silence him.

Blood stained the boy's tunic and the robe on which he lay his head. There was dried blood between Hope's fingers and smeared over her chin and cheek. Yet . . . there was no evidence that a wound had ever existed on Daniel's brow.

"God's blood," Roger whispered, turning his gaze up to Roland's. "Do my eyes deceive me—"

"Nay, they don't deceive you, Roger. The wound is healed.''

Roger caught Roland's arm and propelled him back out the door. His face in Roland's, Roger whispered, "This puts a different light on the matter, don't you think?"

"Meaning?"

" 'Tis true. The gal is a saint. The men are sure to mutiny should they discover—"

"Matilda has been known to heal. Is she a saint?"

"Good God, you have a point. She is as far from being a saint as I am from becoming archbishop. Matilda is a hag. A witch. A hexess." He paced before stopping short and slowly looking back at Roland. "If what we have witnessed in that room be truth, saint or sorceress, Hope of Châteauroux is worth a figging king's ransom to Philip and the Pope."

Saint or sorceress? Therein lay Roland's quandary.

Roland moved again to the threshold and looked down on the sleeping girl. How easy it would be to believe in her saintly abilities. To think that the divine beauty that radiated from her features was a reflection of goodness, and not evil. Yet even as he gazed upon her countenance his shoulder throbbed with pain, a grim reminder that the knife she had thrust into his shoulder had been meant to destroy him and everything he represented.

As Roger moved up behind him, Roland said, "Her healing of the boy is to remain our secret. Without proof of her abilities the men will have little cause to question our motives. Agreed?"

"Agreed," Roger replied.

"Heretic you may be, Roland, but we won't abide your bringing damnation on this entire army. I speak for the lot of loyal and brave men who have fought by your side through the cruelest of battles. There isn't one of us who wouldn't lay down his life to protect you, and we have done so many times. But this is out of the question. Take the saint of Châteauroux as prisoner? What could you be thinking?"

Astride his destrier, Roland regarded the faces of his men, all of whom glared at him as if he were totally mad. "Would you rather she remain here, a prisoner of the abbot? Besides, who among you truly believes in miracles? Were she capable of performing such, why would she allow herself and her brother to be caged like animals?"

A murmur passed among the men before someone spoke up, "I don't like it. We're surely doomed for such a sacrilege."

Roger exited the building, the girl and her brother trailing at the end of ropes. A spear of disquietude caused the horses to dance in place and roll their eyes wildly, bringing further anxiety to Roland's men, not to mention the villagers who were gathering in clusters, many with cudgels and stones in their hands. Several soldiers were forced to drive their horses into the crowds to reinforce that they would brook no interference of their taking of the girl.

Roger presented Roland with the ropes. "If you don't mind, Sir Knight, I happily decline the offer of dragging the pair from this abbey as if they were recalcitrant pups."

The men exchanged looks. Finally, Roger said softly, "As your second-in-command, Roland, I follow your leave with utmost sobriety and consideration of your stature. However, I must confess as to being totally baffled by your behavior, especially in light of what we've witnessed. If she truly be a saint she deserves better than to be dragged through the mud like a hog."

"She attempted to slaughter me. Is that not reason enough? Would a saint attempt to cut out a man's heart while he's sleeping? Nay, Roger; the cat is no saint. More like a sorceress."

"The only sorcery I see here is in your own head, Roland." Further lowering his voice, Roger added, "The thought has just occurred to me; if she *is* a sorceress, would it not be unwise to unleash her powers on Henry's armies . . . *this* army in particular?"

"Need I remind you that I've looked into the Devil's face too many times to take him seriously?" Roland grinned.

"I've often said you would eventually come up against a force more powerful than your own," Roger warned. "I cannot tell you why, but I feel in the pit of my gut that you've just confronted it." His voice dropping, he added as an afterthought, "I hope we don't come to regret this, good captain. I would hate to find my most illustrious career dimmed by sacrilege, of all things."

As Roland's horse shifted nervously beneath him, Roland

regarded Hope and her brother, and the manner in which Hope held herself, shoulders back, chin up, her magnificent eyes boring like two hot stones into his own. She wore her contempt for him like a shimmering chlamys. All that was missing was a sapphire brooch, the color of her eyes, to secure it around her shoulders.

Roger was wrong, of course. Stupidly wrong. Roland did not find the girl in the least bit attractive. She was much too waiflike. Too fragile. Too white. Too pouty. Her eyes were much too large for her face, and her face was much too oval. And her lips were too red. And full. And he didn't care at all for the tiny cleft in her chin. It made her look too bloody obstinate. No knight worth his shield and banner would tolerate obstinacy from a woman—even one who was purported to be a saint.

Forcing himself to turn away, and refusing to look again at his agitated men, or the villagers who shouted, spat, and flung horse dung at them, Roland nudged his destrier out through the open gates, the woman and her brother following at the end of their tethers.

The rains came, cold and steady, turning the roads to muck and mire. Hope and Daniel stumbled over the muddy terrain, doing their best to keep up with Roland's struggling destrier. Again, Hope stumbled and fell, forcing Daniel to help her to her feet before Roland dragged her through the mush.

"Filthy butcher!" Daniel cried through the downpour. "Coldhearted son of a mange-infested cur! You're a disgrace to your banner, not to mention your king. No chivalrous knight would put the fair maiden through such travails!"

"You'll not better our plight by insulting him," Hope pointed out.

"I would do more than insult him if I could get my hands on his sword. Besides, you're one to talk. Had you not attempted to skewer him as if he were an ox to be roasted we wouldn't be in this predicament now. On the other hand, I suppose we have to look at the bright side.''

Hope barely managed to leap over a fallen tree trunk before staring at her brother in disbelief. ''Pray tell me, Daniel: Is there a bright side to this? For if there is, tell me quick before I give in to self-pity and begin to blubber like a babe. I'm cold. I'm hungry. I'm wet. Right now I would happily trade Roland de Gallienne for ten abbots.''

''I don't believe that. Not after what the abbot subjected you to last eventide, the perverted bastard. Were it in my power I would strangle him with my bare hands.''

The rope around Hope's wrists snapped taut, upsetting her balance so she again fell hard to the ground. There came a chorus of shouts and suddenly the world exploded in thrashing hooves and flying mud that stung her face like nettles. Someone twisted his hands into her robe and lifted her from the mire as if she were light as goose down. She thought of struggling, but her arms and feet felt heavy as mail. Mud clogged her nose and she was forced to gasp for breath amid the flying mud and drenching rain. Blinking water from her eyes, she did her best to focus on Roger, his red beard virtually bristling with anger. His hair plastered to the sides of his head, he glared at his commander and hoisted Hope into his arms.

''Enough is enough, Roland. The girl is exhausted, as is the boy. She can walk no further. She needs food and respite. She's shivering like a newborn calf.''

''As are we all,'' someone shouted.

Roger wrapped his arms around Hope and frowned. ''She trembles, Roland, from cold and fear. I've seen you treat swine with more compassion.''

''The swine didn't try to kill me,'' Roland shouted through the roar of rain and advancing thunder.

Hope watched through her strands of sodden hair as Roland flung the ropes into the mud and spurred the destrier toward her and Roger. Planting her feet, her hands fisting at her sides, she bravely raised her chin and cried, "Blast you to Hades, Roland. I would rot on a gibbet before climbing on that beast with you!"

The horse stumbled, throwing Roland off balance. He hit the ground, face down, his body nearly disappearing in a wave of muddy water.

It seemed in that moment as if the universe careened to a halt. Soldier and camp follower alike froze in their tracks, mouths open, eyes staring as Roland slowly pulled himself out of the muck and raised his dark eyes to Hope with a look that made the blood freeze in her veins. She backed against Roger, who clamped his arm around her waist and muttered something under his breath that sounded like, "Be brave, lass. It'll be over swiftly. I swear you'll not feel a thing."

With mud sucking at his feet, Daniel threw himself between Roland and Hope and lifted his fists. "You'll have to go through me first, Roland."

"Happily," he sneered, then drew back his arm and drove it so hard against Daniel's shoulder that the boy spiraled back over the tree trunk and dove head first into a puddle.

"Daniel!" Hope cried, but before she could spring to her brother's aid, Roland leapt again onto his horse and grabbed Hope's arm, flinging her over his horse's withers. The wind left her in a rush, yet when she fought to lift her head in search of air, he shoved it down again into the horse's shoulder, filling her senses with the smell of sweating hide, as suffocating as the rain running into her nose.

"Be still," Roland growled. "I'm in no mood for your harping. One more utterance from you and I'll drag you by the feet to our destination."

"Despicable idiot. Foul oaf—"

He swatted her buttocks and she jumped, causing the horse to lunge forward, upsetting her balance, forcing her to grab her captor's hard, mud-covered thigh and hang on with all her strength. Too weary to struggle, she rested her head near his knee and did her best to hold on as the army trudged forward through the downpour.

As the army of drenched, agitated men struggled to erect tents beneath the trees, Hope and Daniel shivered together beneath a canopy of oak limbs, their teeth chattering as they wrapped themselves in a rain-heavy horse blanket that made their flesh burn as if from stinging ants.

"I'll jump the fiend at first opportunity," Daniel announced wearily. "Just give me a moment or two to plan my course of attack."

"You'll do no such thing," Hope said, her head nodding with the need to close her eyes and sleep. Perhaps then she would awaken to discover this was all a bad dream. That she was yet sequestered in her tiny dank and dark cell at Châteauroux, fantasizing about her more carefree days in Déols—before her mother's death—before Hope had been burdened by the only "gift" her penniless mother could leave her cherished daughter upon her demise. "Look around you, Daniel. Angry the men may appear to be over Roland's treatment of us, but I venture they won't hesitate to retaliate should you try and dispose of him."

Daniel released a sigh. "Look at them, Hope. Knights all of them. Fearless. Strong. Courageous. There's not a one of them who wouldn't lay down his life to live up to his code of honor . . . except, perhaps, Roland. Still, I'm not so certain he's as evil as he seems."

"Would an honorable man drag a woman tethered at the end of a rope through the mud?"

His fair brow wrinkling, Daniel looked upon his sister with an air of amusement. "Perhaps if you had acted more like a saint and less like a termagant he would have left us at Châteauroux. I ask you again, would that be preferable to a little rain and mud?"

"I care not for your wit, Daniel. Nor your continued appreciation for these heretics. There is little honor or bravery in abusing a woman, not to mention a boy."

"I'm not a boy," he reminded her, then sat up straight as Roger de Ferres exited a striped tent and made his way toward them. "If we're smart," Daniel whispered, "we'll make a friend of this Roger de Ferres. As Roland's second-in-command he has influence on the others."

"I would rather die in a pit of asps than befriend an Englishman."

"Well, I for one haven't got the taste for my own blood, thank you."

Roger regarded them with hooded eyes before pointing to Hope. "You'll come along with me, girl. Roland will have you in yonder tent for the night."

Daniel jumped up. "Fair knight, I beseech you—"

Roger cuffed Daniel on the ear. "Quiet. I'm in no mood to listen to your prattle. The girl comes with me. Albert will be along soon to see you settled for the night." Bending, he grabbed Hope's arm and dragged her to her feet. "As for you, I suggest you learn to bite your tongue where Roland is concerned. He's not above thrashing a woman if necessary. You don't look as if you could stand up to his sort of . . . brutality."

Hope looked back at Daniel, who remained on the knoll, his face twisted in despair. "I'll be fine," she called out. "Behave, Daniel. Promise me?"

He nodded, albeit reluctantly.

Roger shoved her inside the tent, where the damp ground had been covered by animal hides and the light rain made a muted drumming on the roof. She listened hard to the muffled voices of Roland's army, the occasional whinnying of the cold, drenched horses, the clatter of armor and sword as the men prepared themselves for the encroaching night. She would know the moment before Roland entered, and she would prepare herself.

The tent flap was thrown back and a bent old woman wearing black robes shuffled in, her gray hair hanging like knotted yarn around her face. Her yellow eyes glistened like polished amber, and the bags hanging from her wrists by straps made clinking sounds as she moved across the tent toward Hope.

"So," the hag said, "this is the so-called saint, I take it. There is much talk of you among the men."

"I'm no saint," Hope replied, drawing her knees up to her chest and averting her gaze from the old woman's face. Her breathing quickened and her brow began to sweat. The dim light within the tent appeared to pulsate like a gasping flame.

The hag cocked her head and showed her teeth in something short of a smile. "Are you a sorceress?"

"No."

"A healer?"

"Why do you ask?" Hope demanded.

"There must be some reason Roland has brought you here. 'Tis certain it's not because of your beauty. I've seen rats more pleasing to the eye. Roland prefers his women buxom, their hips wide—the better to accommodate him comfortably."

"I'll not accommodate Roland in any manner, least of all that."

The hag cackled and moved closer, so close that Hope could smell the *jabrol* that permeated her ragged robes. A darkness fell over Hope's face that obliterated what little light had remained in the tent until that moment, and suddenly the air smelled foul and felt hot on her skin. "Why are you here?" she demanded.

"Whispered word is you have magical powers. That one

touch of your hand will close a wound. I came to see for myself. Show me your hands.''

Hope raised her hands. "There's no magic in these hands, old woman. Now leave me. I demand an audience with Roland.''

"You have no authority here, least of all with Roland. Roland listens to no one other than King Henry and myself.'' The hag bent close and pointed one crooked finger at Hope's face. "His fate lies in *my* magic. I choose whether he lives or dies on the battlefield.''

"'Twould be a sad day if Roland's life were left up to you, Matilda." Roger stepped into the tent, his clothes and hair dripping water. He carried a bundle under one arm. "I suspect Roland would be less than pleased to find you here with our . . . guest. I suggest you waddle off to your own tent before I inform him.''

"Good and kind knight, I meant no harm to the girl. I only wished to see for myself if what yon soldiers whisper be the truth.''

"Roland has done nothing more than free the girl and her brother from the abbot's tyranny.''

Her eyebrows going up, Matilda smiled. "The rope burns around her wrist speak otherwise . . . Sir Knight." She turned for the opening, paused, and looked back over her stooped and rounded shoulder. "She will cast a spell over these men. They will turn their backs on Roland to protect her. Mark my words, Roger de Ferres, she will bring about the fall of Roland de Gallienne within a fortnight if she remains. As the man closest to Roland, both in heart and the battlefield, you would do him justice by freeing the girl and her brother before she brings the ruination of your friend and all he holds sacred.''

Matilda flung back the tent flap, allowing a cold rush of damp wind and rain to swirl through the opening. For an instant the sides of the tent breathed in and out like a living thing; then the hag disappeared into the dark.

Roger frowned as he turned to Hope. His eyes were hard as he studied her. "Were I to believe Matilda—that you'll bring about the downfall of my friend—I would lift my sword against you this moment."

"Then raise your sword, Sir Knight, for if given the chance I would see him worm's meat before dawn."

"Harsh words for one so fair. 'Twas not Roland who murdered your family." He tossed the bundle into her lap. "He sent you these. I suspect you'll find them finer, not to mention cleaner, than the garb you're wearing."

She flung the bundle to the ground. "I would rather go naked."

A grin flickered across Roger's lips, and he shrugged. "I'm certain none of us would find that aspect too displeasing. I'll wait outside until you've changed. I suggest you hurry; Roland is an impatient man."

As Roger stepped from the tent, Hope jumped to her feet, kicking the bundle as hard as she could. "Beastly man. He binds me in ropes, then expects me to tremble in gratitude over a lot of rags."

"You haven't much time," came Roger's voice.

She glanced again at the clothes, which lay scattered over the ground. She snatched at a garment and held it toward the light. The material was cloth woven with silk and gold, more suited for a chatelaine than a captive peasant such as herself. On further inspection she found linen underthings: a chemise, white as the lily of the field, with a light tinge of yellow that was not disagreeable even to the most critical eyes. There, too, was a pair of embroidered slippers.

"Does Roland always dress his prisoners in such finery?" she called to Roger.

"Only if they're female," came his amused response.

Looking down the mud-caked robe that had been her only

frock since the day she had arrived at Châteauroux and pleaded with the abbot for respite, she recalled a recent time when she had yearned to don the feminine frocks—although far less splendid than those at her feet—that she had worn before that fateful day when her village had been burned to the ground. But to contemplate accepting such finery from one of King Henry's knights seemed a sacrilege to her mother's memory.

Still . . . the wool robe, heavy with rain and mud, made her skin itch. The prospect of spending the night wrapped in the cloying folds was not a pleasant one. As her mother had once said, "To rebel against good judgment, just for the sake of rebelling, is cutting one's nose off to spite his face." If she prayed hard enough, perhaps God, and her mother, would understand.

With rainwater she washed the mud from her feet and legs, then dressed quickly. Roger's surprise was evident on his face when he stepped into the tent. For a moment, he stood speechless.

"Am I acceptable?" she asked.

"Yes." He nodded and repeated, "Yes."

"Is something wrong?"

"Far from it. I suspect Roland will be pleased."

"I care not what Roland thinks."

"You should. After the men see you, I fear their . . . ad-miration will be surpassed only by their respect for Roland's wishes that they keep a goodly distance from you. If you looked as lovely when stumbling into the abbot's lair, I don't doubt he kept you under lock and key."

FIVE

Most knights of Roland's notoriety would have demanded the finest and most opulent tent made of colors as varied as a peacock's tail. Hung upon the walls would be tapestries, most depicting the knight's greatest and most successful battles. Roland, however, cared not for such displays of grandeur. He knew too well that amid the great successes were far too many defeats.

As was custom, Roland's tent was much separated from the others in case of an unexpected attack on their encampment. Perched under a tree on a high knoll, it reflected none of the infamous knight's reputation. Still and all, the Black Flame's tent always caused a certain degree of nervousness, be the visitor Roland's second-in-command or the bright-eyed young falconer, whose dedication to the care of Roland's hawks was as fervent as de Gallienne's desire to please his king. In truth, the falconer was normally welcomed more warmly than most into the leader's chamber. If there was anything that could take a knight's thoughts from war and death, the sight of his beautiful birds could normally do it.

Days had passed since Roland had last spent time with his hawks; he needed something to avert his thoughts, which had been caught up in some strange tumult since leaving the abbey. Alas, Matilda wasn't helping with her prattling about his cursing the men by bringing the "sorceress" Hope of Châteauroux into their midst. His head was beginning to pound.

"Heed me well, good knight; yon men's angst and anger mount by the minute. They fear the Black Flame acts without reason and care for his people's welfare." Matilda shuffled up beside him and tugged on his sleeve. "By the looks of you, I'd say the tendrils of her magic have already sunk to the very heart of you. Yer skin is yellow as saffron and yer eyes—"

"My eyes have long since grown weary of looking at you, old woman." Roland studied the beautiful gyrfalcon that perched splendidly on its *sedile*. He stroked its white plumage before nodding to Renaud, who hurried to offer fresh meat to the alert bird. It grabbed the bloody flesh with its talons, causing the tiny silver campanelle on its foot to tinkle lightly. Only then did Roland turn his attention back to the hag. "My men are my business. If they have reservations about my bringing the girl along then they should discuss them with me. You have my permission to tell them so."

"Mayhap your father was right," Matilda wheezed. "He said you would turn out to be your own worst enemy—that your cursed stars would bring the ruination of your army and ultimately your king."

"My father is an ignorant old man too caught up in his foul ale to know what he's saying—or why."

Matilda flung the contents of her pouch onto the ground. The stones and bones and withered leaves scattered at Roland's feet, and she sank to her knees to study them closely. "There is evil here, my lord. Its cold and fetid fingers even now are worming through these campsites. It will twist these stalwart soldiers' minds and crush their bodies. They will eventually turn on you—"

"My men would never turn on me," he said through his teeth.

"Cursed you be so that you will be forced to watch them fall one by one. Their loyalty will be like water in your hands. Even your closest friend will be your enemy." Pointing to a solitary piece of fine blue glass amid the bones, Matilda turned her gaze up to Roland's. "Her presence appears pure and true, her beauty a priceless treasure that would grasp the heart of any man."

"Beauty?" He laughed and scratched the gyrfalcon's breast. "I fear you've been nipping your own henbane, old woman. I've seen starving hedgehogs with more allure, and I'm certain their spines weren't nearly so lethal."

"I tell you true, Roland. Her magic be not from Heaven— her attempts to murder you are evidence of that. While your army be dazzled now by the whispers of ignorant villagers, soon their admiration will turn to suspicion and fear as foul Fate drives them to their graves. Hope of Châteauroux will rent this army apart. Get her gone now, Roland, while you have the chance—before she brings about the ruination of all you hold dear!"

"Silence!" Roland shouted, grabbing a handful of the hag's matted hair and snapping back her head, exposing her throat. Then he grabbed from the nearby wooden table the knife he had earlier used to cut up the gyrfalcon's meat, and he pressed the bloody tip to her jugular. "Vile old woman, were you not so revered by my idiot father I would cut you now and let that bird eat you while I watch."

Her yellow eyes darted to the *sedile* where the hawk cocked its head and danced on its perch, filling the tent with a wild tinkling of the campanelle. "'Tis bad fortune to kill a seeress, good knight."

"Perhaps. But where is it said that bad fortune befalls the

man who cuts out her tongue?'' He flung her aside so she sprawled on her back, her hair like a gray web around her head. ''Now get you out of my presence, hag. And you tell those among my men that if they have complaints about my decisions they should bring them to me.''

She rolled first to her hands and knees, clawed the bones and stones from the dirt, then scrambled to her feet. She looked back at Roland and sneered, ''You will soon see the evidence of her sorcery, I vow. And so will your men.''

The hag scurried from the tent. Roland followed, flinging back the tent door and allowing a thick gray fog to tumble around his legs.

''Idiot woman,'' he said to himself, even as his eyes scanned the landscape, registering each shadow and blur.

Roger materialized through the mist, his face concerned. ''The hag runs like a rabbit, Roland. What have you done to her now?''

''Threatened to feed her to my bird,'' Roland drawled. ''As if the fowl would have her.''

Roland glanced at Renaud, who attempted to soothe the agitated falcon. He dismissed the young man with a nod, then offered his forearm to the bird, which hopped upon it with a flutter of its wings. ''Have you come to scold me as well, Roger? Am I to believe that my army is intent on mutiny over my allowing the girl to remain here?''

'' 'Allowing?' God's teeth, Roland, you've taken the lass captive. She detests us, in case you haven't noticed. If the hag be right, and Hope's magic prove to be more sinful than saintly, I fear we'll be dead by the morrow.''

''And the little dragon Daniel? How does he fare?''

''As curious as he is angry. I've given him over to Albert. If anyone can tame him, Albert can.''

''Albert is little more than a boy himself.''

''You knighted him. Why? Because he reminded you of

you. Albert, however, is not so intent on his own destruction.''

''Albert hasn't yet seen enough men die in battle. Give him time.'' Roland dropped into a chair. The falcon fluttered to the chair back and danced momentarily before settling lightly atop the scrolled wood depicting a sword aflame.

Roger retrieved a vessel of ale from the table and filled two tankards. He handed one to Roland, turned the other up to his mouth and drank deeply, then wiped his chin with the sleeve of his shirt. Roland regarded him closely before speaking.

''You have something on your mind.''

Roger nodded. ''The hag wasn't lying, Roland. I've listened to the men. Even as we speak there's a growing division among them, neither of which bodes well for you. Those who believe she's a saint fear your actions will bring God's wrath on them. Those who claim her a sorceress believe she'll curse us all with black magic. I don't have to remind you that there was unrest among the men even before we ventured to Châteauroux. They all feel your behavior toward the abbot was reason enough for anathema.''

His mouth thinning, Roland frowned. ''I'll not stop any man who desires to withdraw his oath to me.''

''They fear that you're showing signs of your father's affliction.''

His gaze going to Roger's, Roland asked quietly, ''Is that what you think? That my father's lunacy has begun eating away at my reason?''

A moment passed. At last, Roger wearily ran one hand over his eyes and shook his head. ''The occasional madness I see in your face has little to do with insanity, I think. 'Tis more your anger over this constant warring.''

Roland laughed sharply. ''You give me too much credit, Roger. Half the time I feel quite the lunatic. I feel like howling at the moon. I want to drive my sword through the heart of every man who looks at me as if I *am* crazy." He drummed his fingers on the chair arm. "Where is the girl?"

"Waiting in her tent."

"Did she accept the gift?"

"With reluctance."

"Do the clothes suit her?"

Roger took a deep breath and released it slowly.

"Well?" Roland said. "Do the clothes suit her?"

"Yes." Roger swallowed. "I think you'll find that they suit her splendidly."

Slowly rising from the chair, Roland studied his friend closely. "Do I detect a touch of dry mouth and sweaty palms? Could it be that the trusted husband of Gwyneth has found himself attracted to another woman?"

His eyes rounding and his cheeks blushing as red as his beard, Roger shook his head.

Roland slapped his hand on Roger's shoulder, and squeezed. "As I recall, Roger, your wife is most comely. I would have trouble believing that the foul-tempered and murderous little termagant we dragged from the bowels of the abbey could come close to rivaling your wife's beauty."

Clearing his throat, Roger shrugged and stepped away. "As I said, Roland: the clothes suit her splendidly."

"Fine. Then go and fetch her. Once she and I have discussed this . . . situation like two adults, then perhaps, depending on my mood, of course, I may reconsider my decision to keep her with us. Who knows; I may feel so generous as to forget the fact that Philip might be willing to pay a fortune for her return and send her and her toothless little dragon of a brother on their merry way—before either of them causes us any more trouble than they already have."

With an abrupt nod of his head, Roger backed out of the tent, leaving Roland to stare after him, a smirk on his face. "Smitten fool," he said aloud, then drank deeply of his ale.

As he turned to collect his bird and return it to the *sedile*, his eye was caught by a flash of blue light near his foot. He bent to one knee and reached for the sliver of ice-blue glass that had earlier spilled from the hag's pouch. He held it in the palm of his hand as he studied it—its faceted sides, the purity that caught the dim light inside the tent and sent it shooting in golden streaks in a hundred directions. For an instant, its radiance grew brighter—so bright he was forced to briefly close his eyes. Yet, when he looked again, there was nothing but cold dull glass, and somehow its sharp edges had cut into his skin, bringing a sudden bead of blood that fell like a raindrop onto the tip of his boot.

Roland lay on his back, his eyes closed, when Roger stepped into the tent with Hope in his arms. The girl, her eyes wide with anticipation, shrank against Roger's chest as Roland propped himself up on one elbow and stared at them without speaking. In truth, he was momentarily taken aback with confusion, not to mention the drugged effect the vessel of mead had had on his reasoning. He wondered, too, if Matilda had slipped him a sprinkling of nightshade, for certainly his brain was wont to convulse with a certain twinge of delirium as he focused on the beauty in Roger's arms.

"Who have we here?" he asked softly, his lips curling sleepily, his body rousing not so sleepily as it acknowledged the perfection of her delicately boned face and generously rounded breasts, made all the more alluring by her gown. "Don't tell me some farmer has sent me his daughter in hopes of inviting my favor. If so, you may tell him for me that his efforts are appreciated. Give me his name and I'll reward him substantially."

Roger made an amused sound and raised one eyebrow. "No farmer's daughter this, captain. As requested, I have brought you 'the termagant.' " He dropped Hope onto her bare feet, allowing her moon-silver hair to spill over her shoulders. Like an ethereal cloud, it settled around her hips, which were slenderly curved and silhouetted beneath the frail material of the dress. "Do you think you can handle her alone," Roger drawled, "or should I stand guard under yonder tree?"

"I'm not amused," Roland snapped, his eyes narrowing as the realization of Roger's meaning sank in. *This* was Hope of Châteauroux? The drab, cowled little mouse with poison fangs who thought nothing of murdering a man in his sleep? Then again, why should he be surprised when even her behavior was the very antithesis of her saintly reputation?

Roger smiled, apparently finding humor in Roland's discomposure, then he noted the blood-soaked bandage around Roland's hand.

" 'Tis nothing," Roland assured him, his gaze still locked on Hope's features. "The injury is simply an annoyance. I allowed my admiration over a pretty bauble to interfere with my better judgment. You might keep that in mind, Roger, the next time you find yourself smitten speechless by a pretty face."

As if to say, *Speak for yourself,* Roger gave him a flat smile, then turned on his heels and quit the tent. Hope watched Roger go, obviously restraining herself from running after his second-in-command.

"I wouldn't if I were you," Roland stated matter-of-factly, his perusal continuing to take in the transformation Hope had gone through since he'd last seen her mere hours before. The realization struck him, too, that beautiful as she was, she was little more than a child, and trembling with a fear she was trying desperately to hide. "While Roger is chivalrous to a fault when it comes to fair damsels in distress, I fear you would find him quite the ogre when asked to put another's desires over mine. In short, if you think to escape me, or this encampment, he'll search you down with no more thought than if you were a boar and he were starving. Then, of course, you would have *me* to deal with. Although a patient man, I have my limits. Be warned that you've pushed mine to their endurance.''

She took a deep breath and met Roland's eyes directly. ''Before we progress, Englishman, I demand to know what you've done with my brother.''

He raised one brow.

''He's young. I trust you'll forgive him his warrish enthusiasm. He has aspirations of becoming a knight.''

Roland laughed in his throat, and his voice dropped an octave. ''Everyone aspires to be a knight. Few have the diligence to accomplish the task. Even fewer have the stomach for it.''

''I suppose ravishing women and burning villages would have a tendency to bother some, though obviously not *all*.''

He sat up abruptly. Her eyes widening, Hope stepped back and clinched her hands, her gaze darting to the sword and dagger lying near his mat. ''Careful,'' he said smoothly. ''Your gratitude is showing again.''

''Am I to be thankful for being held against my will?''

''You should be thankful you need not concern yourself any longer that the abbot will visit you during the night with his strops and torments.''

Her fair cheeks flushed with color, and she averted her gaze. Lower lip trembling, she took a quick, ragged breath before managing to look at him again, her eyes blazing all the more with her emotions.

Standing, Roland picked up his sword, then offered it to her, jeweled hilt first. Hope's eyes widened and her lips parted. She took a cautious step back before stopping herself and setting her heels. ''Go on,'' he ordered. ''Take it.''

She stared, her fine brows drawing together in distrust and confusion.

''I said take it. Once this need for retribution is satisfied, then perhaps we can get on with our conversation. *Take it*.''

With a catlike growl, she grabbed it, crying out as the

weight of it nearly toppled her over. Her arms trembled as she attempted to raise the tip off the floor, to no avail. Furious, she dropped the sword and dove for the dagger on the table, only to be stopped short as Roland grabbed her around the waist, dragging her back against his chest. Her hair sprayed over his chest and shoulders, filling his nostrils with a fragrance that made his inebriated mind all the dizzier.

"I want to know the truth," he said in her ear. "How did you heal your brother's wound? What magic did you use? Was it truly of Heaven, or is the angelic beauty and innocence you portray before me now simply a guise to confound my army?"

"I don't know what you mean—"

"Your brother's head was bloodied. I saw it with my own eyes."

"You're mistaken, de Gallienne. 'Twas nothing more than a sleight of hand to make you think he was injured."

"I don't believe you."

She struggled. He held her tighter, so tightly her ribs felt crushable beneath his arm. Her heart beat wildly and her breathing became shallow. For an instant her entire being sagged against his, allowing him to experience the sensation of her little buttocks pressed softly against his loins, which responded with a jolt that made his body go rock hard. Suddenly the air in the tent became thin and hot, and it was all he could do to ignore the shamefully base need to toss her to the rug and mount her. He was not, after all, a man known for monkishness when it came to turning away a willing body.

Except . . . hers was *not* willing, he reminded himself. Or was it? Just how far would she go to win favor for herself and her brother? Perhaps the gruesome details Daniel had spun about the abuse she was forced to tolerate at the abbot's hands was nothing more than a ploy for sympathy.

He cupped her breast in his palm, stroked the nubby little

peak that felt hard as a cherry pit beneath his thumb. Her
body tensed. The breath left her in a rush. A half-scream
worked its way up her constricted throat, but she swallowed
it back and did her best to remain still, even as he squeezed
her nipple between his fingers.

"Blackhearted son of Satan that I am, I could mount you
right now and there would not be a damnable thing you could
do about it. I could tear these pretty clothes from your
shapely little body and twist yon rope around your neck and
lead you about this camp as if you were a pet lamb. Could
I not, Hope of Châteauroux?"

"Y—yes," she managed.

"I could snap your frail pretty neck with one jerk of my
hands."

"Then do so, for I grow weary of your bullying me."

"Do what, love? Snap your neck or mount you?"

"Snap my neck. I would rather die a thousand horrible,
painful deaths than be mounted by an English infidel."

He spun her around, closed his fingers around her neck,
and backed her against the table. The color drained from her
cheeks, and her pink lips parted. He could not breathe, suddenly. He could not tear his gaze from hers as he was flooded
by the dizzying need to ravish her enticing mouth and body.
"My smitten friend Roger said these clothes suit you. He
was right. They suit you far better than a monk's robes, and
I trust feel gentler against the flesh. If you're a good girl, I
might gift you with a pretty pelisse or perhaps a bliaut to
match the color of your eyes."

"I care nothing for your gifts."

"Then you must not be of this earth, because I've not met
a woman yet whose head wasn't turned by a bit of embroidered frippery or the prospect of owning a jeweled girdle."

"What need do I have for such excess?"

"To please a man, of course. Even hardened warriors enjoy looking on a beautiful woman. Of course, we much prefer to enjoy our women *without* clothes.''

"Do you not fear your men's actions should they learn you misused me?''

"The Black Flame fears no man, little one.''

"He fears one,'' she said breathlessly. "His father.''

His fingers tightened around her throat and her head fell back. He felt her pulse escalate beneath his palm, and the color of her face became white as lilies. Still, she refused to whimper, to show the least amount of fear or respect for her predicament. Indeed, she had the audacity to manage to further taunt him with a smile as she focused hard on his eyes—too hard, as if she were purposefully plunging headlong into his mind.

"You've feared him since you were a child,'' she whispered. "He loathed you and you knew it. Many nights you lay awake, listening to his drunken, incoherent tirades, terrified that he would make good on his threat to get rid of you once and for all. Even now, your reasons for remaining so long removed from England are less due to your love of war and defending your blessed king than they are over confronting Godfrey again, for a terror fills you that you will at last be forced to raise your sword against him—''

"Silence!'' he hissed. "Tell me who's been filling your mind with these ideas? I'll cut out the bastard's tongue.''

"It is there,'' she replied in a barely audible voice, "writhing like worms in your eyes.''

"I would never raise my sword against my father. Never!'' He shook her and her eyelids fluttered closed as she sank like a stone to the floor.

With a gasp of breath, she awakened slowly—the pain in her head too intense to allow her to move for a moment. Where was she? Back at the abbey? Where was Daniel?

"Daniel?'' she cried out and gripped her head with both

hands. "Bring me the tablets. What do they read? What detestable and insane visions have I seen now? Dear merciful God in Heaven, why have I been so cursed with such sight . . . and pain? Why me, Daniel? Why?"

Someone pressed a cup of water to her lips, and she drank deeply. Almost immediately, the pounding, mind-splitting agony in her temples diminished, and the memory of her visions came rushing upon her like water through a burst dam. Her eyes flew open. She lay on her back on the ground; de Gallienne stooped beside her, cradling the back of her head with one of his big hands.

"*You.*" She struggled to sit up.

Roland pushed her back down. "Be still. I said to be still. Infidel I may be, but I'm not in the habit of abusing women . . . normally. Although I suspect I could make an exception where you're concerned."

"Liar." Hope coughed and grabbed her neck, wincing at the horrible fire burning her throat. Her skin throbbed. Her jaw felt like fractured glass. She did her best not to look at the intimidating foe, for fear the horrible pain and darkness would descend on her again. Yet his presence swirled around her like a storm, full of roiling black clouds and streaks of lightning. It was as if every nerve ending in her body had expanded to the point of exploding. Her senses magnified tenfold. No matter how she struggled, she could not help but be drawn again into the tumult that was his eyes.

Framed by a leonine mane of black hair, Roland's features were sharp and slightly gaunt, his lips full and his eyes heavily lashed. She struggled not to faint again.

"Wh—what do you intend to do with me now?" she managed in a hoarse whisper.

"What would any blackhearted heretic do who hasn't held a beautiful woman in his arms for months?"

"I'll die before I submit to you willingly." She planted her hands on his chest and did her best to push him away.

"I invite you to scream if you'd like. That should bring at least a dozen of my men running. There's nothing we infidels enjoy more than a good orgy."

Her struggling ceased. "Son of a dog, Roland. You mock me! If you touch me I'll make certain you burn in Hell."

"I'm a heretic, remember? I doubt your curse would worsen my plight. Besides, I have every right to punish you. First you attempt to murder me . . . and now you make accusations that I'm a coward—fearing my own father. Already my men fight among themselves because of you."

"Then allow me and my brother to leave."

She flinched as he stroked her cheek with one fingertip; his eyelids grew heavy. "Another time and another woman and I might find this abhorrence to my touch amusing. But I'm tired, and my shoulder where you stabbed me is pounding like Lucifer. I have five hundred men outside this tent who are even now debating among themselves over who, or what you are." Lowering his head to hers, he breathed against her lips. "I've been trying to convince myself that the best thing I could do for my men, and myself, at this time is to let you go. Send you away with your little dragon brother in tow before I allow either of you the opportunity to try to kill me again—or to destroy this army, as Matilda has predicted. The only assurance I have that you aren't so daft as to do such a thing is the reality of your circumstances. Were you to attempt to murder me again, my soldiers would separate your head from your body so fast you wouldn't know what hit you."

"Would they raise their sword against a saint?"

His eyes narrowed. "As Matilda points out, a saint would hardly stoop to cold-blooded killing, would she?"

"Matilda is evil—so evil the stench sickens me. Mind me well, Englishman. The cloud that hovers about her is foul and deceptive. If you and your men look to her power for enlightenment and protection it is no wonder you've met with such catastrophic defeat the last months.''

He raised one dark eyebrow and laughed shortly. ''Matilda says the same about you. 'Tis her opinion we should burn you at the stake while we still have the chance—before you bring the ruination of all of England.

''Frankly, the thought of your body burning to an ugly ash disturbs me. What a waste of something so beautiful; something that could bring us both such incredible pleasure.'' He peeled the cloth of her skirt up her leg, allowed his fingers to lightly trail along the smooth, soft skin of her inner thigh. Her eyes widened and her nostrils flared. Her body appeared to turn as fragile as glass.

Then he found the cleft between her legs.

Hope made a sound, a gasp of surprise—of fear—of anger. She tried to close her legs, but he nudged them apart, imprisoning them with his knees as he slid his massive, muscular body over hers, and continued with the exploration of her private body as if this invasion were natural, and normal. Her cheeks grew hot and her heart thumped like a rabbit in her breast, and though her mind screamed to fight him, to claw his face, her body rebelled. It seemed to her in that instant that it had become a stranger to her, as vulnerable to his animal maleness and overwhelming power as she was appalled by her own weakness. Watching her through half-closed eyes, his sensual mouth curled in something short of a smile, Roland lowered his head and parted his lips, covering her mouth with his. His tongue invaded her, thrust like a spear against her own, sending through her body unnerving arrowlike points of pain.

He tasted like wine.

He smelled of rain and smoke and horse.

The heat of his body permeated her own and caused a disconcerting somersault in her stomach and she struggled to reinforce to her flailing senses that Roland de Gallienne was the enemy—an English infidel—as guilty of slaughtering her mother as the godless animals who had swept upon the sleeping village and raped or murdered any sleepy villager who had not been fortunate enough to escape.

At last, she managed to turn her face away, groaning as he buried his lips against the pulse of her throat and swirled his tongue over the yet-sensitive bruises he had earlier inflicted on her skin. As she struggled, he caught her wrists and pinned them above her head, settling the weight of his hips between her thighs, and nudging open her legs with his knees. His manhood, still bound within his braies, felt full and hard and insistent pressed against her achingly sensitive mound. One shift of his clothing and he could take her with a swift, fierce thrust of his body into hers.

"Be still," he whispered in her ear, and moved his hips gently against her, tightening his grip on her wrists as she squirmed beneath him. He brushed her cheek with his soft lips, then kissed the corner of her trembling mouth. "You shake like a virgin, Hope. Am I that terrifying? Would you rather give yourself to a man like the abbot than afford me the luxury of enjoying your lovely little body, especially since I have control over whether you live or die?"

Her eyes flew open wide and she did her best to wrench free of his grip. "Fiend! I never submitted to the abbot. Never!"

"That, of course, can be disproved. In truth, you haven't the body of a saint. A seductress, yes. A whore, definitely. If you learn to behave, I might even consider taking you for my own lover."

"I would rather fornicate with a—"

"Shh! Best to be careful what you would 'rather' do. You might get your 'rathers' whether you want them or not." He kissed her again, this time not so gently.

She bit his lip.

He cursed and thrust his bulge hard against her. His eyes became hooded. The contours of his face appeared to sharpen, and his jaw worked. Blood beaded upon his lip and ran down his chin. His lips drawing back over his teeth, he growled, "Be nice. Be very nice. I've taken just about as much as I'm going to from you. Never for a moment forget that should I grow weary of your pretty face and tempting body, not to mention your annoying behavior, I can snap you in two as if you were nothing more significant than a splinter. And should I desire to enjoy what's between your legs, I have every right to do so. You, little captive, are at my mercy. Therefore, if you do have any saintly connections to God, I suggest that you call on Him for help. Go on." He released her wrists. "I await a burst of spiritual light that will whisk you away from this Devil incarnate."

She opened her fingers. They brushed against an object, then closed around it.

"Naughty girl. I wouldn't if I were you."

The sound of Roger's voice brought Roland's head up to discover Roger's foot pinning Hope's arm to the floor. She gripped Roland's dagger in her hand.

"I fear this is becoming a habit," Roger said, then bent and took the knife from Hope's hand before removing his foot from her arm.

Hope shoved Roland aside and stumbled to her feet. She backed toward the opening, her hair a tumble of waves over her face and shoulders. Smiling, Roger added, "You'll thank me tomorrow, Hope, once you've pondered the eventuality of your corpse hanging from a gibbet for murdering our beloved Roland."

With a cry of exasperation, Hope fled the tent.

Roland rolled to his back and closed his eyes.

"That was hardly chivalrous," Roger pointed out.

"You needn't remind me."

"Such behavior isn't like you, Roland. She's hardly a slattern or tavern wench. Had I waited a minute longer to make my entrance your soul would be flaming in Hell by now."

"I suspect that it already is."

Roger pared his thumbnail with the dagger and laughed. "Shall I send out for a woman?"

Roland climbed to his feet and adjusted his shirt. "I've no desire to bed some wench who smells of stale ale and crawls with fleas." He took his dagger from Roger and slid it into the leather sleeve on his belt, then he turned for the tent flap, flung it back, and allowed the drizzle to put out the fire in his face. Below him stretched his battalions, their fires flickering intermittently amid the haze of mist and drizzle. He could just make out the dark shapes of the conical tents; he heard the trumpets proclaiming nightfall, the clatter of sentries marching to their posts and the subsequent calls of the watchmen announcing that all be safe within their encampment.

Roland took a weary breath and turned his face toward the sky, allowing the rain to kiss his closed eyelids. His lip throbbed where Hope had bit him, and he licked the blood from the wound. "Mayhap the tongue waggers are right, Roger. Mayhap I've turned into some heartless, godless devil whose soul is driven only by hatred and the need to destroy. Perhaps I've been about warring so long, I've forgotten compassion." Roland looked at his friend at last. "Then again, if Hope of Châteauroux were some sorceress or saint, she wouldn't need a dagger to slay me. Would she?"

Hope lay curled on her mat in the dark, her bowl of untouched stew grown cold and her bread hard. The rain fell steadily on the roof, the only sound to disturb the silence as she thought of those moments in Roland's tent. Where was her outrage? Why, as he'd pressed his body down on hers, had she experienced a flutter of something other than anger, no matter how briefly?

Cursed enemy.

Imagine his believing she would actually succumb like

some wanton to the taste and feel of his mouth on hers.

She touched her lips with the tip of her finger and the air around her seemed to warm. Her hand traveled down her waist to her hip, and she thought again of his loins pressed against hers, his rock-hard thigh wedged between her legs, the immensity of his shoulders obliterating the world beyond him, and the ruthlessness of his eyes.

Except, there had been a brief moment when those eyes had reflected something other than coldness.

A sound.

She sat upright and grabbed for a blanket, pulling it up to her chin. "Who's there?" she called.

"Daniel."

Hope squinted to see her brother in the dark. "Daniel?"

He scrambled through the tent opening and hurried to her. They hugged fiercely. "How came you to be here?" she whispered. "Have you escaped?"

"Hardly. Albert allowed me to see you. I haven't much time, so I'll make this quick."

"Hurry!" came Albert's voice from outside the tent. "If Roger discovers I've brought you here I'll not sit a horse for a fortnight."

Settling on the mat beside her, Daniel took Hope's face in his hands. "There was talk that Roland took you to his tent. Is it true?"

"It's true," she replied.

Silence, then, "Did he—"

"No!" She shook her head.

"Because if he did—"

"He kissed me. Nothing more."

"Filthy dog. I'll defend your honor if you like."

Recalling the weight of Roland's sword, Hope smiled and took Daniel's hand in hers. "Good brother, there is nothing to defend. I swear it."

There came a sigh of relief, then Daniel bowed his head,

spilling his pale hair over his shoulders. "Word of your healing gift has been whispered among the men. There's mounting discord over Roland's keeping us here. They fear God
will retaliate against Roland's blasphemy and allow Philip's
armies to destroy them."

"What about the tablets?"

"Albert has secured them."

Hope frowned and lowered her voice. "Have you be-
friended this Albert?"

"He's promised to teach me the ways of chivalry—"

"He is the enemy, Daniel!"

After a moment, Daniel released a long breath. "You're
right, of course. I'm sorry. It's just that Albert isn't so different from me, Hope."

"You're both children rushing too quickly into manhood." Laying her palm against Daniel's cheek, she said,
"Sword and armor do not make the man, Daniel. It's what
good or evil resides in his heart that makes him what he is."

Albert called, "Quickly, Daniel! Roger is about his
rounds."

Hope grabbed her brother's shoulders. "Promise me you'll
think about what I've just said."

Without speaking again, Daniel hastened from the tent,
allowing the flap to fall closed behind him. Hope followed,
peered through the opening, and watched as her brother and
Albert ran through the dark and the puddles of rainwater
toward Albert's tent in the distance. Then her gaze was
drawn to the solitary tent at the top of the knoll, and she
watched as lightning danced in jagged spears across the sky
beyond it.

The sudden unwelcome images came as bright and erratic
as the explosive lightning plunging toward the earth outside
her tent: *men on horseback, their pennants fluttering at the
ends of their lances as they bear down on fallen soldiers who
plead for mercy.*

She groaned. The pain, oh the pain. Please, God, make it

stop. I don't want to know. I don't want to see. Relieve me of this unbearable burden once and for all and allow me to feel human once in my life.

The runnels of rain stream with blood.

King Henry's banner rises in ashes into a flaming sky.

Daniel. Daniel. Help me, please. Make the pain and nightmares cease. Why have I been burdened with this curse?

A child's grave, a tiny stone monument engraved simply:

ROLAND
BELOVED SON

Her eyes flying open, her hands twisted in her hair, Hope rocked from side to side, hopelessly willing the excruciating pressure in her temples to subside. The visions continued to wing at her from the gray fog, bursting like shattering glass into light so bright it seemed as if her eyes were being forced from their sockets. She turned her face toward the sky, hoping the knifing wet spears would alleviate the agony, only to be driven to her knees by the vision of a fiery lance streaking from the boiling clouds, straight at Roland de Gallienne.

"I'll tell you true, Roland. Her magic be not from heaven— her attempts to murder you are evidence of that. While your army be dazzled now by the whispers of ignorant villagers, soon their admiration will turn to suspicion and fear as foul Fate drives them to their graves. Hope of Châteauroux will rent this army apart. Get her gone now, Roland, while you have the chance—before she brings about the ruination of all you hold dear!"

Roland awoke in a sweat. Lying in the dark, he listened to thunder crack so fiercely that the ground trembled beneath him. His disquietude had begun shortly after Roger had left his tent. He was not a man to abuse a woman, yet, something about Hope of Châteauroux had driven him to the verge of violence and rape—had eroded all common sense from his beleaguered mind. For a fractional moment he had wanted to bury his body into hers even more than he yearned for this cursed war to be over . . . even more than he wanted to live.

Matilda—cursed hag. *She* had planted these seeds of disquietude. *She* had poisoned his dreams.

Still, the hag was right about one thing. There was enough discord among his men without aggravating the situation by keeping Hope and her brother prisoner, regardless of the ransom he might collect from King Philip for her return.

And he sure as the Devil had horns did not care for the idea that he was attracted to a she-demon who on one hand found pleasure in murdering an English knight, and on the other flushed with pleasure when the same knight stroked her most intimate body.

Oh, yes. She had flushed with pleasure. Just as her body had responded to his fingers with a rush of heat and moisture that had very nearly driven him beyond reason.

He could hardly deny that the girl was strange. Very strange. But was her ethereal allure saintly? How effortlessly she had unearthed the worms of his greatest turmoil—his father.

How had she known?

Who among his men would have so blithely discussed his relationship with Godfrey? Who among his men even knew about his nightmarish childhood, and of the fear that had burdened his young shoulders from the time he was old enough to comprehend his father's insane and terrifying rantings?

Roger.

Roland frowned.

Surely his second-in-command—his closest friend— would not be so free of tongue as to discuss Roland's personal feelings, and fears, with one who loathed him so intensely she had attempted to kill him.

But if not Roger . . . then who?

How did she know?

Was he to believe that she was truly a seeress or sorceress, as Matilda vowed? If so, Hope's powers would far exceed Matilda's. And if she did indeed have such abilities, then perhaps the hag was right . . . for a change. Hope might well prove to be the downfall of his army.

He thought of the odd predictions Daniel had scribbled onto the pages of the tablets Roland had hidden deep in his war trunks—a place no one would dare trespass. Shocking predictions. Visions of lunacy, certainly. Were his men to discover the outrageous prophecies, they would panic. All suspicions of her being saintly would evaporate like smoke in a gale. They would rope Hope to the nearest tree and burn her alive.

It was one thing to foresee the outcome of a battle, or even a foe's strategy—the hag had once been very good at reading stones and bones and birds' beaks so as to predict how best to wage an attack—but visions of flying machines and underwater ships would make even a jongleur raise his eyebrows in disbelief.

Impossibilities.

Prattling of a lunatic.

It was simple luck that she had stumbled on the truth of his cursed relationship with Godfrey. It wasn't as if the Lunatic wasn't well known for his unpredictability.

Roland's eyelids drifted closed again as the wound in his shoulder began to throb. He saw Hope stretched out beneath him, smelled the sweet perfume of her skin, felt the silken texture of her hair brushing his face. But as he imagined lowering his body onto hers, her eyes transformed into those unnatural lights she had turned on him in her cell at the abbey, and she screamed:

"Your condemnation will come, Sir Roland de Gallienne—friend of Henry, son of the lunatic Godfrey. Surely as your mother died giving birth to a cur, your destruction will come like a bolt from the turbulent sky as you sleep!"

Outside Roland's tent, thunder exploded overhead and lightning ignited the dark like a thousand brilliant flames. He groaned and tried to waken. Yet sleep's talons dragged him down . . . down, where visions of his father merged with the alabaster image of the abbey saint, sorceress, seeress. Her face a mask of fury and condemnation, she pointed to him and cried:

"Your destruction will come like a bolt from the turbulent sky—"

Roland's eyes flew open and he rolled from his mat. He grabbed his sword and ran from the tent just as the night erupted in an ear-splitting crash. A bolt of light ripped through the low black clouds and speared the tree under which Roland had been sleeping seconds before. With a hiss like a viper, the blade traveled down the tree and danced like dragon's breath across the ground toward the tent, which glowed for an instant like some unearthly specter before incinerating in an explosion of fire. The impact lifted Roland from his feet and flung him partially down the slippery knoll.

There were shouting voices, screaming horses and women, the sound of running feet and barked commands. Groaning, Roland managed to get to his feet just as Roger reached him.

"For the love of all Christendom, Roland, you were nearly killed. Had you not escaped when you did—"

Roland shoved Roger aside and moved drunkenly, numbly through the rain and air that smelled like burning sulphur, toward the figures crouched outside Hope's tent.

Daniel held Hope fast, rocking her comfortingly as, on her hands and knees in the mud, she wept against his shoulder. His eyes widening, Daniel jumped up and put himself between Roland and Hope in a futile attempt to hide her. Roland swung his fist against Daniel's cheek, sending the boy facedown in the mud.

Slowly, Hope raised herself to her knees. Her sodden clothes clinging to her body, her face streaked with tears and mud, she lifted her gaze to the sword in his hand, then to his eyes. She drew back her shoulders.

"I beg you, Roland," Daniel cried in the distance. "In the name of all that is holy, spare her!"

Roland placed the tip of his sword against Hope's pale throat and said through his teeth, "She knew . . . she knew."

SIX

"Did I not foretell she would bring your destruction, Sir Roland? See yonder scorched tent and you'll know now that I speak the truth. I've seen it with my own eyes. I was there, after all." Matilda cocked her head and smiled at Roland, adding, "Would I lie?"

Roland moved through the cluster of soldiers and camp followers, all of whom whispered behind their hands as he passed. Many diverted their eyes. Still others gave him a wide berth, fearing that whatever curse Hope of Châteauroux had inflicted on him would somehow harm them.

He had listened to their heated discourses through the long, rain-drenched day. The feelings among his men were raw. More than once he had been forced to stop arguments before they broke out into physical confrontations. In the end, they had turned their sour moods on him, but while they had been cautious not to rebuke him to his face, their condemnation had been apparent in their eyes. They believed that by taking Hope captive, Roland had openly invited a plethora of calamitous events that would ultimately bring great loss and destruction to his army. Still, Roland suspected that Matilda had a great deal to do with the men's mounting distress. Her harping on about sorcery and black magic had every normally stalwart soldier glancing toward the gray sky in anticipation that he, too, would be incinerated by a lightning bolt if he so much as looked at Hope of Châteauroux.

A woman called Rosamunde followed at Roland's heels, a basket of food propped on her ample hip. Her hair, a tangle of bright red strands, hung to her waist. As she labored with the meat- and bread-filled basket, Roland took it from her and headed for her crude little campsite situated amid the vast numbers of camp followers, all of whom stopped what they were doing and stared at him as if he were a leper.

Without looking at Matilda, who shuffled along beside him, he said, "I fully suspect you would lie if you thought your place in my army might be jeopardized."

"But why would I think that?"

"Because if the girl turns out to be a true seeress, your place in this army might well be questioned."

"Surely you would not trust the visions of your enemy, Roland. She would lead you and your men down the true path of death and destruction. After witnessing the occurrence last eventide, I suspect this army would fling themselves on flaming stakes before believing one utterance from her mouth. Besides, you know as well as I that I'm here by order of your father. 'Tis my duty and loyalty to him that I protect you and this army."

Roland's step slowed. "I need no reminders that your allegiance is for Godfrey, old woman, but if you've any intelligence in that twisted old mind you won't remind me of that fact too often."

Rosamunde ran ahead. By the time Roland arrived at her camp she had fetched him a cup of wine, which she presented to him with a coy smile. He took it and drank thirstily. Though the day was yet dreary, his throat felt tight and dry and had since the incident the previous night. He handed the empty vessel back to her and smiled into her eager eyes. Her fair face blushed, prompting him to stroke her cheek gently with one finger.

Glancing down at the hag, he said, "If you truly foresaw my demise, why did you not warn me?"

"But you misunderstand, sir. 'Twas not my stones that told me."

"Then the stars, perhaps? The moon? The waters of yon river? Speak up, hag. My lack of respite the last days has left me in no mood to tolerate your riddles."

The hag wrung her hands and glanced around the busy encampment of soldiers, squires, and grooms intermingling with camp followers. "You've said yourself that the girl is odd. The men whisper among themselves that she's a saint. But would a saint attempt to slay you? Nay, my lord. She is a demon. Kill her before she takes control of your army and brings about the destruction of our king and all Christendom."

As if to drive home the memory of Hope's previous behavior, a pain shot through his shoulder as hot as the lightning bolt that had nearly killed him the night before, reminding him that the beautiful prisoner with hair like moonbeams and lips as sweet as honey was definitely capable of murder.

Oh, yes, she was definitely capable. But of what? Capable of *conjuring* the hateful lightning in order to destroy him? Or simply capable of *predicting* that he would be struck by the storm? One could destroy him and his army. The other would make her worth a king's ransom.

"I saw her with mine own eyes," the hag repeated, and tugged on his sleeve.

"What do you mean, you saw her?"

"I was there, good knight. I witnessed for myself the odd and awful convulsions before she cried out for all the demons in Hell to gather their forces and smite you with the terrible bolt. I swear on your father's good name.''

''My father is a lunatic.'' Pushing by the hag, Roland walked to Rosamunde's tent before looking back. ''Still, I'll give your warning some thought.''

''I trust you will, sir, for my stars have predicted further grief for you if she remains.''

For the first time in weeks Roland's dreams were not of war and pain and death, but of the lovemaking he had earlier made with Rosamunde. Sweet Rosamunde. She was always willing, eager, hungry for his touch—no doubt because he was Roland, the Black Flame, who could easily strike down his foe with a single swipe of his sword. To lie with him on his mat would make her the envy of her peers. Still, he knew there was more to her willingness than that. She loved him unconditionally, though she knew there was no future for them. A man of his stature could never marry a woman of her lowly position.

He dreamt again that he held her white body with its voluptuous curves hard against his, felt her silken legs open voluntarily and allow him to slide effortlessly into her. Yet, as he turned his head to bury his face in her hair, he was surprised that the locks spread across his chest were not those of red flames, but of gold, as fair as the soft yellow sunlight on a spring morning.

Waking with a start, he glanced down at Rosamunde, who slept with her head on his shoulder. He ran his finger along the curve of her cheek, down along her jawline to the ragged red scar that ran from the back of her ear to the hollow of her throat. Opening her sleepy eyes, she smiled and purred like a cat.

He kissed the tip of her nose. ''You treat me too well, I fear. 'Tis all I can do to leave after I've held you through the night.''

She smiled again, and her eyes twinkled.

He cupped her small face between her hands. "Were I capable I would search out the bastard who cut your throat and robbed you of voice. I miss your singing to me."

Her green eyes misted over, then she lightly pressed her lips to his. Her tongue teased the edges of his teeth and the roof of his mouth. Yet as she twisted her fingers into his hair and kissed him fiercely, pressing her full white breasts against his dark chest, the image to flood his senses and rouse his body was not her fiery comeliness, but the same vision—pale and cool as blue ice—that had taunted him just before waking.

With a guttural curse, he wrapped his hard arms around Rosamunde and rolled her to her back, just as Roger's voice hailed him outside the tent.

"Roland, come quickly!"

Rosamunde whimpered and sank her nails into his shoulders. She offered up her breasts, their nipples rosy as spring buds, then clamped her thighs around his hips.

"I have to go," he whispered.

She shook her head, ran one hand between their bodies and closed her fingers around his member. She slid it into her then thrust as hard as she could up against him.

He groaned.

"Roland!" Roger shouted.

She kissed his mouth.

He groaned again.

She ground her mound against his, taking all of him, her deep, wet chasm working him like a mouth.

"God's teeth, Roland, don't make me come in there to get you."

Finally, he managed to pull Rosamunde's arms from around him, pinned them out to her sides as he braced himself. "A moment!" he shouted, then grinned into Rosamunde's eyes. "My friend grows impatient. As do you, I think. Very well. Perhaps this will keep you content for a while.''

He shoved her legs open further, then rode her hard, his thrusts driving her across the blanket until her flesh grew red and sweating, until she arched her body and a scream tore from her throat. Only then did he retreat, leaving her stretched over her mat like a sleepy, contented cat . . . until she noted that he obviously had not found the respite he had given her. As he stood and reached for his braies, she rolled onto her knees and reached for him.

''No.'' He swatted her hand away and dragged the braies up over his hips, caught his breath as he managed somewhat painfully to adjust the clothing over his body. Her lips pouted, and he laughed. ''Insatiable wench. You're enough to rob a man of his last bit of strength . . . not to mention his judgment.''

I love you, she mouthed, and cupped his hand upon her cheek. Her eyes regarded him intensely, her features hopeful—almost desperate—as she waited for his response.

Bending, he pressed a kiss to her forehead and whispered, ''Thank you.''

The light dimmed in her eyes. She sank back on the mat and turned her head, doing her best not to allow her disappointment to show.

Dragging his shirt on, Roland joined Roger outside, where the encampment as well as the surrounding forest was covered in a heavy gray mist. Roger paced, but stopped upon seeing Roland, his brow damp with sweat and his skin still flush from his exertion.

''I trust you rested well,'' Roger said.

''Rosamunde was, as usual, obliging.''

''Obviously.''

''Your envy is showing, de Ferres.''

''I wonder what it is about you that these women find so attractive.''

"They like my sword?"

Roger shook his head. "Don't you love her just a little?"

"Would that make our relationship any more acceptable to you, Roger?"

Roger glanced toward Rosamunde's tent. "I knew her husband. We were friends."

"I knew her husband, too."

"And you were friends . . . too."

"Charles is dead. He's been dead for four years."

"Then get her married off. Every time you go to her tent you ruin her for the next man. She'll never find a worthy husband as long as you're fucking her."

Roland grabbed Roger by his tunic and shoved him against a wagon. "Were you not my friend, Roger, I might kill you. Need I remind you that I'm well capable of making my own decisions. As for Rose . . . I suggest that you keep your opinions to yourself, lest I be forced to defend her reputation."

"She has no reputation, thanks to you. Were you just a little in love with her, it might be different. But to see her pining away from a relationship that is doomed to go nowhere makes me think Charles is no doubt tossing in his grave. Besides," he added with a short laugh. "Need I remind you about Hildegard—your future wife?"

"I think I *will* kill you," Roland sneered, and slammed Roger against the wagon again before turning him loose. "My thanks for reminding me exactly why I choose not to return to England."

Roger adjusted his clothing, then smoothed the wrinkles from his tunic. "My apologies. You're well aware of my displeasure over your relationship with Rosamunde. I suppose I needn't harp on it."

"No, you needn't. Were you not so in love with Gwyneth I would think you to be in love with Rose yourself."

Roger's face flushed, and his lips thinned.

Roland narrowed his eyes. "But if I were to believe *that,*

then I might also believe that the interest you've recently shown in Hope is more due to infatuation than over any concern you might have for what her presence in this camp might cost *me*. And that would be a terrible shame, wouldn't it? I would hate to think of what that sort of breach between myself and my second-in-command would do to our friendship.''

Roger took a step back and remained silent for a moment, his face lacking any expression whatsoever. His countenance looked suddenly peaked, and his shoulders slumped. ''You have a cruel streak, Roland,'' he finally said. ''You know I would lay down my life for you.''

Looking out over the misty countryside, Roland took a deep breath and ran one hand through his dark hair. ''What is it you wanted, Roger?''

''To let you know that our scouts have returned with news that not a half day's ride ahead is a battalion of Philip's soldiers. I hesitate to add that they are led by Lacurne de Palaye.''

Lacurne.

''Roland, considering the mood of this camp, I suggest you hold off confronting Lacurne. Our men are weary. Too weary. To confront Lacurne now is to invite defeat.'' As Roland turned away, Roger grabbed him. ''The last time we met Lacurne we buried nearly one hundred men.''

''Are you suggesting that we run? That Roland de Gallienne, the Black Flame, tuck his tail between his legs and flee like a coward?''

''I'm suggesting that we wait until this upheaval over Hope has passed. Until then, we search out some haven where we can rest and recover, and become one army— undivided—again. And perhaps in the meantime . . . you might finally come to your senses and send the girl and her brother on their way.''

Roland shook his head. ''Hasn't it occurred to you, Roger,

that she thinks us English dogs? What would keep her from searching Lacurne out? From taking him by the hand and leading him directly to us?''

''She won't. Such actions are simply not in her.''

Roland walked away. Roger hurried to catch up. ''I know that look, Roland. You've every right to hate Lacurne—''

''I have never met a foe more heartless. He makes a mockery of knighthood.''

''He does what he's paid to do. Just as we do.''

''He slaughters women and children. I do not slaughter women and children.''

''To march now against Lacurne is inviting slaughter,'' Roger yelled after Roland.

''Send the hag to me immediately,'' Roland shouted back. ''And prepare the men and arms.''

Hope sat quietly as Daniel brushed her hair and plaited it into a long golden rope. ''There's talk of war,'' he said. ''Many of the men are preparing to ride out to meet Lacurne de Palaye.''

Partially turning, Hope frowned. ''Lacurne will destroy him.''

''Have you a vision, or is such a comment simply wishful thinking?''

''It's common knowledge that Lacurne is undefeated on the battlefield.''

''Then you should take delight over the prospect of Roland's dying. Or perhaps that's changed.''

Hope said nothing.

Daniel sat down beside her. ''The men talk of Roland's extreme hate for Lacurne. They say the last time they met, Lacurne killed a hundred of Roland's men, including a number of innocent camp followers.'' Daniel sighed. ''And even some children.''

"Says who? Albert? He would have you believe the worst about our countrymen."

"Rumor is rampant that if Roland confronts Lacurne now, he'll surely be cut down. They whisper that Roland hasn't the heart for fighting." Daniel caught Hope's chin with his finger and turned her face toward his. "Tell me true, Hope. Would it please you to see Roland cut down?"

"I care not for the death of any man, Daniel. You know that."

"What happened between you, Hope?"

"What do you mean?"

"Since Roland took you to his tent, you've reacted differently toward him. I've seen you watching him with an odd expression: a far cry from the previous anger you held for him."

"Does me no good to harbor such anger. 'Twould only make our circumstances worse."

"He's a handsome devil, wouldn't you agree?"

"I find him crude."

"The women camp followers whisper about him."

"That he's a brute and an animal, no doubt, who has the manners and disposition of a swine."

"Quite the contrary. They say that while he's ruthless on the battlefield, he has the heart of a kitten when it comes to women and children."

"I've seen no evidence of that."

Daniel shrugged. "If he were as heartless as you claim him to be, would he position sentries outside your tent for your protection? A barbarian would have thrown you to the lot of dogs by now."

"My reputation as a saint protects me."

"I fear after the lightning incident he is apt to think you more a sorceress than a saint, as do a mounting number of his men."

There came shouting voices, and Hope and Daniel scrambled to the tent opening to witness a sea of mounted knights, all equipped with armor and lances, their shields polished and emblazoned with King Henry's crest. Amid the throng of crossbowmen and infantrymen Roland sat astride his giant destrier, looking out across his army with a sense of resoluteness.

A silence fell over the crowd as Roger de Ferres took his place beside Roland and lifted his lance high in the air. "Fellow soldiers and barons," he began. "You are on the brink of the battle which you have so desired. Remember the ills you have endured, to which this will put an end. Your foes are numerous, but look up to Heaven and remember that God will send you legions of angels as he has done before. When you are in the battle, strike and spare not, till you have penetrated your enemy's ranks. Remember, you are the soldiers of God. You have received absolution; let your penitence be shown in your striking down the enemy. Now go!"

A roar so loud erupted from the men that Hope was forced to cover her ears. Daniel regarded it all with wide eyes that flashed with excitement. "To be a knight," he cried. "To raise my lance in the name of God and king."

A group of men peeled away from the swarms of soldiers and turned their steeds directly toward Hope. Albert approached, his youthful face oddly serene. To Hope's surprise, he slowly lowered the tip of his lance to her shoulder. "I ask for your blessings as I go to war. Protect me. And if I should die, ask that my soul be forgiven for all wrongs I have committed against my brothers. Let me not die in vain."

Albert turned his horse away and rejoined the suddenly silent army. Another knight approached.

"What are they doing?" she whispered to Daniel.

"They ask the saint for absolution and protection," he replied.

"But I'm no saint," she replied urgently.

"Does it matter? Perhaps they'll fight more bravely if they believe you've blessed them. If they die, they won't fear death so desperately."

One by one the men paraded by her, each repeating the same phrase until all who were left were those who refused to believe that Hope was anything more than a portent of trouble. Amid them, Roland watched, his gaze never leaving Hope's. When the last infantryman and knight had again taken their place in the ranks, Roland spurred his horse through the parted crowd and rode directly to her. He said nothing. Did nothing. Just pinned her with eyes so intense she was forced to set her heels for fear she would flee.

At last, he smiled coldly. "Tell me, *saint*, or sorceress. Do you see victory on the battlefield for these men?"

"I have no way of knowing such things, Roland."

"Do you deny you predicted that I would be struck by lightning and killed?"

"Coincidence!" Daniel exclaimed.

"Then perhaps I should presume that you conjured the storm up in an effort to destroy me."

"But that's ridiculous," Daniel said.

"Quiet!" Roland snapped, causing Daniel to take a step back. "Answer me, woman: do you see victory for these men in the upcoming battle?"

"To answer would be foolish. Whether the outcome be good or bad, if it is opposite to what I tell you you'll have cause to condemn me further."

"You realize that if I'm killed, these men will war among themselves over you. Half will claim you cursed me. The other half will lay down their lives to protect you because they believe you to be holy."

"It's my understanding that these men were divided long before you arrived at Châteauroux."

"Meaning?"

"Many of these men believe you to be a heretic. I should

watch my back for that reason alone. After all, an army divided is not an army, but an enemy to themselves.''

His dark jaw worked and his eyes narrowed. As if sensing his anger, the horse pranced in place beneath him. Finally, he turned back to his men. Hope stepped forward and called:

"Roland!''

He looked around. But as she opened her mouth to speak, a woman ran from the crowd, her long hair like a burnished robe around her shoulders. She flung herself upon Roland's leg, causing him to steady his mount before laying his hand atop her head. Bending low, he kissed her mouth, yet it was to Hope that he looked, his eyes like two burning black pits.

"Is something wrong?'' Daniel whispered.

She swallowed, and shook her head, her gaze still locked on Roland and the woman, who clung to him with a familiarity that turned the air hot in Hope's lungs.

"You're white as chalk,'' Daniel said. "Are you in pain? Are you having a vision?''

"No vision,'' she replied, forcing herself to turn away.

Roland looked to the dozens of men who watched him, their countenances emotionless, but their eyes speaking volumes. Without another word, he spurred his horse toward the road, his army falling in behind him.

Hope watched until the last riders and infantrymen disappeared from sight. Only then did she notice Matilda lurking in the shadows of the distant trees, her yellow eyes fixed on Hope and Daniel. A feeling of disquietude rolled in Hope's stomach, and her knees began to shake.

Daniel sighed. "Someday I'll ride into war with men such as these. My foes will tremble with the mere mention of my name—as they do Roland's.''

Hope focused on her brother, noting the flush of emotion in his normally fair cheeks, the flash of excitement in his eyes. "Am I hearing admiration for Roland in your voice, Daniel?"

He shrugged. "I've not seen him hurt another soul since we've been here."

"He's English. He just rode from this camp with the intention of striking a blow against our king." Looking again toward the hag, Hope released a relieved breath to discover her gone. "That should be reason enough to despise him, Daniel," she added thoughtfully. "Never forget . . . Roland is our enemy.

The pain. Oh God, the pain.

The river lay peaceful and gray in the mist. The only sound to disrupt the chirping of birds and the scurry of animals through the undergrowth was the invasive noise of distant marching.

Closer and closer came the army. Darker and darker swirled the mist that blanketed the river and walls of rock jutting up from the earth.

The trees moved. Like specters they floated through the fog, and from their midst came a rider, lance raised and banner reflecting some unknown light like crystal stone reflects the sun . . . King Philip's *banner.*

Her eyes flying open, Hope fought for a breath as a solitary pain tore through her temples. Just as quickly, the discomfort subsided and she lay back on her mat, thinking of the odd vision, and what it might mean.

The battalion returned just after midnight. Hope ran from her tent to discover scores of men scattered over the ground, their armor bloody, their groans of pain filling the darkness like howls of wolves. The sight of so many hurt and dying made Hope's knees grow weak and a shudder of revulsion ran up her spine. She yearned to bury herself in her tent, but even that would not help her escape the cries of agony ripping the night asunder.

Stepping carefully amid the fallen men, her gaze swept the battalion, or what was left of it. The campfires distorted the men's faces, making even the familiar seem like strangers. Daniel moved up beside her. His eyes looked glazed, his face frozen in disbelief.

"Regard this carefully, sweet brother. This is the destiny you so crave. What glory could come from such carnage and slaughter?"

Daniel bent over and vomited. Hope laid a comforting hand on his shoulder as she looked out across the field of suffering men, searching for . . . what? What odd fear pounded in her chest, and for whom? Certainly not Roland— cursed warrior. He deserved no less than crumbling under Lacurne's mighty sword.

"Yonder hill," came Daniel's voice.

Frowning, Hope looked around.

Daniel wiped his mouth with his sleeve. "You asked about Roland."

She shook her head. "Why would I do that? I care not what happened to Roland."

He pointed to the knoll where two nights before Roland had nearly lost his life by lightning. "He was there, offering succor to the dying."

Hope released her breath, annoyed that the first sensation to rush over her felt suspiciously like relief. "Was he wounded?"

Daniel frowned and regarded the fallen soldiers before replying. "Do you ask because you care or because you yet hold the hope that he be mortally stricken?"

She glared at her brother.

"Spare me your outrage, Hope. You've cursed the English since they killed our mother. You took up a knife and attempted to kill Roland as he slept. Why would you not welcome his death?"

Standing silent, she watched as Daniel turned on his heels and walked away.

"Witch," came a weak voice. " 'Twas her doing—her curse that brought us this despair."

Hope looked down into the eyes of a mortally wounded soldier. The splintered shaft of a lance jutted up from his shoulder. Blood ran in thick runnels down his neck, his ear having been sliced from his head. Raising one trembling hand, he pointed directly at Hope and hissed, "You did this. You and your vile magic condemned us all."

She backed away, her gaze flying to the gathering of injured men forming a circle around her.

"How did you do it?" another shouted. "How did you manage to warn Lacurne we were coming?"

Shaking her head, Hope looked frantically for Daniel.

"I say it's Roland's fault," someone argued. "He's the one who brought the curse upon us by bringing her along. We should burn them both—"

Hope fled through the crowd, dodging her way around the press of wounded men, doing her best to remain as inconspicuous as possible. By the time she had weaved through the dead and dying bodies to reach the knoll, the hem of her gown had become soaked with blood.

Many of the wounded had been confined to the care of the doctors and camp followers who hurried from man to man, dressing their wounds and offering water to assuage their thirst. No sooner was one man treated than another was delivered by litter or ambulance, their bodies disarmed of their weapons and armor, their hurts washed. Women hurried to cleanse the wounds with white wine and unguents, then fed them sleeping draughts that rendered them insensible to pain.

Hope had no time to question her reason for searching

Roland out. She simply told herself that he would offer her protection, should the men decide to make good on their threat to kill her. Yet, after an hour's search and still no Roland, she was forced to acknowledge her mounting concern, and again focused her attention on the scores of wounded men laid out across the ground.

She discovered Roland at the edge of the forest, his sword raised over a crouching, cowering Matilda. "Have mercy, Roland! I relayed all that the stones and stars predicted."

"Your stones and stars predicted victory, old woman. See yonder victory. It drowns in my army's blood! For the love of God, Lacurne was ready for us. We were ambushed. Why did your stars not predict that?"

Trembling, one arm thrown up to shield her face, Matlida searched about wildly for some means of escape. Then her eyes locked with Hope's. "There is your doom, Roland!"

Hope's gaze flew to Roland's as he looked around. The gyrating fires scattered over the ground painted his bloody face with tongues of light that made him appear demonic. His rage emanated from him in waves.

"Did I not portend, Roland, that she would bring your ruination?" Matilda cried. "Mayhap her powers are stronger than mine. Did she not gather the forces of the universe to murder you? Kill her now before her evil destroys us all!"

Roland released his grip on the hag.

Hope stepped back, tripping on the hem of her gown as he moved toward her, his bloody sword in one massive hand reflecting the firelight.

"Kill her!" the hag screeched. "Kill her before it's too late for us all!"

Hope spun to flee. Roland caught her arm and dragged her body up against his. His breastplate, covered with streaks of blood, bit into her flesh. His dark eyes blazed with such anger her knees buckled. He sneered, "Saint or sorceress? Which are you, Hope of Châteauroux?"

"Neither," she managed in a dry voice.

"The evidence would prove otherwise."

She struggled as his fingers dug more cruelly into her arm. "The hag is lying, Roland. I'm not evil. I did not curse these men."

With a growl of anger, Roland forced her toward a groaning soldier, his throat and face laid open in wounds that made Hope feel faint. Roland shoved her to her knees, and burying his hand in her hair, forced her to look down on the suffering man. "Look upon your English foe. See what brutality your kind and caring king inflicts on his enemy. This man is a husband and father . . . and my friend. When he dies we'll toss his body and those of fifty other brave men into a common pit—"

"Stop!" she cried and attempted to cover her ears.

Roland stooped beside her, his hand still in her hair. He forced her tear-streaked face toward his and said through his teeth, "*Heal* him."

She shook her head.

"*Heal him* or I declare you a sorceress and therefore champion the hag's claim that this is all your doing."

"I—I cannot—"

"I witnessed the healing of your brother."

"It was only a minor cut."

"Then you admit it."

"Yes!" she cried, and struck at his hand. "I care not that he's English, Roland. If I could heal him I would. It's not in me to enjoy the suffering of any human being."

She looked directly into his eyes and did her best not to give into the pain he inflicted on her. In that moment she thought she had never seen a man's face so tortured. His eyes glistened, not with fury now, but with tears.

He stood, dragging her to her feet and causing her to whimper and claw at his hand. "Albert!" he roared.

Albert ran through the darkness toward them, his step hesitating when he saw Hope.

Roland shoved her toward the stunned young man, who caught her in his arms. "Take her to my tent and shackle her."

"Sir? But why—"

"Your position here is not to question my authority."

Albert backed away. "I intend no disrespect, Roland."

Finding her feet, Hope turned on Roland, her anger snapping in her eyes. "What now? Do you intend to torch me at dawn? Starve me? Strip me bare and lay leather to my flesh? Tell me, Roland. How do the English treat a suspected sorceress? I might remind you that it's your own doing that I'm here. If there's any misfortune plaguing these men it's you they should blame, not me. *You* are their leader. *You* led them into battle. Their deaths lie on your conscience, not mine."

He said nothing, just stared down at her with eyes that were now void of all feelings but the mute expression of grief. His shoulders sinking, he turned his gaze out on the fields of men and the squires and grooms who moved among them, torches in hand as they searched for their beloved friends. In that instant it seemed as if the soul of every dead man rose up and, as swiftly as a bird in flight, swept into Roland's body, driving the pain of the lost into his chest. Dropping the sword to the ground, he moved away, disappearing into the darkness.

At first light the living gathered along the pit where the bodies of those comrades who had died during the night had been laid shoulder-to-shoulder, their feet pointed to the rising sun. Roger de Ferres stood amid the human rubble, his ravaged, grief-stricken face uplifted to the heavens as he recited the funeral prayer.

"Here be the brave men and allies of our gracious and most respected King Henry, those men who go forth to fight for the righteous and the sanctity of God and England. Brave men and lovely youth, may God rest thy soul in holy flowers in Paradise, amongst the beautiful and glorified above.''

Hope watched the sad event from Roland's tent atop the knoll. The mournful wailing of the camp followers sent chills up her spine. Odd that she had never allowed herself to consider that the English were as capable as the French of grieving for lost loved ones. Men like Roland de Gallienne had represented only ruthless, cold-blooded murderers. She had never thought to witness the sort of pain she had seen in Roland's eyes the night before.

''Where is Roland?'' Daniel asked as he sat near Hope and frowned at the shackles on her ankles.

''I know not,'' she replied wearily. ''Perhaps he's preparing to burn me at the stake. After last eventide, I would not be surprised.''

''He's taken this defeat hard.''

''Yes. I imagine he has.''

Daniel tugged on the chain anchoring her to the ground.

''Do they blame me for this catastrophe, Daniel?''

''There are discussions . . .'' He pulled again.

''Does *he* blame me?''

''Roland?''

She nodded.

''I . . . don't know. Few have seen him since dawn.'' Sitting back on his heels, Daniel regarded Hope closely. ''Why do you care what he thinks?''

''That's obvious, of course.'' She averted her eyes. ''It's up to him whether I live or die.''

''I've seen no pyres built. That should relieve you.''

''The day is yet young.'' She sighed. ''He knows about my ability to heal. He demanded that I heal the wounds of his friend.''

''And did you?''

''You know I didn't. I couldn't. They were far too severe.'' She rested her head in his lap and smiled as he stroked her hair. "Why have I been cursed so with this . . . affliction?''

"Why was our mother so cursed? Her mother before that? Some good must eventually come from it. Of course . . . there is a way. You simply marry.''

"The decision to marry must be made for love, not convenience. Which is where our mother failed. We both know she married our father for one reason only: to end this terrible torment.''

"Then, if I were you, I would concentrate on falling in love.''

"I'm hardly in a position to scour the countryside for a love match. Besides, if Roland has his way I'm certain to rot of old age in these awful shackles—if he doesn't toss me to the lot of bloodthirsty soldiers first. Even now I suspect they're putting their heads together attempting to come up with some way to have done with me once and for all.''

"Roland doesn't strike me as a man whose opinion could be swayed by others. I'm certain he knows deep in his heart that you had nothing to do with this defeat.'' He patted her cheek and stood up. "I'm sorry to have to leave you here, but I'm to meet Albert soon. He's going to lend me his horse. I'm told a knight is not a knight unless he's mastered sitting a steed.''

As her brother turned for the door, Hope said, "I have a dreadful confession, Daniel.''

He paused and looked back.

Hope took a breath and admitted, "I had a premonition.''

"Of what?''

"The ambush on Roland's men.''

Daniel's face clouded over, and his brow knitted in concern. There was an edge of anger to his voice when he spoke again. "Jesu, Hope. Are you admitting that you knew—''

"There was only a brief moment as they were riding out—"

Daniel shook his head, his features incredulous. "Why did you not stop them?"

"It came and went so swiftly. It was only a feeling in my belly, and then only when I saw Matilda lurking in the shadows. Oh God, Daniel, please don't doubt me. The vision came late in the night, too cryptic even for my own understanding. Even if I had understood, they were too far gone to save. We could never have reached them in time."

"Would you have warned them had you known?"

Hope swallowed, unable to force her gaze away from her brother's intense eyes. How much older and mature he appeared in that moment. But, most important, how disappointed. The emotion cut to her very heart.

"I . . . I think I would not knowingly allow any man, no matter what banner he fights under, to ride unwittingly into such slaughter as I have seen here. Such a proclamation is hard to digest, I suppose, especially in light of the fact that I attempted to kill Roland before. But I'm sorry for that. My anger over his invading the abbey thwarted my better judgment. All I could think of was our blessed mother, and the awful way she was murdered. If I could take it back I would, Daniel. You must believe me."

The tent flap was thrown back in that instant. Roland filled up the opening, his countenance dark as he looked first as Daniel, then at Hope. "Get out," he growled at Daniel.

SEVEN

The smell of baked bread, roasted venison, and highly spiced stew woke her, as did the sound of someone talking in little more than a whisper.

Roger?

"A messenger arrived earlier. Lacurne has limped to Anjou to lick his wounds and recover. Word is he'll ride soon to Chinon."

Both men remained silent until Roger added with hesitance, "Henry has withdrawn from Le Mans."

"Henry would never withdraw from Le Mans, Roger. Le Mans is his birthplace. For him to do so is as good as admitting defeat."

"Henry and William the Marshal were forced to flee Le Mans for Fresnay two days ago. The worst part is, William fell back to cover Henry's retreat and found himself face to face with Richard."

Roland drank his ale, then shook his head. "Traitorous son. What sort of man turns his back on his own father?"

"A future king, that's who. A man who desires power more than he craves loyalty. Richard would have Philip his friend instead of his enemy."

"William should have lopped off his head."

"He considered it. But I'm told Richard pled for his life: 'By God, marshal, do not kill me; it would not be a good deed, because I am unarmed.' The marshal smiled grimly, and replied, 'I shall not kill you: I leave that to the Devil!' He then plunged his spear into Richard's horse."

"What of Henry? How does he fare?"

"Not well. After Le Mans fell he retreated to Sainte-Suzanne. He's there now, fallen ill again. He's totally reliant on his bastard son Geoffrey of Lincoln to see that his orders are carried out." Roger took a deep breath and slowly released it. " 'Tis only a matter of time, Roland. We should begin to accept the fact that Richard will soon be king. Henry looks for respite from this war. We both know that. His heart is in England, as is mine. Regardless, I suspect Henry and Philip will meet soon and try to put this fighting behind them. Too many men have died on both sides. Which brings me to reason that we should rethink this scheme regarding Hope. If it's true that Philip and the Pope regard her as saintly, would our taking her not further provoke their desire for blood? Our own army's unrest mounts by the day. Their injuries are there to remind them of what misfortune awaits them should Hope remain here, inviting Philip's attention. Besides that, her brother worries for her health. As do I. She barely eats. With every hour she spends in this tent she grows more pale and feeble. If one can will oneself dead, I fear she intends to do just that."

"She wills your sympathy," Roland replied. "And by the sounds of it, she has it."

"Would you have her death on your conscience?"

"What is one more death when my conscience is already plagued by a thousand deaths?"

"When has the Black Flame treated any woman with such callousness?"

"When has any woman attempted to murder me? When

has any woman forseen the fall of this army and yet allowed it to ride into slaughter?''

"I fear you listen too much to Matilda, who thinks of nothing more than her own future in this army."

Hope opened her eyes a little, just enough to focus on Roland, where he sat at a table, his back to her. Roger sat across from him, dipping bread into his stew and stuffing it into his mouth so eagerly that gravy dribbled from the corners of his lips and pooled on the tips of his red beard. He continued to regard Roland sharply, his brow lined with concern.

"Why do you not eat, Roland? You look terrible. Are you ill? Should I send for Matilda? Mayhap a touch of her hemlock will cure what ails you."

Roland briefly gripped his side, curling his fingers into the material of his tunic before returning his slightly trembling hand to the table. Hope frowned as a sudden sharp ache seeped along her side and settled amid her ribs. Heat sluiced through her body and beaded her brow with sweat, causing her to catch her breath and think that perhaps she had allowed her muleheadedness to get the better of her at last. If she did not eat soon, she would not have the strength to walk away from this predicament, should Roland come to his senses and set her and Daniel free.

Roland shook his head. "Matilda's mood hardly lends itself to remedying what may or may not be ailing me. I would rather go up against a she-bear, thank you very much."

There was food placed beside Hope's pelt —as there had been for the last days. She had refused to eat, thinking that Roland would react like any gallant knight and send her back to her own tent, perhaps even release her.

But after three days of starving, Hope was forced to surmise that Roland de Gallienne was not like other knights. As the smell of the roasted venison assaulted her, she grabbed it hungrily and sat up. The venison was tough, but well seasoned, and her mouth watered almost painfully as she chewed it, her gaze fixed on Roland as he partially turned to watch her, giving her a profile of his face, dark and lined with fatigue.

For an instant she forgot her food, and the hunger that had gnawed in her belly for the last days—since Roland's army had returned from their disastrous confrontation with La-curne; she stared at Roland as fixedly as she did her cursed tripod, mesmerized, disturbed . . . fascinated, only vaguely aware that the food seemed to stick in her throat and the air inside the tent felt stifling hot.

The shackles around her ankles bit into her skin as Roland slowly turned to face her completely. His eyes looked hard and black as onyx, and the sudden, unexpected memory of his kissing her brought an odd, breathless anticipation with it that set fire to her flesh, and something—not quite fear or anger—to rolling in her belly. Forgetting about food, she fixed her gaze on his slightly turned-down lips and took a ragged breath.

"Why do you stare at me like that?" she demanded in a dry voice.

"I'm not certain I have ever seen a more beautiful seeress, or one so blessed that she can heal without potions or elix-irs." He left his chair and moved toward her, his step un-steady. Hope scurried back as far as her shackles would allow as Roland withdrew a tiny key from a slit in his tunic, stooped, and unlocked the cuffs. He ran his fingers lightly over the bruised and abraded flesh before she drew her feet up under her gown.

"You must be very hungry and thirsty," he said.

She thought of lying. "Yes," she replied.

"Then join me. You might find the stew more to your liking than the dry venison."

He offered his hand. She ignored it, but as nonchalantly as possible stood and smoothed the wrinkles from her skirt while doing her best not to look too eager to dash for the table of bread trenchers filled with steaming stew. She waited as he returned to his seat, then walked to a place near Roger, who smiled in encouragement.

The smell of spices and hot bread made her feel heady. She dropped like a stone onto the seat and grabbed a handful of bread and plunged it into the stew. Her eyes rolled shut as the melange slid down the back of her throat and dripped from the corners of her mouth; she swiped the brown gravy from her chin with her sleeve then ate again. Only when she had slowed to take a breath did she turn her attention to Roland.

"My hunger must bring you a great deal of satisfaction," she said with her mouth full. Her eyes narrowed and she tore another chunk of bread. "Perhaps you've decided to feed me one last meal before setting fire to my feet."

He shook his head.

"Then you've decided to throw me to yon infidels."

"There are no infidels in this camp."

"Aside from you, that is."

His jaw flexed and she swallowed hard. The next mouthful of stew burned her tongue.

Roland propped his elbows on the table and made a tent of his fingertips. "You knew Lacurne's men waited in ambush for us in the forest. I overheard you tell your brother as much. *How* did you know?"

Hope shrugged and fished for a turnip. "I dreamt it."

"Would you have warned us had you known in time?"

She lifted her gaze to discover his countenance one of simmering anger. "Do you expect that I would warn my enemy of impending doom? An enemy who keeps me caged and chained like an animal?"

"Perhaps you *planned* the destruction of my men."

The bread crust fell from her fingertips. "How could I have done such a deed when I'm—"

"Sent word to Lacurne of our plans."

"Which means someone among you is traitor. Or perhaps my spiritual self soared from my body—"

He came over the table and grabbed her jaw. A pain sluiced through her temples and down her neck as she clawed at his arm.

Pulling her near so she was forced to plant her hands on the table, one sinking in the hot stew, he said through his teeth, "They knew we were coming, and when. They clothed themselves with branches of leaves so that my men rode amid them like lambs to the slaughter!"

"It wasn't I who assured your victory, Roland. Nor did I portend that you would confront them near the river. Look to your own seeress if you desire to cast blame!"

Roland gradually eased his grip on Hope. Still, he did not release her, but appeared to lose himself momentarily in thought as his fingers lingered along the curve of her neck.

Roger cleared his throat and offered Hope a cloth with which to clean the stew from her hand. Only then did Roland drop down onto his chair. His features appeared pale, his eyes hollow, the lines in his face deepening.

Her jaw throbbing, her appetite gone, Hope regarded the food as if it were poison. With a heavy sigh, she said, "If you believe me capable of these crimes, why do you continue to keep me here?"

"And allow you to use your . . . *gift* for the benefit of Philip?"

"Gift?" She laughed sharply and shook her head. Her eyes began to burn and her chin to quiver. "Were it a gift I would gladly give it back." Hot tears spilled down her cheeks; she did nothing to check them, but bowed her head and let them drip from her chin and nose. "You would do me a favor by setting me afire, I think. I would rather tolerate a moment's pain than a lifetime of it."

Roland pushed away from the table so suddenly the tankards of ale toppled over. Running both hands through his black hair, he glanced at Hope. Her eyes were wide with uncertainty, her cheeks suddenly pale.

Roger frowned. "There's no reason to take out your anger on her."

"No?"

"She has no fault in any of this."

Roland laughed. "As you said, Roger, a growing number of my men feel otherwise."

"Then release her. Send her on her way. Be done with her once and for all. If you truly believe she has some power to destroy us, then to keep her here only invites our destruction."

Roland moved toward Hope, a thin smile curling one side of his mouth as she stood and backed as far as possible into the shadows. "Do you know, Roger, that our little 'saint' admitted to her brother that she regrets having tried to kill me. Should I believe her? Or should I believe 'tis all a sly ploy to win my favor?"

"You should follow what's in your own heart, Roland."

Roland's eyebrows rose, and he laughed, low and deep in his throat. "According to Hope, I have no heart. No soul. No hopes of heavenly bliss when I die. I'm a hated heretic doomed to roast in Hell for all eternity for the pain and destruction I've wrought on mankind. Why would she not desire to destroy me and take pleasure in it?"

Again he gripped his side, and his face went white. Just as swiftly Hope was awash with pain, causing her to stagger back and sink to the floor, blackness crashing in on her like an avalanche.

Roger lined the cuffs on Hope's ankles with fur, then cushioned her mat with a plush bear pelt. There were cuts and abrasions on his face, and a deeper laceration across the top of his hand—injuries obtained from his army's skirmish with

Lacurne. Hope was tempted to lay her hand upon them, to return the favor he was showing her in that moment; then she reminded herself that, though Roger was kind and sympathetic to her predicament, he was the enemy, and friend to Roland. Should Roland decide to execute her, Roger would not stand in his way. Besides, to openly reveal her ability to heal even so minor a wound would jeopardize any hope that Roland would rethink his reasons for keeping her captive.

Forcing a smile, Hope said, "This is kind of you, Roger de Ferres, but it would be kinder to let me go."

He turned his concerned eyes up to hers. "It's Roland's desire that you remain here. At least for the time being."

"And you would never go against Roland."

"No."

"Because you're his friend, or because your loyalty to your king dictates that you follow his directives without question, be they right or wrong?"

"Both." He sat back and smiled. "Roland is a fair man. I've never known him to behave in a manner that would purposefully jeopardize his men's well-being."

"Yet he would take a woman captive and chain her."

"I admit that his reasoning where you're concerned is a bit odd. Then again, you did try to murder him. Another man in his position would have every right to kill you, and would have done so."

"He may yet kill me."

"Perhaps."

Frowning, Hope laid back on the rug. "You're not very comforting, Roger."

"It's hard to tell what's going on in his mind right now. He suffered a great loss those nights ago. He grows weary of death, as do we all. 'Tis been a long time since we last saw England and our families. But until Roland is prepared to return home, then we continue to fight as long as Henry needs us."

"His loyalty to King Henry will destroy him, not to mention his men."

Roger sighed; his brow creased with worry and fatigue. "Henry is his friend. In truth, Henry has been more of a father to Roland than Godfrey has. Until Henry himself releases Roland from his command, Roland will remain here to fight, or die."

Hope turned her cheek into the fur and enjoyed the feel of it on her skin as Roger regarded her. Her lids grew heavy and she sighed sleepily. "I'm sorry about your men, Roger. It must have been a terrible shock to discover that the forest was Philip's army prepared for ambush."

"It's our lot, Hope. Be we English or French, we face every day with the possibility that it may be our last." Roger tucked a blanket over Hope's shoulders. "Roland isn't a bad man. He's simply doing what is expected of him, just as Lacurne does. You should try better to know and understand him before judging him too severely."

Rosamunde hurried to Roland and proceeded to pour wine into a cup. Only after she had handed the vessel to Roland did she turn her attention on Hope. Somewhat tenuously, Rosamunde poured another cup of wine, then offered it to Hope. Hope shook her head, but Rosamunde encouraged her with a nod and finally Hope took it, turning it up to her mouth and drinking like one who had not felt liquid pass her parched lips in days.

Rosamunde refilled the cup and Hope softly said, "Thank you." Then her gaze slid past the watchful woman, to Roland, who sipped at the ambrosia and regarded Hope over the rim of his cup, his brow beaded with sweat, his expression hooded—until Rosamunde drew his attention back to her. She sat on his lap, took his face in her hands, and kissed his mouth.

Gripping the vessel in both hands, Hope sank into the

deepening shadows and did her best to ignore Roland and his lover. It wasn't easy, especially when with every glance their way Hope recalled those moments when Roland had fondled her, had kissed her with far more passion and hunger than he did Rosamunde.

Why?

Because his attentions that day had been driven by anger, instead of love?

Because he meant for his caresses and kisses to brutalize her emotionally? To torment her physically?

Arrogant bull.

For hours Roland and Rosamunde sat at the table and fed each other stew and bread. They drank from each other's wine as Rosamunde sat on Roland's lap and laid her head on his shoulder. Occasionally, he kissed Rosamunde's forehead, and, once, the tip of her nose. More than once his gaze shifted to Hope, and the air warmed against Hope's skin as she made haste to divert her eyes and pretend to sleep.

The wine made Hope groggy.

As nightfall encroached, her head began to hurt—the wine, surely. Please, dear merciful Savior, let it not be a vision, not now. It was enough to tolerate the disturbing going-on between Roland and Rosamunde. She knew the ways of men and women—had slept in the same room as her parents before her father died, and after, when men occasionally visited her mother.

The wine dragged her down and she slept fitfully, only to be awakened what seemed like hours later. Her throat felt tight, her mouth dry. What at first felt like little more than a cramp in her side suddenly cut into her ribs like a knife, and she gasped and sat upright, just as Rosamunde stumbled over Hope's leg chains.

Her hair a wild array, her eyes wide, and her body clad in little more than a coarse shift that exposed most of her breasts, Rosamunde shook Hope hard and pointed toward the back of the tent. She made a sound in her throat before scrambling for the door.

Hope crawled to her knees and did her best to see through the shadows, barely making out Roland's form lying oddly limp on his mattress. The pain in her side grew intense and, like a sliver of cold ice, streaked up through her chest and speared into her temples. The agony rocked her backward.

"Roland?" she finally managed, and crawled toward his cot.

The vision came like a flurry of crows, stark and black against a pale sky.

Fire.

Men screaming.

Women and children begging for mercy.

Roland on his knees, blood pouring from his eyes.

"Roland?" she cried again and reached out through the dark, praying the leg irons would not impede her ability to reach him. Her hand touched his face.

He made a sound.

She managed to crawl to her knees beside him.

Roland's skin felt hot. His breathing sounded ragged as he clutched his side with bloody fingers and groaned. Her breath trapped in her throat, Hope peeled aside his hand, allowing the thick, blood-heavy linen to fall to the ground, exposing a festering, putrid wound in his flesh. Its stench made her stomach turn over.

Roger entered the tent, a burning sconce in one hand. He stopped short upon seeing Hope, her hands cradling Roland's flushed, sweating face. "Holy Mother of God," he whispered.

Hope closed her fingers over the wound, steeling herself against the sickening feeling of his hot, slick blood pooling against her skin. His eyelids fluttered; his dry lips parted.

Roger bent over them, his shock and concern apparent. "Roland, can you speak?"

He nodded.

"When did this happen? How?"

"Lacurne," he managed to whisper.

Roger drew back, his look incredulous. "What were you thinking, Roland, to allow this wound to fester?"

"That he would punish himself for surviving when so many of his men died," Hope said softly, smoothing the hair back from Roland's brow.

Roger remained silent for a long moment, then turned on his heels and left the tent. "Where the devil is Matilda!" he roared at no one in particular, then added, "I'll personally rip off her arms if she isn't here in two minutes!"

Silence.

Roland's heart beat against her hand.

She regarded Roland's face, etched with deep creases of pain . . . and sorrow. The lines of fatigue on his brow made him appear much older than his years. The sudden startling need to press her fingertips to his brow made her tremble; yet struggle as she might against the overwhelming urge, her hand was drawn to the noble brow that radiated a heat that felt like smoldering ash to her sensitive flesh.

With no warning, visions winged at her like bats from a cave—hundreds, thousands, a mass of black wildness that bombarded her from every side. And with it pain and fear so excruciating she felt as if her heart were being ripped from her chest.

A small boy standing bravely at the bedside of his mother, his eyes squeezed closed as he gripped her hand. "Don't die, Mama. I beg you. Don't leave me here with Father. He hates me. He wants to kill me. Why does he despise me so? Why?"

"Stand before me like a man and take your whipping. Loathed stars that condemn me with your cursed birth. Now that your blessed mother is gone I'll see that those wretched stars be rent from their damned orbit and flung to burning

Hell. You'll not know one moment's satisfaction as my first-
born, but will find contentment only in the scraps that my
son Harold tosses you. From this moment on, you will never
again know me as father.''

"Don't beat me again, Godfrey. If there is any sane and
human heart left in you, I ask you, don't beat me again."

Like one waking from a dream, Hope struggled to drag
herself from the dark and terrible pit of Roland's past, knowing even as she did that whatever fears, whatever tragic
memories squirmed like snakes in his mind were now buried
in hers as well. Even as she forced the last bit of fog from
her consciousness, she could feel the seed of his memory
begin to germinate.

Bending to his ear, she whispered, "Sleep deeply, Roland.
Tomorrow there will be no more pain. I swear it."

His eyes drifted closed. His body went limp as death, and
for an instant Hope was awash with a concern she had rarely
experienced. Only the frighteningly shallow beat of his heart
against her hand rallied her; Hope laid her hands on his
wound and closed her eyes, bracing herself against the on-
slaught of misery that would certainly consume her.

The pain came, roiling around her like black smoke, cutting off her breath and obliterating all thought.

Dear God, it was much worse than she had thought, for
this was more than a simple, festering wound. The memories
that had earlier assaulted her streaked like fiery spears
through the smoke, impaling her with images of a boy's awful abuse at the hands of his father, of a young man's white-
hot anger, of men screaming for mercy as they writhed in
death throes, all fallen from a flaming black sword. And
through it all came the vision of a grave swathed in mist, its
tombstone rising ghostlike from the ground and engraved
simply with:

HERE BE ROLAND
SON OF THE LUNATIC GODFREY

Roger returned. "Damnable drunken old hag. She'll be no good to us toni—" He focused on Hope's pale face as she stood by Roland's bed, her body trembling uncontrollably. "God, no," Roger groaned. "He isn't dead . . . ?"

Pushing by her, Roger fell beside his captain. A moment of total quiet passed before he slowly stood up and turned to Hope, his face a colorless mask of incredulity. "Jesu," he whispered, then dropped to one knee before her and genuflected.

"No." She stepped away, shaking her head almost frantically. "Pay me no homage, Roger de Ferres! I swear to you, I'm no saint."

"But you—"

"Did nothing more than anyone of true faith could have done." She lightly placed her bloody hand atop his head. "You must never tell anyone what you've seen here tonight. My life depends on it, Roger."

He nodded and grabbed her hand, pressing it to his cheek.

Hope swayed. She did her best to draw herself upright before saying, "Bring me my brother. Quickly! I beseech you, before . . ." With a groan, she toppled into Roger's arms.

EIGHT

"What have you done, Hope?" His voice thick with emotion, Daniel cried, "Foul curse! Despicable gift! You've let it destroy you. Wake up. Wake up, I tell you!"

She tried to open her eyes. Daniel's face swam before her like a mirage.

He sat her up and gently slapped her face, then pressed a cup to her lips. Cool water slid down her hot throat, and she coughed.

Sinking down beside her, Daniel shook his head and frowned at the bloodstained bandages scattered around Roland's bed. Only then did he address Roger, who continued to regard them in stunned silence. "You must collect these evidences and destroy them. No one but ourselves must know what's gone on here tonight."

"What *has* gone on here tonight?" Roger whispered

"What do you think?"

"A miracle. Aye. A damned miracle. I've seen it with my own eyes, for certain. There was a hole in Roland's side that I could put my fist in. Now . . ." He buried his face in his hands and shook his head. "Now he's . . . healed. How do you expect me to explain this to my men?"

"It's your word against theirs."

"But they heard from my own mouth—"

"You were mistaken. It was only a trick of the firelight that made you think you saw blood."

Roger rolled his eyes in disbelief and regarded the still-sleeping Roland a long time. He tugged on his beard as he contemplated the situation. "What about Roland? How do we explain it to him?"

"The memory of his injury will be nothing more than some distant inconsequential dream, I assure you."

Roger laughed humorlessly and a look of fear settled over his pale countenance. Standing, his hands opening and closing, he focused on Hope's face. "What *are* you?" he demanded. "Are we to be blessed or cursed by your presence in this army?"

"Neither," she responded softly, and smiled her thanks as Daniel offered her another drink.

"My most humble apologies for believing otherwise," Roger declared. He walked to Roland's bed, where Roland continued to sleep as if in a trance. Bending, Roger examined the place that earlier had been a grievous wound. There was yet blood on Roland's clothes to attest to the fact that Roger had in no way imagined the injury. Finally, he looked upon Daniel and Hope again, his features becoming angry. "Try not to convince me that this is normal."

"Hardly normal," Daniel replied. "And if we could explain it we would. This ability has been passed on for generations, from one mother to the next. It remained hidden well enough . . . until the abbot discovered Hope's . . . gift. He used her to bring great acclaim to Châteauroux, forcing her to call on her abilities knowing the kind of distress and pain it causes her. When she refused . . . he beat her." His voice dropping, he added, "Had I been more of a man, I might have killed him for his cruelty, my soul be damned."

Roger moved to the doorway. Outside the tent the night

was alive with activity—soldiers crowded shoulder-to-shoulder as they awaited word of Roland's welfare. "Roland will remember none of this?" he asked.

"Virtually nothing. He'll probably not remember having been injured at all."

Without looking around, Roger said, "Gather up those bloody linens. I'll have Rosamunde remove his soiled clothes and destroy them."

Daniel did so, then watched as Roger stuffed the bandages under his shirt and tunic before leaving the tent. There came a quiet murmur of voices before someone yelled, "A trick of firelight? You lie, Roger! What are you trying to hide? If Roland still be alive and well, then let him show himself!"

"I say the sorceress has killed him—"

"You're protecting the woman, Roger—"

Daniel shook his head and closed his eyes. "This will do nothing to help your reputation, Hope. I fear that by dawn you'll either be canonized or burned at the stake."

The voices faded to a drone as Hope lightly touched her fingertips to Roland's cool brow. She smiled.

Daniel dropped down beside her. "Why? Why have you risked everything for a man you claim to despise? The very act of taking his pain could have killed you."

Rosamunde returned in that moment. With her gaze locked on Hope, her back to the tent wall, she cautiously moved toward Roland, her countenance reflecting both awe and fear. Hope moved away, back into the farthest corner her shackles would allow as Rosamunde made haste to change Roland's clothes. Once done, Rosamunde shoved the soiled garments into a pouch and hid them deep in one of Roland's chests.

Roland stirred. Rosamunde hurried to his side.

Hope turned her back on the couple as Daniel took her hand in his. Her fingers were yet bloody. Grabbing up a cloth, he attempted to cleanse them—scrubbing harder . . .

then harder, cursing through his teeth as the stains remained on her skin.

"What the devil is going on?" came Roland's voice. "What's wrong with the men? Why are they arguing?"

Daniel dropped the cloth. Hope caught her breath.

Roland sat up, glancing first at Rosamunde, whose face looked pale as wax, then at Hope and Daniel. His eyes were sleepy, but his brow without pain. As another burst of angry voices sounded outside the tent, Roland stood up, swaying for a moment before finding his balance.

Daniel scrambled to his feet and placed himself between Roland and Hope. "Sir . . . some rumor has flourished that you've been wounded, and are near death. Silly . . . isn't it?"

Frowning, Roland looked down his person. He shook his head as if to clear his thoughts.

"I fear you and Roger had a bit too much ale," Daniel hurried to add.

Roland turned his gaze down to Hope. Her heartbeat quickened. A sudden warmth radiated from her bloodstained hands into her chest.

Roger returned, stopping short at discovering Roland awake and standing. "Good God," he said before catching himself. ". . . You're . . . awake. Good. Very good!" He laughed lightly. "You might step outside and assure your men that your soul is yet with us . . . that you haven't some-how been murdered in your sleep."

Roland walked over to Roger and, standing toe-to-toe with him, studied Roger's face. "You don't look drunk to me."

" 'Tis well known I'm able to hold my ale better than any man in this army," he replied, then cleared his throat. "What, exactly, do you last remember?"

Closing his eyes briefly, Roland took a deep breath and shook his head. "I'm . . . not certain." He glanced at Hope and muttered, "Odd dream. Like I was caught up in a whirl-pool."

Roger slapped Roland on the back and nudged him toward the door. "Yes, well, it was a potent keg to be sure. I wouldn't have put it past the hag to have dispensed a pinch or two of her dog's-ear wax, or perhaps even jabrol into the brew."

Again, Roland glanced back, his gaze locking momentarily with Hope's before Roger shoved him through the tent flap. After a slight hesitation, Rosamunde ran after him, leaving Hope and Daniel alone.

Hope sank to the floor. Her fingers curling into fists, she pressed her hands to her breast.

"Are you all right?" Daniel asked.

It was a moment before Hope managed to catch her breath. Closing her eyes, she whispered, "I feel as if the sun has just risen in my heart. What could it mean, Daniel? Pray, tell me. What could it mean?"

Roland's army marched at dawn.

The rains fell, turning the road to mire and forcing the carts and wagons full of camp followers to fall behind the soldiers' struggling horses as they made their way toward Chinon, where rumor had it Roland's beloved King Henry had requested Roland to meet him as soon as possible. Whispers were rampant that Henry was prepared to bow to Philip in defeat. Still others ventured that Roland would at last ask for Henry's blessing to return to England. All speculated that after their latest defeat, Roland no longer had the courage to fight, nor the heart.

Stumbling along at the end of a tether, sinking to her shins in mud, Hope did her best to keep up with Roland's laboring horse as they fought their way over the winding route toward Chinon. Roland's men eyed her speculatively, obviously concerned over the fact that their leader would mistreat a woman, perhaps a saint, in such a way. Still others muttered among themselves about the odd and disturbing occurrences the night before, vowing that what might have transpired inside Roland's tent had not been the work of a saint, but of a sorceress. Because Roland had apparently dismissed their accusations as mere folly brought on by one of Matilda's foul concoctions caused heated debate over the possibility that Roland was in league with the sorceress. Why else would he protect her?

Not until the army reached the swollen Vienne River did Roger de Ferres ride up to Roland and yell through the downpour, "Will you drag the girl through the water as if she were a herring? I fear many of these men will mutiny for certain if you propose to drown her."

Roland looked back at Hope. His black hair was plastered to his head and his lashes were spiked with rain. "She's a saint, isn't she?" he replied with a smirk. " 'Tis my understanding that saints walk on water."

"Don't bother yourself, Roger," Hope cried. "I wouldn't ride with the cur even if he was to allow it."

"Then she'll ride with me," Roger declared.

"She won't," Roland snapped.

Teeth clenched, his beard dripping runnels of water, Roger shook his head. "Had I not seen you fight the most fearsome enemies, Roland, I would begin to suspect that you were afraid of the girl."

Thunder crashed overhead.

Roland whirled his horse toward Hope, causing her to stagger aside for fear of being trampled. He caught her arm and swung her up onto the back of his nervous horse; she was forced to grab Roland around the chest as he spurred the destrier forward through the rain.

Throughout the following days, Roland moved like one in a dream; his senses felt blunted—all but that portion of his mind that continued to acknowledge his mounting disquietude. Around him the tumbled stone walls of the fallen and long-deserted Heribert Castle were like objects seen through a veil. His men had not been pleased that he had chosen to camp instead of pushing toward Chinon. They were eager to confront Lacurne—while the anger over his ambush still boiled their blood. More than once had Roland acknowledged a snarled insult hissed through some soldier's teeth: traitor, coward, *heretic* . . .

Yet he had chosen to ignore them.

Why?

More and more he retreated to one of the crumbling old castle's dreary, secluded little chambers that overlooked his vast, increasingly unhappy army scattered over the hillsides. He sat on the ledge of a fenestral window, with its remnants of lattice frames and tattered tallowed linen, and allowed the wind to kiss his cheeks. Occasionally, the sound of music touched his ear: the beat of a naker, the thrum of the lute, the heavenly, harplike hum of a psaltery.

The idea suddenly occurred to him that his mood, which of late had plagued him with a burdensome darkness, felt . . . lighter somehow. The great weight that had once pressed on his chest felt little more than a feather—a wispy cloud. Odd that a man such as himself, who once found little peace in such passiveness as lounging about dimly lit chambers, now avoided the very activities that once had filled his every waking minute: preparing his next war strategy, practicing the quintain, strolling about his encampment, reminiscing over previous battle wins, or losses, with his soldiers—or spending wild, lustful hours in Rosamunde's eager arms.

Mayhap he should not so lightly dismiss the whispered rumors he had heard in passing through his troops. Mayhap, like Henry, he had lost the heart to fight. Mayhap he had become soft. Why else would a knight of his esteem prefer the company of . . . what?

What, exactly, lured him to this dismal cell, to spend time with a girl with fair hair and crystalline eyes, whose unnerving company somehow compensated for his normal need to prowl?

Drowsily, he turned his gaze to Hope. As if moving to the rhythm of the faint music, the sconce light and shadow danced over her bowed head. She had agreed to spend her long hours as his prisoner repairing his men's tattered clothing. Rarely did she speak when spoken to; she simply turned her big blue eyes up to his and regarded him with an emotion that had begun to disturb his dreams.

Dreams? How could he possibly dream when he could rarely sleep? When he could but lie in the dark and listen to Hope's occasional soft sighs as she slept? When the very air in the room pulsed like a living thing with the scent of her sex?

Releasing a heavy sigh, he said to himself, "Shall I never be out of this hateful country?"

"It's my understanding that you're free to return to England any time you so desire," came the soft response.

Roland raised an eyebrow. "She speaks. I'm not certain whether I should be pleased or fear that I'll be struck by lightning again."

"I had nothing to do with the lightning."

"But you knew it would come—"

"I was on my way to warn you when it hit." She looked up and stared at him steadily. "You have no reason to believe me, of course. Why should you?"

He did not respond and she returned to her sewing. Her braided hair fell over one shoulder, and the memory of it flowing freely beyond her hips caused him to frown. Leaving the ledge, he proceeded to pace.

"Are you sorry that I took you away from Châteauroux?" he asked.

No response; not even a shake of her head.

"Would you care to go back?" he prompted angrily.

Her hands briefly stopped mending, then began again. Finally, she replied in a more tentative voice, "If I must remain a prisoner here or there, then I suppose it would matter little where I am."

"That would depend on whose company you prefer, the abbot's . . . or *mine*."

"That's like asking whether I care to be hanged by the neck or burned at the stake."

He strode across the room and stopped before her. "You've been treated fairly, considering you attempted to *murder* me."

"If you consider being dragged through the mud at the end of a tether fair treatment, then I agree. If being bound by chains about my ankles be fair treatment, then I agree." Her pale eyebrows drew together and she nibbled her lower lip as she contemplated her next words. "Does the injury bother you over much?"

"Only when I move. Or breathe. Occasionally I get a twinge when I talk. Other than that, it feels perfectly fine."

"I had a right to kill you. I still do."

"It was not I who murdered your family, Hope."

"But you would have in the name of your king."

"I've never raised my hand against a woman or child." He stared at her pink mouth before returning to the embrasure. Sinking against the fenestral frame, he crossed his arms over his chest and did his best to focus again on the distant music. The breeze did much to cool the film of sweat that had suddenly risen upon his brow, and he took a deep steadying breath before speaking again. "I swear to you that I have never hurt a woman or child."

"I have trouble believing that a man of such honor would chain a woman as if she were an animal."

"Were I assured you wouldn't attempt escape, perhaps I would release you."

"Where would I go? How could I evade an army of men?"

"And if I granted you your freedom, where would you go?"

Hope took a deep breath and slowly released it. Her hands lay quietly amid the folds of Roger's tunic. Finally, she shrugged. "I don't know. I suppose I would travel with my brother until we found a place to settle."

"I fear you may find that persuading your brother to leave would prove to be more difficult than you imagine."

"Meaning?"

"He's found a great many friends among my men. I think he fancies himself Albert's squire."

"Daniel would never forsake me for his enemy."

"That's my point, dearest. He no longer considers these men his enemy."

Her cheeks flushed with color and she set her chin. "I would ask him to tell me that himself before I would believe you."

He smiled.

She narrowed her eyes.

Roland looked away, over the hundreds of smoky fires dotting the horizon.

Hearing the chains around Hope's ankles clatter on the planked floor, he discovered her standing near a distant window, the shackle preventing her from reaching the ledge completely. The dark outside the room painted her face with deep shadows. Her expression was of such intense yearning that a knot formed in his chest, squeezing off his breath.

"What do you see out there?" he asked more softly.

"Freedom," she replied.

Reaching for the tiny key in his tunic, he slid from the window and moved toward her. She backed away, her eyes growing large in her exquisite face. Coming up against the wall, she raised her chin and squared her shoulders, obviously prepared for the worst.

Roland dropped to his knee and unlocked the cuffs.

Still on one knee, he looked up into her eyes, which were wide with confusion. "You're free," he told her.

"What trick—"

"No trick."

She took a sideward step, appeared to totter, then glanced toward the door.

Roland slowly stood. "Go on. Leave if you so desire. I'll not stop you. I'll even provide you a horse."

Her fingers moved nervously against her skirt as she peered again toward the door.

"Of course . . . you're welcome to stay," he added, slowly drawing his fingers along the curve of her jaw. "I'll provide you comfortable shelter. Splendid clothes that will compliment your beauty and frailty. I'll buy you ribbons of every imaginable color for your hair."

Her countenance became rigid, and she shied from his hand. A moment passed before she asked in a wooden voice, "And in turn I'll be expected to do what?"

He smiled. "Remain with me, day and night. You'll be at my beck and call at all times. You'll eat with me. And sleep with me."

"You expect me to become like—"

There was a movement at the door and Hope bit off her words. Rosamunde stepped into the chamber holding a tray of food and a cask of wine. She looked first at Roland. Then her gaze dropped to the discarded shackles on the floor.

Finally, Roland walked to Rosamunde and took the tray. She closed her fingers around his arm, her expression one of eager anticipation.

"Not tonight," he told her softly, and disappointment fell like a shroud over Rosamunde's features. "Perhaps I'll see you later," he said gently.

Rosamunde looked again at Hope, then reluctantly left the room.

Silence filled up the chamber, then Roland placed the tray

on the floor and dropped down beside it. "I'm starved," he said and reached for a round of bread.

Hope moved into the light. "She's in love with you, Roland."

"Sit down and eat before the food grows cold."

After a moment's hesitation, Hope sat across from him. Still, she did not eat. "Are you in love with her, Roland?"

The abruptness of her query brought his head up, and he shrugged. "Once love was defined to me by an acquaintance who discovered himself smitten of some fair daughter of a burgher: 'Love is a certain inborn suffering derived from the sight of and excessive meditation upon the beauty of the opposite sex, which causes each one to wish above all things the embraces of the other and by common desire to carry out all of love's precepts in the other's embrace.' If that be certain, then I must declare that while I care for Rosamunde very much, I don't love her."

"Yet . . . she often shares your bed."

He tore a piece of meat in two with his fingers.

Hope said, "You hold her and kiss her and . . . is that not love? And if not, then what is it?"

"You talk too much for your own good, Hope. Just eat and be content with your freedom."

"Not until you tell me exactly what it is you feel for Rosamunde."

"Why do you care?" he shouted.

"I simply desire to understand how a man can take such liberties with a woman's body, not to mention her heart, and yet feel . . . nothing for her here?" She pressed one hand against her heart.

"The same way a woman can take pleasure in a man's body and feel nothing here." He thumped his chest. "It's called lust. We all experience it from time to time . . . at least most of us."

"And what is that supposed to mean?"

"Nothing." He flung his bread into his pottage and reached for his wine.

"Can one not experience lust and love at once?"

"I wouldn't know. I suppose it's possible." He flashed her a hooded look. "My friend also provided me with a series of rules, each of which should be considered while deciding whether or not a man be truly in love:

"One: Marriage is no real excuse for not loving.

"Two: He who is not jealous cannot love.

"Three: It is well known that love is always increasing or decreasing.

"Four: That which a lover takes against the will of his beloved has no relish.

"Five: A true lover does not desire to embrace in love anyone except his beloved.

"Six: When made public, love rarely endures.

"Seven: The easy attainment of love makes it of little value; difficulty of attainment makes it prized.

"Eight: Every lover regularly turns pale in the presence of his beloved.

"Nine: When a lover suddenly catches sight of his beloved, his heart palpitates.

"Ten: Real jealousy always increases the feeling of love.

"Eleven: A true lover considers nothing good except what he thinks will please his beloved.

"Twelve: A lover can never have enough of the solaces of his beloved."

With a lift of one eyebrow, Roland added, "I suspect it's all a lot of ox dung, but then again he was known to fall in love at least once every new moon."

Quiet for a moment, her expression one of intense concentration, Hope chewed her lip and studied Roland through her tawny lashes. "Do you expect me to take Rosamunde's place in your bed?"

Her bluntness caught him ill-prepared for an instant. Then

he swallowed and nodded. " 'Twould not be unpleasant for you, I assure you. You would be justly and amply rewarded."

"I would rather wander the earth like a blind man racked by leprosy for the remainder of my life!"

Hope jumped to her feet. She snatched up a length of material and draped it over her head, wound it around her shoulders like a mantle, and started for the doorway.

Roland frowned. "What are you doing?"

"Leaving. Did you not just give me permission to do so? Or could it be that Roland's word proves to be even less trustworthy than his faithfulness to his lovers?" She moved toward the door, her stride angry.

"You should know that there are many among my men who are far less cordial than I," he called after her.

"Meaning?" She stopped at the threshold, her face partially hidden by the cowl.

Reaching for the wine cask, Roland shrugged. "They won't be so nice as to ask before mounting you."

Hope stormed from the chamber.

"You'll change your mind soon enough," Roland remarked to himself, then relaxed with his wine.

Vast numbers of soldiers and camp followers sat around campfires, while others wandered about the grounds with comrades as they discussed the business of war. As Hope jostled her way through the masses looking for Daniel, the smell of horse dung and roasting meat was thick in the air, as was the smell of ale and urine.

The troop of traveling jongleurs who had happened upon Roland's army while on their way to Poitiers moved amid the crowds with a boisterous glee that seemed at odds with the foul mood prevailing the encampment. They performed handsprings and tumbles, offered imitations of bird calls and sleight-of-hand tricks, while still others strode through the clusters of men and sang at the top of their voices, accompanied by lute and viol, or occasionally tabor pipe and tabor.

Where was Daniel?

What, exactly, would she tell him when—if—she found him?

And what would she do if he refused to leave with her?

She spun around, plowing directly into her brother. Her relieved smile faded to shock as Daniel, with his arm thrown around a woman at least twice his age, did his best to stand up straight, despite the fact that he was obviously drunk.

"Daniel?" she whispered.

The wench hanging off his shoulder planted a kiss on his cheek and rubbed her breasts against him. She flashed Hope a vexed look and said, "Off with ya, ya saucy tart. Find yer own man and leave this un t' me." The wretch planted her hand on Daniel's crotch and squeezed. " 'E's taken, I vow."

"Daniel!" Hope cried, causing Daniel to focus at last on her partially covered face. His eyes widened. His jaw dropped.

Hope grabbed the woman and shoved her, taking little notice that the wench landed flat on her back with her skirts up over her face. Hope grabbed Daniel's hand and led him to a place that was shadowed and quiet. Only then did she back her brother up against a wagon and shake him.

"What are you doing? What are you thinking? Have you lost your senses? Have you no shame? No dignity? Have you forgotten all that my mother and I have taught you?"

He blinked hard, then reached for the cowl hiding her face. "Hope? Is that you?"

"Imbecile. Drunken fool."

"Jesu. It *is* you!" He crossed himself and tried to draw himself upright, failing miserably. He swayed back against the wagon and groaned.

Her face near his, she whispered, "How low have you sunk, Daniel?"

"Pretty damn low," he moaned.

"Did you bed the disgusting wench?"

He swallowed and averted his eyes.

Hope stepped back, shaking her head in disbelief. "What have they done to you, Daniel? This foul enemy and their evil ways have polluted you—"

"*They* have done nothing," he snapped. "I'm not a boy any longer, Hope, to be dragged about by my hand like some wayward orphan. I'm grown enough to make my own way . . . and my own mistakes." Running one hand through his fair hair, he took a deep breath and tried to smile. "*They* are not my enemy any longer."

"They're English—"

"Do you know," he interrupted, "that while on Crusade, Lacurne ate the corpses of the Turks he killed? Some of them he disemboweled while they were yet alive. They were forced to watch as he roasted their intestines on a spit."

"Vile lies—"

"No lies," he shouted, causing Hope to stumble back and the cowl to slide from her head. "It was not these friends whom I heard speak of Lacurne's evil . . . but the abbot himself at Châteauroux. And something else you should know," he slurred as his eyes filled with tears. "It wasn't the English who raided our home and killed our mother."

"What are you saying?"

"That the men who sacked Déols and burned it to the ground were French mercenaries. They believed our village to be protecting English soldiers."

Hope covered her mouth with her hand.

Daniel wiped his nose and cheek with his shirt sleeve. "How could I tell you? We were already without home. Were we to be without country as well?"

A burst of ribald laughter erupted nearby. Hope turned just as a dozen men stumbled around a wagon, their eyes widening with pleasure upon discovering her in the shadows.

She grabbed for the cowl too late; it slipped off her shoulders and fell to the ground.

"Well now, wot have we got here?"

"Appears to me like she's lookin' a bit lonely."

"Run," Daniel whispered behind her, then shoved her to one side and put himself between Hope and the soldiers. "Begging your pardon, milords, but the young lady is my sister and—"

"Shut the blazes up," the tallest sneered, then backhanded Daniel hard enough to send him flying against a nearby tree.

Hope turned to flee, only to find herself swept off her feet and crushed against a man's sweating bare chest. He leered at her with a toothless smile. "I don't reckon I know this one."

"I demand that you release me this moment," she ordered, and kicked at her captor's shins.

"She's a feisty one," someone yelled.

"I like 'em feisty," another replied.

"Let me have a go at her first," came the cry. "By the time I'm done she won't have a taste for the rest of you. She'll be pleadin' with me for more, I vow." He made lewd thrusts with his hips, causing his companions to laugh up roariously and Hope to squirm more furiously. Someone twisted his hand into her bodice and ripped it from her shoulder. His fingernails tore at her skin and she cried aloud, her heart hammering so loudly that the din of raucous laughter seemed to diminish.

The giant holding her backed away from his friends. "I'm the one who found her so I'm the one to have her first."

Frantic, Hope looked up into his scarred, bearded face that was there one moment, laughing grotesquely, then *gone*. A scream lodging in her throat, she watched as his head fell from his body and thumped at her feet. His body followed, limbs twitching as blood gushed like a waterfall from his throat.

The night became suddenly silent as Hope stared first into the man's gaping, lifeless eyes, then up into Roland's face, strangely masked of all emotion as he stood with legs slightly spread, his bloody sword in one hand.

"Come here," he ordered her.

Hope forced herself to step over the still-twitching body and walk to Roland's side. His hand closed around her arm and she leaned against him as her knees threatened to buckle. As if from some great distance, she heard him say, "The same punishment awaits any man who thinks to misuse a woman in any way while in my army. Am I understood?"

There came a muttered response.

"Bury him," Roland snapped.

"My brother! Where is he?" Hope cried.

"Daniel will be seen to," Roland said, then ushered Hope back toward the castle.

Hope stood in the middle of the chamber, her body shaking uncontrollably, her voice still caught somewhere deep in her throat. Having thrown his sword as hard as he could against the wall, Roland paced, jaw knotted, fists clinched, his black hair spilling over his brow to the bridge of his nose.

"Bloody idiot," he roared. "I should have known better than to release you. Now thanks to you I'm left with one less soldier. A good one at that, as I recall."

At last finding her voice, she managed weakly, "You cut off his head . . ."

"What did you expect me to do. Swat his hand?"

"But you *cut off his head*."

He grabbed her shoulders and shook her, causing her hair to slide from its braid and tumble over his hands. "Pretty little fool. Don't you understand my position here? If I allowed one man to get away with such behavior then I would be faced with a hundred who would expect to do the same. Soon I would have no authority over these men whatsoever."

"But did you have to cut off his head?"

Little by little the fury melted from his features. His fingers eased their grip. Still, he did not release her, but appeared to search every tiny nuance of her face. "I would kill any man who thought to lift a hand against you," he finally said, allowing his hands to fall away.

He backed to the embrasure before turning his face into the wind. Leaning upon his hands, head bowed, he remained silent for a long moment. "I realized once you left me that I didn't care much for the idea . . . of you leaving, that is." He laughed quietly to himself. "I was outraged that you would do it. How very arrogant of me to believe that you would want to stay." He added thoughtfully, "There have been wars waged over women. I never understood why, until . . ."

At last, he turned to regard her through his fringe of disheveled hair. "You'll remain here, under my protection, until I decide what to do with you. You're free to wander the grounds only if attended by Roger or myself. Do you fully understand me?"

She nodded. "I'm to remain your prisoner."

He gently caught her chin with his fingers. A full minute passed before her lashes lifted to reveal her eyes that were like two liquid pools. Tears spilled down her cheeks and fell on his hand. Her lower lip trembled.

Softly, he asked, "Do you despise me so much, Hope?"

Her lips parted, yet she said nothing.

"I'm not a bad man, Hope. What I was forced to do tonight brings me no pleasure. But I would do it again to protect you."

Curling his hand around her nape, he eased her closer, or tried to. She braced her hands against his chest and did her best to pull away. He gripped her tighter, his fingers twisting into her fallen hair. "Hope, listen to me."

"No." She shook her head.

He pulled her hard against him, his sudden rush of anger and frustration and . . . something else eroding his patience. "Blast you," he said through his teeth. "I've just killed a man because of you—because I allowed myself to be struck senseless by your pretty eyes and pouting lips and goddamn ethereal beauty. The least you can do is kiss me."

Crushing his mouth onto hers, he kissed her brutally, forcing his tongue between her lips until the taste and scent of her filled his head like a fire raging. She beat his chest and shoulders and did her best to twist her face away.

Finally, he released her. She stumbled slightly before regaining her balance. Her cheeks were as red as embers, her small mouth swollen, the skin around her lips abraded by the roughness of his stubble. "Bastard," she hissed, then slapped his face as hard as she could.

Slowly, slowly, Roland's reason returned. His cheek burned with the impression of her hand. He tasted blood on his tongue. "It seems my manners leave a great deal to be desired," he said softly, touching his fingers to his face. "As I recall I just killed a man for treating you as shabbily." Bowing slightly, he swallowed and said, "My apologies. You've been more than frank about your feelings regarding us heathens and heretics. I stand by my earlier vow. I give you my solemn word that I'll in no way force my . . . attentions on you . . . again. Is there anything I can provide you that will make your stay more tolerable—aside from my dropping dead, of course?"

Hope backed away, her hand pressed to her mouth. "I would like to see my brother more often. Also, I would like my tripod and tablets."

He did not touch her again. He simply moved past her, and without another word, walked off into the darkness, leaving Hope to contemplate her fiercely racing heart, and the dizzy sensation of lightness that spun in her head when she touched her tongue to her lips, and tasted Roland.

What was it about Roland de Gallienne that triggered such strange, frightening, shocking sensations in her? Why did she continually voice her hatred for the arrogant knight, and at the same time pace her miserable little chamber in frustration because too many hours had passed since he'd last visited her?

Why did she spend her long nights tossing and turning on her mat as images of him holding Rosamunde tapped at her memory? Why had she lain awake deep into the night, unable to sleep until Roland returned to fall wearily onto his cot—but not until walking quietly as a cat to her mat to secretly study her while she pretended to sleep.

Cursed enemy.

Except, according to Daniel, Roland was not her enemy. Nor was his army, nor his country. Should she believe Daniel? If the English had won him over, would he not lie to protect them?

Nay, he would not lie to her.

Hope went to her mat and lay down. She stared at the ceiling, focusing her thoughts on her brother's confession and not on the memory of a man's head rolling from his body, or even Roland's brazen behavior where she was concerned.

Her thoughts floated back.

Hope and Daniel ran like the wind over the countryside, their arms outstretched like birds, the breeze in their hair and the dawn light sparkling from the dew on the meadow as their laughter reverberated over the hilltops. 'Twas rare that their mother allowed them such freedom so early. Normally they would be fetching water from the village well, gathering eggs, and milking the cow. But that morning their mother had awakened them long before daylight, dressed them warmly and handed them a bundle of buns and pork, and told them sternly to go play where the forest crowded the river. She had kissed them and hugged them and vowed that she loved them more than life. Then, softly, she had whispered in Hope's ear, "Forgive me, child, for what I must now bequeath you."

The soldiers came, laying waste to the village while Hope and Daniel, safely removed from the carnage, waded in the shallow river and chased tadpoles.

Closing her eyes, Hope wept.

NINE

"But I don't want a companion, Roger. Nor do I need one. I'm not in the habit of depending on anyone to feed me or dress me or—God forbid—bathe me." Hope glanced at the mouselike young girl named Estelle who hovered near the door. For the last few days the child had catered to Hope's every whim. But while the girl's company had not been totally unwelcome, especially late in the evening when solitude had most plagued Hope, Estelle's nervous trembling at Hope's every move had long since made her weary.

"'Tis more for your welfare than your comfort," Roger explained. "Despite my best attempts to disarm the rumors, there are those among this army who believe your presence among us is bound to lead us down a dark road. Especially in light of what most recently took place."

They glanced at Estelle, who continued to pace and chew her thumbnail.

Lowering her voice, Hope asked, "Am I in danger? Tell me true, Roger. I have a right to know."

"No one would dare lift a hand against you, Hope. Can you doubt it after witnessing Roland's retribution on the man who attempted it? While they question his hunger to fight, they wouldn't dare doubt his ruthlessness when it comes to revenge.''

Hope shivered.

''Simply put, Roland feels the girl's companionship will lessen the tediousness of your somewhat cloistered existence. Although . . .'' He glanced around the chamber. ''You've apparently kept yourself busy enough. The window dressings are very nice.''

She smiled. ''Do you like them?''

''That appears to be material Roland purchased in Tours. He imagined it would make someone a lovely bliaut, as I recall.''

''It isn't proper for a woman to accept such a gift from a man like Roland.''

''I think he called it a peace offering.''

''A bribe is more likely.''

There came a knock at the door. Renaud stepped in, Roland's gyrfalcon balanced on his gloved forearm.

''Roland's not here,'' Roger said.

''I've not come to see Roland,'' Renaud announced. ''I've brought the lady a gift. From the captain himself.'' With a bounce of his arm, Renaud sent the great white bird flapping into the air, the campanelle tinkling on its feet. It soared once around the room, then settled on an overhead rafter.

''God's teeth,'' Roger declared. ''What did our Roland do to win such disfavor in your eyes, Hope? It must have been drastic for him to give over his most prized bird, not to mention half of his stores of materials.''

Hope sat on a stool.

Estelle dashed to join her. She grabbed a handful of Hope's hair and proceeded to comb it. Hope sighed. ''She follows on my heels like a puppy. She cuts my meat. She cleans my shoes. She brushes my hair every time I sit. She even beds me down at night and tucks the blanket under my chin. She's there when I go to sleep at night, and there when I awake in the morning."

"Most women enjoy being pampered."

"I'm not most women."

Roger smiled and appeared to consider her words. "I can speak to Roland if you like. I don't think it will do any good."

"I would tell Roland myself if I ever saw him." Hope winced as Estelle pulled her hair. "Where is he, anyway?"

"Attempting to keep his mind on his business, I suppose."

"I haven't seen him for days."

"No doubt."

As Roger walked toward the door, Hope asked, "Is he with Rosamunde?"

"I don't know."

"Well . . . he's obviously with someone. He hasn't slept *here* for nights."

Pausing at the threshold, Roger said, "You sound like a wife. If I didn't know better I'd think you were jealous."

As Roger left the room, Hope ran after him, calling, "Will you escort me on a walk this afternoon?"

"Sorry," he responded. "I cannot. Would you like me to send Roland—?"

"I would rather walk with a skunk!"

"Very well then." Roger laughed.

Slamming the door, Hope turned to find Estelle cowering in the corner, her eyes wide as two moonstones as she anticipated Hope striking her dead with a bolt of lightning. Her brow creasing in as much aggravation as frustration, Hope crossed her arms and continued to glare at Estelle until the servant girl began to outwardly tremble and inch toward the door with every intention of making a quick getaway.

"Hold," Hope commanded, freezing the girl in her tracks. Her hands on her hips, Hope assessed Estelle's clothing, which was little more than a lot of rags sewn together, as were her shoes. Her eyes narrowed and her lips curving, she ordered softly, "Take off your clothes. I should like to borrow them, I think."

"Will you agree, Roland?" Albert asked. "Will you allow Daniel to squire for me?"

With his arms crossed, Roland regarded the tall, thin young man at Albert's side. There was much about Daniel that reminded Roland of Hope. The eyes were the same. The fairness of hair. The identical stubborn set of his jaw . . . not to mention the flagrant ambivalence the boy felt toward Roland.

"You trust too easily, Albert," Roland said. "He's been with us barely a month—"

"He's quick to learn, sir."

"His alliance is to Philip."

Albert and Daniel exchanged glances. After a moment's contemplation, Albert shook his head and appeared to mentally formulate his response before addressing Roland again. "Daniel has made a great many friends the last weeks. He's learned to respect us. He realizes no man should be judged wrongly for his opinions or beliefs."

Roland raised one eyebrow and shifted his weight from one hip to the other. "If that's true, then why does he look at me as if he would like to cut my throat while I sleep?"

"Because of what you've done to my sister," Daniel blurted, causing Albert to cringe.

"And what, exactly, have I done to your sister?"

"You know what you've done. I shouldn't have to spell it out for you."

Albert's shoulders sank and he rolled his eyes in resignation.

His hands clenched, Daniel took a combative step toward Roland. "She hasn't been the same since you imprisoned her in your chamber. I can only imagine to what sort of gruesome and appalling tortures you've subjected her."

Roland smiled thinly. "Is that what she's insinuated?"

"Not in so many words. But there's a difference to her. She moons about as if she's . . ." Frowning, Daniel shook his head. "You've robbed her of spirit. She no longer has an interest in anything."

"If your accusations proved to be true, just what do you think you could do about it?"

"Challenge you, of course."

Albert let out a groan and covered his face with his hands. "Now you've done it," he muttered.

"Challenge me?" Roland responded in a flat tone.

"Albert's schooled me well the last weeks. Roger de Ferres has stated most emphatically that I'm the best young swordsman he's come across in a very long time."

"Did he." It wasn't a question. "Then I take it Roger has sanctioned your squiring for Albert."

"Not exactly," Albert hurried to assure him.

Drawing back his shoulders, Daniel raised his chin and narrowed his eyes. "Sir, the duty of the knight is to constitute himself as guardian and protector of the poor, so that the rich shall never injure them. The duty of the knight is to sustain the weak so that the strong shall never oppress them. Every knight is bound to accompany the frightened and solitary stranger so that no one molests him or strikes him." Drawing himself up, Daniel added, "All good knights are to be the defender and the bold champion of the Church, the widow, and the orphan!"

Looking at Albert, Roland said, "You've taught him well, Albert. However, I fear you forgot to teach him that wise silence is better than foolish talking."

"Yes, sir."

"How well have you taught him to sword?"

A veil of uneasiness crossed Albert's brow.

A smile curling his lip, Roland focused again on Daniel.

"You do realize that a knight never backs down from a challenge."

"Roland," Albert nervously intruded.

"Quiet," Roland snapped. "We'll see just how far your young squire has come these last weeks. Give him your sword, Albert."

"But—"

"Now."

Reluctantly, Albert removed his sword from his belt and offered it to Daniel hilt first. Hot color suffused Daniel's cheeks as he accepted it.

Roland's steel blade sang as he whipped it through the air, its pointed tip *whoosh*ing just in front of Daniel's nose. Then he took his stance, legs slightly scissored and bent, balancing his weight perfectly on the balls of his feet.

Albert swallowed and glanced at Daniel. "Did I happen to mention that Roland has never fallen beneath another knight's sword?"

Daniel, his gaze fixed on Roland's face, shook his head, then wrapped both hands around the hilt of Albert's heavy sword and raised it between himself and Roland.

"En garde, Roland de Gallienne. For the honor of my sweet sister, I challenge you. Should I draw first blood, you will release my sister and allow her her freedom to leave."

"And if *I* draw first blood?"

He thought a moment. "Then my life will be one of complete servitude to you and your precious King Henry."

"Unless rumors prove to be wrong, I doubt that would be much of a sacrifice," Roland remarked dryly, "but then what sort of sacrifice could I expect from a mere . . . child."

"En garde," Daniel shouted again, then swung the blade of his sword as hard as he could against Roland's. Roland responded with a halfhearted movement of his own, which did little more than deflect Daniel's sword with a clank that appeared to vibrate Daniel to the bottoms of his feet.

"Hear me well, Daniel: Young people love danger, but you must tell yourself that some prudence is right and necessary, and that he who would warm himself burns himself sometimes."

His face red and sweating, Daniel lifted the blade and struck again. Again, Roland deflected it only to have Daniel strike again, then again, each time with greater vigor, forcing Roland to the defense.

A crowd formed around them. Shoulder-to-shoulder, Roland's men looked on, smiles on their faces, an occasional laugh. They hooted each time Daniel slammed Albert's sword against Roland's. They jeered when he stumbled, and mocked appreciation when he thrust.

"Roland," someone shouted. "Why do you not run the young ass through and be done with it? Or perhaps you have at last met your match?"

The men shouted in laughter, and Roland grinned, dancing to one side as Daniel labored with trembling arms to swing the sword again, to no avail. His shoulders stooped, his head bowed and dripping sweat, Daniel could not lift the tip of his blade off the ground.

Lowering his sword, Roland slapped Daniel on the back and flashed his cheering men a smile. "What think you, men? Shall I give him another go in say . . . five or seven years?"

They roared in laughter. Roland bowed and lifted his sword triumphantly, just as a voice cried, "Roland, watch your back!"

He spun on his heels just as Daniel's blade sliced through his forearm. The crowd fell silent as Roland stumbled back and stared at his blood-soaked sleeve.

His mouth open, his face suddenly ashen, Daniel raised his gaze to Roland's and swallowed.

Roland swung his sword and struck Daniel's weapon with enough force to knock it from his trembling hands. Daniel retreated, tripped on his feet and landed flat on his back, throwing up his arms in defense as Roland drew back his blade.

"Stop!" Appearing from nowhere, a raggedly dressed wench flung herself across the boy. Her eyes aflame, she tossed back her scarf-wrapped head and cried, "Would you murder a child, Roland? You would strike down a boy who believes duels are little more than games?"

Daniel pushed the woman aside. "First blood, good knight. You know our agreement."

"Your agreement can burn in eternal Hell," he sneered, then dragged the interfering little shrew to her feet, holding her at arm's length as he continued to glare down at Daniel.

"And you call yourself a knight?" Daniel sneered. "What knight would forget his pledge?"

Roland glanced at his men's silent, watchful faces. Finding Albert, he said through his teeth, "If you value your protégé's life, you'll teach him about the consequences of impulsiveness when it comes to challenge, and that the next man he confronts won't be so tolerant of his recklessness."

Roland shoved his way through the crowd, dragging the struggling young woman with him.

"Let me go!" she cried. "You're hurting me, for Heaven's sake. Roland, I demand that you release me this instant."

He stopped and slowly turned his head, his jaw tensing as he at last recognized Hope.

Her lips pouting and her cheeks flushed with color, Hope rubbed her arm. "Cursed brute. I'll be bruised tomorrow. If this is any indication how you treat common women then I'm surprised you ever find a willing body to mount."

His gaze raked her, and still he said nothing, just stared as his eyes became more and more hooded and a tic began to play with his cheek. Finally, drawing her closer and slowly dragging the scarf from her head, releasing her hair in a

tumble of pale waves, he said, "Would you truly like for me
to show you how I treat *most* common women, Hope? Would
you like for me to show you how I treat women who *blatantly* disobey me? Women who meddle in my business?
Who spite me? Who spit and claw like a cat? Who attempt
to *murder* me in my sleep? Shall I go on?"

She shook her head. "I think not, Roland."

"Good," he replied softly. "Very good."

Hope washed Roland's injury with a mixture of warm water
and powdered marjoram that she dug from a small leather
bag. His arm was massive and brown, the muscles hard as
rock beneath her fingers. As carefully as possible, she packed
the injury with a bloodroot poultice that Estelle hurried to
provide her.

"It's little more than a scratch, Roland. Would you have
killed Daniel over such a menial wound?"

"Even menial injuries hurt." He flinched and watched as
Estelle, drapped in Hope's discarded gown, fetched a clean
linen and laid it across Hope's open hand.

"The only hurt I see at this moment, Sir Knight, is your
pride." Hope's eyes reflected her amusement. Her skin appeared paler than usual, which accentuated her delicately
sculptured face and wide eyes. The fact that her shoddy
clothes only enhanced her comeliness provoked an irritation
in him that he was hard pressed to understand. In truth, they
gave her an earthiness that made his blood surge, as did the
sight of the too-tight bodice, which exaggerated and revealed
far too much of her round, white breasts. God's teeth, but if
he did not know better he might think that she was purposefully flaunting her attributes.

As she turned away, Roland grabbed her wrist. He expected her to struggle, to flail, to squirm, to slap his face
again. Only her lips parted, allowing him to smell her honey-
sweet breath as he slid his arm around her waist and pulled

her close. "You do realize that I could still have my revenge on your brother. 'Tis my right. He attacked me while my back was turned."

"But you won't. Will you? It's only a scratch, Roland. Your men will find no weakness in pardoning his error in judgment. He has much to learn about the ways of a knight."

"As do you, I think."

"I care not for learning, sir."

"No? You should. Then you would know just how unwise it is to go flouncing about lonely men with your breasts half-exposed. 'Tis enough to drive a man to his limits, methinks."

He grinned and ran the tip of one finger over the curve of her breast, tracing the blue vein he could see just beneath the skin. She quivered, yet did not flee. Her flesh flushed with heat, effecting a wash of female scent that seemed to permeate from her every pore and rouse from his own body a kind of hunger he had rarely if ever experienced—at least, not since he had kissed and so brazenly caressed her those many nights ago.

What trick was this? Where was her normal response of outrage and resistance? Did she truly believe that he would have revenge on her brother for his foolish ignorance? And was this her way of winning his favor in hopes of changing his mind?

Drawing her closer still, until her small body nestled between his thighs, he lowered his head and breathed softly against her breasts, feeling the steam of his breath rise up to kiss his lips, along with her taste and smell that was like a wildflower. Her body tensed and trembled in his arms that he locked around her, and when he looked up to her face he found her head fallen back and her eyes closed, as if she were offering up her body for some strange ritualistic sacrifice.

He kissed her breasts, and she gasped.

He ran his tongue along the edge of the dress and felt her shiver, heard her murmur an incoherent denial even as she buried her hands in his hair and twisted it around her fingers. It was then that the sting of Daniel's wound made Roland acknowledge the thin stream of blood running down his arm.

"Heal it," he said to Hope. "Just as you did before."

"Before . . . ?" she replied drowsily.

"Rumors abound that you worked some magic on me. They whisper that I had a wound in my side—"

"Why would I care to heal you, Englishman?"

"My question exactly." He tugged her closer, so close that the juncture of her thighs pressed intimately against his. "Perhaps for the same reason you allow me now to touch you, and hold you, and drift my breath and mouth across your breasts. Odd that my memory fails me to such extremes. Odd that I can vaguely even recall my battle with Lacurne. Odd that every time I try to recall my returning to camp I can see little more than some misty image of you, and of our souls colliding for one brief moment. I don't, for a moment, believe that Roger and I drank too much that evening. Tell me true, Hope. Did you heal me?"

For a moment, her body relaxed into his, her eyes became drowsy, her lips parted. She looked on the verge of speaking . . . just as Estelle dropped to her knees beside Hope and began plaiting her hair. As if rousing from a dream, Hope shook her head and suddenly drew away, leaving Estelle staring into Roland's dark face.

"Thank you," he quietly sneered at Estelle.

"Milord?"

"What the devil are you doing here, anyway?"

"You sent me here, milord, to see to Hope's needs . . . and to make certain she weren't bothered by anyone."

"It seems you're performing the task remarkably well."

She beamed. "Thank you, milord."

"Now get out."

"Milord?"

"Get out. *Now*. Before I forget my vow to champion right and good against injustice and evil and squash you like a bug."

Estelle scrambled from the room.

Hope carefully repacked her pouches of medicinals into the chest that had accompanied her from Châteauroux. Her shoulders looked rigid, her movements wooden. Still, her skin looked flushed. Her hands trembled. She glanced over her shoulder repeatedly, as if she expected him to advance on her at any moment.

"Answer me," he said. "Did you heal me?"

"Would my doing so help my cause?" She laughed tightly. "I think not. To heal the man who has taken me prisoner would seem foolish. And even if I had, to admit it would be even more foolish. Would not my value be greater to the Black Flame if I could perform such miracles?"

Roland's eyes narrowed and his lips curled. "Your value to me as a woman would be greater, I think."

Her hands stilled.

Roland moved up behind her, but did not touch her. "I would not have killed Daniel," Roland said softly. "Any more than I would take you against your will."

"I'm relieved to hear it."

"He has a great deal to learn about war . . . and men who wage it. Given time he might prove to be a worthy adversary. You, on the other hand, have a great deal to learn about men."

"Meaning?"

Running one hand up her back, Roland allowed his fingers to trail along her spine, causing Hope to catch her breath. His lips near her ear, he whispered, "When you allow a man to hold you, you invite his interest. When you allow him to breathe on your skin and taste the flesh of your breasts with his tongue, you invite his lust. When you grow weak with enjoyment over his touch and allow your body to quiver with enjoyment and pleasure, you invite him to take you in his arms and make impassioned love to you. Is that what you want, Hope?''

A moment passed, and Hope said nothing. Roland moved nearer. ''What were you doing out there alone? Who were you searching for?'' he asked.

''I simply grow weary of spending my entire day bending over torn tunics. I asked Roger to escort me, but he hadn't the time.''

''So you were searching for Roger?'' he demanded in a sharper tone, causing Hope to step away. Her eyes grew wide and her cheeks flushed as she backed against the trunk and no further. Roland took a steadying breath, willed away the sudden rise of irritation that came with the thought of her risking Roland's anger to search out his second-in-command. ''Roger should return by nightfall. Will that please you?''

''Yes.'' She nodded. ''I like Roger.''

''So it seems.''

''He's most cordial.''

''He's also married. With *seven* children.''

Hope cautiously moved to a pile of tunics and hose to be mended, her gaze still focused on Roland and his darkening mood.

''Roger tells me that of late you show little interest in your tripod.''

''It simply seems like a waste of time. As you can see, there are a great many more important matters to attend to. Roger tore a hole in his favorite tunic when he was hunting boar with Albert and Gerald. Gerald caught his sleeve on a bramble and punctured it with a thorn. Louis, on the other hand, is quite certain that his braies have grown too large for him and wonders if I might alter them. Oh, then there is Hardre—''

''Are you unhappy with these conditions?'' He motioned

around the room. "Perhaps the mattress is not plump enough for you? I'm certain the one you slept on in the abbey was far superior. Do these carpets, which are my very own, not cushion your feet against the splintered floors? Do yon furs not keep you warm enough at night? Is the food I bring you—which you repeatedly refuse to eat—not savorful enough? Does the pheasant not pleasure you, milady?" He grabbed her arm and dragged her to the window. "Look and see, Hope. There are a hundred women there who would happily trade places with you."

A brief moment of silence passed before Hope responded with a hint of her old belligerence. "Would they truly, sir? Would they give up their freedom to reside night and day in a cell, no matter that the cell be carpeted and the walls bright with tapestries? Would they not trade this grandeur for the opportunity to move among their peers, to participate in the most mundane conversation, to feel the wind in their hair and the sun on their face?" She did her best to compose herself, yet the sudden glint of bright tears in her eyes belied her bravado. "You ask that of a prisoner, Roland? You truly believe I find pleasure in these cloistered walls, and in the expressions of yon army as I move among them? I'm little more than one of your birds, free only to fly at your whim and pleasure. I'm surprised you haven't yet tied a campanelle to my ankle, or better yet shroud me within a maileolet."

"I offered you your freedom."

"You took it back."

"Only to protect you."

"Had you not taken me prisoner in the first place, I would not need protection. Why am I here, Roland? What do you intend to do with me?"

Briefly, Roland closed his eyes, shutting out the vision of Hope's face. Finally, he turned away.

"I'm sorry you're lonely. Would you like me to stay with you until Roger returns?"

Hope rubbed her arm where he had held her, then she nodded. "Yes. I would like that very much, I think."

"Fine," he snapped, then grabbed up the demure gown she had worn the day before and flung it at her. "Put it on before I do something I'll be sorry for in the morning."

"The tripod was passed on to me by my mother." Hope studied the stream of oily smoke that rose up from the gold flame dancing within the brass tripod. "Her mother passed it on to her, along with her curse of foresight."

Stretched out on his side, propped upon his elbow, Roland watched as Hope bent over the flame and stared hard into it. Her brow wrinkled and began to sweat.

"I don't always see visions of the future in the flame. Occasionally they come to me in my dreams. Odd . . ." She gazed off into space, then added, "The last days I've been plagued little by the visions, and none have come to me in the tripod. I wonder what that means?" Her voice trailed off and she frowned as Daniel's young face roused before her mind's eye. The memory of their conversation many nights before tapped at her consciousness, reminding her that with love came the diminishment of her powers.

She glanced at Roland, his dark, somber face and black-as-night eyes—his lips that she had allowed to caress her bare skin just hours before. A few days ago he had been her most vile enemy, capable of razing a countryside, of annihilating families with no more thought than if they were insects to be wiped off God's earth—or so she had believed. Would the animal she had believed him to be hold her so gently? Would he speak to her so softly? Would he slay his own valued soldier in defense of her life?

Her breath caught and her heartbeat quickened. The idea that she would like nothing more than for him to touch her like that again made reality swirl like a whirlpool in her head . . . as did the absurd idea that she had actually grown fond of the arrogant, brutal English knight.

"The predictions I read in the tablets . . . they came to you in the tripod?" he asked, rousing her from her musing.

She nodded, still unable to speak.

"They're dumb."

Hope smiled and managed to nod. "Possibly."

"How can you expect a rational man to believe that men will travel in horseless wagons? Or that lances will someday spit deathly fire that can strike warriors down hundreds of feet away?"

"I can only tell you what I see. Only the future will determine whether I was right."

"What future have you seen for me, aside from my being struck by lightning?"

Hope stared again into the flame, choosing to ignore the amused tone of his voice. "Visions of the near future don't come to me in the tripod, but from my own dreams. Since they cause me great pain I choose not to invite them, though they often come to me regardless. They are the worst and most painful and frightening. They are the visions I cannot control or often understand."

"Surely you've seen something of my past and future."

Rubbing her eyes, Hope sat back from the flame and sighed resignedly. "As I said, the last days there's been little sight, and what was there was obscured by an unusual fog. To have forced the vision would have brought severe consequences that I choose not to experience."

Roland reached out and closed his hand around one of the tripod legs. "The truth, Hope. Have you seen nothing of my future?"

Finally, Hope sighed and nodded, resigned to the fact that Roland would give her no peace until she confessed. "It is a strange vision, Roland: A child's grave."

"A child's grave and nothing more?"

"There's a man who weeps at the grave and begs God to forgive him."

"Who is the man?"

"I know not for certain. Only that he has the eyes of a lunatic."

Roland's eyebrows drew together. "My father. Yes, I suppose he *would* pray to God for forgiveness since he considers me more like devil's spawn. So tell me, wise seeress, what, if anything, do you foresee for my army?"

A moment's hesitation passed as Hope gathered her instrument. Roland took her chin in his fingers and forced her to look at him squarely. "Answer me," he demanded in a flat tone.

"I see them scattered like feathers in a gale." She swallowed, and when she lifted her lashes to meet his dark gaze directly, her body began to tremble. "I see King Henry dead of a broken heart, and his sons John and Richard in league with Philip Augustus." Hope regarded him closely. "The men talk of your loyalty to Henry. That you love him like a father."

"Had Henry not taken me to squire I would be dead by now. As for my men, they would never desert me, or Henry. And as far as his sons . . . while Richard is capable of turning on his father, John never would."

Roland stood and walked to the window. Hope moved up beside him. "Do you not miss your family, Roland? Are you not eager to return to England?"

"I'm certain you can gaze into your tripod and discover the answer to that," he said through his teeth, then turned on his heels and quit the chamber, leaving Hope to stare after him, her heart yet racing wildly in her breast.

TEN

A heightened sense of expectation hovered in the night air as Hope walked at Roger's side. Three dozen men were preparing to ride at first light—their duty to patrol the roads and make certain Roland's army met no enemy on their journey to Chinon, which would commence in three days. The eager soldiers crowded around Matilda's tent, their expressions intent as they listened to her predictions, which were favorable, judging by the relief on their faces. They laughed and slapped one another on the back. They raised their tankards of ale and mead high in the air and howled insults at King Philip and made crude threats to Lacurne.

Amid the wild celebration, Matilda bent over her collection of stones, bones, and crystals and turned her tiny yellow eyes toward the rowdy soldiers. "I see naught but success for Roland from this night forward. Philip's army grows weak and soon will crumble under the mighty power of our King Henry."

"But what of the rumors that Henry grows weak and ill?" someone shouted.

" 'Tis a ruse. Nothing more. A ruse to lure Philip into a

state of complacency. When the time is right, Henry will rise and strike down his fierce enemy with a solitary blow.'' She tossed powder into the fire, causing a bloom of bright green smoke to coil into the night air. "I see this army of weary men returning to England within the year. They will soon know the pleasure of holding their wives and children in their arms again!''

The men roared their approval.

Frowning, Hope turned to Roger, who regarded the celebration with an expression of slight irritation. "They hang on her every word even after their comrades fell to Lacurne.''

"They cling to anything that will give them the courage to face their possible death,'' he replied wearily. "Brave they may be, but who among us cherishes the certain possibility of dying?''

She searched the crowd—the men bowed over their chess or backgammon boards, those flown with wine and staggering from one boisterous group to another—even those men and women who had found their way to some secluded shadow in hopes of sating their more base hungers.

"He isn't there," Roger said.

"Who?"

"Roland, of course.''

Hope laughed lightly. "What makes you think I search for Roland?''

"You always search for Roland." Roger grinned. "Anytime he's out of your sight your eye scans each and every face. And when you find him . . .''

Hope walked away. "Surely you jest with me, Roger. Or perhaps the mead turns your thoughts to idiocy. As it apparently does with this entire lot of ruffians. I care not where Roland is, or who he's with. He's a blackguard. A charlatan. A rogue knight who apparently enjoys bullying little boys and refuses to live up to his pledges.''

" 'Twas Daniel who challenged Roland," Roger replied, falling in beside her. "And had Roland been so inclined he could have slain your brother for the simple reason that the lad was stupid enough to challenge Roland in the first place—let alone attacking Roland while his back was turned. A man of honor *never* strikes another while his back is turned. I've seen men beheaded for lesser crimes."

Hope stopped abruptly as Rosamunde appeared through the crowd. She had obviously taken great care with her appearance, her hair being braided neatly into a long red rope that fell across one shoulder. Hope recognized her emerald-green skirt as the same garment Roland had offered Hope just days before. Hope, of course, had turned the gift away.

Bending near Hope's ear, Roger whispered, "It seems our Roland is well sought out this eve, does it not? What fate to be desired by the two most beautiful women in camp. I envy him. But such is the good fortune that comes with Roland's looks and reputation, eh?"

Hope flashed him a hot look. "You're a wedded man, Roger de Ferres."

"Wedded, yes. But too long without a wife. Such depravation weakens even the strongest warrior. 'Tis a woman's body who gives a man life. 'Tis a woman's love that gives him his will to live."

Rosamunde spotted them at that moment. Her eyes grew large; her hands nervously smoothed the folds in her skirt as she locked gazes with Roger, then with Hope. "Roland is down by the horses," he called.

Rosamunde flashed Hope a last tentative look before turning away and melting into the dark beyond the campfires. Gently, Roger took Hope's arm. "For one who considers Roland a blackguard, a charlatan, and generally unfit to walk amid anyone other than lepers, thy lady's lovely cheeks be suddenly flush with color. You wouldn't be jealous, would you?"

Hope jerked her arm away and lengthened her stride. Behind her, Roger laughed and hurried to catch up. "Ah, but 'tis a lovely night for lovers, sweet Hope. The sky is scattered with stars and yon moon is full and brilliant. I swear 'tis enough to steal a man's heart away . . . were he to set eyes on the woman of his dreams."

"I fear, Roger, that you've missed your true calling," she told him with an arch of one eyebrow.

"Pray tell me, Hope. What better calling would I have other than brave and most heroic of knights?"

"Jongleur," she retorted, causing Roger to toss back his head in laughter.

The throng of the rowdy crowd grew as the night deepened. Roger returned Hope to the castle much too early for her liking, but she demurred nevertheless. She surmised that rather than acting as companion to some drab, displaced prisoner, a man such as Roger would prefer to spend his nights gambling and jousting and drinking with his fellow soldiers. Still, as he prepared to take his leave, she stopped him by asking:

"What does Roland intend to do with me?"

Roger regarded her closely for a long, silent moment, his features expressionless but his eyes intense. "I know not, Hope."

"Of course you do. I suspect you're the only man in this entire army in whom he will openly and honestly confide. Nor would he make his decisions without first discussing them with you."

Roger stepped away and averted his eyes. "Why don't you ask him?"

"I have. This very afternoon."

Roger looked thoughtful and replied more to himself than to Hope. "I suspect that in his present frame of mind he would be hard pressed to know the answer to that himself."

He searched Hope's face. "Do you hunger much for freedom? Would you be pleased if Roland handed you over to Philip . . . or the Pope?"

Hope bit her lip, inwardly shocked that any eagerness that might have met Roger's question did not come. Instead, a spear of some emotion that felt surprisingly like dread settled in the pit of her chest.

"Well?" Roger raised one eyebrow as Hope continued to remain silent. "Have you grown fond of our Roland, Hope? Can it be you would rather linger away your youth following him on his knightly jaunts across country, sharing his life with Rosamunde and all the others who catch his roving eye now and again?"

"Certainly not." She squared her shoulders, aware that her face had grown red with embarrassment, not to mention the irritation and chagrin she felt over the idea that Roland kept a bevy of women at his beck and call who no doubt became as quivering and featherheaded as she did in his presence. "I . . . think only of Daniel, of course. He has grown fond of these men."

"God's mustache. I would never have believed it—not you, the saint of Châteauroux—"

"I'm *not* a saint, and *what* do you not believe? Why do you look at me that way, Roger?"

"You're falling in love with Roland," he declared with an edge of anger. "That's why you healed him—not for fear that he was somehow your protector, or even because some divine voice instructed you to turn the other cheek and heal thine enemy, but because you've actually grown fond of the surly bastard."

"Oh, you're wrong," she told him dryly. "Very wrong. Why, if you told me this very moment that you intended to return me to the abbey I would . . . I would . . ." She chewed her lip.

"You would what?" Roger glared at her, his jaw

clenched. When she continued to offer no reply, he shook his head and turned for the door, muttering under his breath as he quit the room, leaving Hope to stare after him and listen to the music and laughter that occasionally found its way through the fenestral window.

Roger was wrong, of course. She was not even remotely fond of Roland, much less in love with him. She did *not* find him attractive. She did *not* approve of his brutish behavior or his thirst to make war.

His kisses had *not* made her lose her breath.

His touch had *not* turned her skin to fire.

She had *not* gone weak as a quivering, trembling lamb when he slid his tongue over her breasts.

She did *not* awaken at night reliving the sensation of his hand between her legs, or aching to again experience the forbidden touch.

And she certainly did not feel even the slightest twinge of jealousy over the prospect that, even at that very moment, he might be lying with Rosamunde: kissing her, touching her, sliding his tongue over her breasts and running his warm, strong hands up the insides of her thighs.

Hope paced. She perched on the window embrasure and absorbed the feel of the wind in her face and the cool kiss of night on her closed eyelids and did her best not to think of how pretty Rosamunde had looked tonight—all for Roland, no doubt. She knew how to please him: how to make him smile, to sigh . . . to make him tremble with desire.

As the night wore on there was much talk of the upcoming march to Chinon, and much speculation over what Roland's army would confront there.

King Henry and rumors of his failing health prevailed. The king was now forced to rely on his bastard son, Geoffrey, who had been chancellor of England for the past years, to see that his father's orders were carried out. Henry had gone

so far as to order that all his Norman castles were only to
be surrendered to John, and that a levy of Welsh mercenaries
was to be brought from England with the hopes of stabilizing
his dwindling forces abroad.

As always, there was conversation about Hope, the men
squarely divided over whether she be good or evil. Many
believed that she had cast some spell over Roland—for he
had not been himself since their sojourn to the abbey of the
Miracles. Others were quick to add that Roland had been
cursed since the day of his birth, and that it was Roland's
very existence that had driven the great Godfrey insane.

Roland inspected the line of horses, finding them well
tended and healthy. The coals of the blacksmith's fire still
glowed in the dark, however, telling him that his trusted
blacksmith would soon return to take up iron and hammer
and finish the shoeing of his soldiers' war animals. Finding
his own horse amid the group, Roland ran his hand down
the black's massive shoulder and recalled the day King
Henry had presented Roland with the magnificent beast.
Roland had been only a little older than Daniel. Young.
Brash. Arrogant. Like Daniel. Innocent in the ways of life
and death . . . as well as love.

Like Roland, the horse showed evidence of previous wars.
The fire that had once burned in its eyes was now more like
an ember. The scars marring its beautiful sleek black skin
were healed but apparent. When Roland ran his hand up the
animal's crest and scratched behind its ears, the horse turned
its muzzle into Roland's chest and nickered softly. Grinning,
Roland pressed his face against the black's massive neck and
breathed in its scent, allowed the sweat of its body to warm
his cheek and chase away the chill that had crept into his
joints.

God, but he felt weary. The sleep that had eluded him so
long pressed at his eyelids.

He thought of Hope, holed up in her stagnant chamber—

alone, bent over her odd little tripod with its strange glowing flame of light. Part of him yearned to wrap his hands around her throat and murder her—wipe the image of her disturbing eyes and beautiful mouth from his mind. Perhaps then the desire to take up sword and shield against Philip would return.

Another part of him—the hot painful center of his chest that of late had bothered him more than any physical wound—yearned only to bask in her nearness and absorb the golden heat that her presence emanated. What sweet lethargy overtook him when she was near! He felt like a boy again, made drowsy by warm summer sun. He wanted only to float in the sublimity of her infrequent smile.

A roar of the crowd brought his head around. In the distance a group of revelers had congregated around a singular figure—a woman. No doubt the lot of drunkards had enticed some little wench with too many meads and ales to totally forget her inhibitions and entertain them with a peeling off of her clothes.

With a final scratch to his horse's withers, Roland moved to the fascinated, albeit drunken onlookers who let out a whoop of appreciation as Roger, encouraged by the crowd, stumbled into the circle and swept the woman up into his arms. They danced in rhythm with the spectators' chants and music until each sprawled to the ground, a tangle of arms and legs, the woman's skirts flown up like tulip petals around her armpits.

Someone shouted. "Are ye blind, de Ferres? Can ye not see that the bitch is pining for ye? If she were any wetter ye'd be drowning by now!"

Roland barely noticed as Matilda pressed close—so close that the air swam with the scent of her medicinal herbs and the perpetual stink of her aged, unwashed body and rotting teeth. "The men are particularly restless this eventide, wouldn't you agree, Roland?"

"Stand away from me, hag. Had I desired your opinion I would have asked for it."

"Do you wonder on the behavior of your second-in-command?"

"Why should I?"

"The men talk of Roger de Ferres and Hope of Châteauroux; how Roger takes such pleasure in accompanying her. They say he no longer speaks of his family. That he hangs on the seeress's every move. The men worry that she's cast some spell on him. Look at him, de Gallienne. Your friend and second-in-command is no longer himself."

Roland flashed the old woman a dark look.

"When have you last seen Roger so loose of his judgment that he would flounder on his belly like a carp?" she goaded. "And before his men at that?"

Roland flung his empty tankard to the ground. Matilda replaced it with another. The liquid burned the inside of his mouth and throat, and it hit his belly like a hot stone. He staggered back before setting his heels. The dark beyond the campfire breathed in and out like a living thing.

"Witch," he managed to murmur, then did his best to focus on the hag's features. "What have you done to us? What vile concoction have you put in this drink?"

" 'Tis not my doing. She's bewitched you all," came Matilda's voice through the rising cacophony. "Soon she'll have them all exactly where she wants them."

Wiping his mouth with the back of his hand, Roland asked, "And where would that be?"

"Dead and buried in yonder common grave, my good knight. Where else? It's quite simple, de Gallienne. They no longer look to you as their leader and protector, but to her as their salvation. Instead of rallying for Henry, they follow her like stupid sheep to the slaughter. Look about you if you don't believe me. Are these soldiers the brave and splendid knights who have fought by you for so many years? Nay, they are more like mindless eels. Need I remind you that she has already brought about the death of one of your best soldiers?''

Roland quaffed the cooling mead and shoved the empty tankard at Matilda as she made some final comment that buzzed past his ears. Beyond the campfires the shapes of tents and wagons were masked by midnight darkness. Figures moved here and yon, their voices as much a blur as their hidden faces.

A pressure mounted inside him like a coil twisted to its endurance. His head pounded and every nerve ending on his skin felt as if it were on fire.

''She will cast her spell on each and every one of them,'' came the hag's voice from somewhere behind him. ''Mark my words, Roland. Soon you'll not trust even your closest friend. She'll use her charms to seduce you all, and when you've weakened, she will cut out your soul and devour it . . .''

''Get out of my sight,'' Roland sneered, then shoved the hag aside, taking no notice as she spilled to the ground. He focused his gaze on Roger, who stumbled to his feet and grabbed his partner's buttock, causing her to squeal and slap his hand. Then Roger's gaze met Roland's, and his laughter died. Attempting to stand tall, Roger walked unsteadily toward Roland, his smile set and his fists clamped at his sides.

''If it's not our fearless leader,'' Roger greeted. ''Have you come to join the ranks of your inebriated army, Sir Roland? Or have you, perhaps, better things to do . . . such as seducing saints and widows and horny whores who believe you God's gift to womankind?''

''I might ask you the same,'' Roland replied with thin patience. ''But then I remind myself that you're a married man. So any sense of jealousy I might note in your tone is nothing more than my imagination.''

Sidling up next to Roland, Roger slapped one hand on

Roland's shoulder and squeezed hard. " 'Tis good that we can talk like this—as friends. There are a great many problems we should discuss."

"I'm aware of no problems, other than that my army appears to have forgotten that their drunkenness leaves us vulnerable as a motherless fawn. Have you forgotten there are wolves in the forests who would like nothing more than to tear out our throats?"

"Are we not protected, Roland? For God's sake, we have a saint living among us. One who apparently has acquired a certain fondness for us. And if she cannot protect us from an attack, then she can at least heal our wounds, if not our hearts. Need I remind you what she is worth in ransom? Or does the idea of our growing wealthier than Henry himself no longer appeal to the Black Flame?"

Roland knocked Roger's hand aside. "You need remind me of nothing."

"I'm not so certain," Roger slurred, his lips thinning in something less than a smile. "I think you don't realize just how valuable our little saint is to Philip . . . or the Pope."

"She's no saint," Roland declared and attempted to step away, only to be stopped short as Roger grabbed his tunic in one fist and held him fast. Thrusting his face near Roland's, Roger whispered:

"Saint or sorceress, I care little, Roland. I know only that you're alive now because of her. Aye, the rumors you've heard are true. She healed a wound in your side as big as my fist. A lance wound gifted to you by Lacurne himself. She took your memory of it along with the pain and blood and scar. She has more power in her lovely little hand than all the armies in England and France combined. We could purchase our own bloody country with the reward Philip and the Pope will happily pay to get her back."

Roland looked at Roger's hand twisted in his tunic, then focused again on his second-in-command's eyes. "Were you not my friend, Roger, I would kill you for touching me in such a way. But since you are my friend, I'll allow you to keep your head if you release me . . . *now*."

Gradually, Roger lessened his grip on Roland's tunic, his mouth a thin slash of anger as he stepped away.

"Go back to your ale and whores," Roland ordered softly. "The morrow will see us both in better minds and dispositions. Then we'll speak of your apparent dissatisfaction with my decisions and what we might do to remedy this breach in our relationship."

"Do you mean our relationship as friends or soldiers?" Roger sneered.

"Both."

"Do you mean to demote me, Captain? Am I so useless to you as second-in-command? Then again, by the way you fight these days perhaps even Daniel would be capable of guarding your back."

Roland drew his bollock from his scabbard, and before Roger could blink, pressed it against Roger's throat.

"Have you something to say about my capabilities of leading this army, then say it. If not, you'll be wise to keep such opinions to yourself."

Roger stared into Roland's face, his own beginning to sweat as the point of Roland's knife blade bit into his skin, drawing a bead of blood. At last, Roger backed off and shrugged.

"I fear you're right, Roland. Seems I've had far too much to drink. That, however, won't stop me from partaking in at least one or two more before I crawl to my tent." With a short bow and a smile that did not reach his eyes, Roger turned and walked unsteadily toward the group of men who had congregated around a pair of dice.

The ground trembles, and trees and buildings crumble.
The night shadows shift around Hope—foggy forms black

against an eerily lit sky the color of flames. A roaring comes, washing over the decimated land, rolling like invisible waves.

The horsemen cometh, swords raised and bloody, their banners burning flames.

Run. Run! Don't stop. Don't look back.

Roland!

From the ashes Matilda rises amid the fallen men, her smile twisting with malice, her terrible laugh as shrieking and awful as a murder of crows. She points directly at Hope, and her vicious eye is a prism of terrible melee.

Hope sat up, gasping for breath, her face sweating and her body shaking.

She held her head, praying that the pain of the gruesome vision would ease. Yet it remained, throbbing at her temples as if her head would explode at any minute.

Where was Estelle?

She crawled on her hands and knees to the sleeping girl. "Estelle, awaken! Estelle!" Nothing. The girl lay as limp as death, refusing to be roused.

Hope covered her eyes with her hands. Was she dreaming still? Was this yet some vision from which she could not awaken?

Hope ran to the window.

Flames dance before her eyes.

Bodies lay strewn upon the ground, their corpses charred and bloody.

Hope stumbled back, covering her face with her hands. No heat.

Only voices. Laughing. Only campfires—distant, dim . . . nothing wrong.

Why could she not awaken?

The walls run with blood.

She had to warn them.

But *they* are the enemy.

Get dressed. Quickly. Time is running out.

Hope dragged her clothes on, kicking over the half-full tankard of mead she had drunk with her meal. Vague memory returns—*she's drinking the ale some strange little woman had brought with her evening meal and listening to the voices that occasionally drift in through the window.*

Where is Roland? *she wonders.*

Holding Rosamunde?

Kissing her?

The mead tastes odd. Bitter. The room is spinning and she feels so desperately tired . . .

She must warn them!

Roland won't believe her—not about the vision. He won't trust that she would help his army.

Roger will believe her. He'll persuade Roland to prepare the soldiers before it's too late, before the flaming horsemen, led by Lacurne, swoop upon yonder army and burn it to the ground.

Upon arriving at the camp grounds Hope was momentarily filled with dread as she scanned the scattering of procumbent forms, believing them already dead. There was an odd smokiness in the air that made her feel dizzy and sick, and the horrifying images that had come to her moments ago roused before her mind's eye and made her begin to shake.

Roger lay sprawled on his back, eyes staring blankly at the sky as Hope shook him, then slapped his cheeks. "Wake up, Roger. I fear there's little time. Something terrible is about to happen and—"

"Gwyneth is that you?" He grinned and touched Hope's face. "You're much prettier than I remember."

"Get up." Hope struggled to sit Roger up. His head bobbed back and forth, and he belched. "Where is Roland, Roger? You must find Roland and warn him."

Raising both eyebrows, Roger looked at Hope squarely. "Warn him of what?"

Hope took his face in her hands. "I've had a vision, Roger. A terrible vision. I saw this army decimated—"

He grabbed her wrist, and his features tensed as he glanced around. The campfire had dwindled to little more than coals. Men lay scattered about the ground where they had fallen. "This is hardly the place to talk of your visions, Hope. Help me up. There will be privacy by the river . . . if I can make it that far. Come here. Give me your shoulder. God's grace, but I can't remember a time when I've so lost my good senses. 'Tis no wonder Roland threatened to cut me."

With her arm around Roger's waist, his draped around her shoulder, Hope did her best to lead Roger to the river—not an easy task in the dark. They tripped on gnarled tree roots. Thrice they wandered from the beaten path and became snarled in wild undergrowth. At last, her patience at an end, she led Roger down the rocky shoal and dropped him into the shallow water, then fell to her knees beside him. The water felt shockingly cold and revived her lethargic mind.

Hope bathed Roger's face with her hands, and poured water from her cupped palm down the back of his nape. Finally, he raised his shaggy head and smiled.

"The moonlight suits you, lass."

"I've not brought you here to talk of moonlight, Roger."

He looked at the sky and the moon that cast soft light over the rippling river. "That's a terrible shame. There's nothing I would like more than to tell you that you have an exquisite face and the most alluring body I've ever seen. Is it a wonder that most men look at you and think you're an angel?"

"Listen to me, Roger." She sat down in the water. "I've had a vision."

"You *are* a vision."

"We must find Roland and warn him."

"Warn him of what? That you're falling in love with

him?'' He laughed. ''You needn't look so shocked. You become green every time you see him with Rosamunde. Besides—'' He swiped one wet hand over his eyes. ''Had you
not cared for him more deeply than you pretend, you
wouldn't have risked your life by healing the wound in his
side. That wasn't particularly wise, Hope. Don't you know
there are greedy bastards around who would use that knowledge to their advantage?''

''I trust you and Roland would not allow that to happen,''
she replied, offering him her hand.

Roger regarded her extended hand, his jaw tensing.
''Would you trust your enemy so easily, Hope? Should *we*
trust *you*?''

''Would I care to see you destroyed I would not be here
now. I would allow your enemy to ravage this army so that
I and my brother could go free.''

''Have you already spoken to Roland—''

''No. I fear he would not believe me.''

Roger took Hope's hand and stumbled to his feet, ''Very
well, Hope of Châteauroux, tell me about your vision.''

Estelle cowered in the corner as Roland paced. ''Where is
Hope and why aren't you with her?'' he demanded. ''Speak
up, for God's sake. Why do you tremble like a mouse every
time I walk into this bloody room?''

''You frighten me, milord.''

''Obviously.'' Hands on his hips, he glared at the timid
girl. ''Where is Hope?''

''I don't know, milord. I drank yonder ale and . . . I don't
remember anything after that.''

Roland forced himself to take a deep breath as he closed
his eyes.

''Mayhap she went for a walk,'' Estelle said. ''She were
feelin' a bit lonely earlier . . . like she was tired of bein'
holed up in this dreary chamber.''

He cursed and quit the room, stood for a while in the dark outside the chamber while he attempted to clear his thoughts. He would find the hag and kill her for planting insane notions in his head about Hope and Roger—notions that Hope desired nothing more than to destroy his army—and that by allowing her to remain among them the Black Flame invited his and his army's destruction—notions that Hope and Roger had somehow become . . . close. Already he had allowed such insane suspicion to cloud his reasoning with dealing with his friend and second-in-command. Roger had been like a brother to him over the years. They had never passed a solitary cross word, yet over the past days a friction had formed between them that too swiftly flared when Hope's name came up.

Hope.

Why could he not think of anything but the smell of her skin and the taste of her lips? Why did the memory of her yielding her body to his make the blood boil in his veins? Why did the thought of her with Roger fill him with such fury that he would happily cut Roger's throat if his friend so much as touched her?

Mayhap the hag was right. Mayhap the saintly seeress had cast some spell on him, robbing him of his ability to reason—and to rally his defenses against these feelings that Hope of Châteauroux inspired in him.

By the time Roland returned to the camp, revelers lay strewn upon the ground as still as corpses. The stench of some familiar odor hung in the air.

A man on the ground began to moan. He thrashed at the air and screamed as if he were drowning in a pit of snakes. Then, as quickly, he fell silent, eyes closed as if in a deep sleep. His body twitched one last time; then he lay still as death.

Roland frowned and backed away, suspicion worming its way into his reason.

Matilda materialized through the smoke, her yellow eyes aglitter.

"What have you done to my men?" Roland demanded, drawing his sword. "Speak true, Matilda, or I swear to all the saints in Heaven that I'll kill you where you stand. I know the smell of jabrol. I've seen you feed it to my injured men enough times to recognize the insensibility it produces."

"But only to alleviate their pain, Roland. What reason would I have to incapacitate this army? What would I gain but your disfavor? Think! Who among us would have more reason to produce stupor in these men's minds?"

"Say what you mean for once in your miserable life."

"Hope of Châteauroux, of course." She smiled. "How better to control her destiny? How better to control your men? You'll find her at the river. *With Roger.* I should hurry, de Gallienne, before your second-in-command is lost to you for good."

His legs felt like wood as Roland slowly turned toward the forest. His vision spun as he stumbled over the prone bodies of his groaning men, then through the twisted trunks of the ancient trees and the curtain of darkness blanketing his way. At last, after what seemed like an eternity, he found himself on the rocky shoal of the river, the water lapping gently around his ankles and moonlight so bright in his eyes that he was forced to shield them with his arm.

There came a sound of splashing water. He clumsily turned, slipping on moss-covered stones and nearly falling. Before him stood a couple—a man and woman knee-deep in the water, the man's torso bare, the woman touching his face very gently with her hands. Her long hair reflected the moonlight so it shimmered like white fire.

A sound worked up Roland's throat and he waded deeper into the water. Startled, Hope looked around, her eyes shadowed, her skin like alabaster. Her lips parted as if she might speak.

Roland hit Roger with a force that sent his friend flying backward, sprawling in the shallows.

"Stop!" Hope cried, attempting to grab his arm. "Your anger at Roger is misplaced. I searched him out because I feared you wouldn't listen to me. Roland, I had a vision. I saw this army—these men, wasted—"

"So did I. They're mindless because of the jabrol you put in their drink."

Hope stumbled back, shaking her head in disbelief. "Why would I do such a thing? What would I accomplish?"

"That's what I intend to find out," he replied through his teeth.

"Roland, please, you must listen to me—"

He pushed her aside, causing her to fall to one knee amid the rushes. Struggling to stand, her gown dripping water and mud, she glared up at Roland and shook her head. "You arrogant bull. I should have known better than to help you. See how far you get by trusting *Matilda's* lies. Your destruction by Lacurne's army will be nothing more than you deserve."

Roger lunged for Roland. They struggled, splashing in the muddied water before Roland managed to shove Roger away and draw his sword.

Roger's eyes widened and he stumbled back, slipping on the slick mud and stones as he raised his arms to shield himself. "Would you lift a weapon against a friend, Roland? Would you slay me without allowing me to defend myself?"

"There is no defense for what I witnessed."

"You witnessed nothing but my ministering him," Hope cried behind him. "Roger is ill, Roland—"

"And who made him so?" he shouted, turning on Hope as she struggled to fight her way to better footing.

"Why would I care to harm Roger, who is my friend?"

"Friend?" He laughed, then slowly raised the tip of his sword, catching the frail material of her blouse and dragging it down over her shoulder. "Is that all he is to you, Hope? Simply a friend?"

"Yes," she replied softly, and nodded.

"You needn't defend me, Hope," Roger stated, at last finding the strength to stand straight. "Roland is right, of course, and has every reason to confront me. As your protector I should have used better judgment than to bring you here alone."

"Quiet," Roland snarled, turning the tip of his sword to Roger's throat, then stepped close and lowered his voice. "When our heads have cleared of this rank ale and our thoughts are again our own, we'll sit down as two soldiers and discuss this unseemly incident. Until then, get you out of my sight. If I see you again while this anger is eating at my chest, I may well kill you."

Roger backed through the rushes, his beard dripping water and his hands curled into fists. "Were we not friends, my lord, I might think you had just challenged me."

"Think what you will," Roland snapped, lifting his sword between them.

Roger bit back any further comment before turning on his heels and stumbling out of the water. He did not look back before disappearing into the dark copse, leaving Roland standing thigh-deep in the river, his unconscionable anger pressing as sharply as the point of a sword into his gut.

What the devil had come over him?

What insanity had gripped him the moment he saw his best friend and second-in-command in such a scene with Hope of Châteauroux?

He turned to confront Hope.

She was gone.

ELEVEN

Hope could not find Daniel among the drunken soldiers. After an hour's search, she finally gave up, deciding to return to the castle.

Somehow she had to find a way to communicate with Roland—to warn him that his life and the lives of his soldiers were in danger, that the prattle that Matilda continued to feed them was wrong—deadly wrong. Roger had been her only hope; he would believe her, but she dare not attempt to seek him out again—not when Roland's behavior proved so irrational.

As Hope hurried along the dark path to the castle, her thoughts focused on Roland's confusing behavior and his shocking anger at Roger. Matilda stepped from the shadows, bringing Hope up short with a startled gasp.

"Foolish child," the crone wheezed. "Do you think they care what you see? Do you think they trust you? There are those among these men who would sell you for a pittance to the Devil just to be rid of your presence."

"It's not I who fills these desperate men with false hope and promise," Hope declared. "Why do you mislead them?

How can you prepare them for victory when you know as
well as I that little but destruction and death awaits them at
the hands of Lacurne?''

"Are we to believe our enemy? One who attempted to
murder Roland in his sleep. Look to yonder oblivious soldiers. When they awaken in the morning they'll believe you
to be the culprit behind their sorry moods. Who else would
have cause to sprinkle jabrol in their mead?''

Hope tried to step around Matilda. The hag caught her
arm, her bony fingers digging into Hope's skin.

"You question why Roland keeps you. Why he would
suffer his men's anger over harboring you. Foolish little twit.
The Black Flame and Roger de Ferres care for only one thing
and that is the fortune you'll bring them soon. I will tell you
true, Hope of Châteauroux. Roland intends to ransom you to
King Philip. You'll bring him enough wealth that he can
return to England and give up this life of mayhem and destruction.''

"I don't believe you. Why should I when I know you to
lie even to Roland?''

Matilda cocked her head and narrowed her eyes. She
laughed softly. "Mayhap you had come to think he fancies
you, hmm? That his reasons for locking you in yon chamber
and treating you like a queen is because of some fondness
he harbors in his heart.''

Hope pulled away. "Witch! I care not what Roland thinks
or feels for me. Why should I? He is my enemy.''

"If we believe that, then we must believe that your predictions be not for friend, but for foe.''

Hope backed away, rubbing her arm where the hag's nails
had left small bloody scratches in her skin. She tried to
breathe, to stop the flush of emotion turning her skin fever-
ishly hot. She did her best to ignore the hag's words but they
pricked at her consciousness like a sharp thorn.

Why else would Roland continue to keep her here, to risk

the condemnation of his army, if not for the lure of incredible wealth that might come to him by ransoming her to Philip? Yes, yes. It all made sense now.

She was nothing more than costly chattel—plunder of war.

"When reason returns to Roland he'll realize that my predictions were right. You've cast some spell on this army, and his friend Roger. You have turned friend into foe, and soldiers into mindless, spineless eels. There won't be mounted knight or foot soldier who will look at you as anything more than an evil, capable of corrupting hearts and souls."

Matilda lifted her fist, and with a flip of her wrist, cast a powder into Hope's face. Hope gasped and coughed as she stumbled back, the world instantly becoming a blur that crashed in on her like a black, exploding universe.

Dawn. Slowly, slowly, reality returned in a heavy blanket of gray silence that felt damp and cloying against Hope's shivering skin. There was a bitter taste in her mouth—like cold metal—causing her teeth to chatter and her stomach to roll.

Where was Estelle? Why was the timid child not here to tuck the blanket under Hope's chin, to fetch her water to soothe this rancid taste in her mouth and the odd fever burning her brow?

She stretched her arms and legs, confused by the feel of wet and sharpness biting into her skin. Opening her eyes, she tried hard to focus on her surroundings.

A gray rabbit huddled in a bush near her head, its whiskered nose bobbing rapidly up and down as the animal nibbled on a dew-kissed piece of grass. Overhead a bird trilled—not a cheerful tune, but a long, shrill cry that rent the deep silence of the forest.

Hope groaned. Her body hurt. Her temples throbbed.

Where was she, and how long had she been sleeping?

For minutes? Hours? Days . . . ?

She felt weak with hunger and burning with thirst.

Try to think.

Yes, yes, it was coming back to her now. Matilda had confronted her with the truth, that Roland intended to ransom her to Philip, and she'd realized with a flash of dismay that what the hag told her must be true, and that Roland's reasons for keeping her had nothing whatsoever to do with any feelings he might have for her.

Oh, to admit even to herself that such a revelation had crushed her made her head swim and her heart beat heavily. To acknowledge her pain and disappointment forced her to confront her awakening feelings for Roland—and the thrill his kiss and touch had brought her. For an instant the previous night she had been filled with a raging desire to claw Matilda's face, then . . . the hag had, with a swipe of her clawed hand, cast some vile powder into her eyes.

Memories speared through Hope's groggy mind.

Images of her fighting her way through the dense black forest, thinking only that she had to escape Roland and his army.

She would not allow Roland to use her in any way against Philip.

She would not allow Roland to again make her heart skip a beat in his presence, would not experience again the surge of excitement and pleasure his smile and touch brought her.

Nor would she ever again seethe with certain jealousy over the idea of his being with another woman.

Other memories—more vague—like images of dreams that come late at night while deep in sleep—too distant to grasp and hold, leaving the mind to flounder in an attempt to recall them . . .

Roland on his destrier, thrashing with his sword through the weeds and trees, roaring her name as she curled up in the bushes and remained silent.

Wearily, blackness again tapping at her consciousness, Hope curled her knees into her chest and closed her eyes.

Fog rises from the bloodied ground, taking the form of soldiers, their faces masks of death, twisted in pain.

A boy approaches, his eye sockets gaping and black but still weeping tears. He holds his hand out to Hope and his mouth opens in a terrible wail.

Daniel?

Behind him comes a knight—a ghostly vision on horseback, sword raised and glinting with an odd iridescence as bright as the sun. Like a falcon on a rabbit, he sweeps down on the boy, and with a solitary swipe of his sword, cuts off his head.

Her eyes flying open, Hope gasped and cried aloud. Oh God, she had forgotten the vision, the horrible vision.

Merciful God, she was too late!

Through the thick smoke that rose up from the bloody ground, the decimation of Roland's army materialized around Hope. Everywhere there were bodies of men and horses. Cries of pain assaulted her ears and the stench of dead flesh sickened her stomach. Around her, the familiar faces she had come to recognize through the last many days stared up at her with gaping, lifeless eyes, their frozen expressions reflecting their shock and anguish at dying so ill-prepared. Covering her mouth with her hand, Hope stumbled over the corpses, only vaguely aware of the cries of pain and fury resonating from the living.

"Daniel!" she cried, swiping at her burning eyes, which were fast becoming swollen from the fierce bite of the consuming, suffocating smoke.

She tripped and fell, landing hard on her stomach, so hard that the breath left her in a rush.

Little by little the death stare materialized before her—mouth frozen open in a silent scream of fear and pain. His eyes seem to stare accusingly into hers.

Oh, God, *Albert.*

Clawing her way to her feet, Hope turned round and round, her terror flooding through her in a mindless rush.

"Daniel," she chanted to herself, or perhaps it was only the voice in her mind, the scream that would not surface, but spun rapidly in her head like whirling water. "Roland? Roger? God, oh God, please . . . someone answer me!"

Where were the visions now?

Why would they not come?

Focus!

They would show her the fate of her brother and Roland— be they alive . . . or dead.

The horrible visions had tried to warn her, had shown her the terrible melee to be, yet she had allowed her own foolish anger and hurt pride over Roland's intentions to ransom her to Philip to get in the way of her helping his army.

This destruction was her crucifying rod to bear.

A movement behind her—she started to turn just as the flesh-abrading sack crashed down over her head, and the muffled voice whispered near her ear, "Don't fight, Hope. 'Twill do you no good."

Hope could not move, as her hands were tied. She could not see because of the blindfold strapped over her eyes. Gradually, as she worked hard to clear her foggy mind of its confusion, voices came to her, muted by the hum of ribald laughter and conversation outside the tent in which she lay huddled on the damp ground.

"I care little about so-called saints, or have you not paid close enough heed to the rumors running rampant about this country. I am a mercenary—a soldier for hire. I kill for the love of money, not principles or respect for religion. You can take your religion and your pious aspirations and fling them into the sea. Saint? Ha! Look at her. She's little more than a child. A scrawny one at that. Even if I were inclined to believe in miracles and visions and all that wag I would expect something a little more substantial than *that* pitiful, ragged-looking creature. Besides, aren't saints supposed to glow or some such rot? Get her up and have her work a miracle for me. Then I shall believe you."

"That scrawny child will make you the wealthiest lord in Philip's reign. I've seen her abilities with mine own eyes. She can heal with a touch of her hand. She can see the future as clearly as you see me this moment. She envisioned your attack."

A woman's voice.

But whose?

"If that be so, then why was Roland's army so ill-prepared for my invasion?"

"Like you, there are—were—many nonbelievers among Roland's army."

"Including Roland, apparently."

Laughter—coarse and cajoling.

"You may scoff, but need I remind you that the last time you and Roland met, you injured him with your lance? A wound . . . here. He might have been dead by now, but Hope of Châteauroux healed the injury."

"Sounds like a lot of hog swill to me. If she were so gifted, why would Roland even consider ransoming her to the king? Why would he not desire to keep her for himself?"

"I'll tell you why," sounded a far-too-familiar voice, causing Hope's heart to rise in her throat.

Roger?

"Roland has become soft. His desire to love women is greater than his hunger to fight. I fear he is too much like Henry, unwilling to concede that their time has come and gone. While neither has the appetite to confront the enemy, they are far too stubborn and concerned with their pride to voluntarily lay down their lances."

"Remove the girl's blindfold and unbind her hands. I'll see for myself if what you say is true."

"I would caution you," the woman said. "She wields a knife with great efficiency. She thrice attempted to murder Roland."

"Since when do saints wield knives and murder knights?" More laughter. "Besides, what have I to fear if she in truth favors Philip? Would she not be pleased to be returned to her king and countrymen?"

Hands grabbed Hope and sat her up. Her wrists were unbound and the cloth removed from her eyes.

She blinked and tried to focus on the image before her. Little by little the features became clear, revealing a countenance that was heavily scarred and sneering with cold amusement. But it was the faces beyond his that made her chest constrict.

Roger regarded her emotionlessly.

Rosamunde smiled with a smugness that turned Hope's blood cold.

Her voice dry with dread, Hope whispered, "My brother. Is he dead?"

"I don't know," Roger replied.

Turning her gaze to Rosamunde, Hope swallowed and shook her head. "It was you all along. You held Roland in your arms, listened to his secrets, pretended you could not speak, and then betrayed him. Why?"

"Greed," Roger answered for Rosamunde, who looked at him with a cold smile. "I fear the lust for gold far outweighs her lust for a virile body. As for me, I'm wise enough, unlike Roland, to realize and accept that Henry's reign is finished. Even now Henry meets with Philip to discuss his possible capitulation. I suspect Henry will be willing enough when learning both of his sons, Richard *and* John, have sided with Philip."

"Is Roland dead?"

Roger crossed his arms over his chest, and shrugged. "I know not, Hope."

Her voice trembling with emotion and disbelief, Hope said, "Nor do you care, Roger?"

The scarred stranger stepped forward. "I sense something less than relief that Hope finds herself in the company of her countrymen. Could it be that you're not so pleased with being rescued from your enemy's clutches?"

Frowning, Hope looked the soldier up and down. "Who are you?"

His eyebrows shot up and he threw back his head in a howl of laughter, then he offered her a bow and a thin smile. "Lacurne to the mademoiselle's rescue."

She gasped.

His grin widened. "It seems my reputation precedes me. Dare I hope that your gasp stems from admiration and not repulsion? Pray tell us, saintly one: be you lover of France . . . or *England*?"

Hope glanced toward Roger and Rosamunde. Her face felt icy and her throat constricted. She did not respond, but fixed Roger with a look that made him avert his eyes.

"How much?" she finally whispered. "How much am I worth to you, Roger? More than your country? More than the family you left in England? More than the love of your friend Roland, who would lay down his life to protect you?"

Lacurne turned to Roger and Rosamunde. "I'll speak to your saint alone."

As Roger and Rosamunde left the tent, Lacurne paced. He glanced at Hope occasionally, his small gray eyes assessing her up and down. Finally, he said, "You want to know if Roland is dead. Could it be that you've grown fond of my nemesis?"

Hope said nothing, but continued to regard Lacurne with a cautiousness that crept like cold fingers along her spine.

"Why do you look at me in such a way?" he demanded.

"I've heard terrible stories about Lacurne."

"Such as . . . ?"

"Of brutality and torture. Of the rape and destruction of innocent women and children. That you're known to cook and eat your enemy."

"There is little as satisfying as braised gut of Turk. I enjoy roasting their livers with rosemary and turnips. The English, on the other hand, are complimented best with cabbage and onions with a touch of mint. The mint, you see, kills the bitterness of the gall."

Hope shuddered as Lacurne smiled and slowly circled her, each step bringing him closer, until his body, clothed in hauberk and chausses, hovered so near she could smell the sourness of his sweat. "So you see, Hope de Châteauroux, I am not overly impressed by talk of saintliness and miracles. I am concerned only with what plum awaits me for dutifully fulfilling my role in this grievous war with Henry. I care little what Philip thinks of me, as long as he rewards me for my accomplishments."

He drew one finger down the side of her face, and she flinched and stepped away.

"Perhaps you cared more for Roland's touch, *oui*?"

"Roland did not torture. Nor did he harm women and children."

"Roland is soft, and grows softer with his age. No respectable knight considers Roland a threat any longer." Twisting one hand into her hair, he forced her head around so she had no choice but to look at him. "To answer your question: Roland was not found among the dead of his army. And do you know why? Because he was not with his army at the time of my attack. A shame and disappointment. I had every intention of returning to my camp with his head on my glaive. Have you any idea just how much his head is worth to Philip? No? Then I shall tell you: A chateau in Boulogne and a winery in Ponthieu. The estates would add immensely to my holdings."

"What a shame." Her lips curving, Hope fixed him with

a look and added, "It seems the great Lacurne must wait to reap the benefits of his plunder until another time."

"Perhaps," he said softly, yet curling his fingers more cruelly into her hair. "And perhaps not. If what Roger de Ferres tells me is truth, that Philip would regard your return with high favor, then *you* might do just as well to win me those holdings." His voice dropping, he mused more to himself than to Hope, "There is the little matter of de Ferres and that slut Rosamunde. They'll want a partial of my reward. That could muddle my chances of winning Philip's full appreciation. He might even be inclined to look more favorably on their endeavors."

He tapped his foot, his hands pulling so hard against her scalp that her eyes began to tear.

Shoving her aside, Lacurne stalked to the tent opening and shouted orders to his guard to fetch him Roger and Rosamunde. There were muted conversations and the sound of running feet and clattering armor. Hope looked frantically for any means of escape, her mind racing with the thought that Roland was yet alive. And if Roland be alive, then, perhaps, so was Daniel. Relief and hope sluiced through her with a weakness that made her knees shake.

Soldiers entered, dragging Roger and Rosamunde with them. Her red hair a tangle and her face flushed with anger, Rosamunde squirmed and spit obscenities that made Lacurne's men roar with laughter.

"What is the meaning of this?" Roger demanded, yanking his arm from his captor.

Smirking, Lacurne crossed his arms over his chest and raised one eyebrow. "I've given your proposition some thought. The idea that Philip would amply reward us for the girl's return inspires me. Still, we have a problem."

Roger frowned. "That being?"

Wagging a finger at Roger and Rosamunde, he said simply, "The two of you."

The color drained from Roger's face, and he glanced warily at Hope.

"You see, de Ferres, while such a reward be ample for the girl's return, be it divided three ways would be hardly worth my effort."

"Need I remind you, Lacurne, that I am personal friends with Richard, who stands by Philip against his father in this war?"

"Think you I care about Richard Lionheart? He's a traitor. He would stab Henry in the back if he thought it would win him more favor with Philip. Do you think such a man would overly worry about the death of one of Henry's not-so-esteemed knights?"

Flinging herself at Lacurne's feet, Rosamunde grabbed his legs and looked up at him tearfully. "Did our nights together mean nothing to you? Would you ignore the information I brought you through these last months?"

Grinning, Lacurne shook his head. "I think you enjoyed spreading your legs for Roland too much for me to take your mission seriously."

"But why kill us?" she cried.

He shrugged. "Why not? Do you think I would trust you when you so easily turned your back on Roland, not to mention your king? Would you not do the same to me if the reward be handsome enough?"

" 'Twas not for the reward that we treasoned. 'Twas for the love of Philip and France."

With a sharp laugh, Lacurne kicked Rosamunde aside. She spilled at Roger's feet. Roger regarded her emotionlessly before turning his gaze up to Hope's, and smiled sadly. " 'Tis nothing more than I deserve, I suppose. Should you see Roland again, which I suspect you will, I would appreciate your telling him that 'twas nothing personal. I only did what he had not the heart to do—give you up."

"He was your friend," Hope said softly. "He loved you."

Lacurne motioned to the guards, who grabbed Roger's arms and dragged Rosamunde to her feet. As they shoved Roger toward the door, he set his heels and looked back at Hope. His cheeks colorless and his eyes slightly glazed with fear and resignation, he did his best to smile. "If you care to work another miracle, perhaps you'll conjure up another one of your lightning bolts and save me from a less-than-divine fate."

"I would if I could," she told him kindly, her voice closing off with emotion.

"Tell Roland that the reward meant nothing to me. That I simply grew weary of the war."

"I shall tell him that you're sorry, and that if you were given another chance you would do it all differently."

Roger looked away, and squared his shoulders. He left the tent with the swagger of Roland's second-in-command. Rosamunde, however, fought tooth and nail as the soldiers dragged her out of the tent by her arms and hair. Only then did Hope focus her attention on Lacurne as he regarded her keenly, his mouth a slash of smugness in his grime-streaked face.

"So . . . you are a healer. A miracle worker. A seeress, and a saint."

"No." She shook her head. "I am not a saint. Nor can I work miracles."

"If that be so, then you will hardly be worth a ransom to me, will you?" With the snap of Lacurne's fingers, a servant appeared, a girl younger than Hope, with black hair and dark eyes as round as a doe's. "Clean her up," Lacurne ordered the girl. "Make her presentable. She'll join me for food and mead . . . at which time I'll decide just what her worth is to me."

With hot water steaming about her pink shoulders, Hope closed her eyes and did her best to enjoy the scrubbing of

her back with a cloth of coarse gunny. Still, what might have
been pleasurable felt little more than torture in light of the
emotions twisting inside her.

She was, at last, free of Roland, the Black Flame. Even
now he was no doubt collecting the bodies of his dead soldiers and burying them. He would grieve horribly, as he had
suffered before, blaming himself for their deaths, cursing foul
Fate that would strike down so many.

The girl with black hair and doe eyes was named Jeanne,
and she regarded Hope closely as she poured rose-scented
oil over Hope's bare back. "Why do you weep?" Jeanne
asked. "Are you not pleased to be back with your countrymen?"

"I grieve for those who died."

"Your tears won't bring them back." Jeanne ran her hand
lightly over Hope's spine. "I see the rumors I've heard about
Roland be true. He does not whip women like Lacurne
does."

Frowning, Hope partially turned and regarded the young
woman. "Lacurne beats you?"

Nudging down the material of her shirt, Jeanne exposed
the puckered pink whip scars on her shoulder, then she
smiled. "Tell me about Roland de Gallienne. Are the rumors
of his gentleness toward women and children true? Is it true
that he eats the same meager meals as his soldiers? That he
refuses to embellish his tent with the spoils of his enemies?
That he offers sanctuary to his foes who would yield their
fealty to Philip and lay down their arms to Henry?" Sinking
down beside the wood tub, Jeanne propped her elbow on the
edge and sighed. "I saw him once. He was carrying a child
on his shoulders. His hair was black and shiny as a raven's
wing, and he had a smile as brilliant as summer clouds. For
nigh on a score of nights I dreamt of him kissing me. Tell
me true, have you kissed him?"

Hope sank deeper into the tub, until the steam tickled her

nose and caused her scalp to tingle. She thought, how odd to discuss such things as kisses so openly. Did all young women converse so? Had she been so cloistered from reality the last years that she could not appreciate the simplest thrill over the possibility of sharing a secret with so eager a confidante as Jeanne?

Biting her lip and trying not to smile, Hope nodded.

Jeanne's eyes grew big. "Oh, lucky you. Tell me: what was it like? Were his lips soft? Was he gentle? Was his breath bad, or good?"

"His lips were hard, and soft. He was rough . . . and gentle. His breath smelled of . . . mint."

Jeanne sighed again and stared dreamily into the rising steam.

TWELVE

There were no visions. No single flash of knowing. No pain. Only the dull ache of not knowing the fate of her brother and Roland . . . and the even greater pain that gnawed at her each time she thought of never seeing them again.

How ironic that she should grieve for the possible passing of the very man she had attempted to kill.

But *was* Roland dead? And why should she care? His plans to ransom her to Philip had hardly been heroic.

Should she believe Lacurne when he told her that Roland had not been with his army at the time of the attack? Roger had become aware of her mounting feelings for Roland, and he was obviously capable of dupery; would he and Lacurne simply tell her what they thought she wanted to hear in hopes of winning her favor?

Lacurne's tent felt suffocatingly hot as Hope stood just inside the threshold and tried hard to focus on her surroundings. A thin, hump-shouldered man with twisted hands bent over a pile of red coals and poured onto them an ocher-colored liquid that spewed and spat in the heat before rising in a plume of acrid steam that blanketed the tent with a yellow haze.

At last, her eyes and nose burning, Hope located Lacurne where he rested on a bed on the far side of the tent. He lay totally naked amid plush fur bedding.

"Come here," he ordered her.

"Cover yourself," she replied sharply, "and I shall do so."

He made a grunting noise before grabbing a fur and tossing it across his loins. Only then did Hope join him, still remaining more than an arm's length from him. His eyes narrowed as he looked her up and down.

"So tell me, Hope de Châteauroux . . . what do your visions show you of my future?"

"I need no visions to determine that you're unwell, sir. The vile concoction your healer spills onto the embers stinks of lungwort, and you sweat as if you have recently taken in lemon balm."

He coughed up phlegm and spat it on the ground.

"Cursed rotting lungs are the least of my problems. It's this that plagues me most." Flinging the pelt aside, he exposed his grotesquely distended belly. "Foul gut keeps me afoot most of the time. My clothes barely fit and should I straddle my horse to fight it is done so with grievous pain. I hardly managed to kill me a dozen Englishmen last battle."

"Pity," she replied with an edge of acerbity, causing Lacurne to raise his eyebrows and sneer.

"I think you've grown too fond of your enemy."

"I found them as human as you or I. Perhaps more so."

"Human, perhaps, but infested with greed, as Roger de Ferres has proven. But then again, who among us is opposed to a touch of greed now and then?" Groaning and grabbing his belly, Lacurne clenched his jaw and held his breath until the pain passed. Only then did he lift his eyes to look directly into Hope's. "Tell me true. Did you heal the wound I gave to Roland?"

Hope remained silent, even as Lacurne grabbed his belly

again and twisted in pain. "Will you not help me?" he shouted. "Would you rather I call my man and have you skewered alongside Roger and Rosamunde?"

"You won't skewer me, sir. Not as long as you hold hope of winning favor with Philip."

"I care not what Philip thinks of me. Only what Philip's money will buy me. Not to mention that you'll make a tasty tidbit to lure Roland out of hiding. If Roger is correct about Roland's interest in you, I suspect we'll be hearing from the Black Flame before long."

"Philip's reward will do you no good if you're dead."

The healer, who had continued to pour diluted lungwort onto the embers, tossed down his foul potion and ran to Lacurne.

"Away with you," Lacurne shouted, and shoved the frail man away. "Idiot. If you attempt to bleed me once more I'll thrust your blasted knife through your scrawny neck and eat your gizzard with pottage and leeks."

The healer scrambled from the tent, leaving Hope to watch Lacurne writhe and mumble curses. Only when the pain passed enough so he lay limp and exhausted did she approach him and lay her hand on his belly, which was marked by open oozing wounds. Her touch sent a shock through him as sharp and unexpected as the agony biting at his insides. His body went rigid, his eyes round. He stared up at Hope as if he expected her to plunge a blade into his chest at any moment.

Stretched to its endurance, Lacurne's flesh felt tight and appeared nearly transparent, the swollen veins running like blue spider webs across his bloated bowel. It was then she discerned the movement beneath her fingers. The skin roiled as if alive and she snatched her hand away, only to have Lacurne grab her wrist with a cruelty that made her cry out and fall to her knees beside him.

His face in hers, he sneered, "Tell me, *saint,* if you cherish your life you will answer me truthfully: What foul soul has infested me? Can you, who are known to heal, rid me of this monster, or need I send for a priest to exorcise what squirms in my gut like some demon's seed?''

"No priest or saint can heal what eats you," she managed. "There is no demon there, only worms. Your gut crawls with them, Lacurne.''

A look of horror and repulsion swept his sweating features. Drawing her closer, so his rank breath, like rotting flesh, filled her senses and made her stomach turn, he hissed, "Worms? Do you mean . . . *worms*?''

"Maggots, perhaps. Ingested by eating foul meat.''

Wordlessly, his mouth opened and closed as his fingers dug deeper into her skin. Then he hissed through his rotting teeth, "Damned Turks. I thought the lot of bastards tasted a bit putrid.''

"Have the old man mix up a compound of wormwood and willow leaves. Taken with vinegar it should help kill and pass the creatures, but I must warn you: There is no promise that the injuries already done won't continue to fester.''

At last, he released her, fell back on his pelts, and closed his eyes. Hope backed away, shivering, doing her best to swallow back the disgust creeping up her throat.

Fleeing the tent, Hope paused long enough to gulp in the clean air, to allow her eyes to adjust to the sunlight spilling through the overhead tree branches. It was then that the vision swept upon her with the force of a battering ram, knocking her back and driving through her temples like a spike.

Thunder and lightning rip apart the black sky.

Through the rent in the clouds spills blinding light, and from the light comes the flame, incinerating the earth, turning the world into ashes.

Paralyzed by the sudden and unexpected pain, Hope held her head as the agony washed over and through her, then, as quickly, subsided—like a wave pulled by its turbulent current back out to sea.

An overwhelming sense of euphoria filled her next as she thought, *Roland is yet alive . . . and he's coming soon for me!*

Days passed and still Roland did not come for Hope as her visions had proclaimed. He did not burst from some blinding flash of light and fire to save her. He did not conquer his enemy to proclaim her as his prize. Nor did word arrive assuring her that he and Daniel were even alive. She wanted desperately to speak with Roger one last time—to assuage her fear that Daniel and Roland were dead, that the tale of Roland's being absent from the army during the attack was false.

Yet a final meeting with Roger was not to be. On the third day he and Rosamunde were executed by hanging. Their bodies were left to rot at the end of their ropes—with not a solitary prayer to mark their passing, other than that which Hope whispered to herself.

Lacurne made certain that Hope's every move was guarded by his soldiers. He made no secret to her, or his men, that he suspected she would bolt at the first opportunity and return to Roland. Lacurne vowed that he would have the man's head who allowed it. Hope of Châteauroux was a two-fold treasure. Not only would Lacurne reap a hefty reward for presenting her to Philip, but the extra bounty for capturing Roland would give him the means to purchase enough lands to make him as wealthy as Philip. Not only that, but Henry would gladly pay a high ransom to buy Roland's freedom.

The very idea of Hope's attempting to return to Roland would have, at one time, brought her much amusement. But not now. As the long hours plodded by and still no sign or word arrived of Roland's or Daniel's well-being, her spirits dimmed as did her faith. Had the visions not continued their barrage on her mind, she would have long since lost all hope of ever seeing either of them again.

Her only companion was Jeanne, who catered to Hope's every whim—who occupied her tedious days with light-hearted conversation that revolved mostly around Roland. The girl took Hope's mind off the fact that Roland had yet to appear and sweep her away from Lacurne, whose behavior grew more erratic every day.

Hope suspected that the worms that infected his gut were working on his brain as well. She had seen such infestation before, and the acknowledgment of Lacurne's illness grew more frightening every day. Judging by the way he stumbled around his army, carrying on rambling conversations with himself, showing irrational anger toward anyone he perceived as a threat, Hope suspected that he would soon lose all grip on reality and go totally mad.

A week of interminable days and nights passed. The nights were the worst, for it seemed Lacurne's madness magnified when the sun set. He prowled the camp like some predator, his eyes glazed and his teeth showing as he growled utterances that sounded more bestial than human.

Then the rumors started: that Lacurne's health had begun to deteriorate upon Hope's arrival in the camp. Perhaps Lacurne's madness was God's punishment for his treating Hope in such a manner. If God would punish Lacurne in such a horrible fashion, what rod would He raise against Lacurne's army?

Or, perhaps, Hope had the power to cast the grievous disease on Lacurne. If so, be her magic good . . . or evil?

On the evening of her seventh night in Lacurne's camp, Hope lay on her fur bed and drifted to an uneasy sleep, only to be roused suddenly and repeatedly by dreams that left her heart racing with fear and an odd anticipation.

Again and again she saw Daniel dressed in hauberk and chausses, bloody sword in his hand . . . and Roland standing behind him, his black eyes blazing like burning coal. Stepping toward her and raising his hand, Daniel whispered, "Flee, good sister. Roland be your only hope for freedom."

She awakened with a start as someone shook her. Jeanne, her features showing despair, cried, "Lacurne is gravely ill. He demands to see you immediately. Quickly! Toss this robe over your shoulders; there's little time to spare."

Groggily, Hope followed Jeanne into the odd silent night. Lacurne's soldiers stood shoulder-to-shoulder, their gazes following her as she ran beside Jeanne to Lacurne's tent. Inside, Lacurne lay on his back, his putrid flesh sweating and stinking of foul decay. His healer stood at his side, a filthy knife poised over Lacurne's naked arm.

"Stop him," Lacurne wailed. "I've no more than a drop of blood left and the scrawny bastard intends to bleed it from me."

"I have healed as many men by bleeding as you have killed on the battlefield. 'Twas no more than a year past that I healed a man of leprosy, and do you know how, my lord? By bleeding him behind the ear. That's how, so there."

"You've bled my ear! You've bled my toe! You've bled each and every one of my fingers! You'll soon be bleeding my damned *balls* if I let you! And what good has it done me? There is squirming in my brain, I tell you! I can hear it in my ears! Get out. Get out, I say! Bring me that frail wisp of a saint. I'll see that she heals me of this infestation or I'll send her the way of Roger de Ferres!"

"Do my ears hear correctly?" the healer hissed, shaking his fist in Lacurne's bloated face. "Do you reject my skills, my lord?"

"I reject your skills, you bumbling idiot. I reject your name. I reject your filthy, scum-sucking little body."

His eyes wide and bulging, the healer backed toward the tent door, brushing Hope and Jeanne in the process. "You feebleminded and foolish jackass. Reject me and you'll not see another sunrise, I vow. Your ugly head will explode like an overripe melon and your carotids will spew like geysers.''

Lacurne bared his teeth and howled. He labored to rise, to no avail, falling back on his bed and coughing up enough phlegm to make him choke.

''You'll be begging me to bleed you,'' the healer sneered. ''But I'll not do it. I'll rise to cheer each time the malady mounts to twist your stomach like a vise, and when the bilious vomit burns into your brain so your thoughts are little more than mush. And then the convulsions—ha! You'll flounder about like a headless hawk until all vital functions cease and plummet like a hailstone to death, at which time I send my condolences to Lucifer for having to tolerate your company for eternity.''

''Out! Out, I say. Get him out! Chop off his damned head and use my bollock to do it. I want to see him atop my pike before I die.''

Soldiers appeared at the tent door, stopping the escaping healer in his tracks. As they grabbed his arms, he turned his bony face toward Lacurne and hissed, ''Look to your own sins and desecration for the cause of your madness.''

''I'll eat your scrotum for breakfast,'' Lacurne sneered, then watched in concentrated spite as the physician was dragged from the tent.

Lacurne closed his eyes and took several labored breaths before slowly raising his head and focusing on Hope and Jeanne. ''Who is there?'' he demanded. ''Step forth and show yourself.''

Clutching the robe tightly about her shoulders, Hope moved cautiously toward him.

He blinked at her stupidly as drool ran from the corners of his mouth. ''Ah, the saint of Châteauroux, is it? Have you come here to cure me again, or perhaps you intend to suggest that I drink more wormwood and vinegar?''

''I take it the mixture did little to help you.''

"I shat out my brains for three days and look where it got me, worse now than then. Were you not French and supposedly holy I would believe you intentionally poisoned me. Then again . . . what proof do I own that you have these supposed healing powers from God Almighty? You might well be nothing more than some pretty little bait planted here by Roland to do me in." His eyes widened and his body began to tremble. "That's it! What a fool I've been. Of course. Why did I not see it before now? I should have realized that de Ferres would never turn on Roland. He sent you here to hex me!"

Jeanne grabbed Hope's arm and whispered urgently, "He's gone mad. Come away before—"

"What vile thing have you put in my brain?" Lacurne roared as he rolled from his cot.

"Come away," Jeanne cried, tugging hard on Hope's arm.

"I heard whispers of your witchery—how you cast your spell on Roland and made his brain soft as a swine's. Now you have infested me with vermin and intend to ravage my army. Guards!"

Hope turned as a pair of soldiers entered the tent.

"Burn her!" Lacurne shouted.

The soldiers swallowed. Their brows began to sweat and their hands to shake as Hope regarded them steadily, her chin set and her shoulders square—her look daring them to advance.

"Damned cowards," Lacurne sneered, then grabbed Hope from behind, his sweaty fingers closing around her neck like pincers as he shoved her out the tent door and into the crowd of snoopers, who fell back as if they expected her to strike them dead at any moment.

"Prepare to roast her," Lacurne declared, then shoved Hope to the ground. "The first man who refuses my order will burn along with her."

•   •   •

Hope sat alone in her tent, her wrists and ankles bound as she listened to the escalating commotion outside, and among it all Lacurne's incoherent ranting. Jeanne entered, her face white and her eyes glazed with emotion. She fell to her knees beside Hope and took Hope's face in her hands.

"Good Hope. Kind friend. Will you sit here and do nothing to save yourself?"

"Courage, Jeanne. If I'm to die in this manner, then so be it." She smiled. "Do you expect that I can conjure up some spell to make me vanish into thin air? Do you think that God will reach down from heaven and pluck me from this destiny, if, indeed, this is my destiny?"

"Are you not afraid?"

Hope shook her head. "Odd that there is no fear. Not yet."

Jeanne scrambled to the tent opening and looked out. Hope took a deep breath and slowly released it as she closed her eyes and wondered to herself over the strange calmness that cradled her with a warm serenity she had rarely known. It wrapped around her like some comforting hand, even as Roland's image materialized before her mind's eye, along with the same vision that had haunted her dreams for the last many nights—of Roland rising from flames and laying down his enemy with a blow of his battle-ax.

A cry from Jeanne brought her thoughts around. Two men entered the tent and approached her. Their hands trembled as they gently took her arms and lifted her to her feet. A young man no older than Albert looked at his comrade and said:

"We're doomed if we do this, I tell you. Lacurne is mad. What ever ails him has done so for longer than she has been here."

"He'll kill us if we don't."

"I don't much care for the thought of roasting a woman.

What if she is a saint? Mother Mary, our souls will burn for eternity."

Their faces gray as ash, they glanced at Hope. She returned their look with equanimity that, deep in the pit of her stomach, was gradually beginning to erode. Fear fluttered in her breast. Her knees became weak. Her senses expanded so acutely that the sounds of shouting men outside her tent crashed against her ears like thunder.

The soldier on her right lowered his mouth near her ear and whispered, "Save yourself. Work some magic on Lacurne and he'll spare you."

"No magic that I could perform would cure his madness," she said, "nor remove the vermin squirming in his brain."

The crowd outside fell silent as Hope stepped from the tent. Lacurne stood unsteadily among them, barely able to hold his head up as he lifted one finger and pointed directly at her.

"I condemn you to die by fire for treason and witchery, Hope de Châteauroux. May your soul burn in Hell for the wretched plague you have cast on me!"

THIRTEEN

From the end of the fraying rope, Roger's lifeless, bloated face stared down at Roland, as did Rosamunde's, hidden partially by her fall of dark red hair over her gaping eyes. How often had he peered into those eyes . . . and trusted? How many times had he held that body and experienced, for a moment, a flicker of intense fondness? And as for Roger . . . his friend. What price glory when the cost was the lives of so many?

His horse pranced nervously in place as Roland turned to watch Daniel slip silently from a copse of bushes and approach.

Bending at the waist and attempting to catch his breath, Daniel said, "Lacurne has just sentenced Hope to burn. Blast you, Roland. How long will you continue to hide here and do nothing for my sister?" Straightening, curling his hands into fists, he declared, "You continue to blame her for the decimation of your army when the truth is there." He pointed to Roger. "There is your traitor. Not Hope. It was he who sold you out."

Roland looked away.

Stepping closer, his mouth curling under, Daniel said, "Why don't you admit that you blame Hope for one reason only—because in a jealous rage you were out beating the bushes trying to find her when Lacurne swept on your camp. You're feeling guilty because you weren't there for your men. You want to take out that guilt on Hope. You want her to suffer as badly as you're suffering."

"Careful," Roland sneered.

"How can you still believe that she and Roger were some-how involved in all of this when the truth is there?" He motioned toward Rosamunde. "It was Rosamunde and Roger. Not Roger and Hope. *They* are—were—your ene-mies. Not my good sister who came to care for you too much. Who came to accept the fact that you were not the sort of man who would ravage our home and family. Who regretted having hurt you, or doubted your honor."

Roland turned his horse away, giving Daniel his back.

His fury rising, Daniel shouted, "Be you coward, Ro-land?"

Roland stopped, but did not turn.

"A knight worth his shield would strike Lacurne now."

Silence. Roland glanced to his watchful soldiers.

Daniel moved up beside Roland's horse. "These brave soldiers lost friend and family as well, Roland. For them alone you should seek retribution and finally end this fiend's havoc on Henry's armies. If you don't stop Lacurne now, he'll eventually destroy you." In a quieter voice, Daniel added, "Surely you have enough heart for one last fight. If not for me or your men, then for Henry your king."

Roland took a weary breath, looked again around the circle of tense soldiers, then in a flat voice announced, "Henry our king is dead."

There came gasps from the men. They stared at Roland as if he were mad.

"Word was brought me three nights ago. 'Tis true. Henry

is dead. This war is finished with Philip. Richard is king now and Richard is Philip's friend. There is no more reason to raise our swords against Lacurne. And no more reason to sacrifice the lives of my men for a cause that is . . . personal." Drawing back his shoulders, Roland looked from one face to another, acknowledging the expression of relief in their battle-weary eyes. "This campaign is ended," he shouted, then added in a tighter voice, "Go home to England and your wives and families. There will not be another widow made this day or any other because of me."

The men looked from one to the other, uncertain and unbalanced by the sudden turn of events. Many turned and disappeared into the forest. Others fell to their knees, genuflected, and began to pray.

Daniel slowly turned away, his face white. Roland noted the slump of the young man's shoulders, the trembling of his body. He reined his horse over to where Daniel leaned against a tree, covering his eyes with his hands.

"Daniel," he said.

Daniel sobbed.

" 'Tis a weakness to weep," Roland said. "Tears won't help your sister."

"Nor will you, apparently," Daniel sneered.

"Collect yourself and return to camp."

"I would rather burn in Hell."

"Do you think to storm Lacurne alone? Do you think that one child will succeed in overthrowing an army? Would you have Hope watch you struck down before her eyes?" His voice softened. "She would rather you live to someday confront such evil as Lacurne and save a thousand lives."

His hand going to his sword hilt, Roland withdrew the bloodstained weapon. His horse snorted and arched its neck, prancing in place as if anticipating Roland's next move. Daniel's eyes slowly turned up to Roland's, and his brows drew together.

Roland smiled. "Heed me well, Daniel. There is a vast difference between a fool and a hero. A fool cares little about the consequences of his actions on others."

Roland spurred his horse into the copse, his sword blade resting lightly on his thigh, the horse's soft footfalls on the rotting vegetation and the clink of Roland's mail the only sound in the forest's vast silence.

At last he came to the verge of the meadow and looked down on the army spread as far as he could see, their dew-damp tents and colorful banners sparkling in the morning sunlight. Lacurne's tent was easily recognizable as it glistened splendidly in the intensifying daylight. Its silk materials, in brilliant hues as varied as a peacock's tail, sparkled with gaudy frivolousness. On the top was a golden sphere surmounted by eagles.

Lacurne's men formed a circle around a frail form, her body tied to a post and surrounded by brush that was beginning to smolder—still too damp from the night's condensation to catch fire easily. How calmly and proudly she stood— as proud and dignified at death's threshold as any knight— her chin up, her eyes directed forward, her look one of supreme dauntlessness in the face of what would cause even the bravest knight to tremble in terror.

Turning his eyes toward Heaven, Roland prayed aloud, "Look up to Heaven and remember that God will send you legions of angels as He has done before. Fear not death, but, for the honor of Him who suffered for you, seek it. Should I survive I will sin no more. Nor will I lift up my sword to bring death upon another soul. But should the sword of my enemy strike me the fatal blow, let my foe inscribe upon my tomb, 'Ce fu li mieudres qui sor destrier sist.' Amen."

Roland spurred his horse forward. He prepared his sword.

The brush surrounding Hope sputtered fire. Flames danced from one bush to another, grew brighter and higher, gobbled up the kindling like a rousing, hungry serpent. Lacurne's army looked on in silence, their expressions fearful as Lacurne paced back and forth before the mounting heat. He beat the air with his fists. He ranted incoherently. Grabbing his head and holding it, his eyes rolling wildly, he screamed condemnation against Hope for poisoning his brain and body.

The smoke burning her eyes, the flames licking at her feet and singing her flesh, Hope looked out through the smoke and fire, focused on the distant green hills, and prayed aloud—or tried to. Fear mounted. Her faith eroded with each spark that drifted like a dust mote into the swirling air around her. How long could she continue to be brave? How long would she trust that God would save her from this torturous death by fire?

The hot air scorched her nostrils and the smoke crawled into her mouth with suffocating purposefulness. She gasped and choked. Her eyes swelled and teared until the red, wavering world became as foggy as her consciousness.

It was then that the image came to her. A vision, surely. The last she would have before succumbing to the burning death. The same vision that had nagged her the last days, filling her with false hope and promise.

Through the flames and smoke comes Roland astride his destrier, sword raised, his face resolute and his eyes blazing. He carries his shield before him—the Black Flame—yet he does not need it. The French soldiers part before him like the waters of the Red Sea. His horse canters virtually in place, neck bowed, nostrils flaring, hooves flashing as he awaits Roland's command.

Beyond Roland there is movement. The trees and stones and hills become a human mass moving like insects over the ground, swarming around Lacurne's unprepared army, their swords and lances with flying banners glittering in the sunlight.

A young man on horseback approaches, his fair hair flying in the wind.

Daniel?

Lacurne raises his fists and cries, "Kill him! Strike him now! Finish him, I command you!"

Yet no one moves. They turn their eyes away from their raving leader and back away.

Through the flames and smoke she sees Roland drive his horse toward Lacurne. He swings his gilded and jeweled sword. His army roars. Lacurne's men drop to their knees, and amid the rising flames she glimpses Roland, lifting his sword high in the air, and on it Lacurne's head, his eyes gaping, his mouth open in a soundless frozen scream.

Then there is light. Brilliant and blinding. Through the flames comes the horse. Its black, frothed flesh shimmers with fire, as does the shield of the Black Flame. She lifts her nearly blinded eyes up to his . . . and darkness descends.

Hope roused and groaned. The pain in her head and chest was crucifying. Her throat felt raw and scratchy. And her eyes—dear God, was she blind?

She touched her swollen lids and barely managed to open them enough to make out the fuzzy yet familiar surroundings of Roland's chamber. There was movement. Someone knelt at her side and took her hand, smoothed the frayed hair back from her forehead. "Kind and brave friend, you are alive and for that we thank God."

"Who's there?" Hope whispered.

"It is Jeanne."

Fear and confusion clutched her. "Lacurne—"

"Is dead, Hope. Roland killed him."

"But why are you—"

"It was my own idea to come. Your brother Daniel allowed it when I assured him I was your friend and would see you through this dreadful ordeal."

"Daniel?"

"Yes," Jeanne replied with the same dreaminess she had once used when speaking of Roland. "Your brother is quite brave. He rode into camp with nothing more than a bollock to protect himself."

Hope smiled. "I often question Daniel's common sense."

"He is as handsome as he is brave."

Hope tried to lift her head, but pain stabbed her. She gasped and clutched at the bedding beneath her. A moment passed before she could catch her breath. "Where is Roland?" she finally asked.

"With his men. They prepare to return to England."

Hope flinched as a spear of pain stabbed through her head, then the flash of sight as quick as the flicker of a firefly:

A crypt rising out of mist, and upon it is engraved:

ROLAND

"King Henry is dead," Jeanne told her. "Richard is king. The war is over for now."

"No. No, he mustn't return to England." Hope grabbed Jeanne and tried to sit up. "I've seen it again, the vision. If Roland returns to England he'll die."

"But England is his home—"

"I must see Roland. I must convince him—"

"Convince him of what?" came Roland's voice from the threshold.

Pushing Jeanne aside, Hope did her best to open her eyes and sit up. Roland stood inside the doorway, his thumbs hooked over his belt, his eyes hooded with suspicion. Despite the pain that stung her flesh like bees, Hope managed to smile. "Roland," she managed. "I had almost lost hope that you would come for me."

Roland glanced at Jeanne. She hurried from the room, closing the door behind her.

Hope studied his dark expression. "Why do you regard me so angrily?"

"Your brother has yet to fully convince me that you were in no way involved with Roger and the annihilation of three hundred of my men."

"Do you think me capable of such slaughter?"

"How do you explain that I found you together at the river and that you conveniently disappeared shortly before the attack?"

Hope struggled to sit up. The room spun as she staggered to her feet. Tears burning her eyes, she cried, "Dear God, you *do* believe me capable of such butchery!"

Roland crossed the room in three strides. He grabbed her arms and shook her. "Why else would you be meeting Roger on the sly, then disappear?"

"Because I learned exactly what you intended to do with me," she cried. "Because I had allowed myself to grow overly fond of a man who wanted nothing more from me than the fortune he would attain by ransoming me to Philip." She struggled. He held her more tightly, his fingers bruising her fair flesh and causing her to lose her breath. Throwing back her head, she glared up into his black eyes and did her best to control the anger making her tremble. "I was naïve enough to think you cared for me. Well, I won't allow you to blame me for the guilt eating away at your conscience, Sir Knight. Had you not been so concerned over losing the fortune you would have received by dumping me on Philip's lap, you would have been with your army when it was attacked."

He grabbed her throat with one hand, snapping back her head and cutting off her breath. She clutched at his fingers frantically as he lowered his face over hers. "Is that what you think, Hope? That I was thrashing through the forest like a madman in search of you because of some fortune you might bring me?" He laughed coldly. "Were it that simple

I might be able to sleep at night. Instead I'm racked by the thought that I allowed my actions to be manipulated by my feelings for you. I committed the most unforgivable mistake a leader of men can make. I put my own desires above the welfare of my army.''

He backed her toward the cot. ''I should have gotten rid of you long ago, the moment I realized that my hunger to confront Lacurne was minuscule compared to my hunger to spend time in your company. To lurk about shadows like some love-struck youth and watch you work your magic on my men. I wanted to kill Roger every time I saw you with him. Every time you smiled at him. Or touched him. Even now, when I remember seeing the two of you at the river I experience a madness that I never felt in battle—a hunger to murder that I've never known, even for my enemy. Had Lacurne not killed Roger for his greediness, then surely I would have.''

Releasing the grip on her throat, Roland smoothed his thumb over the swellings on her skin. He traced the line of her jaw, then lightly brushed her parched, red lips that fell open slightly at his touch. ''Sometimes I feel you inside me,'' he whispered, catching one of her hands and pressing it to his side where she had healed him.

''What are you, Hope? Are you real? Are you human? Are you simply some beautiful temptation sent by God to test me? Or protect me? Just how saintly are you, Hope of Châteauroux? How divine your feelings? Are you incapable of sin? Could a human being have stood tied to that sacrificial pole and so bravely faced burning to death?''

''I knew you would come,'' she whispered almost drowsily, mesmerized by his eyes and the crooning tone of his deep voice.

''More visions?'' His lips curled sardonically. ''Tell me, angel. What visions have you now?''

She shook her head. ''I have no visions while in your company, Roland. It is impossible for me to do so.'' She touched his cheek with her fingertips. "The lightness that your presence brings me is like a rebirth. The vast freedom I experience even now is like a soaring bird. I am . . . as weightless as a spirit. As unencumbered as wind. I feel truly human for the first time in my life—too human, I fear, with dreams and desires that are far too shameful to be saintly."

Hope leaned her body against Roland's, felt him tense, watched his eyes narrow and his lips part with some soundless word that made her shiver with heat.

"Roland, you can end my pain forever. You can take the visions from me, shatter the chains of their awful responsibilities. Free me, Roland. You're the only one who can." Rising to her toes, Hope pressed her lips to his. He groaned. His arms went around her and drew her up, even as his mouth parted over hers and his tongue slid inside her, danced along the inside of her lips like a soft, hot flame.

Hope stepped away, vaguely aware of her unsteadiness, of the discomfort of her blistered skin or the burning of her eyes. She drew her sleeping gown up over her head and dropped it to the floor. Naked, trembling, she smiled. "Will you have me, Roland?"

He could not find the words to speak. How could he? The perfection of her body robbed him of thought. Her breasts were ivory globes tipped by small rosy nipples that, even as he watched, grew hard and erect in anticipation of his touch. Her waist was tiny, easily spanned by his hands, and below, at the juncture of her shapely thighs, her nest of pale silken hair barely concealed her womanhood.

"Is something wrong?" she asked. "Do I not please you?"

Blinking, his gaze still locked on her womanly mound, Roland shook his head. "Hope, I . . ." He swallowed and tried to ignore the pressure growing between his legs and the almost overwhelming hunger to toss her to the bed and

mount her as if she were one of the wenches who normally
sated his lust.

"This isn't . . . right. What I mean is . . . you're not like
the others. A man of my rank is vowed to protect innocence,
and I . . . Jesu help me, you *are* beautiful. Far too fair to be
human. I have often thought of having you. Dreamt of it.
Shook with it. Even when I held others, 'twas your lips I
kissed. Your skin I smelled. Your body I imagined wrapped
around me."

"Do you *care* for me, Roland?"

He sighed and lightly laid his hand upon her breast.
"Yes," he murmured. "I fear I've gone mad caring for
you."

"Do you *love* me, Roland?"

His jaw flexed. His teeth clenched. His hand inched down
her little waist, hesitated at her navel, then dropped to the
downy nest that quivered at his touch.

"Do you *love* me, Roland?" she whispered more urgently.

His fingers parted the warm folds, dipped into the slick
crevice that responded to his touch with a drop of hot moisture that trickled over his skin.

With a soft curse he caught her shoulders and lowered her
to the bed, pressed her into the fur pelts that caressed her
pale body as he clawed at the ties on his stockings and
breeches, kicking them aside as they slid down his legs. Then
he snatched the wool shirt off over his head and tossed it to
the floor.

With her hair spread like rays of moonlight over the dark
pelts, Hope regarded Roland's naked body with a breath-
lessness that made her heart hesitate: the muscles of his chest
that flexed with the most minute movement, the dark hair
that formed an arrow down his flat belly to the aroused member that thrust from between his legs like a lance.

Roland eased onto the bed and between her legs. He gently
kissed her tender eyelids. He teased her sweet nipples with

his tongue. He breathed a path along her belly to her mound, lightly sank his teeth into the sensitive flesh and filled up his senses with her feminine scent.

Hope groaned. She twisted. She arched her back and opened her legs in shameless invitation, and still he did not take her, but continued to titillate with his fingers, his lips, his tongue, turning her skin into raw nerves that was as painful as it was glorious. And just as it seemed she could stand no more, he rose up on his knees, turned his dark eyes up to hers and whispered, "Forgive me, Hope. The pain will be but brief and then done forever."

He thrust.

Her mouth flew open in a silent cry. She grabbed his arms, sank her nails into his skin as he pressed into her again, and again, insistent, his skin shimmering with sweat, muscles taut with the suppressed hunger to bury himself completely and sate the maddening need.

At last, at last. He felt the barrier give. He sank deep, dizzied by the heat and tightness of her body around his. Dropping onto her, burying his face in her fragrant hair, he groaned like a man dying.

Hope closed her arms around his shoulders and curled her fingers into his hair. The pain had passed. Only the sensation of his body stretching hers remained, along with the yet-unsettled sensation that his slightest movement roused inside her. It mounted as he moved his hips, forward and back, rocking her gently, then not so gently, until she thrashed helplessly for some culmination that she did not understand, but hungered for, nevertheless.

It came upon her like a rush of wind, lifting, spiraling, robbing her of control and consciousness and toppling her over an edge that was as brilliant as Heaven itself. Then the words came, scattered like leaves in a gale, as impossible to grasp and hold as sunlight.

"I love you, Hope. God help us both. I love you."

FOURTEEN

Naked, sated, wrapped within her cocoon of soft fur, Hope awoke, reborn.

The unbearable lightness of her soul brought tears to her eyes. The gladness filled her up. The power and the visions that had once tottered on the ledge of her consciousness—hour upon hour, day upon day, tapping and taunting at her reality—were little more than a memory, extinguished by the hotter and more brilliant flame of love.

Rolling from bed, the pelt draped from her shoulders like a robe, Hope spun around on her tiptoes and laughed aloud. The act startled her, the sound of her own laughter strange in the cavernous, mostly hollow chamber that she had shared the last weeks with her enemy.

No, not enemy. Not any longer.

Lover. Savior. Future.

From this day forward she would live a normal life. Experience normal fear, and pain. She would look into her neighbors' eyes and see them for what they are, not what they would become. There would be no more excruciating headaches. No more terrifying premonitions.

Squeezing her eyes closed, she tried desperately to conjure even the remotest spark of cognition.

Nothing.

She ran to Roland's war chest, flung it open and dug out the tripod, hastily erected it and struck the flame. For long minutes she stared into the oily smoke, searched the dim, flickering flare and saw . . . nothing. No horrifying revelations of war, of plagues, of holocausts.

The door opened, and Daniel stepped in.

Hope jumped up. "Daniel! Daniel, 'tis true! The sight is lifted. 'Tis gone! I'm free of the visions at long last."

Daniel's eyes flew wide, and Hope realized she was yet naked. With a girlish "Oops," she grabbed up her gown and dragged it over her head. Then she flew as if on wings across the room to hug her befuddled brother.

"You were right, Daniel. I feel . . . young. I feel . . . alive. I want to sing out to the entire world that I'm free at long last to be human again."

Daniel stepped back, and his eyes narrowed. "Have you fever, Hope? Should I fetch you some lemon balm? Or mayhap the barber should bleed you?"

She danced again on her toes and twirled. "I'm in love, Daniel. You were right. Love has unbound me. If I had wings I would fly out yon window and soar above the clouds. I feel as if I'm soaring now." She leapt across the floor like a fairy, her gown fluttering around her knees like butterfly wings.

"I think I should get Jeanne," he said flatly, backing toward the door.

"I feel dizzy." She giggled. "I feel . . . delirious." She danced in place.

"Right," Daniel murmured. "I'll fetch Jeanne."

Hope ran to the window and crawled upon the wide embrasure. On her hands and knees, her hair whipped by the morning wind, she searched the grounds below and the army that was making haste to prepare to break camp. She searched for Roland among his men, closed her eyes and focused on the sounds, thinking the breeze might lift his voice to her. Yet she could hear little beyond the twittering birds in the nearby trees and the hum of voices that sounded more insect than human from this distance.

Dreamily, she turned back to the room, and gasped.

Matilda stared at Hope with yellow, malicious eyes that glittered with a kind of mirth, sending shivers crawling up Hope's spine. "Well, well," the hag wheezed. "Seems there's no ridding ourselves of misfortune." She glanced toward the bed. Shoulders stooped, fingers crooked, Matilda waddled to the pelts where Hope and Roland had made love throughout the night. She swiped one finger along the fur, then lifted it high to show a tinge of blood.

"A virgin's blood, is it?" She cackled and cocked her head. "Has the saintly one sacrificed her heart, not to mention her magic, for the love of the Black Flame? What did he promise you, my dear? Fortune? Undying devotion?"

"Stand away," Hope declared, backing toward the door. "Roland vowed his love to me. I expect nothing more."

She cackled again and waggled her finger in the air. "Surely there is something. Such an offering as your virginity and magic will warrant the gift of some juicy plum. What is it, Hope of Châteauroux? An estate in England? Gems? Furs? What will it take to keep you happy through the years?"

Lifting her chin and righting her shoulders, she replied, "Nothing more than his name, witch."

Her eyebrows lifted. "His name? Did you say . . . his name?"

Hope frowned.

"Did he actually promise you with banns?"

"He vowed he loved me—"

"Since when has our Church permitted multiple wives?"

Hope slowly blinked and did her best to breathe, even as Matilda sidled close—so close that Hope could smell the rank mustiness of her wrinkled skin. In a voice barely above a whisper, the hag said:

"He is plighted to another. Has been for years. The contract was signed and sealed by Henry himself."

"Liar," Hope managed, even as her earlier dizziness began to swirl in her head like a whirlpool. She tried to move. She could not. It was as if her body had suddenly petrified, and although her mind raced with the memory of his love-making and love words in an attempt to grasp any tiny detail that would assure her that Matilda lied, there was nothing. No assurances. No promises of tomorrow, or forever.

"Hildegard is her name, daughter of Arnold of Cheswyck, Roland's father's greatest nemesis. For years Arnold and Godfrey have warred for territory and power. It wasn't until the promised union between Roland and Hildegard that the fighting ceased and the land once again knew peace. It was Henry's wish that they marry, to end the turmoil, and so they shall as soon as Roland returns to Wytham."

Shuffling closer still, Matilda smiled. "I see by your countenance that you doubt me. Do you wonder about the fine cloth and rare jewels that Roland has collected along his journeys? 'Twas gifts to his affianced. For their wedding night."

Hope turned away, a wave of nausea rolling over her, exaggerating the spinning in her head. "I will ask Roland myself," she declared with a surprisingly steady voice. When she looked around again, the hag was gone.

There was great jubilation among the soldiers as they prepared for the journey home. Having slept little the last many days, his head swimming with too much ale and far too little food, Roland sat atop a hill and watched his army until the sun topped the trees and the air became warm on his face.

His inebriated thoughts continued to stray back to Henry— his friend. The king had died virtually alone, learning at the end that both of his sons, Richard and John, had turned against him. Even now Richard was sailing for England, to declare himself king to his father's people. Parents would wait in anticipation for the return of their sons from war. Many—most—would wait forever. Roland himself would break the news to Gywneth that Roger was dead, but how would he explain to her that her husband and the father of her children had died a traitor's death? Such shame would scar their sons and daughters for generations.

   In truth, he cared little for witnessing the pain and resig- nation in the faces of far too many mothers and wives. Jesu, he dreaded returning to Wytham—for more reasons than he cared to confront at the moment. Still . . . he could only put off the inevitable for so long. He could drink stale ale and souring mead until he was oblivious, but such idiocy was not going to change the fact that he would be forced to return to England and confront his dreaded obligations where his father was concerned. Holy Mother, he would rather en- counter a thousand worm-infested Lacurnes than be faced with the lunacy in Godfrey's eyes—not to mention Arnold of Cheswyck's ugly daughter. The very thought of the dreaded ordeal pricked his irritation, made all the more raw by his drunken mood.

   He shuddered, quaffed the remainder of his ale, then tossed the cup to the ground.

   With the memory of Hope's body clinging to his, the scent of her skin and hair still burning his nostrils from the night before, Roland clumsily climbed to his feet and returned to the castle, barely managing the crumbling, winding old stairs to the second floor, where he was forced to lean against the wall momentarily for support. He took a deep breath, did his best to focus on his chamber door, and walked.

   The door was jammed.

He rammed it with his shoulder. It hardly budged.

With a growling curse, he kicked it, sending it winging back with a crash, then stumbled into the room.

Hope stood near his war chest, his collection of silks, linens, and precious velvets scattered around her feet. She had wrapped a length of emerald-green silk around her so it clutched her form like a second skin. Her shoulders and arms were bare but for the soft blond hair flowing down her back and sides. Her eyes were large and glassy. But for two bright spots of hot color on her cheeks, her face was chalk white.

"Mademoiselle," he slurred with a wicked smile, and bowed at the waist. "I trust you missed me."

Her chin went up, as did one eyebrow.

"The color suits you," he said. "As does the silk. You should wear nothing else, I think."

"Do you always so compliment your mistresses, sir?"

"Only if they are deserving of such compliments, lady."

Gracefully, almost regally, Hope moved toward him, the silk rustling around her ankles. Stopping a hand's space from him, she squared her shoulders. "I was under the impression that these silks and velvets were for your affianced . . . sir. A wedding gift? Her name is Hildegard, is it not? Daughter of your father's most feared rival, Arnold of Cheswyck."

Roland set his jaw, and his face flushed with heat. *Matilda.* Damn the hag to burning perdition. He would strangle her yet.

"When, exactly, did you propose to tell me that I was to be nothing more than a replacement in your bed for Rosamunde?" Hope asked in a deadly calm voice.

"When I thought the time appropriate," he replied as calmly.

"I suppose worming such news in between whispering love words and robbing me of my virginity would have proved inconvenient . . . sir."

"I robbed you of your virginity? I beg to differ . . . lady. As I recall, you begged me to take you—"

Hope slapped his cheek.

His head snapped back, and he clenched his teeth. " 'Tis a knight's duty to oblige—"

She slapped him again.

He caught her wrist. "If you hit me again I'm liable to get mad."

Her eyes clouded with tears and her chin began to quiver. "You said you loved me, Roland."

"I do."

"But with love comes commitment."

"I have committed my heart and soul to you, Hope. At this time they are all I can give."

"Heart and soul are not enough. I demand your name. I demand your children."

"And you shall have my children."

"Not without your name," she hissed, then yanked her arm away.

The ale rolling in his belly, Roland took an unsteady breath.

Hope turned away. She walked to the window and looked down on Roland's army. The shaft of soft morning sunlight through the opening turned her skin butter-yellow and reflected off the tear streaks on her cheeks. "I have always imagined falling in love. How the giving of my heart and soul would free me to feel human at long last. I simply never imagined love would hurt so very much. 'Tis far more painful than the visions. I cannot think why people crave it so."

"She means nothing to me," he confessed softly.

"How very sad for you." Hope swallowed and swiped the tears from her eyes. "Wedding someone you don't love must be heartbreaking."

"Not as heartbreaking as not being able to wed the one you love."

She looked at him with big blue eyes full of sadness and a tinge of her earlier anger.

"The joining was agreed upon years ago, Hope. It was the only way to end the war between her family and mine. Henry asked it of me."

"And you would sacrifice anything for Henry because he was like a father to you." She looked away and added more angrily, "Henry is dead. Do you intend to fulfill your obligations to a dead man?"

"There are contracts—"

"Are you afraid of your father?" she blurted.

Roland's face turned dark; his hands became fists.

Hope approached him again, her fair flesh colored by her mounting fury. "Well? Speak to me, brave knight—he who slaughters on a whim. Who carries men's heads about on the tip of his sword as war medals. Whose name makes men, women, and children tremble with awe and fear. Are you afraid of your father? Or are you simply so desirous of his affections that you would sacrifice your life and happiness in hope that such a union will win his appreciation and love at long last?"

"Careful," he whispered in so ominous a tone that Hope took a step back.

More cautiously, she said, "You wasted years fighting for Henry, and for what? Will you waste the rest of your life attempting to win what is not there to give?"

" 'Tis my decision to make," he snapped.

"And you've already made it . . . haven't you? You'll return to England and marry this woman . . . Then I wish you much happiness, sir. I pray that the children she gives you grow strong and as damnably faithful to their father and king as you have been. I wish only one thing for them: that they grow to be happy men, unlike their father."

Turning on her heels, giving Roland her back, Hope started for the door.

"Where the blazes do you think you're going?" he shouted.

"I'm leaving. You've humiliated me enough. I shan't tolerate it again."

"I think not," he growled.

He caught up to her in three strides, grabbed the tail of material she had tucked into the back of her makeshift silk gown, and yanked it—hard. She spun like a top, unraveling the cloth as she spilled to the floor.

Naked, arms and legs splayed, her hair tangled around her breasts and hips, she glared up at him through tear-spiked lashes. "I'll not allow you to turn me into a harlot like you did Rosamunde," she wept. "No wonder she turned to Lacurne. You used her as if she were some tavern whore. I should have killed you after all. I will if I get the chance!"

His lips curled. "I think not, milady. Not unless you wish for my men to finish what Lacurne started."

"Stand away. Don't touch me or I—"

He grabbed a handful of her hair and twisted his fingers into it.

She cried out and raked at his hand with her nails and kicked at his shins.

He dragged her by the hair to the dark corner where once he had imprisoned her in chains. They remained still, the serpentlike coils of heavy links clinking and clanking as Roland pinned Hope's feet to the floor and clamped the cuffs around her ankles. She swung at his jaw with her fist— missed—he knocked her arm away as if it were nothing more than a pesky insect—then he straddled her, one big, dark hand planted between her breasts, holding her against the floor, the other drawing the bollock from the scabbard on his belt. The knife blade glinted in the streak of light spilling through the window as he lightly pressed the keen point to her throat and showed his teeth in something short of a smile.

"I'm not a man accustomed to taking orders," he

breathed. "Nor am I accustomed to tolerating threats, especially from someone who has thrice attempted to murder me—in my sleep, no less. The truth is, love, I fancy your company, not to mention your body. Fiend that I am, I would be foolish to let you go now, when I've only begun to sample the ripe, juicy little plum between your legs. It's most intoxicating. Tastier than ale and warmer than mead."

Her eyes grew wide; her breathing quickened.

Roland lowered his knife to the tip of her erect nipple, cautiously slid the point around the aureole until it puckered like little pebbles and flushed red as wine. "You'll come with me to England," he whispered, lowering his lips to the feminine peak, taking it gently, then not so gently between his teeth, tugging, stroking it with his tongue.

"I won't." She shook her head and bowed her back, caught off-guard by the sluice of heat that streaked from her breast to the cleft between her legs.

Roland laughed—a wicked sound that rumbled like thunder in his chest. Then he straddled her as he plucked at the strings on his leggings, allowing the enormous swelling within the fine linen to spring free.

Hope tried to kick. Impossible, thanks to the irons around her ankles, pinning her to the floor. She struck at his chest with her fists. He caught her wrists and stretched her arms out to her sides. Her breathing became rapid and uneven. Her skin became moist, her eyes liquid and feverish as mercury.

"I shall loathe you forever if you do this," she murmured breathlessly.

"If I do what, love?" He slid his body inside hers, eased in and out, in and out until her eyes rolled and a whimper fled her lips.

"Take me against my will," she finally managed, even as she lifted her hips to his thrust that became more demanding and powerful in response.

"Is that what I'm doing, Hope?" Sliding his knees under her thighs, he lifted her lower body, wrapped her knees around his waist and rocked her until her hunger for sublimity eclipsed even her immense fury over his brutish arrogance—and the fact that she had fallen in love with a man who was destined to leave her for another.

The climax rushed through her with blinding finality, the control shattered. Her mouth open in a soundless scream, she curled her fingers into his chest and dug deep, until the trenches in his skin filled with blood that trickled like tears down his ribs. Spent, strengthless, she fell back and stared up into the dark, shockingly handsome and forbidding face of her enemy lover and said softly:

"I hate you. Now kiss me like you mean it . . . and never touch me again."

FIFTEEN

England, Wytham Castle

Royce Goodman had hair black as coal, the shoulders of a bull, and fists the size of ham hocks—all the good to shape hot iron into horseshoes or pound out the deadly keen blades of weapons that his liege lord, Godfrey de Gallienne, used to protect Wytham Castle from the growing number of enemies who would like nothing more than to murder the Lunatic in his sleep. Royce's voice rumbled like thunder when he spoke, yet his tone was as gentle as a priest's. He towered a foot taller than his wife Mary, who, after thirty years of marriage, still regarded her husband with something just short of worship. With eyes as dark as onyx she sat near the fire in their small two-room house, and studied Roland with a concern and fondness that had offered him consolation through his years of tolerating his father Godfrey's cruelty.

Roland walked through night's shadows to the bedroom door and peered into the dimly lit quarter. Asleep, exhausted from the grueling journey to Wytham the last weeks, Hope lay on the bed, snuggled beneath woolen blankets. Her cheeks appeared sunken, the dark circles around her eyes exaggerated by the shadows in the room. She seemed a mere relic of the woman she had been those final days in France.

"Never let her out of your sight, Mary," he said. "I'm not certain what I would do if I lost her."

"You're much in love with this woman," Mary replied softly.

"Yes." He nodded.

"And she loves you?"

"She did." Turning back to his godparents, Roland shook his head. "No longer, I think."

"Chaining her as if she were an animal won't help, sir," Royce declared with a hint of irritation. "I'm surprised at you, Roland. You have never been a man to show cruelty to a woman."

"Neither have I ever had a woman who so chafed me. Who takes such pleasure in driving me beyond my capabilities to tolerate her behavior. I swear to you, she lives to thwart my every attempt to make amends for this situation."

"Which is?" Mary asked.

Roland paced.

Royce and Mary exchanged looks.

Leaving her stool by the fire, Mary tiptoed to the bedroom door and peeked inside, regarded Hope a long moment without speaking, then turned back to Roland. "Is she with child, Roland?"

Roland lowered his eyes. "I cannot discount the possibility."

Royce made a sound and pressed his lips together. "There is much that has changed about you since you left here those years ago. Among other things, did I not teach you the worth of a woman's chastity?"

"You did, and until Hope I never forgot the lessons. But from the moment I first saw her, I could think of nothing else but having her. It's all I think about now."

"I take it she doesn't feel the same," Mary said, "considering you keep her chained like some wayward goat."

"And I'll continue to chain her as long as she threatens to leave me." Roland kicked a table leg, causing Royce to raise his eyebrows. "There must be some way out of this damnable situation with Hildegard. I would rather marry a goat than spend one minute between that drab's thighs." He glanced apologetically toward Mary, who rewarded him with a stern look.

Royce crossed his arms over his chest and set his jaw. "You could go to King Richard—"

"I would go to Hell before I would ask favor of Richard for anything."

"You were like brothers growing up."

"He broke Henry's heart. He sided with Philip against England's armies. Now you expect me to go to my knee for such a traitor and ask him to release me from my bond with Hildegard?"

"You were always too proud for your own good," Mary pointed out. "And far too stubborn, I might add."

Roland walked to the open window and gazed out on the village spread out within the castle's walls. There were howls of drunken laughter. A woman screamed. "This village is wasted," Roland said. "Wytham is dying."

"It will die," Royce replied. "Unless you stop it."

"How do you propose that I do that? My father despises me. What makes you think he'll allow me to end this nightmare?"

"He'll die some day," Mary said bitterly. "And the sooner the better."

Royce glared at his wife. "Enough, woman! You forget yourself. You forget to whom you are speaking."

"Nay, I do not forget!" Her anger mounting, her cheeks flushing with hot color, Mary focused on Roland and squared her shoulders in belligerence. "I have watched Godfrey's mind go to rot and ruin, and with it his respect for Roland. He's treated the lad like—''

''Hush!'' Royce leapt to his feet.

Lowering her voice, she said, '' 'Tis Roland's right as Godfrey's eldest son to inherit his father's lands and wealth upon his father's death. I say someone should kill Godfrey. Before he destroys this land and these people completely. But mostly before he destroys Roland's future.''

Roland stared at Mary in disbelief, and his voice trembled in anger. ''Are you suggesting that I kill my father?''

Royce stepped between them. ''She speaks from her heart and not her head, Roland. We've known Wytham once to be one of the most vast and powerful of all Henry's strongholds. We've known Godfrey to be feared and respected, and as honorable a friend and knight to king and serf as any in this or any other country. We've seen, too, the crumbling of his empire, not to mention his mind. We've watched him turn to your brother Harold the last years, allowing him more and more control of this land and these people. We've seen Harold maliciously destroy what would ultimately become yours. He taxes us heavily, and grows fat off the villagers' sweat and blood. When he's drained our coffers completely, he takes our crops and livestock—for the love of God, we have children in Wytham who are starving. Our wives and daughters live in fear of the unspeakable crimes his men perpetrate against them.''

Royce's eyes clouded and his broad shoulders sank. ''Those who pledge themselves to Harold, who are willing to turn on their neighbors, are rewarded; they're taxed little and their crops are untouched. Those who refuse to cow to his thievery ultimately give up and leave Wytham. Were I not faithful to Godfrey, I would have murdered Harold myself.'' Turning again to his wife, Royce touched her face gently, and smiled. ''As your godparents, Roland, we took oath to protect you and raise you as we would our own son.

Surely, we cannot be faulted now for worrying overmuch about your welfare, and future. As Godfrey's . . . firstborn son, it is your right of primogeniture to inherit all that belongs to your father upon his death, but I fear Harold is determined that you'll gather little more than ruin when Godfrey passes.''

"Harold won't be pleased that you've returned," Mary said, her brow creasing with worry. "He's ruled us at will, with Godfrey's blessing. Wickedness and cruelty are a way of life in Wytham. The few of us who stubbornly remain, refusing to give up our homes, live in fear that Harold will find cause to turn on us as he has the neighboring lords. 'Tis only our deep-rooted bond with Godfrey that keeps us safe, for the time being. If Harold still controls Wytham when Godfrey passes . . .''

Turning away, Mary walked to the small hearth where low flames licked up at a bubbling cauldron of pottage hanging from a ratchet. Her body shook, and her eyes filled with tears.

Roland walked to her, gently took her in his arms, and held her close, saying nothing. The memories poured back to him, all the years she had held him in her arms, supporting him, banishing his fear and heartbreak over Godfrey's bewildering behavior. He had wept countless tears on her breast, and she had vowed to him that she would never let Godfrey, or any man, harm him. That she would lay down her life to protect him.

"Hush," he whispered as she cried as quietly as possible. "I'm home now, Mary. You needn't fear Harold or Godfrey any longer."

She cried harder, her sobs causing her frail body to draw in on itself. Her fingers twisted into his shirt and she shook her head. "God forgive me. Forgive us for doing this to you. Had I known. Had I only known."

Royce dragged her away, wrapped his big arms around

her, and cradled her face into his shoulder. "Hush, Mary. Sweet Mary. What's done is done. Please . . . stop this before all is destroyed."

Furious, she backed away. "What good is there in continuing, husband? The dream is gone. There is no kingdom here worth inheriting. Look yonder. The fields are waste. The people are destitute and hungry. Day after day they live in fear, not of starving to death, but of dying of some felony committed by Harold's cohorts. Rape and murder are as common in Wytham as the sun rising on yon east horizon."

Royce looked at Roland. "Your godmother is hysterical. The last years have taken a toll on us all. Now that you've returned, Roland, I know in my heart that this siege of unhappiness will end. You, and only you, can bring Wytham back to its former worth."

Roland dragged one hand through his black hair, then walked again to the bedroom door, leaned against the wall and gazed for a long while into the dim room where Hope continued to sleep. "Cursed fate," he whispered.

Standing half a head shorter than Roland, and with a body that had grown grotesquely bloated the last years of Roland's absence, Harold sprawled in his father's ornate chair, his greasy blond hair hanging over his right eye as he looked Roland up and down. "He returns in all his glory. The Black Flame. Brave knight and savior of lost kingdoms. I once heard you were skewered by Lacurne's longbow."

"Obviously you heard wrong," Roland replied.

"Obviously." Harold feigned a yawn as his blue eyes continued to study Roland closely. "You look none the worse for wear for having spent the last years of your life warring for lost causes."

"I'm older and wiser. And not nearly so patient."

"Your return to Wytham has caused quite a stir. The village simpletons are a-titter about how you intend to step into my boots and save them from their dreadful, dreary existences.''

Roland's eyes narrowed and he gave Harold a flat smile. ''The village simpletons could be right.''

Harold drummed the chair arm with his fingers. His jaw worked.

Roland glanced around the great hall. The straw strewn over the floor smelled of rot and urine. The priceless tapestries that had once decorated the stone walls so splendidly were tattered and stained by food and wine. A half-dozen mongrels congregated in a corner, all gnawing on bones they had been tossed after dinner.

At last, Harold left the chair and stepped from the dais to stand before Roland. ''Father won't be happy that you've returned. I think he was hoping you would honor him by dying in battle.''

''When have I ever lived up to Father's expectations?''

''You continue to exist simply to spite him. Father's words, not mine.''

Roland took a deep breath and slowly released it, allowing the flicker of emotion Harold's jabs had roused to dissipate before it could take root and cloud his reason. ''Where is our father?'' he finally asked.

''In his chamber, as always. He rarely ventures out, other than to occasionally visit Mother's grave. He's totally insane, you know. Incompetent. Incoherent. An idiot. He babbles to ghosts. He spends hours a day on his knees praying for God to forgive him for some mysterious crime he confesses he committed long ago. The priest is little help, as Father refuses to see him. He rants of excommunication and burning in Hell for his sins. He hasn't stepped foot in the chapel in years. Someone would do him a favor by killing him, I think.''

''And how have you occupied your years, Harold? Aside from plundering and raping Wytham and her neighbors?''

Harold laughed. ''Ah, me hears whispers of Royce and

Mary Goodman, I think. One day I'll grow weary of their wagging, traitorous tongues and hang them from the gibbet for maggots to breed in their rotting corpses.''

"Over my dead body.''

"That, dear brother, can be easily arranged.'' Harold smiled again. "In case you haven't noticed, a new age has dawned in Wytham. The time of compliance and tolerance is gone. Men in our position are meant to dominate and control. We are the law, and the power. We are God.''

"You've grown as insane as Father,'' Roland said.

"Perhaps.''

"I won't allow you to destroy this village or these people.''

"How very knightlike of you. Are you challenging me? Should I run for my glaive and pike, call my men to arms?'' Harold laughed. "I doubt it. Is it not written somewhere in your precious oath that a knight worth his shield never raises his arms against father or brother?''

Roland turned his back on Harold and started for the stairs.

"Rumor has it you brought a woman with you to Wytham,'' Harold called. "You've tucked her away at the Goodmans'. Surely you haven't forgotten Hildegard? The poor dear has wasted away waiting for the return of her beloved Roland. Personally, I can't wait to see the two of you wed. 'Twill be a match made in Heaven!''

With a roar of laughter, Harold dropped back into the chair and yelled for a hovering servant to fetch him more wine. Roland mounted the stone steps, Harold's laughter echoing off the walls and clashing against his ears. The anger simmering in his belly crawled into his chest until his heart pounded painfully against his ribs. Still, he forced himself not to look back, not to give in to his need to run Harold through with his bollock—though he shook with the desire in that instant. How easy it would be to lop off the bastard's head and be done with his vexatiousness once and for all.

But Harold was his brother, after all. No man—no knight—would dare take up a weapon against his brother. No castle, no kingdom was worth the dishonor of striking down his own flesh and blood.

The second floor of Wytham Castle was as filthy and stinking as the first. Feeling his way along the walls, Roland moved down the unlit corridor until he reached his father's chamber. For a long while he stood, frozen, on the threshold, afraid to enter, afraid of who, or what, would confront him. All the years of his boyhood washed over him in waves—his body shook, sweat beaded on his brow. Vomit filled up his throat and he thought—prayed—briefly that he might suffocate before being forced to face Godfrey again.

Christ, he had slain a thousand men on the battlefield—had faced the most fierce of Philip's warriors. None had wrought the dread in his gut that he experienced in that moment.

Placing his hands flat against the door, he shoved it open.

Hope sat upright in bed, her heart racing, the odd dream squirming disturbingly on the edge of her memory. She struggled desperately to grasp it, to hold it long enough to see it clearly, to understand it.

A dream?

Or a vision?

No. No vision. There would be no more visions. Remember? By falling in love with Roland, by acknowledging her love for Roland, she had given up her gift. There were only dreams now. Vague. Confusing. Images twisted and roiling like a pit of snakes.

How odd that she should feel sadness over the loss of something she had cursed for the last years of her life. How many times had she turned her anger to God, demanding to know why she and her mothers before her had been burdened with such a curse . . . such a gift?

Where was Roland?

A pain throbbed in her temples and grew stronger as Hope tried desperately once again to recall her dream. For the last weeks it had nagged her, teased her, awoke her with pounding heart and a sense of suffocating. Yet, the moment she had opened her eyes the images had fled, leaving her feeling like one stumbling along in the dark and knowing that somewhere before her lay a bottomless abyss.

Leaving the bed, she walked to the window. Sounds crept through the heavy shutter: dogs barking, raucous laughter, children crying.

Voices came to her from another room. Cautiously, she moved to the door and opened it slightly, allowing the smell of cooking food to waft over her as she focused on the couple near the fire. For an instant, her heart stopped as the tall man with his back to her wrapped his arms around a woman and held her close.

"Roland?" Hope whispered.

The man turned. Their eyes met.

For an instant, she could not breathe, or move. The stranger's black eyes sucked her into a vortex where reality became splintered by flashes of light and images that, like her dreams, vanished before she could grasp them. Her knees buckled.

The woman gasped. The man caught Hope before she hit the floor.

"Sit her here, before the fire," the woman said.

"She's as light as a leaf, Mary. Bring her a bowl of pottage and a slab of cheese." He gently slapped Hope's cheek until she managed to open her eyes. Again, she caught her breath, unable to take her gaze from his.

"You're exhausted, lass," he said, and the sound of his voice caused reality to ripple like water in her head. She thrashed as if she were drowning. "Hush. Hush, girl. Be still. There is nothing here to harm you."

"Roland," Hope gasped, and grabbed the man fiercely. "Roland."

"He'll be back," came the woman's voice.

Soft hands cradled Hope's face. They were not unlike her mother's hands. They felt cool against her hot skin. There was a gentleness in the touch that calmed her, and she managed at last to breathe. The flurry of confusion and scattered images that had whirled in her brain settled like snowflakes on a windless day.

"Can you sit up?" the woman asked.

Hope nodded. The man helped her, then tucked a blanket across her knees before backing away. Glancing at his wife, he said, "I'll see to the livestock, Mary."

Mary nodded and smiled at Hope. "I'll see she's fed properly. Then we'll do something about cleaning her up."

As the man left, Hope frowned. Mary ladled pottage into a bowl and handed it to Hope, along with a horn spoon. "My husband can be a bit intimidating at first. But he's as kind and gentle a man as you'll ever meet."

"Where am I?" Hope asked. "Where is Roland?"

"I'm Mary Goodman. 'Twas my husband Royce who scared you out of your senses. You've come to Wytham, Roland's home." Mary sat on the bench beside her. "Eat. You're far too thin. To be healthy a woman should have meat on her bones."

"I've little hunger of late." Hope looked at the thick pea soup, and felt her stomach turn over.

Mary took the bowl and set it aside. She then placed a slice of warm bread in Hope's hand. "Warm bread is good for the soul, not to mention the hips."

Hope broke off a piece and put it in her mouth. Her jaws ached in response, and it was all she could do to swallow.

Regarding Hope closely, Mary smiled. "We're Roland's godparents. He brought you to us for safekeeping."

"If Roland cared for my well-being he would not have

dragged me halfway across the world in shackles. France is my home. Not England."

"It matters not where you live as long as you're with the man you love."

"I don't love Roland!" she cried, and tossed the bread into the fire.

Mary smiled. "The tears in your eyes tell me otherwise."

"He's a barbarian. A liar. A thief of hearts. He takes pleasure in making women fall in love with him."

"Then you *are* in love with him."

Hope looked around the room, noting the wooden salt chest and the collection of pots hanging near the fire. She sighed. "I must be. Although my thoughts tell me no, my heart and soul say otherwise."

"One can hardly deny the feelings of the heart. 'Tis what gives us life." Mary patted Hope's hand. "If it's any consolation, I happen to know that Roland cares for you deeply."

"What good does that do me?" Hope said, her voice taking on a bitter tone. "I have given up all that I am, or was, for a man who is destined to belong to another."

"Was what you gave up so important? Did it bring you more joy than the pleasure you get from being with Roland? Was your life complete, fulfilled, and happy?"

"I would rather suffer the agonies of damnation than watch another bear him children."

Mary's look became distant as she gazed down into the fire. "Yes. 'Twould be difficult to watch another raise the son or daughter who should have been yours."

There was a sad desperation in Mary's voice that caused Hope to study her closely. The firelight accentuated the creases in Mary's brow, and for an instant Hope thought she saw the glimmer of tears in her eyes. A glance around the room told her why. "You have no children, Mary?"

Mary flinched. She left Hope's side and paced the room,

her face turning gray as ash. "There was a child—a boy. Dear God, but we had so looked forward to his birth. We were terribly poor in those days, with little to offer a child but love. But we had dreams, as do all parents, that we could some how provide our children with the means to far exceed our humble existence. Then, we believed that fortune and power were all one needed to be happy.

"But our son was born weak, the cord around his throat. I held him in my arms only briefly before . . . We named him William, after Royce's father."

"He died?" Hope asked, feeling her heart turn over at the stricken expression on Mary's face. For a brief moment their gazes locked. Just as briefly, Hope again experienced the sensation of falling into a pinpoint of pulsating light. She grabbed the table edge, closed her eyes, willing the spinning in her head to stop. Vaguely, Mary's voice came to her, rousing the sudden bombardment of confusing and frightening images that momentarily obliterated reality. Were they simply flashes of the distant and troubling dreams that had plagued her the last weeks? Or were the visions returning?

"We thought for certain there would be other children. And there was. A girl two years later. She died of a fever when she was only three months old. There were no more babies." Mary frowned as Hope pressed her fingertips to her temple. "You stare at me strangely, Hope."

"You seem so . . . familiar to me," Hope replied. "It's as if there is some bond, as if I know you already."

"Perhaps it's our mutual love for Roland."

"How came you to be Roland's godparents?"

Mary again sat at Hope's side. "Royce and Godfrey were children together. They became trusted friends. As close as if not closer than brothers. Godfrey knew that of all men, Royce would sacrifice his own life to protect him."

"Was it not unusual for a man of such esteem to entrust the welfare of his firstborn son to a simple blacksmith, no matter the thread of friendship that tied them?'' Hope asked.

"Many were stunned. At first the church forbade it.'' Her voice dropping and her eyes becoming hard, Mary said, "Even priests are known to look the other way if it means a new chapel or a generous donation to the church's coffers.''

The memory of Châteauroux and the hateful abbot made Hope shiver.

"What of Roland's mother?''

A cloud passed over Mary's face. "Alais, daughter of Raoul de Cambrai. She was as fragile as the eggshell of a bluebird. Godfrey worshipped her. He would do anything to protect her, kill anyone—even his own flesh and blood— with his bare hands to ensure her well-being and happiness. She died soon after giving birth to Harold. 'Tis just as well. Her heart would have broken over what has become of her husband and son.''

"Why does Godfrey so hate Roland?'' Hope asked.

Mary reached for the head shawl hanging from a peg near the door. She wrapped it over her head, secured the stray hairs at her temples beneath the wool, then opened the door. She paused, her back to Hope, her gaze fixed on some distant point in the dark. "Because Roland is a reminder of Godfrey's greatest sin—his burden to bear for loving his wife more than God,'' she replied in a chillingly flat voice, then quit the house, closing the door behind her.

SIXTEEN

The Lunatic squatted before a replica of the Virgin Mary hanging on the wall, his naked, wasted body rocking back and forth as he prayed into his scarred and knotted hands. Over the last years his hair had grown white as snow. Left uncut, it hung in limp, tangled, thinning threads to the middle of his back, which was little more than open, oozing wounds. The chamber that had once sparkled with the resplendence of Henry's most respected and successful earl and knight appeared as filthy as the rest of the castle. The straw on the floor crawled with vermin. Human waste and decaying food fouled the air, turning Roland's stomach.

Cautious, Roland moved up behind Godfrey. Once he might have ached to touch him, hoping that for once his father would open his arms in acceptance to Roland. But the last years had dulled the hunger for Godfrey's love. The only emotion turning over in his chest at that moment felt unnervingly like repulsion. The thought of drawing his bollock and cutting the old man's throat—if for nothing more than to end Godfrey's suffering—made Roland's mouth go dry.

"Father," Roland said.

Godfrey rocked and prayed more loudly.

Roland walked slowly around him, placing himself before Godfrey and the Virgin on the wall. Moments passed, yet he could not find the ability to speak.

Gradually, Godfrey's gaze lifted. His eyes were hollow and glassy. Drool dribbled from the corners of his mouth, into the unkempt beard that hung like a dank white bib over his chest.

"I've come home, Father."

Godfrey tipped his head one way, then the other as he regarded Roland with a blank expression.

Roland knelt before Godfrey so they were face-to-face. Still, Godfrey stared at him emotionlessly, uncomprehending.

"There were times I prayed to live long enough to see you suffer for your treatment of me," Roland said. "It seems that I have done so."

Godfrey frowned and clasped his hands tighter. He resumed rocking, though he did not take his eyes from Roland's.

" 'Tis odd that I take no pleasure in it," Roland continued. "I would walk away now and leave you to succumb to this mephitic insanity, allow your madness to eat away your brain, but the hunger in me to understand you continues to gnaw at me like some cursed pestilence." The old anger shivering through him, Roland grabbed Godfrey's face in his hands, ceasing the old man's rocking. "Why, old man? Why have you hated me? Why did you turn my life into a living hell although I continued to respect and love you?"

Godfrey blinked and his eyes became distant. He appeared to stare through Roland, focusing on some vision visible only to him. "Alais?" he called in a pitifully weak voice. "Sweet wife, I will defy the damnable stars to assure your well-being and happiness. I would destroy Henry himself to keep you safe from harm." Grabbing Roland's wrists, his long, ragged nails digging into Roland's flesh, Godfrey sneered, "He is cursed, the child. The seeress warned me. He will ruin this house and bring the demise of my dear Alais. I won't allow it, I tell you!''

Like a wild animal, Godfrey sprang to his feet, thrashing his arms, his eyes rolling. ''The seeress predicted it. The boy will grow to destroy all that is good of Wytham. His birth will bring the destruction of my lady.''

Roland grabbed Godfrey's thin shoulders and shook him. ''Blast you to perdition, old man. I did not destroy Alais. 'Twas Harold's birth that killed her. Look around you here. Harold has brought the ruination of Wytham. He savages the land and has wrought distrust among those who once were your allies.''

Godfrey's eyes grew large and frantic. He stared at Roland as if he had transformed into some demon. ''How was I to know? Foul Fate. *Treacherous hag!* She has condemned me to Hell's fires.'' Wrenching away, Godfrey stumbled across the floor, his hands upturned like claws. ''Blood on my hands. Always the blood. Will it not leave me alone?'' He pressed his flattened palms to his ears and wagged his head from side to side. ''Hush! Cease thy pitiful squalling. Poor child. Poor cursed babe. Blood of my blood and bone of my bone. I would rather cut out my own heart than hurt you but I cannot allow you to destroy her—my wife—my sweet Alais. Hush thy crying, oh my soul. My own. My son. Hush, hush, and go to sleep before my resolve is conquered.''

As Godfrey fell silent, his strength vanished as quickly as it had come, causing him to sink to the floor in a heap of sagging flesh and trembling bone. Roland slowly walked to him, bent to one knee, and took his father into his arms. He pressed the old man's face into his shoulder and stroked his hair.

Godfrey clung to Roland like a child awash in grief, his heavy tears soaking Roland's shirt. Roland held him fiercely until the sobbing ceased and Godfrey lay quiet and still against him. Finally, Godfrey lifted his head. His pale gray eyes met Roland's, and for an infinitesimal moment a look of sanity flickered in their depths. The hate with which he had always regarded Roland was replaced with a look of sad resignation . . . and repentance.

"God help you. God help us both," he whispered, touching Roland's cheek. "You should have died, then I could have buried you in yonder grave and be done with it. Struck the terrible deed from my mind and grieved with sweet Alais at your passing. But you refused to die, cursed boy. 'Twas God's will. He would have me look into your eyes every day of my life and be reminded of my sin."

"No sin is so awful that God, or I, won't forgive it," Roland told him. "Confess and repent, Father, and you will be free. Let me get the priest—"

"No priest, damn you! 'Tis my burden to bear. I am deserved of Hell and welcome its eternal damnation." Godfrey's head drooped weakly and tears leaked from his eyes. "My time is near, Roland. Embrace me. Quickly, for as brave as I once was, the fear of Satan's touch fills me with desperation."

Roland gripped Godfrey's body fiercely to his. The old man's skin felt cold and brittle, as if death had knitted its lifeless threads around him long ago.

"Have care," came Godfrey's thin words. "Her stars are evil. She is in league with Satan and will lead you down the path of destruction, as will he. I should have killed him long ago, when I first realized my mistake."

"Who, Father? For the love of God, what are you trying to say?"

Raising his eyes to Roland, Godfrey hissed, "Harold. Kill him as I should have done the night of his birth."

Stunned, Roland shook his head. "I couldn't kill my brother any more than I could kill you."

Godfrey's face twisted and his body contorted in a spasm

that wrenched him free of Roland's arms and flung him to the floor, where he writhed in pain. Roland grabbed his hands until the fit passed, leaving Godfrey to lie deathlike, still, his eyes glazed and staring up into Roland's. His lips moved in a whisper so quiet that Roland was forced to lower his ear to better hear him.

"Then you are as damned as I," Godfrey said.

Daniel paced from one end of the Goodmans' kitchen to the other. "Are you certain that we're alone?"

Hope nodded. "Royce and Mary have joined the others to harvest corn. I don't expect them until dark."

Daniel closed the window shutter, casting the room into shadows. Only then did he face Hope completely. Gone was the boy he had been at Châteauroux—the one who had patiently sat at her side inscribing visions on a tablet. In his place was a man whose body had matured the last many weeks, hardened by his many hours on horseback and the unending tutoring expected of a squire who would someday, praise God, become a knight worthy of his sword, shield, and destrier. A sprinkling of pale beard studded his chin and jaw, and his eyes burned with a fierceness that took Hope aback.

"I think you should leave Wytham," he said. "As soon as possible. Rumors are spreading through the village like fire. There are those among Roland's men who are convinced still that you bear evil instead of good. Matilda isn't helping the situation. She's intent on frightening the life out of the villagers with tales of your summoning lightning demons and spell casting."

He sat beside Hope and took her hand. Hope smiled. "The problem you speak of is hardly new to me, Daniel. There is something else bothering you."

"Have your visions returned?" He grinned.

"I have never needed visions to know when something is

bothering you, or when you're not being totally truthful. You wear deceit on your brow like a brand.''

Frustrated, Daniel paced again. "Wytham is rife with debauchery, depravity, and malevolence.''

"And?''

"Corruption festers like a boil.''

"And?''

Daniel paused and looked at her reluctantly. "Roland's affianced is to arrive within a fortnight.'' He kicked the salt box, upsetting a stack of bowls that clattered to the floor. "Bastard. I should run him through for what he's done to you. I might yet.''

"I think not, Daniel.''

"How can you sit there so calmly when he's treated you as if you were little more than chattel? Your ankles yet bear the blisters of his shackles. He broke your heart, for God's sake. You should despise him.''

"I should. Sometimes I think I do. I convince myself that I do. But then I tremble with the need to see him. To touch him. I think that I would become anything, even his mistress, for the opportunity to share a small portion of his life. What else do I have, Daniel? Where would I go? By falling in love with Roland, I gladly gave up all that I was. I sacrificed my soul for something far more powerful than my gift of sight and healing.''

"Are you certain, Hope? Perhaps if you tried very, very hard—''

"Why would I welcome back the pain?''

"Was that pain any greater than what you feel now? For the love of Mary, you're a shadow of yourself, as if you're slowly evaporating into air. If you love him so much, why don't you fight for him?''

"Our futures arc destined, Daniel. He's pledged to marry Hildegard. It was contracted by Henry.''

"Henry is dead. Besides, we know true destiny is illusive

to the normal soul. What we think is destiny is ofttimes no more than a confusing crossroads. Life is nothing more than a lot of wrong paths we take on our journey to discover our ultimate destiny. You, on the other hand, were blessed by God to glimpse our destinies.''

"Roland is too honorable a man to break his promise.''

"Honorable my ass. Would an honorable man bed a virgin?'' Crossing his arms over his chest, Daniel frowned. "Besides . . . how do you know he's destined to marry Hildegard? Did you see it in a vision?''

"I never chose to look. I was . . . afraid to.''

"It would be a shame if he went through with the marriage, and he wasn't meant to.'' With a lift of one eyebrow, Daniel added, "Perhaps that's why you're here, Hope. To stop him from marrying Hildegard.''

Silence filled the room momentarily as the weight of Daniel's words settled around them. His eyes narrowed. His brow creased. With a muttered *Holy Mary, Mother of God,* he dropped to his knees and took hold of Hope's shoulders.

"That's exactly why you're here,'' he said breathlessly. "It's all clear to me now, Hope. Why the visions cease only when the seer falls in true love. Because they have realized their destiny. Their future is in order. Christ, this . . . gift you have; we all have it, Hope. We're just too damned blind to realize it. You were simply blessed with the ability to see it more clearly than the rest of us.''

"But my ability to heal—''

"Faith. Love. Charity. You inspired the sick and desperate with all of those things. In believing in your abilities, they cured themselves. Because to believe in you was to believe in God's miracles.'' Taking Hope's face in his hands, Daniel searched her eyes. "There comes a time in our lives when we must acknowledge our destiny. Succumb to it. Only then will we know true peace and contentment.''

• • •

Matilda cowered in the corner of her filthy hut with its collection of mystic charms and powders stacked in clutters against the walls. Strings of bird beaks and wolves' teeth glittered in the firelight.

Roland fixed the hag with a look that made her tremble and offer him her meekest smile. "Sir, I am honored that you would seek me out—"

"I came here to wring your neck, old woman, if you don't tell me the truth."

"I am incapable of lying to one so noble and powerful, sir. 'Twould be foolish of me. Hmm?"

"Very foolish."

She opened her hands in compliance. "I will answer you as truthfully as I have endeavored to protect you these last years."

"That is hardly comforting, considering the number of brave men who perished the last years."

She shrugged. "But you, sir, are alive. 'Twas *your* destiny, and *your* stars that concerned me."

Roland paced, the foulness of the air in the cramped, over-hot room making him queazy. "I should have realized long ago that you held the answer to my dilemma. Father never did anything before seeking your advisement. Tell me, hag, what has driven my father insane? Why does he look at me with fear and hatred? And above all else, why has he turned his back on God?"

Her eyes grew wide. She looked beyond him to the door, as if she thought to flee.

Roland drew his bollock. "I'll cut your throat before you can squawk."

Matilda scrambled to a corner and crouched, peering up at Roland from the corners of her yellow eyes. "The stars foretold the fall of Wytham. The stars never lie, sir. On the eve of your birth, I did but tell him that his son would bring his ruination. That he would ravage the land and people

would be left bloodied behind him like lambs of slaughter
. . . I did but tell him that his son would destroy his beloved
Alais.''

"But 'tis Harold, not I, who has brought bad fortune.
'Twas Harold's birth that killed our mother.''

"I did but read the future in the stars, sir. They did not
spell out Harold's name. How was I to know what son would
bring Godfrey's destruction? How was Godfrey to know?''

Roland raked one hand through his hair as his frustration
mounted. "The stars foretold Harold's birth, not mine. Yet
when Father looked into my face, 'twas fear and loathing
and madness he felt long after Harold's birth that brought
the ruin of everything he loved. Why? Why even now, when
he looks into my eyes, do I see such torture? Such pain?
Such sadness? Why does the very sight of me drive all ra-
tionale from his mind?'' Covering his eyes with his hands,
Roland groaned. "Merciful God. I fear I will go as mad as
Godfrey if I don't know the truth.''

The dream again.

Hope awoke with a start, her heart racing, her brow sweating. She struggled to focus, to grasp the image that was illusive as smoke. Think.

A baby wrapped in swaddling.

A woman weeping.

A tombstone—a tiny crucifix—and on it a name.

ROLAND

The image scattered, leaving Hope exhausted. She slid
from the bed, noting that the shadows had deepened. How
long had she slept? Mary and Royce would be returning soon
from harvesting their corn. She smiled, thinking of the couple
who had opened their house and arms to her—a stranger.
Roland's godparents. How very tragic that they had had no

living children of their own. What wonderful parents they would have made, as evidenced by their loyalty to Roland.

ROLAND

Hope squeezed her eyes closed, an odd sense of fear and desperation causing her heart to race. Then the first twinge of pain in her temple.

This was no dream. The visions were returning, worming their way into her reluctant consciousness. Was Roland in danger? Did the cryptic message mean death to Roland? Think! It was a child's grave, not a man's.

Hope hurried to the door. Dusk was falling fast over the village, casting long shadows over the streets. Taking a deep breath, she began walking, her instincts leading her out of the *enceinte* and over the drawbridge, which spanned a murky moat where several children were bathing while their mothers looked on. To her left were a scattering of houses and shops, and beyond that was the vast demesne belonging to Godfrey. Farther still were the more meager holdings of the tenants, who were toiling to harvest their corn crop. To her right . . . she searched the horizon until she found the church spire.

Hope ran, her breath burning her lungs and the rising night wind biting her cheeks.

The small church was set amid the tombstones of what seemed like a thousand graves spread out over the undulating hills. Even as she watched, darkness crept over the barrows, swallowing the stone markers that would identify what body lay within the earthen mounds.

What could she have been thinking to come here?

What had she hoped to find?

Hopelessness assailed her as the countless crosses became blurred by shadows. She turned to leave.

Not yet, whispered the voice in her head. As if held in

place by a cold hand, Hope closed her eyes, as she had a thousand times in the past, and allowed the shiver of pain to creep into her thoughts.

ROLAND

A child's grave.
Open now.
She can smell the wet, musty earth.
She moves closer and looks in. Her body trembles in fear.
But the grave is empty.
Or is it?
Closer.
She drops to her hands and knees, feels the cold dirt against her flesh as she leans over the grave, searching the darkness. There is something there. A hand reaching up out of the blackness. A child's hand. An infant's, with dirt beneath its tiny blue fingernails. She cannot breathe. Or move. She is paralyzed with dread.

Hope opened her eyes.

She heard it then, the wail of suffering coming from a distant knoll. Her feet moved, reluctantly at first, then faster, the sound of misery drawing her through the dark until she topped the hillock overlooking a grouping of tiny graves. A solitary cross seemed to reflect some nonexistent moonlight, and on it was chiseled:

WILLIAM GOODMAN
BELOVED SON

Yet it was not the name that caused her heart to momentarily cease beating, but the huddled figure that bent over the tiny barrow, weeping and praying:

"May God have mercy on my soul."

"Mary?" Hope called.

The figure, hidden within a cowl and robe, collapsed.

Hope dropped to the ground and took the mourner into her arms. The cowl slid back from his brow, and Hope gasped.

The old man stared up at her with impending death stamped upon his features. " 'Tis ended," he whispered. "Wytham is as dead as I."

"Godfrey?"

"My sweet Alais. Cherished wife. 'Twas all for you. Please, forgive me."

Gently, Hope laid him back, tucked the robe closely around his sunken chest, then ran for the castle.

She met Royce and Mary on the road as they returned from their farming. Seeing Hope running at them from the dark caused Mary to drop her sickle and Royce to grab his wife protectively before recognizing Hope.

Doing her best to catch her breath, Hope said, "The cemetery. Quickly! He's dying."

"Who's dying?" Royce demanded.

"Godfrey. At your son's grave."

Mary closed the bedroom door behind her and leaned against it. She regarded Hope where she sat near the fire. "What were you doing at William's grave?" she asked.

"Curiosity," Hope replied, refusing to meet Mary's eyes.

Mary moved across the room, her gaze never leaving Hope. "There are rumors about you, Hope. Not all of them welcome."

"I'm not evil, Mary, despite what Matilda says."

"You're a seeress. You foresee the future."

"I have dreams occasionally. Visions. Which is what led me to your son's grave."

Mary circled her, her countenance wary.

"One dream has plagued me since I first met Roland. It's

that of a child's grave and a tombstone inscribed with Roland's name.''

Mary stopped. Her eyes became round.

"I worried that Roland was in danger. I feared the vision was a portent of his death. But it doesn't make sense. 'Tis a child's grave I see. Not a man's.''

Turning her back on Hope, Mary stared down into the fire. She hugged herself and swallowed back her emotions.

Standing, Hope moved to Mary's side. "Why was Godfrey grieving over your son's grave?'' she asked softly.

"He is a sick, twisted old man. I wish he would die and let us all live our lives in peace. Perhaps then my husband will see reason. Perhaps then he'll be free of Godfrey's hold.''

"Why your son's grave?'' Hope repeated. "Was he in some way responsible for William's death?''

Her head snapping around, her eyes filling with tears, Mary began to tremble. "Had we only known,'' she whispered. "But they were as close as brothers. It seemed right and good that Royce would agree to such a scheme. We were grief-stricken and not thinking clearly. We prepared ourselves for the inevitable, stealing precious moments with the baby when we could. But the inevitable never came—''

"Enough!'' Royce barked, causing Mary and Hope to jump and spin toward the bedroom door where he stood, his face bleached white as linen. He stared at his wife in silence before turning his gaze on Hope. "Find Roland and tell him what has transpired. He should see Godfrey as soon as possible.''

Hope nodded.

She left the Goodmans' house and stood in the dark, her back pressed against the door as Royce and Mary's angry voices came to her.

"You continue to protect him, Royce. And for what?''

"Godfrey is no more at fault for this mess than we are.

He has been forced to live with far worse than we. For the love of God, his soul is tortured.''

"You excuse him even now. After all he has done to Roland. After all the hell he put Roland through. I am weary of the lies, Royce. I crave Godfrey's death with every fiber of my being so the truth can at last be known.''

"And what good will the truth accomplish? Are you so certain Roland will understand and forgive us? What will be left him then, Mary? What will be left for Wytham if it should pass to Harold? Roland is Wytham's only hope.''

SEVENTEEN

The better part of an hour passed before Hope located Roland. He sat atop the crumbling battlement, his back propped against a merlon as he looked down on Wytham's bailey, where once parades had entertained the villagers and families had met on sunny days to while away their few precious hours of leisure with friends. He seemed not the least bit surprised when she carefully sat down beside him; he just opened his arms and pulled her close, shielding her from the cold wind.

Hope allowed herself the pleasure of hearing his heart beat against her ear before speaking. "Godfrey is grave, Roland. Royce feels you should see him."

"He's dying?"

"Yes." She nodded.

A shiver ran through Roland, and he gripped Hope more tightly. "When I was a child, I would sit in this very place and dream of becoming the bravest and most admired knight in Henry's kingdom, worthy of inheriting such a fine castle as Wytham—worthy of filling Godfrey's shoes. Now look at her. What is worth inheriting? Where once children laughed and played, they now cry with hungry bellies and skin pocked with illness. Their fathers pay liege to a man who robs them of hope and dignity. Had I not devoted these lost years to Henry, mayhap this unhappiness they feel could have been avoided.''

He turned his face into the wind. "I ran, Hope. I avoided my responsibilities to Wytham and my father by burying myself in another man's war."

"It's not too late for Wytham. She might well be great again, with your leadership."

"At the cost of what?" He caught her chin with his finger and tipped her face up. His eyes were as dark and cloudy as the sky beyond him. "Is Wytham worth the sin of killing my brother?"

"I would try to persuade you to leave Wytham, but you could no more turn your back on these people again than you could kill Godfrey."

· He kissed her brow. "I love you," he whispered.

"You were destined for this moment, sir. And for this life."

"And you?" He kissed her again. "Are we destined to be together, Hope?"

She looked at the bleak sky that tumbled with clouds. "There is the little matter of Hildegard."

Roland groaned.

Taking his face between her hands, Hope searched his eyes. "Sweet, honorable man. If I must give you up so that yonder people can know peace again, then I shall do so with little regret but for the life we might have shared had destiny smiled on the union."

"You would give me up that easily to another woman?"

"As long as I have your heart, what more can I want?" She pressed her lips against his, then pulled away. "Will you come now to see Godfrey?"

·   ·   ·

The soldiers surrounding Royce Goodman's open door were stone-faced and silent as mutes. Sensing trouble, Roland ordered Hope to remain in the shadows while he cautiously approached Royce's house.

A pair of burly foot soldiers appeared in the doorway, with Mary between them. She flailed at them with her fists, and when she threw back her head her face looked bloodied.

"Animals!" she cried. "If you harm my husband I'll kill you with my own hands."

Roland grabbed the bollock from his belt. "Halt!" he shouted, causing the soldiers to stop short. Mary frantically searched the darkness, her tear-filled eyes widening with relief when she saw him. Roland shoved passed the congregated men until he stood before Mary, who did her best to draw back her thin shoulders and stand straight.

"What the devil is going on here?" he growled. "Take your hands off this woman and stand back."

The soldiers exchanged looks, but refused Roland's order.

Harold stepped from the house, sword drawn. "Roland. We were expecting you. Seems our father is about to do us a great favor and die, at long last."

"What have you done to the Goodmans?" Roland demanded.

"After careful inspection of our records, Goodman appears to have slighted us on his taxes. I simply came here to . . . collect. In doing so I discovered him hiding our sweet father. No doubt in an attempt to make him see reason where you are concerned Royce always did tag about Father's coattails like some nagging conscience regarding his behavior toward you. When I attempted to remove father, Royce forbade it. As Godfrey's son, and ultimate heir, have I not the right to spend these last precious hours with my father?"

"Roland is Godfrey's heir!" Mary cried. "Wytham will bow to Roland and no other!"

Harold grabbed her hair and yanked back her head. "Careful, Mary Goodman. Should I think you to be a source of trouble, I'll be forced to deal with you more harshly than I might have otherwise.''

Roland glanced at the soldiers' faces, none whom he recognized as owing allegiance to Godfrey, or himself. His own soldiers were scattered like starlings throughout the countryside, having returned to their families. The tenants would be little help, as they already lived in fear of Harold. To take sides against him would jeopardize their homes, not to mention their lives.

"Where is Royce?" Roland asked.

"With Godfrey," Mary replied, despite the hold Harold had on her hair. "He refused to leave Godfrey's side when they took him." She struggled and cried, "He's as insane as Godfrey, Roland. He'll murder us all to ensure his hold on Wytham!"

Harold slung Mary to the ground and kicked her. Roland sprang at Harold, only to be brought up short as soldiers grabbed his arms and wrenched the bollock from his hand. Grinning, Harold stepped forward, and smiling into Roland's eyes, drove his fist into Roland's stomach.

Hidden within the shadows, Hope sank against a wall and tried to breathe as Roland fell to his knees. Her body shook. Her mind raced with a thousand images, yet try as she might she could not grasp the most minute thought on which to act. Fear scattered her reasoning. She could not move, though all instincts demanded that she flee.

But where?

A movement behind her.

Her scream was muffled by a hand clamped across her mouth. Then a voice whispered in her ear, "Be very quiet. If they see us we're doomed."

She squeezed her eyes closed and felt the strength melt from her legs.

Daniel!

Cautious, his arm around her waist, Daniel backed down the dark alley, avoiding several crates and barrels stacked near a pile of scaffolding. When certain they were out of sight of Harold's men, he caught her hand and started for the drawbridge that, even now, was beginning to rise.

"No!" Hope set her heels and pulled back. "I won't go. I won't leave him, Daniel."

"We'll do him no good if we're captured. I need time to call the men to arms—"

"I won't go."

"Don't argue with me, Hope. The bridge is closing. We'll be trapped—"

"Then go. Do what you can out there. I vowed to Roland that I would always love him."

"That doesn't mean you have to die for him."

"Daniel." She touched his face and searched his eyes. "You, who no more than a few hours past spoke of destiny, of our ability to recognize our destiny when confronted by it, now ask me to run from my own? I need no visions to tell me that I belong here, with Roland. If our destiny is to die together, then so be it."

He glanced again at the closing drawbridge.

Hope smiled. "Yonder is your destiny, Daniel. You've known it since you first picked up the abbot's quill and stabbed the air as if it were your enemy. You knew even then that you would become a knight who would defend the weak and helpless against such tyranny as Harold's. Go! Please. You are our only hope."

He backed away, his face white in the night, and tortured. "God be with you, Hope, until I return. Have faith."

"I *am* faith. Remember?"

"*Adieu.*" He lifted his hand, then spun on his heels and fled into the dark. Hope thought but could not be certain that she saw him slip through the gate before it crashed shut and the chains locked into place.

The sounds of screaming women and crying children filled the night, along with the shouts of soldiers as they went from house to house, rousting out the few families who might prove to be dangerous to Harold should they continue to hold fealty to Godfrey, or Roland. Hope kept to the shadows and returned to the Goodmans' to discover it empty and ransacked. Blood was spattered over the threshold, and with a sinking heart Hope dropped to her knees, touched the red stains with her fingertips, the horror drumming through her head that the blood might well be Roland's.

"There she is!" came the cry. Hope looked around.

Matilda emerged from the shadows, pointing at Hope with her gnarled hands. Behind her were several of Harold's soldiers. "There is the sorceress. Careful with her. I've seen with my own eyes as she conjured lightning from a clear sky and struck a hundred brave soldiers dead."

The soldiers hesitated. Their eyes narrowed.

Hope stood and faced them, her look defiant. Her smile challenged them, daring them to risk a similar fate.

"Grab her!" Matilda screamed. " 'Tis Harold's orders."

They glanced at the sky, then at each other.

Hope leapt from the doorway and ran for the alley. The men gave chase, hitting her from behind with enough force to drive her to the ground. Pain splintered through her chest and blackness exploded behind her eyes.

Hope awoke, feverish and hungry and wet.

How long had she been here, in this horrible place? How many days and nights?

Where was Roland?

Dead?

She closed her eyes and searched for the visions.

Nothing but blackness.

Above, a singular slit of light peeked through the darkness, vaguely illuminating the circular walls of the pit in which she had existed the last hours. Moss clung to the damp stones, and here and there, far above her head, ferns sprouted from between the rocks, further evidence that the hole in which Harold had locked her was little more than a tomb in the ground. Along the wall at her back were hollow places worn in the stone by the hands and feet of human creatures who, through the weary years of captivity, climbed and clutched and clung to the walls in a pitiful attempt to scale them, to no avail. Around the room at intervals, cut into the stone were the words *Jesus Maria. God help me!* and a pathetic little attempt at an altar scooped out of the rock, with a cross carved above it.

A crash sounded close by. Hope jumped as a door opened, flooding the room with light. She covered her eyes, momentarily blinded as a pair of soldiers dragged her to her feet and propelled her up a flight of narrow stairs. Any thought of rebellion was quashed by the stab of pain from her bruised ribs. She prayed she would not faint again.

Harold sat in a chair on a dais overlooking the great hall. Scattered around him was Hope's tripod and the numerous tablets in which Daniel had inscribed her visions. Harold regarded Hope in silence as the soldiers dumped her at his feet, then he smirked.

"She hardly looks treacherous to me. She's rather pitiful, actually. I'm surprised at Roland. I suspected he would succumb to someone stronger, with a touch more fire."

Matilda waddled from the shadows, making certain to keep a safe distance from Hope. "Read these tablets for yourself, sir. Witness the tripod she uses to conjure up her magic from the very bowels of Hell."

He picked up a tablet and thumbed through it. "Am I really to believe that horses will be replaced by mechanized machines on wheels? That the world will be found to be round in the fifteenth century? That men will fly to the moon in the twentieth century?" He threw back his head in laughter. "If she is so astute at predicting the fate of mankind, what is she doing here?" Tossing the tablet to the floor, Harold slumped in the chair and crossed his legs. He regarded Hope through the fringe of hair over his eyes. "Really, Matilda. I'm starting to suspect you're as crazy as Godfrey."

" 'Tis Roland who brought her," Matilda replied. "See her ankles for yourself. He intended to use her magic to destroy you."

"Liar!" Hope spat, causing Matilda to jump as if goosed.

Harold's eyebrows raised. "So, the little one has a touch of fire after all. Very good. Tell you what, fair sorceress: I'll allow you your freedom this very moment if you burn Matilda to a crisp."

Matilda screeched and cowered behind Harold's chair.

Hope managed to climb to her feet. The room swam, and she stumbled before righting herself. "There is no magic in me," she finally said. "Were I capable of such I would have destroyed you by now, not to mention Matilda," she added with a stab of spite, causing the hag to scramble from the room.

"What a shame." Harold left the chair. He stepped from the dais to stand face-to-face with Hope. "If you are worth nothing to me, then why should I bother keeping you alive?" He smiled. "I have a plan. Prove to me that you can predict the future, and I'll allow you your freedom."

"Is Roland dead?" she asked.

"What difference does that make?"

"If Roland be dead, I care not for living. Therefore you can take your ultimatums and go straight to Hell."

He struck her across the face, knocking her to the floor. Planting his foot on her chest, he grinned down at her. "This is your ultimatum, seeress. If you do *not* tell me my future, I'll cut Roland's throat before your very eyes."

"Prove to me that he's alive," she countered.

"Very well." He snapped his fingers and a door flew open. Roland and Mary were dragged into the room. Mary struggled weakly as she was shoved into a chair. Roland, his hands tied at his back, was forced to his knees. Hope struggled to sit up as Harold walked to Roland, whose head hung between his shoulders. Twisting his hands into Roland's hair, Harold snapped back his head, exposing Roland's beaten face.

"Not so very pretty now, is he?" Harold said. "For the life of me I cannot imagine why his name and reputation sparked such fear among those jelly-livered French the last years. I keep trying to spur some malice in him, but he seems to have been bitten by cowardice."

"Refusing to raise his fist against his brother is hardly cowardice," Hope said. " 'Tis far more noble to turn the other cheek—"

"Save me your Christian blather. I don't believe in God. Never did." Releasing Roland, Harold walked to the tripod.

Roland sank back on his heels and raised his gaze to Hope's. Relief flooded her. There was life yet in his eyes. And strength. Though his features were swollen painfully, there was a calmness about his mien that rallied her spirit, and for the first time in what seemed like an eternity, reason scrambled in her mind for a handhold.

Harold kicked the tripod to her. "Matilda tells me that you gaze into this contraption and visions come to you in streams of smoke." He nodded to a servant in the shadows, who turned over an hourglass. "You have a few minutes before I kill you. Go on. We're waiting." He fell into his chair and yawned.

Reluctantly, Hope dropped to her knees. With a candle she lit the oil in the bottom of the tripod, watched as the first thin stream of gray smoke coiled into the air.

Focus.

Clear your thoughts. Allow the visions to come—the odd

and confusing images. Cryptic. Occasionally full of turmoil, making her tremble.

Nothing.

"This is impossible," she declared angrily. "The visions did not always come."

"The sand is shifting."

"Please understand. I gave it all up—the gift—when I fell in love with Roland. There is nothing here but flame and smoke now. The ability has passed to another."

"Really? Tell me to whom it has passed and I shall go find him."

"I . . . don't know."

"You're lying."

Mary sobbed and buried her face in her hands.

Again, Hope stared hard into the flame, her gaze occasionally drifting back to the hourglass and the sand that was fast seeping to the bottom. Looking at Harold again, she said cautiously, "Godfrey is yet alive."

Harold narrowed his eyes. "The old fool clings to life yet. Yes. But that is not your concern. Your hour is nearly up."

Her brow sweating, Hope watched the thin gray stream of smoke dissipate into the air.

"Time's up," came Harold's voice, as if from a deep well.

The flame sputtered and went out.

Leaping from the chair, drawing his bollock from his belt, Harold strode over to Roland and pressed the knife blade to his throat.

Mary screamed.

Hope jumped to her feet. "As you wish!" she cried, fear and anger making her voice quake. "Remove the knife from Roland's throat and I will relate your destiny as I see it."

Grinning, Harold stepped aside. "Wait. Let my men hear this as well. Then there will be little doubt of to whom they owe their loyalty." He shouted and the doors flew open. Soldiers filed into the room, all dressed in armor and carrying the cultellus and shield. Several wore conical helmets that hid all but their eyes.

"Go on," Harold prompted, throwing open his arms. "You have our undivided attention."

"Your future is this," she declared loudly so all could hear her. "You will die soon, Harold, struck down by one greater than you. More honorable. More powerful."

The smile slid from his face.

The onlooking soldiers gasped and looked from one to the other.

"All men who turn their backs on righteousness and murder for the sake of fortune will die with you."

His face white, his mouth frozen in a sneer, Harold shifted nervously. "Contemptible little bitch," he said. "She lies! There is no man living who can best me."

"Yes. There is." Hope pointed to Roland. "The only coward in this room is you, Harold. You keep Roland tied because you fear him. You would rather murder a bound man than give him the opportunity to defend himself—just as you destroy innocent families who faithfully vow fealty to Godfrey."

Harold glanced at his men.

"You did but ask me to proclaim your destiny, Harold. And I have done so."

He turned on Roland and drew back his dagger. A scream lodged in Hope's throat and she covered her face with her hands.

"Get up," came Harold's voice. "A sword! Throw him a weapon. Do it, idiot, before I run you through."

Hope lowered her hands.

Roland stood, the cut rope dangling from his wrists. A soldier stepped from the crowd and extended to Roland the hilt of a sword. Roland knocked it away. "You won't kill me, Harold. Not here. Not before these witnesses. Not when I have neither sword nor dagger to defend myself. There are men here who won't tolerate murder, even from you. That's why Godfrey lingers on death's edge, isn't it? You would like to kill him but you won't. Because to kill a man such as he would bring Richard Coeur de Lion to Wytham.''

"You underestimate me, Roland.''

Mary leapt to her feet as Royce was dragged into the hall, his hands crushed and bloodied, his face pulverized beyond recognition. Mary flung herself on her husband and cradled him against her breast.

Harold moved up beside Roland and said softly, "My pleasure is not in the kill, Sir Roland, but in the torture. He'll never use his hands again—not, at least, to forge iron. I broke his fingers one by one. They snapped like green tinder.''

Clenching his fists, his body shaking, Roland turned slowly to Harold. Harold smiled. "Kill them!'' he shouted to his men, pointing to Mary and Royce. For an instant no one moved. His eyes bulging, Harold grabbed up a sword and yelled, "Then I shall!''

The double doors of the great hall exploded open in that instant. Soldiers poured forth over the threshold, led by a man on horseback, his blond hair flying as he shouted orders to the advancing forces, all carrying Roland's banner.

"Daniel!'' Hope cried.

Daniel reined back on the black destrier and shouted to Roland. "Your sword, sir!'' He tossed Roland the weapon, then flashed Hope a smile.

Roland turned on Harold. "*En garde.* 'Tis a fight you want. A fight you'll have.''

"To the death,'' Harold sneered.

Hope ran to Royce and Mary. She helped Mary lift her husband and drag him to the door, where he set his heels and shoved them away. "I'll not run like a coward. There is strength left in me yet to help Roland.''

Only then did they realize that Harold's men had put down

their weapons. Only Roland and Harold continued to fight, their swords clashing in the silence again and again—blades slicing the air inches from their faces.

Driven back up the steps of the dais, struggling to block Roland's more powerful blows, Harold slipped and fell. With a fierce swing of his blade, Roland knocked Harold's sword from his hand, then jabbed the point of his own against Harold's throat.

His eyes widening, Harold held his breath, wincing as the keen tip of Roland's blade bit into his skin. "Well? What are you waiting for, Roland? Kill me and get it over with."

Roland swallowed. He tried to breathe. Sweat poured off his brow and into his eyes, blurring his vision.

"You won't kill me," Harold said. "You're too noble. Too honorable to cut your brother's throat."

Gritting his teeth, Roland flicked his sword the tiniest bit, slicing just enough into Harold's skin to make it bleed.

"Go on," Harold cajoled. "You think Father despised you before. Imagine how he'll react to your slaughtering me. His final thoughts will be of your killing his beloved son. He'll curse you with his dying breath."

A moment passed before Roland realized that the pounding in his ears was his heart. He eased the blade tip away from Harold's throat; then, with all of his strength, he drove it into the dais beside Harold's head. "It is finished, Harold. I want no part in your killing."

He turned away as Mary stumbled to her feet. Royce attempted to grab her with his mangled hands, but the pain forbade it.

Mary shoved her way through the silent soldiers. At last standing before Roland, she looked up into his eyes. "Kill him. Kill him now before he rises to destroy us all. Put an end to his cruelty. Put an end to the suffering he has caused us these last years. He does not deserve to live!"

"Mary." Roland gently cradled her cheek in his hand. "I cannot kill my brother. I won't."

Her eyes filled with tears. "He is not your brother, Roland."

Royce got to his feet. "Mary! Not here. Not now. Not like this."

She clutched Roland's hand to her face. "I would take these years back if I could spare you the pain of believing yourself unloved by your parents."

"What are you saying, Mary?"

"*We* are your parents, Roland. Royce and I."

He shook his head. "Your baby died, Mary—"

" 'Tis Godfrey's son who lies in yonder grave. He killed him, Roland. He smothered the life from his tiny body because the seeress predicted that Godfrey's son would destroy Alais and the house of Wytham."

Roland backed away.

Mary grabbed his shirt and shook him. "You were born minutes after Godfrey's son. Yours was a difficult birth. The cord was wrapped around your throat. The nurse, the midwife, the priest—we all thought . . . you were dying. The priest gave you your last rites. I prepared myself for the inevitable. Then Godfrey showed up on our doorstep with his tale of woe. He convinced Royce and me that Wytham was doomed unless we helped him.

"By then he had already killed his son. Since it was known that you were weak, no one was wiser when we announced that our child had died. He took you and put you into Alais's arms, expecting that soon, inexplicably, tragically, you would die."

Mary lowered her eyes. "Days passed and you grew stronger. What could any of us do? To reveal the truth would have disclosed Godfrey's crime. As his firstborn son, Wytham and all its wealth would pass to you someday. What could peasants like us give you?"

"Love," he said softly.

"Do you think we didn't suffer when we were forced to watch Godfrey grow madder with guilt every day? When Alais died after Harold's birth, he realized his mistake—that it was Harold, not his firstborn, who would destroy him. Yet you were there to remind him of his horrible sin. As your godparents, we did our best to provide you with the love Godfrey could not give you, and I prayed every day that somehow, someday, I could come to you and tell you, and hold you only as a mother holds her son."

Harold howled in laughter, the ugly sound bouncing off the walls of the great hall as he slowly stood up. He grabbed the hilt of Roland's sword and yanked it from the floor. "It seems there is an impostor in our midst. A peasant. No, not even that. A mere cottager, the lowest class of peasant. Seems he is deserved of a muck fork instead of a knight's shield. What say you, men? Will you bow to a blacksmith's boy, or to Godfrey's only *legitimate* heir?"

"They will bow now and forever to no one except their rightful liege lord," came the weak but steady voice behind Harold. He turned, his laughter dying in his throat as Godfrey stepped forward. His armor hung upon his shrunken frame. In his left hand he held a bloody sword. From his right swung Matilda's head.

"Jesus Christ, you moronic old lunatic," Harold gasped, just as Godfrey swung his blade, slicing Harold's head from his shoulders.

EIGHTEEN

The letter arrived a week later from Arnold of Cheswyck, Hildegard's father. He proffered his condolences on Godfrey's and Harold's unfortunate passing, then explained curtly that, considering the circumstances of Roland's parentage, and the fact that he was as penniless and landless as a pauper, a marriage between Roland and Hildegard would be unacceptable. He then hinted that he would soon be paying a call on Wytham . . . which meant that Arnold had every intention of parlaying Wytham's vulnerability into an opportunity to seize it for his own.

Standing on the keep's front steps, Roland read the letter aloud to the gathering of villagers and soldiers who had congregated in the bailey to deliberate the future of their home. Mary grabbed Hope and hugged her.

"What wonderful news," Mary cried. "You and Roland are now free to marry."

Her face flushing as all eyes turned on her, Hope laughed. "Hush, Mary. He hasn't asked me yet."

"He'll ask you," Daniel declared with a lift of his eyebrow. "Or he'll answer to me."

Jeanne jabbed him in the ribs. "You grow too big for your chausses, my dear Daniel. 'Tis the Black Flame you challenge—the finest knight in this or any country."

Daniel slid his arm around her waist and narrowed his eyes. "I think I grow weary of your fawning over Roland. Have I true reason to feel jealousy over my sister's future husband?"

Her dark eyes widening, Jeanne smiled and asked breathlessly, "Are you jealous, Daniel?"

Laughing, Hope looked around as Roland moved toward her through the crowd, his black eyes focused on hers and his mouth curling in a smile.

"He comes," Mary whispered, and backed away.

The air warmed. Her heart quickened. She managed a watery smile as he stopped before her and reached for her hand. A long silent moment passed as the villagers pressed close, holding their breath.

Roland dropped to one knee. "Lady, I am landless, and without wealth but for my horse and armor. But if you should agree to marry me I will be the richest man who has ever walked the face of this good earth."

"Our wealth will be enormous, sir. For your name and honor are more valuable to me than vast treasures."

Hope sank into Roland's arms as the villagers cheered. She kissed his bruised lips and laughed as he spun her around. Mary and Jeanne grabbed her arms and dragged her away. "There will be plenty of time for that. There are plans to be made for a wedding."

She threw Roland a kiss and watched as he became swallowed by well-wishers.

The banns were cried and the villagers set forth preparing Wytham for Roland and Hope's wedding day, making their feelings known for the man who, through the years, had brought hope and honor to their village. The fact that Royce

Goodman was Roland's father, and not Godfrey, mattered not at all. 'Twas not the name, but the man himself whom they loved and respected.

With Godfrey's and Harold's deaths, it was as if new life had been breathed into Wytham. The foul streets were cleaned. Houses and shops were repaired. Wives set forth baking and sewing bright banners while children gathered flowers to dry and hang above their doors in celebration of Roland and Hope's joining.

Each morning Hope was presented with a gift from Roland: a fine jewel, a thread of gold, a parcel of exquisite cloth from Persia, Italy, or Spain—all the treasures left to him in the world. Mary toiled day and night to sew Hope's wedding dress, utilizing each and every article in the gown while Roland spent long hours with Royce, learning the fine art of blacksmithing so that he could provide for his young wife in the years to follow.

All seemed well. Hope, however, could not shake the uneasy feeling that something unpleasant was afoot, and mentioned as much to Mary.

"Roland loves you madly," Mary assured her. "Relax, Hope. 'Tis only prewedding jitters that plague you."

"There are times when I wish I could still foresee the future, Mary. Then I could assure myself that Roland and I will at last know happiness together."

"Look in his eyes, Hope. That should be enough to convince you."

She smiled. "I have no doubt that he loves me, Mary. But I've watched him the last days. He gazes out over the land with an odd look in his eyes. A restlessness that unnerves me."

"Perhaps he simply thinks of the years he spent away from Wytham. Of the friends he left buried in France."

"I wonder if a man who has known such freedom, whose life has been so focused on duty and honor, will be happy to settle in one place . . . and with one woman.''

Her hands folded in her lap, Mary smiled sadly. "I wonder how happy he will be as a simple blacksmith's son, when the reality of owning little more than a plot of dirt settles in to remind him that once he might have inherited Wytham and all of the respect it would buy him.''

Hope fell to her knees and grabbed Mary's hands. "He adores you and Royce. You're the mother and father he has ached for all of his life. To have his parents' love is a far greater treasure to him than Wytham.''

"As are you," Mary said. "We simply must have faith that this life and this destiny is what God intended for him.''

Hope smiled. "Yes. We must have faith.''

At last, the day of their marriage arrived. The sun shone in a clear blue September sky as the villagers, dressed in their finest, congregated at the castle's steps where they would follow Hope and Roland to the church.

Hope's dress consisted of a deep red pelisse of silk over a pale yellow chemise. A narrow gold border ornamented the ends of the sleeves, which were tight around her wrists. Tiny jewels trimmed the edge and throat of the pelisse. Over that was added a very light green silk tunic, embroidered with gold. The sleeves were very wide and long, trailing almost to the ground. Roland's final gift to Hope, arriving the morning of the wedding, was a splendid girdle fixed with topazes, agates, and sardonyx stones. On Hope's braided hair, Mary fixed a chaplet of flowers that drooped slightly over her brow, their pale yellow coloring intensifying the brightness of her eyes and the flush of her cheeks.

She curtsied shyly before Roland as she met him on the castle steps. "Are you pleased with me as I am, sir?"

"I am . . . speechless," he replied, his eyes sparkling. "Your beauty humbles me. I am far too poor a man to be

honored by one so fair. I had best hurry and wed you before
you change your mind.''

"How could I deny one so handsome, Roland?''

"Then I please you as well?'' He stepped back, presenting
himself with a bow.

How splendid he looked, his powerful legs encased in
brown silk hose and his shoulders draped in a red pelisson
trimmed in gold. He wore a deep blue tunic over the red silk
that made his black hair look all the blacker, and his dark
eyes all the deeper.

Hope nodded, unable to speak.

Roland took up her hand and kissed it. "To the church
then, my love.''

With Mary and Royce walking behind, the villagers trailing behind them, Roland and Hope rode to the church on
horseback—she on a quiet gray palfrey, he on his prancing,
blowing black warhorse. As they mounted the rose-strewn
steps hand-in-hand they were awash with the heady scent of
perfume.

They took their places beneath the shadow of the statues
of the Savior and the Holy Saints. The priest spoke sternly,
yet calmly as he looked out over the watchful crowd that
spread out of the nave and into the yard far beyond.

"There are no canonical obstacles? This man and woman
are of the proper age? They are not relatives, and are both
Christians? The publications have been made, and the banns
proclaimed three times in this church. You have witnesses?
Yes, yes, of course you do. Several hundred by the looks of
it. If all conditions are complied with, then it only remains
for me to demand from you solemnly your consent to this
marriage. This moment you must reflect, Roland Goodman,
whether you have any greater duties to fulfill than those of
a loyal and lifelong husband to this woman.''

Hope closed her eyes as silence ensued. Her heart beat
like hammers in her ears.

"I have no greater duty than those of husband," came Roland's reply, and Hope released her breath, only then realizing that she gripped Roland's hand like a lifeline. She looked at him askance, noting the wicked grin on his face as he glanced at her and winked.

The priest cleared his throat. "If no one opposes this union, then—"

"I oppose it," came the sudden voice behind them.

Hope and Roland turned, as did the congregation, who gasped as one.

King Richard Coeur de Lion stood in the door, his hard gaze fixed on Roland.

Roland's jaw clenched, and his eyes narrowed. Hope grabbed his arm and felt it tremble in her hands. Royce jumped forward and laid his bandaged hand on Roland's shoulder. "Remember yourself," he whispered urgently in Roland's ear. "He is king, after all."

"I know who the hell he is," Roland said through his teeth.

Richard perused the stunned faces of his subjects. One by one, the women curtsied—albeit reluctantly. The men lowered their eyes, unable to mask their feelings for the man who helped to bring about the fall of Henry.

"Seems someone forgot to invite me to the wedding," Richard declared, moving slowly toward Roland and Hope. " 'Tis a grand occasion when one of my most heralded knights takes a wife, even if he is a blacksmith's son."

Richard looked down his nose at Hope.

She started to curtsy.

Roland grabbed her arm. "Never bend to Richard Coeur de Lion," he ordered her, causing the priest to mutter under his breath and back away.

Richard frowned. "Come now, Roland. We were friends once."

"Before you turned your back on your father and raised weapons against your own countrymen."

"But lest you forget, I *am* king. Henry's death made me so."

"Why have you come here?" Roland demanded.

"To ask your help. I intend to travel to the Holy Land and take up the Crusades. To do so I need the largest, brightest, and most adept army ever assembled to accompany me. It is no secret you are the finest soldier ever to ride for my father. I would ask you to marshal my armies."

Hope turned to Mary, her knees weak, her head swimming. Wrapping her arms around Hope, Mary whispered, "Have faith, dear Hope, and know that he loves you."

Roland remained silent, his eyes never leaving Richard's.

"If the rumors I've heard prove to be true, that you own little more than the clothes on your back," Richard said, "then you might be pleased to know that such a journey will be amply rewarded. Marshal my armies and I will see to it that you're given land and enough wage to build you a fair house when you return to England."

"With all due respect for my liege lord, I would starve before marshaling your armies . . . Your Majesty."

A flicker of anger flashed in Richard's eyes, then he shrugged. "If that's what you desire, Roland." Turning, he walked back toward the door, looking right and left, the lift of his eyebrows acknowledging the dislike and distrust in the villagers' faces.

"'Tis a true shame about Wytham," he said. "Now that Godfrey and Harold are gone, the castle and lands revert to me, and since I plan to leave England soon God only knows what the lot of greedy barons will do to get their hands on it."

A servant dashed up the church steps and handed Richard his gloves. Standing in the open doorway, the sun spilling over his shoulders, he turned back to Roland. "I suppose I owe you and your lovely bride a wedding gift. Would Wytham suffice?''

Cries of surprise erupted through the crowd.

Mary fell into Royce's arms and began to weep.

Roland swallowed and tried to breathe. "What are you saying, Richard?''

"That Wytham is yours. I suppose it's the least I can do to repay you for your loyalty to my father the last years. Overseeing such holdings is such a bother when there are entire continents to conquer. Besides—'' His voice dropped and his eyes became distant. "My father loved and admired you. He often wished that his own sons had been as faithful to him as you were. Yes, yes. Henry would have approved of you having Wytham.''

"Thank you,'' Roland said, taking Hope into his arms and holding her fast.

Richard smiled. "In the meantime, if any of your men yet have an appetite for travel and fighting, there is sufficient need for their services.''

"*I* shall go with you!'' Daniel called, stepping into the aisle.

Jeanne cried, "No! Daniel, what are you saying?''

Hope stared at her brother in disbelief.

"I am more than capable of fighting,'' Daniel announced, "and would relish the opportunity to go to the Holy Land.''

Richard looked over Daniel's head to Roland. "Who is this child?''

"I'm no child, sir,'' Daniel said hotly.

"No?'' Richard sniffed and tugged on his gloves. "Is he capable, Roland?''

"Yes. He is,'' Roland replied, causing Daniel to draw back his shoulders even more and raise his chin. "He has a great deal to learn, sire. But he learns well. He reminds me of myself.''

Daniel smiled and his face flushed with pride.

"Very well," said Richard. "Come along, pup. I'll give you a go, if you like. But mind you, unlike my father, who took Roland in, I'm not nearly so patient, nor so kind. I'll box your ears if you so much as look at me crooked. Do you understand me?"

"Yes, sire."

Richard glared. "Well? What are you waiting for?"

Turning back to Roland and Hope, Daniel looked, for a moment, as if he might cry. "You'll take care of her, sir? She's the only family I've got."

"With my life."

"I'll be back, Hope."

"Yes, you will, Daniel."

He blew her a kiss. "To destiny," he said, then walked from the church into the sunlight.

Hope lay in her husband's arms, listening to the sounds of celebration outside Wytham's keep. She had drifted to sleep with her head on Roland's shoulder. "I have gained a husband and lost a brother," she said sleepily.

He kissed her forehead. "I wish I could assure you that he will come back."

"I know he will."

Rolling her to her back, his body covering hers, Roland searched her eyes. "Having visions again?"

"Perhaps."

"Care to share them?"

"Perhaps." She smiled and curled her arms around his neck.

"What future do you see for us, seeress?"

"That we shall grow old together. That our love will only grow stronger through the years. That you are destined to be an esteemed lord, a tolerant and obliging husband, and a father our children will worship and emulate."

He kissed her breasts, then her stomach, swirled his tongue

around her navel before sliding his hand between her legs. She gasped and twisted her fingers into his hair. "Go on," he murmured. "How many children will we have?"

"Many." She groaned.

"Sons?"

Her back arched and she caught her breath. "All of them," she finally managed.

"And when, exactly, will we be blessed by such an event?"

She smiled at the ceiling and draped one leg over his shoulder. "Oh . . . in about six months."

His head slowly came up.

Hope pouted. "Don't stop now. I was just starting to enjoy it."

"A child? Are you certain?" he said, his sensual mouth curling at one end.

Her fingers in his cloud of black hair, Hope pulled him up until his heart beat against hers and she breathed softly against his warm lips. "Have you ever known me not to be certain about something?" she asked.

EPILOGUE

Montpellier, France

Hope gently put the tripod and tablets into the vault, then nodded to the monk, who with Roland's help shoved the stone door back into position, securing the hiding place from sight. Without speaking, the cowled and robed little man hurried away down the narthex that was lit only by a pitifully few sconces on the wall.

Roland took his wife in his arms. "Are you certain this is what you're to do?" he asked. "Is it what you *want* to do?"

"It was the vision of the Abbey de Montpellier that came to me. I saw this very vault. I was told to bring the tripod and tablets here."

"I thought you gave up the visions when you fell in love with me," he teased. Removing his cloak, he spread the furred folds around Hope's shoulders.

She nodded and shivered with cold. "I have now. The gift is bequeathed to another. Someone more capable than I am will enlighten the world with the gift." The babe moved in her stomach, and Hope hugged herself happily. "No more visions, sir. I swear it."

They moved toward the door.

Hope stopped and turned.

"Is something wrong?" Roland asked.

"I heard a voice."

He looked around the shadows. "I heard nothing. There's no one here."

"The wind plays tricks with my ears. You're right. 'Twas nothing. I thought I heard someone call out a name, is all. *Michel de Nostradamus.*" She smiled up at her husband. "You may take me home to Wytham now."